BOONS
& CURSES

Yugal Joshi is a co-author of the internationally acclaimed book *Singapore Water Story*, which has been translated into Chinese, Japanese and Hindi, and *Creating Shared Value*, on sustainable development. His other books are *Women Warriors in Indian History* and *Ram: the Soul of Time*.

BOONS & CURSES

Legends of the Mythological Mother

YUGAL JOSHI

Published by
Rupa Publications India Pvt. Ltd 2020
7/16, Ansari Road, Daryaganj
New Delhi 110002

Sales Centres:
Allahabad Bengaluru Chennai
Hyderabad Jaipur Kathmandu
Kolkata Mumbai

Copyright © Yugal Joshi 2020

All rights reserved.
No part of this publication may be reproduced, transmitted,
or stored in a retrieval system, in any form or by any means,
electronic, mechanical, photocopying, recording or otherwise,
without the prior permission of the publisher.

This is a work of fiction. Names, characters, places and incidents are either the
product of the author's imagination or are used fictitiously and any resemblance to
any actual person, living or dead, events or locales is entirely coincidental.

ISBN: 978-93-5333-869-5

First impression 2020

10 9 8 7 6 5 4 3 2 1

The moral right of the author has been asserted.

Printed at HT Media Ltd., Gr. Noida

This book is sold subject to the condition that it shall not,
by way of trade or otherwise, be lent, resold, hired out, or otherwise
circulated, without the publisher's prior consent, in any form
of binding or cover other than that in which it is published.

Contents

Ambition/1

Protection/40

Independence/81

Love and Retaliation/140

Sacrifice/215

Bibliography/254

Glossary/255

I

Ambition

'Avarice sticks on the soul forever,' Kunti sighed. She was the strongest woman of her Age. She never cried, in public or in private. Her best quality was the ability to find a trace of light in an otherwise dark and gloomy night. But, that evening, even she had accepted defeat. She wished to cry aloud. But decades of self-control dried her tears.

A maid entered quietly and extinguished the night lamp. Kunti's embellished bedroom turned dark.

'Does the end of desire make us vulnerable?' she wondered. 'Ambitions keep our mind and body agile, but weigh heavily on our soul.'

'Kunti,' her inner self reprimanded, 'what more do you desire? Have not you seen for yourself what your's and others' ambitions have done to the Kuru clan?'

'Krishna… Krishna!' Kunti cried aloud, searching desperately for Krishna's bright and reassuring smile in the dark chamber. 'Krishna… Krishna!' resonated from the other chambers as well. Was it a delusion? Stunned, Kunti went up to the wall that separated Gandhari's room from hers. She heard nothing. The moment she turned back, a loud cry pierced her heart again, 'Krishna… Krishna!'

Kunti's head and heart began to throb heavily. That scared cry, calling Krishna for help, was now coming from everywhere—above the roof, under the floor, within and without the four walls and even her body and soul. 'Krishna…Krishna!' As if countless legions of the dead and the alive were calling out to Krishna for salvation: The Kurus, the Pandavas, the Yadavas, the Vrishnies, the Shoorsenas, the Madras, the Bhojas, the Chetis…millions of their dead came alive in Kunti's dark room. 'Krishna…Krishna!' Everyone was crying so loudly that Kunti's soul became numb and she fell down, unconscious.

~

A few years after the Mahabharata War, Bharatvarsha appeared to be a peaceful, orderly and prosperous state. Famous for his just rule, Dharmaraja Yudhishthira was ably assisted by his four worthy brothers and counselled well by their wife, Draupadi. The Pandava palace appeared majestic and calm to outsiders, perhaps perceived to be the most ideal royal palace in the whole of Aryavarta. However, inside the walls of the palace, the hatred that had caused the greatest war at Kurukshetra had not diminished yet. That simmering hatred had raised its poisonous head yet again, and the souls of all Kurus, alive or dead, called for Krishna.

The oldest Kuru, Dhritarashtra, and his wife Gandhari hesitated to join the Pandavas for dinner that evening. They were apprehensive that mighty Bhima and glamourous Draupadi would again humiliate them, but Kunti insisted, 'Didi, they will not do it again. That was an aberration.'

However, it happened again.

When Dhritarashtra mistakenly bit into a bone, the sound was audible enough for everyone around. Bhima laughed aloud and said, 'That was the sound, uncle. Duryodhana's thigh made exactly that sound when I broke it.' Kunti stared at Bhima, but her second son was in no mood to let the oldest Kuru eat in peace.

Dhritarashtra and Gandhari continued eating with their heads bowed. Bhima ignored his mother's glare. Yudhishthira and the others did not even try to stop Bhima.

Sucking a juicy marrow bone, Bhima showed it to Dhritarashtra and Gandhari. 'Look uncle, this is how I sucked the last drop of blood from wicked Dusshasana's bones.' Bhima laughed like the devil. His cruel laughter reverberated long and loud in the dining hall, shaking the tall stone columns and the floor. The humiliation pierced the wrinkled hearts of the Kuru couple, as well as the tender heart of Parikshita, the son of Abhimanyu and the youngest Pandava.

In the dim light of the flickering candles, Arjuna's grandson Parikshita saw the ghosts of the slain Kurukshetra warriors on the canvas of Bhima's huge face. He could see the mutilated bodies of the Kauravas rising up slowly behind Bhima. Scared, the child looked at his mother Uttara. He was about to cry when Uttara sealed his lips with her finger.

It was not unusual to see Bhima humiliating the old couple during family gatherings. He was not like his elder brother Yudhishthira, and had not forgiven the blind former king for his injustice towards the Pandavas. But tonight's insult had gone too far.

'Bhima, stop this! Are not you in your senses?' Kunti cautioned her son.

'Ha, ha, ha! Poor mother Gandhari!' Bhima was in no mood to stop. He mischeviously looked at Draupadi, urging her to join in.

Emboldened by Bhima's look and enjoying the banter, Draupadi did not miss her chance. 'If mother Gandhari had removed her blindfold in time, perhaps the Kauravas would have been alive today!'

Draupadi's ill-worded comment stunned everybody, but before anyone could speak, Bhima laughed out loud.

'Well-said, Draupadi! But don't you think, but for her counselling, with tacit support from that wicked Shakuni, vile Duryodhana would have separated her head from her body?'

'Bhima, are you insane? Keep your mouth shut!' Yudhishthira shouted.

Bhima and Draupadi looked contemptuously at the Pandava king. Bhima mocked his elder brother, 'Brother, you are dharmaraja: I thought you knew this. There is precedence in our history—on his father Jamadagni's command, Parashurama severed his mother Renuka's neck with one sweep of his axe!'

'Bhima!' Yudhishthira shouted, getting up from his seat in a huff and leaving the dinning hall without finishing his food. Nakul and Sahadeva followed him. Arjuna also got up and stood behind the blind Dhritarashtra, who was trembling with anger, shame and naked helplessness. Gently placing his hand on the weak shoulders of the former king, Arjuna tried to console him. Uttara took Parikshit's hand and dragged him out of the hall.

At the far end of the table, Kunti wondered what was going on. So, this was it: An ignoble end to a turbulent life!

'Blindly chasing ambitions lands you nowhere,' Kunti remembered Krishna's words. 'Krishna, if only you had been here tonight!'

∽

Born as Prutha in Mathura, Kunti's journey to Hastinapur and beyond had been shaped by her ambitions. She was the daughter of Marisha and Shoorsena and one of the younger sisters of Krishna's father, Vasudeva.

A few months after Prutha's birth, Shoorsena's childless friend Kuntibhoja wished to adopt her. Shoorsena obliged. In the palace of Kuntibhoja, people fondly started calling the baby 'Kunti'.

The gods had blessed Kunti with abundant beauty and grace. When she attained puberty, her beauty and caring nature became the talk of the royal palaces. Even Durvasa, a sage infamous for his short temper, could not resist her charms. Once, when Durvasa was visiting Kuntibhoja's palace, Kunti took very good care of him. A mightily-pleased Durvasa taught her a magical formula. Using this formula, Kunti could call any god she wished and have a child with him.

Kunti was too young and immature to understand the consequences of the formula. Her curiosity overpowered her and once, when she was alone in the palace, she decided to try it.

It was a beautiful morning and Kunti was sitting in her garden. 'Whom should I call?' she wondered. The morning sun had just appeared on the eastern horizon. The answer to her dilemma was right before her. 'Surya, I invoke you,' Kunti began casting a charm over the sun god; with each ablution to him, she chanted Durvasa's mantras. Slowly, with the rhythmic chanting of the mantras and with complete devotion, she immersed her soul in her prayers.

Kunti sensed someone next to her and opened her eyes. For a moment bright sunshine blinded her, but soon she could focus her gaze on the extremely handsome man standing before her.

'Prutha, I am Surya,' the divine person introduced himself. 'I know why you have called me here. Come, I will fulfil your wish.' Kunti's first reaction was to run away from the sun god, but his reassuring and measured words stopped her. Charmed by his beauty and manners, she could not utter a word. Wiping the sweat from her forehead with his finger, Surya pulled her tender frame closer.

'You are so young and delicate,' he whispered in her ear.

Kunti did not know how to react. 'Durvasa was right,' she thought proudly, 'I have summoned a deva as mighty and bright as the sun!' She let herself swoon in the warm and caressing arms of Surya.

After the moments of bliss were over, Surya blessed Kunti. 'Prutha, my armour and earrings will be integral parts of our son's body from birth. As long as he possesses them, no one can defeat or kill him.'

The sun god departed as quickly as he had arrived, leaving behind a clueless Kunti. For her, it was like a dream that had ended in a flash. In the evening, when Kuntibhoja and his wife were at the palace, Kunti was unsure about sharing her adventure with them. 'Who would believe me?' she wondered. She decided to keep quiet.

But time was indifferent to her decision. It moved on and began beating its drum, announcing Prutha's pregnancy. With each passing day, her face and body started glowing with increasing intensity, like gold. Very soon, Kuntibhoja's wife alerted the king.

The royal couple adored their daughter. Taking her into confidence, they asked her what had passed. Kunti told them everything that had happened between her and Surya. Kuntibhoja and his wife were aware of Durvasa's mystic powers. The pragmatic king knew where it would lead, and he decided to support his daughter.

'Kunti, my child, it's natural to be curious and try to find out the truth. Something that results from curiosity is not a sin. However, we live among people, and our society is not so large-hearted. Right and wrong are decided by society, on the basis of its traditions,' Kuntibhoja cautiously explained.

Kunti looked at her mother, who nodded in support of her husband. 'Kunti, an unmarried mother is not welcome anywhere. I wish we could change that, but we cannot oppose powerful priests and Kshatriyas. Perhaps, one day you will become strong enough to judge traditions and act wisely.' He paused, and then continued, 'Kunti, I have big dreams for you. I want you to become queen of Hastinapur one day. But if people know you are an unmarried mother, who will marry you?'

'I understand what you are saying, father. I will not mortify you,' Kunti assured her parents. 'But I will give birth to this child.'

After some argument, Kunti's parents agreed. Thus, they made an arrangement. In a secluded and very comfortable part of the palace, Kunti lived out her pregnancy. Kuntibhoja and his wife took every care of her. In course of time, Kunti gave birth to a baby boy. The newborn was handsome like a blossoming lotus and luminous like the morning sun. The royal couple was amazed to see the ears and the broad chest of the boy. As promised by the sun god, the baby was born with a pair of bright shining earrings, which looked like natural extensions of his ears, and his chest was covered by shining, impenetrable armour.

'Kunti was not lying,' the queen whispered in her husband's ear. The baby was indeed Surya's son.

Kuntibhoja's heart melted on seeing the innocent sparkling smile of the newborn. The couple looked questioningly at their daughter to understand if she still wanted to abandon the baby.

'I will keep my word,' Kunti assured her parents with a smile. 'He is the son of Surya and will be taken care of by him.' She kissed the forehead of the extraordinary newborn.

Next day, before dawn, the three of them took the child to the riverbank. They kept the newborn in a cosy basket, well-wrapped in the softest blankets. Very slowly, with trembling hands and a heavy heart, Kunti took out her gold pendant and placed it near the infant. She closed her eyes, looked away and slowly pushed the basket along the smoothly flowing water of the river.

After this, Kuntibhoja quickly arranged a *swayamvara* for Kunti, according to her wishes. In the Yadava council or in the areas under their influence, a *swayamvara* was not the preferred form of marriage. But the ambitious Kunti was no ordinary cowherd princess. She had set her goals much beyond the limits of Yadu's land.

Invitations were sent to all eligible princes and kings of Aryavarta. The most sought-after participant was the young and handsome Pandu, the newly-crowned king of Hastinapur. The eldest Kuru and guardian of Hastinapur's throne, Bhishma, had chosen Pandu to rule the Kuru kingdom, superseding the elder prince Dhritarashtra, who had been born blind and therefore unqualified to rule.

Dhritarashtra never forgave Bhishma for this rejection. However, throughout his life, despite his tremendous ill-will, Dhritarashtra was cautious enough to never utter a word against Bhishma publicly. Dhritarashtra was well-versed in laws and traditions, therefore in public he gracefully accepted his younger brother Pandu as his king.

During the night that followed Pandu's departure to participate in Kunti's *swayamvara*, while making love to his wife Gandhari, Dhritarashtra insisted, 'Give me a son before Pandu's wife produces one, Gandhari. Our son must be the eldest in the family and succeed Pandu to the throne!'

At the *swayamvara*, Kunti was introduced to all the suitors. She looked at Pandu. The king of the second-most powerful state in Aryavarta looked slightly paler than the other assembled royals. The old Jarasandha, king of Magadha, was not there. Kunti did not complain.

'Pandu is young and a better prospect in every sense,' she thought. She disregarded his pale appearance as a temporary trait and garlanded him as her chosen husband.

The whole of Hastinapur rejoiced on the arrival of the newlyweds. Satyavati, the grandmother of Pandu, welcomed the new queen of Hastinapur into her new home. Kunti was happy. Her cherished dream had been fulfilled.

However, everything was not rosy in Kunti's new home. It did not take her long to understand the palace politics. Dhritarashtra's frustration and Gandhari's predicament were reflected in everyday life, but everyone had learnt to live with that. Instead of being a beacon in her husband's life, Gandhari chose to blindfold herself forever: Whether in solidarity with her blind husband or in outrage to protest against her marriage to a blind man, no one knew.

Kunti learnt that Pandu was so named for his pale yellow skin. He was a brave and upright man. However, Kunti quickly discovered that he was impotent. Kunti decided to swallow another secret, that Pandu was incapable of fathering a child.

In a few months, when Satyavati saw no sign of Kunti's pregnancy, she insisted that Pandu remarry. Madri, the younger sister of king Shalya of Madra, was purchased as a second wife for Pandu.

After a few months of marriage, when even Madri showed no signs of pregnancy, Pandu became worried. 'I am cursed. Like my father, I will leave behind two childless widows.' In frustration, Pandu decided to spend some time in a forest.

One day, he went hunting in the forest. Among the trees, he saw an antelope mating with a doe. The scene annoyed the sterile Pandu and he shot a sharp arrow that struck the antelope. The grievously injured antelope and the doe immediately transformed into their original forms. The antelope was actually a sage named Kindama and the doe was his wife.

'Rascal, you have violently interrupted our lovemaking! Sinner, I curse you: You too will die instantly if you ever attempt to make love to anyone,' an enraged Kindama cursed Pandu before dying.

Pandu told this story to his wives and other fellow forest-dwellers. Everyone was sympathetic to the kind king. A distraught Pandu decided to become a hermit and conveyed his wish to the royals in Hastinapur. Bhishma confirmed it through his own spies. Reluctantly, he declared blind Dhritarashtra as the new king.

Kunti and Madri decided to join their husband in the forest. Pandu's inability to procreate and his decision to become a hermit destroyed Kunti's dreams. The unhappiness in Pandu's household gathered like dark clouds. The royal messenger depressed them further when he broke the news of Gandhari's pregnancy.

'What is the worth of a man who cannot procreate? I decided to live in the forest because I cannot bear to hear people's comments behind my back. I lost my crown, but that burns my heart only a little. What burns me like hellfire is the recurring thought of dying without a son. I have failed to repay the debt of my ancestors, how will I face them in heaven?' Pandu lamented before his wives.

Kunti was in a quandary. She had the magical formula, but the question was if she should reveal it or not. Finally, her ambitions overpowered her diffidence. 'I am the first queen of Hastinapur, not Gandhari. My son, not Gandhari's, should have the right to the throne.' She decided to tell Pandu about Durvasa's blessings. Pandu listened to Kunti carefully. The revelation made him happy, but he wanted to be reassured.

'What will people say? Does dharma permit it?' he enquired.

'Lord, the law of marriage was introduced to bind a woman to her husband. It helped society to know who fathered children. But, if a man is unable to give his wife a child, the scriptures prescribe *niyoga*. These rules stipulate that a woman can go to another man chosen by her husband, for the purpose of procreation. The children born of that union belong to her husband, though biologically he has not fathered them.' Kunti scanned her husband's expressions and then reinforced her arguments.

'Lord, this is not unknown to the Kuru family. Grandmother Satyavati sent Vyasa to your widowed mother Ambalika, after your father Vichitravirya's death. That is why you are Vichitravirya's son, not Vyasa's. Your brother Dhritarashtra is also a son born by *niyoga*.' Kunti's words indicated a way out and Pandu reluctantly agreed.

'If you say so, let's identify a suitable sage.'

'There is no need to go to a sage. I can call any god,' Kunti told Pandu and Madri, without disclosing the birth of her first child from Surya. 'If you wish, I can try this formula and have a child from any god of your choice.'

A deity was always better than a worldly sage! A happy Pandu instantly agreed.

'Call Yama,' Pandu said.

'Yama?'

'Yes. He is the protector of dharma. Our son should be a model king, an epitome of truth and justice,' Pandu reasoned.

Kunti used the magical formula and invoked Yama, who obliged her and she became pregnant.

Meanwhile, Dhritarashtra was waiting for the birth of Gandhari's son. He wanted a son to erase the curse of his blindness: A son who would rightfully claim the throne of Hastinapur, unlike the father who got it through Bhishma's mercy. Dhritarashtra was aware of Pandu's physical weakness, but was not ready to take a chance. His ears were desparate to hear the first cry of Gandhari's newborn, and this wait seemed endless.

Kunti gave birth to a boy before Pandu received any news about Dhritarashtra's son. Pandu celebrated. 'My son is the eldest among the new generation of Kurus!' The thought made Pandu immensely happy, and he announced the birth to the forest-dwelling sages. Pandu named the boy Yudhishthira.

'I think we should return to Hastinapur,' Kunti suggested.

Pandu thought long and hard, and finally decided otherwise. However, he sent a messenger to convey the news of Yudhishthira's birth to Bhishma, Dhritarashtra, Gandhari and others in Hastinapur.

In Hastinapur, during Gandhari's long pregnancy, Dhritarashtra picked up a maid for his pleasure. The maid became pregnant and gave birth to a son. Dhritarashtra named him Yuyutsu. Yuyutsu was the eldest among the new generation of the Kauravas and the Pandavas.

Yuyutsu was a worthy man, yet he was disqualified from sitting on the throne. At Kurukshetra, during the battle of Mahabharata, he ultimately joined the Pandavas, thinking that they were on the side of dharma. In the end, frustrated with the immoral conduct of both the sides in the war and their refusal to follow dharma, he committed suicide once the Pandavas were declared winners.

When the news of the birth of Kunti's son reached Hastinapur,

Gandhari's pregnancy was more than a year old, yet there was no sign of a birth.

'Why is your baby so scared to face the world? What kind of mystery is this?' an angry Dhritarashtra shouted at his wife.

Furious at her unduly long pregnancy and with the continuous affronts from her ambitious husband, Gandhari decided to force the child out of her womb. On the instruction of an upset Gandhari, some maids cruelly struck her belly repeatedly with an iron bar, amidst loud and encouraging shouts from the queen herself. Finally something moved: A ball of flesh, as cold as an iron ball, dropped from Gandhari's womb. Cruel fate had played the worst possible trick on the blindfolded mother.

A frightened Gandhari sent messengers to call sage Vyasa to the palace. The sage had once predicted that she would become the mother of a hundred sons.

'Where are my one hundred sons?' she cried before the sage.

The sage inspected the ball of flesh and called the surgeons. He asked them to help him chop the flesh into one hundred equal parts and keep them in one hundred incubators.

'Keep them there for a year. They will transform into babies.'

'Can I have a daughter too?' Gandhari prayed to Vyasa. The sage smiled and divided the flesh into one hundred and one pieces.

This news also reached the forest where Pandu was staying. Everyone there felt bad for Gandhari. However, Pandu decided to have one more child.

'Kunti, I want a son as mighty as Hanuman. Call Hanuman's father Vayu, the god of the wind!'

Being invoked, Vayu arrived and fulfilled Kunti's desire. The son she had from Vayu was named Bhima.

Unaware of Bhima's birth, on the same day in Hastinapur, Vyasa instructed that the first incubator be opened. The moment the child was taken out from the incubator, the palace dog wailed. Considering it a bad omen, Vidura, the stepbrother and minister of Dhritarashtra, advised the parents to get rid of the child, but they refused.

'Vidura, I have got this child after going through hell. Even if God asks me to abandon my baby, I would refuse,' Gandhari rejected Vidura's advice. Dhritarashtra ridiculed him, saying, 'Vidura, why do you always keep your worst advice for me?'

In the forest, after Bhima's birth, Pandu asked Kunti to call Indra for another child.

'Aditya, you are the king of devas and the most opulent. Bless me with a son who will be invincible in the battlefield,' Kunti requested Indra. He liked the beautiful Kunti and blessed her with a son who was called Arjuna.

Meanwhile, from the remaining hundred incubators, Dhritrashtra's ninety-nine sons and one daughter were born. Among them, Dusshasana was the second son and the closest to his elder brother Duryodhana. Gandhari and Dhritarashtra named their only girl child, Dusshala. These one hundred and one children of Dhritarashtra were called the Kauravas.

Pandu's greed for sons did not stop at Arjuna. He wanted more sons. He asked Kunti to invoke one more deva, but she refused.

'I cannot do that. Dharma decrees that a woman can go to four men, at the most. If I go to a fifth, I will be called a whore,' Kunti reasoned.

'But I am permitting you to go to a fifth…and they are not men, they are deities!'

'Lord, even for you I cannot desert my *sati* dharma,' Kunti was steadfast in her decision.

Pandu consulted Madri and asked Kunti to invoke a deva for his second wife. Kunti agreed and asked Madri whom she would like to invoke. Madri thought hard. The number of male progeny mattered in politics: A mother with more sons was always at an advantage. Therefore, Madri decided to invoke the twin Ashvini Kumars.

On Kunti's invocation, instantly, the twin sons of Surya and Sanjana appeared. They fulfilled Madri's desire and she bore twins from them, and the twins came to be called Nakula and Sahadeva. Nakula became the most handsome man in the world and Sahadeva became the most knowledgeable man in the world.

'Invoke another deva for Madri,' Pandu asked Kunti.

Kunti thought for a while and then politely refused. 'Why should Madri have more sons than me?' she thought. She said, 'I don't think we should be more greedy, my lord. Now, you have five sons. Your sons are the five Pandavas and they represent honesty, strength, skill, beauty and wisdom. What else do you need?'

'Do you remember that you wanted a son with the qualities of an ideal king? God has been kind to us and has blessed us with five sons who collectively possess these great qualities,' Kunti pressed her point. 'Our endeavour should be to ensure that the five brothers always remain united. Trust me, if that happens, they will be invincible,' in this way, Kunti convinced Pandu and Madri.

The next few years went by peacefully. A few times, Kunti urged Pandu to return to Hastinapur, but he refused.

'Yudhishthira is the rightful claimant to Hastinapur's crown. He is your son and the eldest among the Kuru princes. Your delay will make it difficult for our sons.'

'Kunti, once relinquished, the throne cannot be reclaimed! I can't go back. Don't worry unnecessarily for Yudhishthira. Bhishma and Satyavati cannot do injustice to him,' Pandu reassured Kunti.

Pandu enjoyed the childhood of his five sons. There were many ashrams close to his hermitage. The Pandavas always had a lot of friends to play with; erudite sages were in the vicinity to teach them history, the *shastra*s and grammar. But their dearest guru was their own father: He taught them the nuances of politics, governance and dharma.

One day, after his teaching session, Pandu addressed his sons to stay for a while, I have spent many years in celibacy and meditation. Nature has blessed me with great knowledge and that knowledge is embedded in my body. Now, listen to me carefully. When I die, eat my flesh and you will be blessed with all the knowledge my body possesses. This will serve you well in the future, because I can see that the coming days will be very harsh on you.'

A couple of days passed. One morning, Pandu went for a bath in a nearby waterfall in the forest. When Pandu reached the waterfall, he saw Madri enjoying the cool water. He could see her beautiful body through her wet clothes. Quietly, he went behind her and clasped her tiny waist.

'Lord, what has happened to you?' Madri shivered from his touch. For a moment, she enjoyed the warmth of Pandu's body, but then she quickly moved away from him. Pandu dragged her down on the grass and started kissing her passionately.

'Leave me, Pandu. Don't you remember the curse?' Madri resisted, but Pandu was in no mood to listen.

'That was many ages ago, Madri. Who cares about that old fool's curse? He has scared us for too long, not any more!' Pandu tried to force himself on her. 'Let me make love to you!'

Slowly, Madri's resistance melted away.

But a curse never gets old. Pandu died while attempting to make love to Madri. Filled with guilt, a mortified Madri became like a cold stone. Later, when Pandu's mortal body was laid on the funeral pyre and the flames rose up into the sky, Madri put Nakul and Sahadeva in Kunti's lap.

'Take care of them, Didi. They are your Pandavas,' she requested Kunti with eyes full of tears. Before anyone could understand and react, she leapt into the fire.

The sudden death of their father and Madri's subsequent self-immolation made the young Pandavas numb. During those extremely testing moments, they forgot what their father had advised them to do with his flesh.

A day after the cremation, little Sahadeva went to the immolation ground. It was a child's quest to find his lost parents. He sat near the burnt logs and waited for their return, crying and calling out to his parents. While sitting there, he saw an army of ants carrying a small piece of his father's flesh. Suddenly, he remembered what his father had advised. He picked up that tiny piece of flesh and ate it. Instantly, he became the one who knew everything about the past, the present and the future.

Sahadeva's mind reeled faster and faster. The little boy could not cope with this sudden influx of knowledge and fell down unconscious. When he awoke after a couple of hours, the knowledge still made him wobble on his feet. He rushed to tell Kunti and his brothers. Before he could reach the cottage, a very attractive stranger stopped him on the way.

'Sahadeva, what you have is an extraordinary gift. It is both a curse and a boon. God gives such exceptional gifts only to a rare genius, to one among billions. Such a rare gift blossoms in silence and demands a certain secrecy. Now, as you know what the future holds for you, you must promise me that you will not foretell it to anyone. You will follow this advice forever. Remember, if someone asks you a question about the future, answer them with another question. Promise me that, and you will be my friend forever.'

Sahadeva looked at the stranger. He recognized him. He would be their greatest friend in the future. Sahadeva promised to do as advised.

When he reached the cottage, an anxious Kunti came running to him. 'Son, where were you? We were searching for you everywhere!' She looked at Sahadeva's pale face. 'Go inside, Arjuna is waiting for you. Eat your food with him. We will go to Hastinapur tomorrow.' Kunti was too busy to notice the look in the youngest Pandava's eyes.

Though overwhelmed by the unfortunate deaths of Pandu and Madri, Kunti was determined to stand up and fight for her sons' legitimate rights. She was firm that a blind Dhritrashtra was no more than a caretaker of the throne.

'He is not qualified to become a king, Yudhishthira. You are the eldest among the Kuru princes. Therefore, you have a legitimate right to wear the crown. Keep this in mind, always,' she said, kissing the forehead of the eldest Pandava.

Yudhishthira nodded in affirmation.

'Bhishma, Satyavati and Vidura are the most influential people in Hastinapur. They are ardent followers of dharma and shall never deviate from their duty. They should be your biggest supporters. Listen, my dear sons, follow the path of truth, be nice to others, work hard and have patience. These virtues will win you more friends and well-wishers,' Kunti advised her sons.

As expected, Bhishma, Satyavati and Vidura welcomed them wholeheartedly. None of the Kauravas liked the homecoming of their cousins. Gandhari met Kunti with some warmth and a frustrated Dhritarashtra completed the formalities.

'The coming days will be difficult,' Kunti said after meeting her relatives. 'All five of you need to live like a single soul, always together through thick and thin. Honesty, strength, skill, beauty and knowledge, you own these virtues. You have to hone them, reinforce them. Education is something anyone can acquire, irrespective of their background. Work hard to acquire knowledge and skill. Try to become the favourite of your gurus and elders.'

~

In a palace full of intrigues, Duryodhana and his brothers ensured that the Pandavas always remained on their toes. However, with the elders' help, the Pandavas survived. They followed what Kunti had taught them. In a very short time, they impressed guru Dronacharya by their simplicity, devotion and hard work. Disciplined and well-mannered, the Pandavas were the guru's delight, compared to the arrogant, haughty and indisciplined Kauravas. Bhishma, Vidura and Drona never masked their liking for the Pandavas.

'Focus on your objective: You must have an unwavering focus, be it in practicing your dharma or honing your skills,' Kunti reiterated.

Following Kunti's lessons always rewarded the Pandavas. An unwavering focus on the goal paid them rich dividends. In an archery competition, when Arjuna replied that he could see only the eye of the bird, it made him the favourite pupil of Dronacharya. Later, it helped them imprison their future father-in-law Drupada, for Dronacharya in *guru-dakshina*. This made Dronacharya forever indebted to them. Yet another time, it helped Arjuna win Draupadi; and finally, his unflinching focus helped him to win Krishna to their side in the Mahabharata War.

After her marriage, Kunti's life had always been tumultuous to say the least. While rearing the five Pandavas, she had forgotten about her firstborn. She was oblivious to the fact that fate was preparing to bring him before her.

Once the education of the princes was completed, Dronacharya proposed to organize a graduation ceremony for his pupils. Bhishma liked the idea and ordered his courtiers to arrange it.

At the graduation ceremony, Arjuna performed like no one else. The demonstration of his unrivalled archery skills filled Kunti with pride and pleased Drona, Bhishma and Vidura. The Kauravas were disheartened, as they did not have a master archer like Arjuna in their ranks. When Dronacharya was about to declare Arjuna the winner, an unknown youth entered the arena and challenged Arjuna.

The intruder wore dazzling armour on his chest, and two radiant jewels in his earlobes illuminated his face. His personality enamoured everyone. Dronacharya was about to allow him to present his skills, when Adhiratha, the royal charioteer, came running inside the arena.

Anxiously running to the youth, he shouted, 'Son, what are you doing here?'

'Who is he, Adhiratha?' Bhishma shouted from the royal pavilion.

'He is my son, Lord. His name is Karna.'

'Adhiratha, how dare your son challenge a kshatriya in a royal archery competition?' Bhishma demanded angrily.

Adhiratha and the youth stood speechless.

'Only kshatriyas can participate in this competition,' Bhishma said, thus declaring Karna disqualified.

'Grandsire, it's an open competition,' Duryodhana quickly came forward to support Karna. 'This youth deserves a chance.'

'You are wrong, Duryodhana. This is a graduation ceremony and this competition is only for Kshatriyas. Even Dronacharya's son Ashwathama cannot participate in it. How can a charioteer's son then do so?' Yudhishthira opposed him.

'I take Karna as my friend. To me, he is as dear as Dusshasana. From now on, I will treat his insult as mine and his enemies will be my enemies,' Duryodhana declared. He then requested his father to declare Karna the king of Anga. Dhritarashtra quickly obliged.

'Now, no one should call my friend a charioteer. He is now

the king of Anga and an equal to us.' Duryodhana hugged and congratulated Karna.

'Let the competition resume,' Duryodhana demanded.

Kunti was watching this drama unfold from the ladies' pavilion. She could spot the shining armour, golden earrings and that dangling golden pendant! Cruel fate had knocked at her door again. A long-forgotten son had returned—not as her son but as an ever-indebted friend of Duryodhana, the sworn enemy of her sons. She could not bear the stress and fainted.

The commotion in the ladies' pavilion halted the duel and gave Bhishma a good reason to declare the graduation ceremony closed.

That evening, Gandhari came to see Kunti, who expressed her anguish at the way Duryodhana had encouraged and promoted a charioteer's son. Gandhari could not see any wrong in what her son had done.

'Arjuna is the best. I don't know why Bhishma did not allow the youth to participate. His participation would have cemented Arjuna's claim of being the best archer in the land,' Gandhari said.

Kunti did not like this. A well-intentioned dialogue soon turned into a heated argument. Kunti accused Duryodhana of plotting endlessly against her sons. Satyavati overheard the argument between Kunti and Gandhari.

A worried Satyavati called Bhishma to her room and expressed her concerns.

'Son, no family lives in complete harmony forever; but it tries. Power and privilege are tempting, and they ignite quarrels among siblings. But, in my household, I see a naked competition for the crown. I expected Kunti to be more sensible towards Gandhari, but I was wrong. Gandhari should have guided Dhritarashtra on the path of dharma, but she chose to follow her husband's blindness. Kunti and her sons will not forsake their claim and Dhritarashtra will encourage his sons to fight for theirs. The only way out, that I can see, is the division of the kingdom. For that, the princes are not prepared. I don't see any good omens in the coming years. I strongly feel that I should leave and become a hermit.'

Bhishma looked at his stepmother. The kingdom had not seen normal times since the death of Bhishma's father, king Shantanu. But, after seeing Kunti's sons, Bhishma had been hopeful for a good future, provided Duryodhana could be restrained.

'Have heart, mother. They are young; things will be alright,' Bhishma consoled the queen mother.

'Bhishma, I can see that this family is on a path of self-destruction. The quarrel between Duryodhana and the Pandavas has become unbearable. I expected Gandhari and Kunti to give some sane advice to their children, but I see that they are no better than their children.'

Satyavati pondered for a moment and then proposed, 'Bhishma, your pledge has become your burden. If you agree, there is a way to save Hastinapur.' Holding Bhishma's hand, she almost prayed to him, 'Bhishma, you become the king. Get married. Let's end this quarrel, let Hastinapur be at peace.'

'I cannot do that, mother,' Bhishma turned away from her.

'Bhishma, the past cannot dictate the future. I am amazed that a person like you puts a personal pledge above national interest. Even your father would have advised you to follow rashtra dharma, my son. If you don't take the reins of this land in your hands, I see a catastrophe coming. How can a wise person like you allow it?'

'Mother, my pledge is sacrosanct.'

'Sacrosanct? At what cost? Bhishma, leave aside the pledge, remember no individual is bigger than the nation!'

Bhishma did not reply. Satyavati looked at him and cried, 'Son, the people you made your pledge to, are not alive today. Your oath was to protect their selfish interests. It was to protect the interests of me and mine. Today, I release you from that bondage. That pledge is no longer binding on you. Agree to my prayer and rule the land!'

'It's not possible, mother. Please don't drive me from the path of my dharma.' Bhishma turned to Satyavati and looked into her eyes, 'But trust me, I will protect the throne of Hastinapur until I pass it on to wiser hands.'

Bhishma's reply angered Satyavati. 'Then so be it, son. I am already past the age of *vanaprastha* and see no role for me in this palace. Therefore, I must enter into *sanyasa* ashrama. I believe I am leaving Hastinapur in your safe hands. Arrange for my travel. I want to go to the Himalayas tomorrow morning.'

Pandu's mother Ambalika and Dhritarashtra's mother Ambika also decided to leave the palace with their mother-in-law Satyavati.

Once their mothers-in-law and grandmother-in-law left the palace to follow *sanyasa*, Gandhari and Kunti became the senior-most royal women in Hastinapur.

The graduation ceremony had brought the enmity between the royal cousins out into the open. It had become a topic of public speculation. Though the people hardly had any say in royal matters, Kunti understood the value of public sympathy in duress. The Pandavas had always been seen as the followers of dharma, as disciplined princes who were always respectful to elders and the public. Kunti had always ensured that not only did the Pandavas behave well, but were also seen to be doing so. Despite their great goodwill and sympathy towards Kunti and her sons, the elders like Bhishma, Vidura and Drona were bound by their duty to the throne. In such a situation, Kunti decided to take the help of her nephew Krishna.

After slaying his evil uncle Kansa, Krishna had become the messiah of the Yadavas. However, when Kunti's messenger reached Mathura to meet Krishna, the Yadavas had already deserted Mathura.

Meanwhile, Duryodhana conspired to kill Bhima by poisoning his food. Once Bhima lost consciousness, the Kauravas tied his limbs and threw him into the Ganga. Fortunately for Bhima, the Nagas living in the water rescued him and drew the poison out of his body. Bhima's survival confirmed Kunti's fear that the Kauravas could go to any extent to harm her children.

Finding herself and her children at sea, a desparate Kunti consulted many astrologers to find a way out: Some solace, a little hope from the stars and constellations, otherwise ever-conspiring against her children! One prominent astrologer suggested that she perform elephant worship for the well-being of her sons. Kunti ordered the city's potters to make one thousand clay models of elephants. When Gandhari learned about this, she also decided to perform a similar ceremony for her children's well-being. Gandhari called all the goldsmiths of the city to make one thousand gold elephant models for her puja.

'You know why she's doing this?' Kunti complained to her sons. 'Queen Gandhari thinks she owns Hastinapur. She is trying to show us our place here. It's so hard to live like beggars in our own kingdom,' she lamented.

'A prayer requires a clean heart. How does it matter what we offer to the gods?' Yudhishthira consoled her.

'Mother, if they can make elephants of gold, why can we not have real elephants?' Nakula suggested.

'I can get you Airawata,' Arjuna offered. Airawata was Indra's elephant, and had never set foot on earth.

'How?' Kunti's smile was bigger than her query.

After many years, the Pandavas saw a smile on their mother's face.

'Let me pray to Indra,' Arjuna said.

Indra agreed to provide Airawata to Arjuna for Kunti's puja.

'How will a celestial elephant descend to earth? How will you create a path for him?' Indra asked.

Arjuna had the answer. He raised his bow and arrows. Shooting arrows into the sky, he made a bridge of arrows, joining sky and earth. This miracle had never been seen in Hastinapur. Everyone came out to see the skills of Arjuna. An amazed Hastinapur saw Indra's Airawata descending to earth and later taking part in Kunti's ritual.

For many weeks, the people of Hastinapur talked about this unbelievable event. It transformed the image of the Pandavas, from kind and pitiable princes to capable and powerful achievers.

This event also made it clear that Kunti and Gandhari could not share the same roof. Vidura brought this issue before the blind king. Dhritarashtra agreed to the suggestion that Kunti and her sons need a separate house. He ordered a big house to be built for the Pandavas at Varnavata, a place not very far from the capital city of Hastinapur.

One day, when Vidura went to inspect the palace under construction, he discovered that the house was being made from lac and other inflammable materials. He immediately warned Kunti.

'It may be a plan to burn you all alive in that lac house,' Vidura alerted her.

'Then why should we go there?' Kunti demanded angrily.

'If you don't, it will be taken as a mark of disrespect against the king. It will go against you,' Vidura advised. He suggested a plan: 'Duryodhana and his uncle are now planning to eliminate you. Here, in Hastinapur, you are vulnerable and at their mercy. I think you should leave and explore new friends.'

'I have built a secret tunnel that leads from that lac palace to a forest,' Vidura described the escape plan. 'Follow Dhritarashtra's wish and go there, but remember that you must escape through the tunnel during the first night itself!'

'Won't they know we have escaped when they see no charred bodies?' Kunti asked.

'Don't worry. I have thought about it. I will arrange something,' Vidura assured her.

Everything happened as per the plan of both parties. The Kauravas set the palace on fire on the first night itself and the Pandavas escaped through the tunnel. Six charred bodies made people believe that the five Pandavas and Kunti had burnt to death in that 'accidental' fire.

Once in the forest, Kunti and her sons lived as impoverished Brahmins. For fear of being recognized, they never stayed in one place for long and continued wandering. Kunti often sobbed about her and her sons' misfortune. Her five sons always tried to keep her happy.

Once, in a Himalayan forest, Bhima killed a rakshasa called Baka and his brother Hidimba. Hidimba's twin sister Hidimbi was enamoured by Bhima's strength and power. Bhima too liked the strong woman with a soft heart. However, he was not sure if Kunti would approve of their union.

After some time, frustrated by Bhima's hesitation, Hidimbi decided to take matters into her own hands. With the help of her magical powers, she took Kunti and her sons to a beautiful place. Her hospitality and good nature floored the widow and her sons. After some time, Hidimbi told Kunti about her and Bhima's relationship.

'I know you will prove to be an ideal daughter-in-law,' Kunti praised her, 'but, you cannot live with Bhima forever. He belongs to Hastinapur and you belong to these forests.'

'I have not loved your son to shackle his life, mother. I know where I belong: Like you people of the Gangetic plains, we forest-dwellers also have our dharma and we follow it sincerely. Our different ways of life do not make us enemies. Let him follow his dharma, I will follow mine,' Hidimbi politely replied.

Kunti got the assurance she was looking for and blessed Hidimbi and Bhima's alliance. After one year, Hidimbi gave birth to a son. She named him Ghatotkacha. Bhima was completely immersed in love for his beautiful and devoted wife and extraordinarily active baby. This worried Kunti: Her aim was to see the Pandavas ruling from the throne of Hastinapur, not ruling the Rakshasas in some obscure forest.

Kunti called her sons and instructed them to return to the plains. On their way back, they met sage Dhaumya and accepted him as their chief priest. Dhaumya told them about the *swayamvara* of Draupadi. Her father Drupada, the king of Panchal, had invited all Kshatriya kings and princes to participate in the *swayamvara* of his daughter. He also told the Pandavas that Draupadi and her twin brother had been born from fire, after a difficult penance by their father. Drupada had undertaken that penance to beget children who could slay his childhood friend-turned-foe Dronacharya and destroy the Kurus.

The Panchal kingdom was similar to Hastinapur in power, prosperity and prestige. An arrogant Drupada was a sworn enemy of the Kurus and more so of their guru Dronacharya. Drupada and Dronacharya had been childhood friends. In his youth, when a penniless Dronacharya had sought monetary help from prince Drupada, the latter had refused to recognize him and insulted the poor Brahmin. Dronacharya had vowed to take revenge.

Dronacharya got his revenge after a decade. He joined Hastinapur as chief teacher to the princes. When they graduated, for *guru dakshina*, Dronacharya asked them to defeat Drupada in battle and bring him before their guru. Led by Arjuna, the princes and the Kuru army defeated the Panchal army and imprisoned Drupada. Dronacharya not only humiliated Drupada in public, but also forced him to hand over half his kingdom.

'If my sons win Draupadi's hand, they will gain a strong ally. We should cultivate strong allies. Hastinapur's rulers are our enemies, so there is no harm in this relationship,' Kunti reasoned. She decided to send her sons to Panchal.

Dhaumya took the Pandavas to Draupadi's *swayamvara* in the disguise of graduate Brahmins. The kings and princes from the whole of Aryavarta were assembled there. The Pandavas knew most of them. However, the centre of attention was a young, dark and extremely handsome man sitting near Drupada's throne. Very soon, they would learn that he was Krishna, a son of their maternal uncle, Vasudeva. The Pandavas sat with the other sages, ascetics and Brahmins. The *swayamvara* included a competition to win Draupadi's hand and it was for Kshatriyas only.

The beautiful Draupadi appeared at the *swayamvara* with a garland in her hands. Her face and limbs glowed like molten gold. When she sat near father, her brother Drishtadhyumna announced the stiff task for the participants.

'To win my sister's hand, the archer has to pierce the eye of the fish rotating on a wheel suspended from the roof while looking at its reflection in a vat of oil. I invite all Kshatriyas assembled here to try their luck.'

Most of the participants looked nervous. Drupada had set a very difficult condition for the winner.

'It is for you,' Bhima whispered in Arjuna's ears.

'Luck has always been cruel to us,' Arjuna responded with a wry smile. 'The competition is for Kshatriyas only!'

'Should we reveal our identity?' Arjuna whispered in Yudhishthira's ears. The temptation was hard to ignore, but Yudhishthira was firm that the Pandavas should not reveal their identity.

'Have patience. Wait and watch,' Dhaumya advised. Arjuna looked dismayed. Except him, every warrior worth his salt was sitting in the pavilion meant for participants.

'Who is that handsome man sitting with Drupada? He is smiling at us,' Yudhishthira wondered.

'He? He is ever-smiling. He is your maternal uncle Vasudeva's son,' Dhaumya replied.

'Krishna?' an amazed Arjuna almost shouted. Dhaumya nodded and squeezed Arjuna's hand. Arjuna saw Krishna smiling at him and his heart instantly recognized a kindred soul.

'Will he participate?' Bhima asked.

'No. Look, he is not sitting in the participants' pavilion. He is sitting with the hosts,' Sahadeva replied.

The competition began. Very soon, it became clear that the task was too stiff for the Kshatriya competitors assembled there. The last two remaining warriors were Duryodhana and Karna.

'I have promised my wife Bhanumati that I will never marry another girl,' Duryodhana said, explaining why he wouldn't participate. 'But, my friend and the king of Anga, Karna will drill the eye of the fish with his sharp arrow.'

Karna stood and walked gracefully towards the oil vat. Draupadi heard Duryodhana and then saw a handsome Karna walking past her towards the oil vat. She had heard a lot about them.

'The competition is for Kshatriyas only,' Krishna whispered to her.

'Stop!' Draupadi commanded. 'I cannot allow the son of a charioteer to participate in my *swayamvara*.'

Karna withdrew and silently vowed never to forgive Draupadi for this humiliation. Drupada then looked towards Krishna, urging him to participate. Krishna inclined his head in a polite refusal.

'It is sad that no Kshatriya warrior is capable of winning my daughter's hand,' Drupada dejectedly said.

'King Drupada, you may invite the willing Brahmins,' Krishna advised.

Hearing the invitation, an elated Arjuna immediately got up, picked up his bow and marched to the oil vat. He looked intently at the reflection of the eye of the rotating fish and shot an arrow. Surprising everyone, the graduate Brahmin's arrow struck the eye of the rotating fish.

The stunned audience shouted in awe. Krishna smiled and gestured at Draupadi to garland the winner and she followed without any hesitation.

※

'Mother, look what we have brought for you!' an excited Arjuna shouted from the door.

Kunti was inside the hut preparing food. For a moment she wondered what it could be, and replied instantly, 'Whatever it is, share equally with your brothers.'

'What?' a shocked Arjuna said, 'it is Draupadi.'

Kunti came out running and saw the beautiful Draupadi standing with Arjuna. A few paces behind the couple, stood the rest of her sons. An epitome of beauty and elegance, one look at Draupadi made Kunti realize all the qualities of Yagyaseni.

'How can I allow her to stay with Arjuna alone? The human mind is fickle and jealousy is the first to eat at it. If we aspire for Hastinapur, I need to keep the five brothers together,' Kunti mused. Suddenly, Pandu's voice reverberated inside her head, 'Kunti, learn to synchronize yourself with the movement of the Universe. Follow the hints that nature sends your way. You will always be at peace.'

'Goddess Saraswati made me speak those words; she showed me what I must do,' Kunti was convinced. 'You have to follow what I have said,' she announced to her sons and then turned to Yudhishthira.

'Does dharma allow it, son?'

'Yes, mother. Vidula married ten Pracheta brothers in the past and no blemish was attached to her.'

Kunti remembered refusing Pandu one more son from *niyoga*. But how can a wise Yudhishthira be wrong? 'It is a pragmatic decision,' she thought. 'It is for the collective good. Why should I play a Bhishma here?'

At that moment, Krishna surprised everyone by his appearance. He had quietly trailed the five Pandavas and Draupadi to their hermitage. Touching Kunti's feet, he introduced himself.

'What Yudhishthira has said is correct. There is no harm in her marrying all five Pandava brothers,' he said with an authority that was impossible to ignore.

'In her past life, Draupadi had completed a tough penance to have an ideal husband who would be truthful, honest, strong, skilled, handsome and knowledgeable. Pleased with her devotion, Lord Shiva had blessed her. "Child, finding all these qualities in one man is impossible. But, I will not disappoint you. You will have five men, each epitomizing one of these qualities, in your next birth."'

Krishna's words made Kunti happy. 'With time, everyone will get used to this,' she thought.

In Krishna, Kunti and her sons found a powerful guide, ally and guru. In a very short period of time, their affection and faith became devotion.

'Will Krishna always be with us, through thick and thin?' Kunti asked Sahadeva.

'Who is a more potent and durable ally than Krishna?' Sahadeva asked her in response. Kunti understood what her wise son meant. By that time, Krishna had become a legend. The stories of his heroism reached mythical proportions and despite him not being the king himself, he had become the supreme and undisputed leader of the Yadavas and related clans.

'Firm ambitions always take shape: Their only mantra is the alignment of *sankalpa* and effort,' Krishna comforted his aunt. 'Look, you wished to be queen and you got that. Now, your five valiant sons are working to attain immortal glory. Life means facing challenges and difficulties fearlessly. You have set very high goals for your sons. Don't be afraid of the difficulties on their path.'

'Drupada will reach here in a few moments,' Krishna said, as if he knew everything. Sahadeva nodded very slightly. He recognized the young man who had forbidden him from revealing his powers to anyone. 'You can now return to Hastinapur. Your strength matches that of the Kauravas. They will not dare harm you again. Go there and demand your rights,' Krishna said.

As predicted, just then, many royal chariots halted outside Kunti's hut, while Krishna was advising the Pandavas.

Drupada was very happy to learn the real identity of the graduate Brahmins, but he became pensive on hearing of Kunti's decision to give five husbands to his beloved daughter. He approached Krishna and expressed his concerns. Krishna told him the stories of Draupadi's past births and the boon she had received from Shiva. He also told Drupada about a curse that Draupadi had received from sage Maudgalya, her husband in a previous birth.

'Disgusted by the insatiable lust of his loving wife Nalayani, Maudgalya had cursed her that in her next birth she would be the wife of many men. Nalayani has been born as Draupadi in this birth,' Krishna told Drupada. 'King, you need not worry. Your daughter is capable enough of managing five husbands. She will be their strength and the cause of their glory.'

Krishna comforted the Panchals in every possible way. Finally, a satisfied Drupada bade farewell to his sons-in-law, with plenty of gifts loaded on hundreds of elephants and chariots.

'Don't worry, the Kuru elders will receive you with love and affection,' Krishna assured Kunti and then added, 'I will convince Vidura that the only way to maintain peace is to divide the kingdom. Bhishma may oppose it, but Dhritarashtra will not disagree.'

Everything happened just as Krishna had predicted. With a little prodding from Vidura, Dhritarashtra reluctantly gave the Pandavas a small share of the kingdom: the barren land of Khandavaprastha, which was devoid of any resources. Bhishma vehemently opposed the division of the kingdom.

'Vidura, your advice has bereaved me. I am alive and helplessly watching this division of my motherland!' he cried.

'Mortals cannot fight against time, grandsire,' Vidura replied. 'You are blessed with the power to choose your moment of death, yet you cannot control the destiny of others. Grandsire, our wills cannot be imposed on time forever. Take heart, protect whatsoever is left in Hastinapur.'

With the help of Krishna, the Pandavas turned a barren and arid land into the most beautiful and prosperous territory on earth, to the envy of their Kaurava cousins. Yudhishthira was now king. Kunti finally found some solace.

'Krishna, now with you in command, I can retire peacefully,' Kunti said to Krishna.

'Come on, aunt! Do you not desire the throne of Hastinapur for your sons?' Krishna smiled. Kunti's face paled. 'Desires never die. Once you desire something, it sticks like glue in your memory,' she thought.

'No, Kanha. I am satisfied with Indraprastha,' she said bravely.

'Your sons have grown up and they are supported by a highly ambitious, competent and determined wife. They will find their way. So, if you desire, you may retire,' Krishna said. 'But... '

'But?'

'You have an old debt to pay,' Krishna said, looking into Kunti's eyes, 'to your first son, Karna. We naturally forget our past deeds, but they always return to haunt us later. We can not liberate ourselves without settling past dues.'

'How does he know that?' a stunned Kunti wondered, speechless.

❧

The happy days evaporated quickly. After establishing themselves at their new capital Indraprastha, the Pandavas conquered a number of states and performed *Rajasuya Yagna*. Yudhishthira had invited kings and princes, including haughty Duryodhana, from the whole of Aryavarta for the *Yagna*. During that *Yagna*, which had not yet been achieved by any of their contemporaries, Krishna and Bhishma declared Yudhishthira a *chakravartin* king. A jealous Duryodhana, in league with Gandhari's scheming brother Shakuni, hatched a plan to usurp the Pandavas' peace, wealth, kingdom and prestige by deceit. Shakuni was a grandmaster in the game of dice and he knew that the game was Yudhishthira's weakness. It was decided that Dhritarashtra would invite his nephews for a game of dice. Yudhishthira would not be able refuse his uncle.

'But how will you ensure that we win?' Duryodhana demanded.

'Trust me, son. The dice will fall only the way I command,' Shakuni reassured him.

This assurance gladdened Duryodhana's heart. No one knew or imagined in their wildest dreams that Shakuni was playing a two-faced game of treachery to destroy the Kuru clan.

～

One day, long ago, when the Kauravas and Pandavas were children, they ended up fighting while playing together, which was quite the norm. Duryodhana abused the Pandavas, 'You call yourself the Pandavas, but you are not Pandu's sons. You are the children of a whore!'

Taken aback, the Pandavas did not know how to react for a few moments. Then, Bhima thundered, 'If so, then you are the children of a widow!'

'Liar!' Duryodhana refused to accept this allegation. 'My mother's only husband is my father. She is not like your mother, who had many partners!'

'Go and ask your mother, she was a widow!' Bhima said confidently.

Surprised, the Kauravas went to Bhishma and narrated the allegation to him. He took it very seriously and investigated.

Bhishma found out that Bhima's allegation was indeed true. When Gandhari was born, the astrologers foretold her father that the girl's first husband would have a very short life. A scared king Suvala, the father of Gandhari, decided to get his daughter married to a goat. Soon after the symbolic marriage, the goat was killed. Thus, in a way, Gandhari was a widow.

This infuriated Bhishma. He called the local astrologers who confirmed the story by studying Gandhari's horoscope. Rubbing salt in Bhishma's injured pride, the astrologers added that the Kauravas were actually the children that the goat would have fathered had he not been sacrificed.

An enraged Bhishma warned the astrologers not to tell this terrible secret to anyone and decided to kill Suvala and his family for hiding the truth. He imprisoned them and instructed the provision of only a fistful of rice for the entire imprisoned family.

'Do you know why Bhishma is allowing us only a handful of rice?' Suvala rhetorically asked his youngest and brightest son, Shakuni.

'Bhishma wants to kill us, but without breaking the code of dharma. It is a sin to kill a relative. So, he gives us only a fistful of rice, so that we starve and die. He knows that it is also a sin for us to ask for more food,' Suvala told Shakuni.

'I hate that old creature. He cares more for dead texts than for living human beings. He is like a static pool that thinks it has stopped the movement of the earth,' Shakuni spat on the ground in anger.

'What are we waiting for? To die of starvation?' a hungry and tired Shakuni asked his father. 'Why don't we run away from this prison?'

'We cannot,' his father replied. 'They are giving us food, howsoever little it is. The *shastras* say that it is a sin to leave your daughter's house while her in-laws are still serving you food.'

'Why are you speaking like that old hat? Do you believe in these books you are referring to, these poems that you dare not dishonour but are ready to die for?'

'Son, my ancestors believed in these scriptures. They made me promise to follow them. I cannot dishonour my ancestors. But I will not bind you to these traditions,' Suvala was almost in tears.

'How cunning this Bhishma is!' Shakuni was filled with limitless hatred for the oldest Kuru. 'Dharma! What kind of dharma is this? He is the biggest manipulator of dharma. He has a black soul behind those white robes!' Young Shakuni vowed, 'Father, I will destroy them all. I will take revenge!'

The family survived for a few more days, and then Suvala took a terrible decision. 'Let us agree not to eat. Only Shakuni eats, because he is the youngest and the most intelligent. Thus, at least one of us will survive.' Then he turned to young Shakuni. 'Son, we are dying so that you can live, to take revenge against Bhishma: A revenge that destroys these arrogant Kurus.' Suvala thus extracted a promise from his son.

All the family starved and died one by one, before the eyes of a young Shakuni. When only Suvala and Shakuni were left alive, the father struck the son's foot and fractured it.

'Shakuni, my son, forgive me for this! Every limping step of yours will remind you of Bhishma's crime and our painful deaths. This limp will not allow you to forget the revenge,' Suvala said, laughing demonically and then bursting into tears.

Young Shakuni looked at his crying father. He was nothing but a skeleton of thin and weak bones. Shakuni shivered with fear. He placed his father's head on his lap. 'How can I?' Shakuni could barely murmur.

Suvala cried out in pain and anger, 'I never thought you were so weak. Everyone died so that you can live. Shame on you!' Then, realizing the pathetic state of his young son, Suvala consoled him and devised a way.

'Son, you have to be more cunning than the Kurus. When I die, take my finger bones and mould them into a dice. These are rage-filled bones and will turn whichever way you command them to. Playing with these dice, you will always win.'

Shakuni looked at his father. Suvala died before his tears were dry.

After Suvala's death, on Gandhari's prayer, Bhishma released Shakuni from prison and raised him like a prince. But Shakuni never forgave Bhishma for what he had done to his family. Now the Pandavas had been invited for a game of dice that would be played with Suvala's bones.

~

Once the Pandavas began gambling, everything changed quickly. They lost their wealth, their kingdom, their people, their prestige and themselves, as well as their wife Draupadi, in the game of dice. Dharmaraja Yudhishthira treated Draupadi as his property and betted on her. Bhishma, Dronacharya, Vidura and the entire Kaurava assembly, chaired by the blind Dhritarashtra, chose to remain silent spectators. None of the Pandava brothers voiced an opinion against Yudhishthira's madness.

Only few months ago, during the *Rajasuya Yagna* at Indraprastha, Draupadi had ridiculed Duryodhana for mistaking between a virtual and a real pond. A laughing Draupadi had mocked, 'A blind man only produces blind children!'

At that time, Duryodhana had swallowed his anger and had chosen not to reply. Today was his chance to take revenge. He asked Dusshasana to bring Draupadi to the royal court. A menstruating Draupadi prayed to him not to take her to the gambling hall, but Dusshasana forcibly grabbed her hair and dragged her there. Barely clothed, she was pushed at Duryodhana's feet. No one came to her rescue.

'Anything can be done with a slave. What do you say, Yudhishthira?' Duryodhana laughed.

'What will he say, Duryodhana?' Vikarna, the younger brother of Duryodhana, got up from his seat. 'Yudhishthira is your slave, so he had no right to stake Draupadi. Once he lost himself in the game, how could he bet on Draupadi? Leave her, Duryodhana,' Vikarna requested.

'Once the master of the house loses, everything that he possesses is transferred to the winner,' Karna rebuked Vikarna. 'And before advocating for her, you should remember that this Draupadi is not a chaste woman. A woman with five husbands is no less than a whore. How can a whore have dignity? Duryodhana can do whatever he wants with her!'

Encouraged by Karna's words, Duryodhana shouted, 'Dusshasana, disrobe this whore and make her sit on my lap!' The vile Dusshashana then began pulling away Draupadi's clothes. She prayed to Krishna to save her.

When Kunti was told what had happened in the Kuru assembly, she too remembered Krishna. She realized that her own son Karna had dishonoured her daughter-in-law.

'Kunti, don't wait. Reveal the truth,' her conscience said. 'Whose well-being and honour is bigger, Kunti? Your's or your family's? Are you not behaving like Bhishma?' But Kunti did not have the courage to follow her heart.

Draupadi's humiliation in the Kuru court created such a disastrous uproar that Dhritarashtra was forced to return to the Pandavas whatever they had gambled away. But a relentless Duryodhana forced his father to invite them again for another game of dice. The Pandavas lost again and this time they were awarded twelve years in exile and one year in hiding.

'If you get recognized in that final year, you shall have to repeat the exile for another twelve years!' This condition was the final stake in the game of dice, and Yudhishthira lost that as well.

'When your children become strong-headed adults, how difficult it becomes to put sense into their heads! How helpless I am!' Kunti lamented. She wanted to follow her sons into exile, but after a discussion with Yudhishthira, she decided to stay back in Hastinapur.

For the next thirteen years, the Pandavas amassed a lot of goodwill, celestial weapons, powerful relatives, influential friends and allies, and a will to win back their lost kingdom. They arrived at the gate of Hastinapur after successfully completing their term and demanded their kingdom back. But Duryodhana was not ready to give them an inch of the land. Hardened by immeasurable sufferings, humiliation and adversity, the Pandavas made one last peaceful effort to regain what was rightfully theirs. Krishna was sent as their peace messenger. Krishna tried everything, but he too failed, as Duryodhana refused to listen to him. After an unsuccessful meeting at the Kuru court, Krishna came to meet Kunti.

'Aunt, we have tried everything, but Duryodhana is not listening. All our attempts to avoid bloodshed have failed.' He looked into Kunti's eyes and said, 'But the war can be avoided if you agree.'

Kunti looked at Krishna with expectation and apprehension.

'Go and meet your eldest son; reveal Karna's true identity. Tell him that you are his mother and request him to come back to you and lead the Pandavas. Tell him that he will rule this land, and the five powerful Pandavas will serve him along with the beautiful Panchali.'

'I cannot, Krishna! How can I?'

'Aunt, if you hesitate now, you and the Pandavas will repent forever. If Karna stays with Duryodhana, then the entire Kuru clan will suffer, there will be millions of widows and orphans. Kuru blood will flood this land and everyone will be a loser,' Krishna warned Kunti.

'Why don't you go, Krishna? Who can convince him better than you?' Kunti urged Krishna. She was too ashamed to go to the innocent child she had abandoned.

'Your wish is my command, aunt. But, think again! Who can substitute a mother?' Kunti did not relent. That night, in hindsight, she thought, 'Even God cannot replace a mother. What if I had gone to meet Karna before the battle began?'

Krishna went to meet Karna and told him everything about his birth. The truth was too grave to bear. Karna had suffered lifelong humiliation because of his birth and his caste. All his qualities had been sacrificed at the altar of his low caste. He was ridiculed in royal assemblies, gatherings and events for being a charioteer's son.

First his own mother had disowned Karna, and then his guru Parashuram had cursed him. When Karna had challenged the royal princes at the graduation ceremony, Bhishma had humiliated him in public. Since then, Bhishma had used every occasion and every opportunity to humiliate Karna. Despite Duryodhana's generosity, Karna knew what Dhritarashtra and Shakuni said about him behind his back.

Krishna's disclosure shook the very foundation of Karna's self-made identity: He was jolted by the revelation that he was a Kshatriya—and Kunti's son on top of that. Destiny had played a cruel joke on him. It was yet another test of his tragic yet robust character, and as always, Karna rose to the occasion. He was not one to be tempted by the gods and their grace. His convictions were his dharma and his way of life. Karna, the son of the sun, rejected Krishna's tempting offer. Krishna tried everything—history, philosophy and dharma—to convince the eldest son of Kunti, but Karna remained unmoved.

'I am Radha's son, Krishna,' Karna smiled wryly.

'Karna, leave Kunti and the Pandavas aside for a moment. Just think, if you choose not to support Duryodhana, he may rethink and settle for a compromise. Then, this war will be avoided and millions of lives will be saved.'

'Krishna, if you think so, you don't understand Duryodhana: He will not compromise. And Vasudeva, even for the empire of heaven, I will never abandon my friend,' Karna replied firmly.

Despite Krishna's persistence and advocacy, Karna did not budge. However, both men agreed to keep Karna's real identity a secret.

In the end, Duryodhana was not ready to give even five villages to his cousins, and Karna refused to join the Pandavas. A war was now inevitable. Pledging never to pick up a weapon in the war, Krishna offered both sides to pick either him or his eighteen-million-strong army. Duryodhana happily took eighteen million men. Arjuna devotedly requested Krishna to drive his chariot in the battlefield.

After a month, a gruesome war began at Kurukshetra. Bhishma was made the chief commander of the Kaurava army and the Pandavas chose Draupadi's brother Drishtadhyumna as their commander-in-chief. However, Bhishma refused to allow Karna to fight under his command and Duryodhana reluctantly agreed after Karna counselled him. Thus, Kunti's eldest son sat away from the war for the first ten days.

'Was Bhishma aware of Karna's true identity?' Kunti wondered.

In the Mahabharata War at Kurukshetra, thousands of soldiers died each day. On the tenth day, Bhishma too fell. Then, Arjuna lost his son Abhimanyu. After commanding the Kauravas in war for five days, Dronacharya was also killed. The three elders Dhritarashtra, Gandhari and Kunti, sitting before Sanjaya, the clairvoyant, saw their ambitions, desires and conflicts killing their kin and friends in the battlefield.

'Dronacharya is dead. Who will be the new commander of the Kauravas now?' Gandhari asked.

'Who else but the charioteer's son!' Dhritarashtra replied.

Kunti's heart sank with those words. The past had presented itself before her at its ugliest form.

'My eldest son, fighting against his own brothers! They don't know that, but he does.' Kunti now repented not following Krishna's advice. 'Is it too late?' she wondered, and decided to talk to Karna. 'Only he can ensure the end of the Kauravas and safety of all my sons!'

Around midnight, she left the palace and by dawn she reached Karna's place of meditation.

A day earlier, Arjuna's father Indra had deceptively stripped Karna of his invincible armour and magical earrings. Karna, who never refused any beggar had happily given away what the cunning king of the Adityas had begged for. Bloodstains were still visible on his broad chest and earlobes.

Both mother and son knew why they were meeting. The initial sarcasm in Karna's voice slowly turned into a sincere desire to help his mother. He was perplexed by the elderly woman who had ignored him all her life. Now, she was standing before him, requesting him to join her other sons, when he was readying himself for the penultimate clash with his archrival, Arjuna.

'Why? Why did you abandon me?' Karna wanted to ask. However, he decided not to ask anything.

'I don't want my sons to die,' Kunti begged her eldest son.

Karna smiled. He was not the one to turn away a beggar emptyhanded. 'The world knows you as the mother of five sons. I promise you, at the end of the war, you will still have five sons. I will not kill any Pandava, except Arjuna,' Karna assured her.

'Why can't I have all six?' Kunti asked with her head bowed.

'Mother, don't snatch away my purpose of life from me,' Karna requested with folded hands and tears in his eyes.

True to his words, Karna fulfilled his promise. He defeated each Pandava brother, except Arjuna, in the battlefield and let them off alive. He granted them their life without a moment's hesitation. However, he made them realize that they owed their life to their sworn enemy, Karna.

At the end of the seventeenth day of war, just before sunset, Karna's chariot wheel got stuck in a wet patch on the field. He asked his charioteer Shalya, the king of Madra, the maternal uncle of Nakul and Sahadeva, to help him pull out the wheel. Shalya refused to help, saying that it was beneath the dignity of a king to help the low caste son of a charioteer. Karna was left with no option, but to descend from the chariot and release the wheel himself. The moment he descended, as he was about to pull out the wheel, Arjuna shot the unarmed Karna on his chest and killed him.

After the war, when Kunti was searching among the Kaurava corpses, her curious sons asked what she was looking for.

'Karna's body,' she replied.

'Why? Why are you looking for the body of that son of a charioteer?' Arjuna was the first to scoff at her.

Then, she revealed the truth to them. Initially, they did not believe her. When the truth sank in, they were devastated.

'For this throne, I killed my elder brother!' Arjuna lamented.

'Why did you not tell us before? Why?' an agitated Yudhishthira demanded. 'My throne is sullied by my elder brother's blood!' he cried, and then cursed all womenfolk, 'Let no woman ever again be able to keep any secret in her belly!'

Kunti remained silent.

'You must have realized that he did not kill you, Yudhishthira,' Krishna came forward and intervened. 'He was your elder brother and he granted you your life. He fulfilled the promise that he had made to his mother.'

'What? You mean he knew that he was our brother?'

'Yes. He knew. He knew it before the battle.'

'Keshava, why did you not tell us this?' Arjuna cried.

'If you knew, would you have fought him? In that case, the

Kauravas would have been victorious, because Karna would never abandon them and Yudhisthira would have refused to fight against his elder brother. How would the reign of dharma have been established?' Krishna explained.

2

Protection

As it had happened many times in the past, like divine magic, a smiling Krishna walked into the royal palace early next morning.

'Aunt, why were you calling me?' he asked.

A surprised Kunti took Krishna to her chamber and arranged for his food. After making him comfortable, Kunti narrated everything that was happening in Yudhishthira's Hastinapur and inside the royal household.

'Why must an old Dhritarashtra suffer so much? Why cannot he, or for that matter Gandhari and I, leave this city? Krishna, guide us. Do you think we still have some worldly desires left?'

'Aunt, if you are in this palace, then you certainly have desires associated with this place. Otherwise, why would the old Kurus suffer so much humiliation?'

'Don't you think it is time for us to proceed on *sanyasa*?' Kunti asked.

'I cannot answer this, you have to decide for yourself,' Krishna said with a smile. 'Reflect if your conscience and existence require this place any more, and then, decide.'

'Krishna, you know everything. Since my sons learnt about Karna, our relationship has not been normal. My sons have the kingdom, but there is no one to share their joy. They cannot keep their elders happy, even after becoming masters of the earth,' Kunti said with a heavy heart. 'I am not at peace, Krishna.'

Krishna held Kunti's hand gently.

'Do our achievements make us happy?' she asked.

'That's the irony, aunt. Accomplishments give you temporary happiness, a momentary high; but the loss you incur in the process of these worldly achievements is often huge. The secret is that all the happiness and pain in life cannot be gauged by a standard yardstick. Accomplishing, achieving and accumulating land, prestige or wealth does not provide a lasting happiness.'

'Is it wrong for a mother to push her sons towards achievements? And when they have achieved, why am I still not at peace?'

'A child's accomplishments always delight a mother. But, if a parent adds her own ambition to her children's, then she cannot be happy.' Krishna looked at Kunti and then added, 'Motherhood is sacred, aunt. Nothing else in this world can even come close to that feeling, and the joy of motherhood comes from giving.'

Kunti remained silent for a long time and then said in a low voice, 'Am I the most unfortunate and unhappiest mother ever?'

Krishna laughed. 'Unfortunate? How can someone who gives life be unfortunate?' Krishna smiled playfully and then said, 'Unhappy? Maybe. But unhappiness is a state of mind and that is a result of your circumstances, actions and the times.'

'I don't agree,' said Kunti. 'Perhaps Gandhari and I are the most unfortunate and aggrieved mothers ever!'

'Aunt, in this world, everyone has to face happiness and sorrow: Only the degree varies, with ambitions and actions. So, it's a choice that an individual makes. Is there anyone better than a mother to understand that there is immense joy in separation? How can new creation be possible without separation? If you understand this, then there is no pain.'

'Krishna, mere *gyana* will not provide me peace. You know both, the beginning and the end. I don't understand your philosophy. Gandhari and I have lost our sons. Now, I realize how useless that war was. I repent not staying in the forest with the learned sages.'

'Aunt, you are not being completely transparent yet,' Krishna smiled. 'I know Karna's memory still haunts you, but you are not the first mother who has seen her son dying before her eyes.'

Kunti did not say a word. She waited for Krishna to continue.

'Aunt, no mother can bear to see her child in pain. A mother's sacrifice for her child is immeasurable. But once a child takes birth, he becomes an independent identity and cannot be controlled by a mother completely. And why should a mother or father try to do so? When Dyaus and Prithvi were young and energetic, they began creating life on land, in the sea and in the air. And they, the most ancient couple, thought they were the wisest and the greatest as well!

'They thought that they would inspire their children to promote righteousness. Therefore, they provided them with lavish gifts for their just behaviour. But, as you know, not all could remain just. Once independent, their children chose their own way of life. Therefore, for a mother, there is always both pain and pleasure.

'Tell me, aunt, what will happen if the children's greed multiplies and they demand their mother's life?'

'She will happily give it,' Kunti instinctively answered.

'Aunt, you forgot,' Krishna smiled again. 'You could not muster the courage to own Karna in his lifetime.'

Kunti said nothing. Krishna moved a little closer to her and apologized, 'I am sorry.'

'Don't be sorry, Kanha. That was the truth. Let us continue the story,' Kunti wiped away her tears.

'A mother cannot afford to die. She will become a ghost, worried for her children's welfare. This earth, this Prithvi, is our primitive mother. Like all mothers, she has always wished if somehow all her children could live forever.'

'But death has no emotion. It is inevitable. Who can prevent death?' Kunti asked.

'Yes, that's the cosmic law and it has always coexisted with the creation of the Universe,' Krishna replied. 'We all know this truth. But when Prithvi and Dyaus began procreating, they wondered if all their children could be immortal.

'Death has been here since the beginning of the cosmos. It is not an intrinsic part of the Divinity, but it is an intrinsic part of creation. Thus, there is no creation without death. Even the creator Brahma is not above this cosmic law. This entire cosmos, that has millions and millions of galaxies, and billions and billions of stars, also goes through this cycle of death and rebirth.'

Boons & Curses

Kunti listened in silence as Krishna continued.

'Aunt, in the beginning when Brahma was producing organisms, and he was pregnant with them, Death appeared and seized the creatures one by one. Death thus overpowered the creator. Brahma saw it as the defeat of the whole purpose of creation.

'To save the process of creation, and to prolong the life of his creations, a scared Brahma practiced *tapa* for one thousand years. Only after this long meditation, did clarity dawn on him, and he realized the distinction between death and desire. He could then see the purpose of death.'

Krishna paused, and then continued.

'Brahma realized that death is hunger and hunger is associated with desire. Now, you know that desire involves killing, for it makes something disappear. Therefore, death became inevitable if the longevity and perpetuation of life were desired. The moment Brahma understood this secret, he defeated Death.'

'When he defeated Death, what happened to him?' Kunti inquired.

'Diti, the mother of the mighty Daityas, also asked this question to Prithvi.'

'Why did she ask Prithvi?'

'Because Prithvi keeps and reveals all secrets. And this is their conversation:

"What happened to Death?" Diti asked Prithvi.

"Diti, in the end, Death took refuge in a woman's hut."

"What?" a shocked Diti exclaimed. "Does this mean that my sons can't be immortal?"

'Prithvi hated answering this question, but replied, "No. Diti, one can prolong life but cannot escape Death."

"I don't understand. Is there another way?" Diti asked.

"Diti, when a victorious Brahma set out to teach the gods and the creatures how to prolong their lives, Death appeared before him and protested. "Now everyone will become immortal and then what will happen to my share?"

'Brahma negotiated and then decided, "From now on, no one will be immortal in their body. They can be immortal only after you have taken the body as your part. One can achieve immortality either through knowledge or through sacred work, after being separated from their body."

'Prithvi consoled Diti. "My dear, no one has seen Death leaving the woman's hut. And Death does not die. So, tell your sons to do good work, attain knowledge and thus become immortal."'

Krishna completed the story of Diti and Prithvi and said, 'And your sons have also been trying to do that, aunt. You should feel happy, because they are trying to achieve immortality through their good deeds. On the other hand, Diti never believed Prithvi. She and her sons continued attempting victory over Death by other means, and failed. Mother Gandhari is an incarnation of Diti.'

'Tell me the story from the beginning,' a curious Kunti urged.

'I will do that.'

Krishna began the story of mothers.

'In the early days, when people behaved like reckless animals, Ven was made the king of human beings. Ven's father Anga was a benevolent man. Ven's mother Sunitha was a daughter of Death and Ven carried the traits of his grandfather. He enjoyed killing creatures, be it an innocent deer or a human being. Frustrated with his son's evil deeds, Anga deserted the palace and settled in a faraway forest.

'Ven was a strict and cruel ruler. When thieves and rioters learnt this, they went into hiding like rats being terrorized by a snake. But this forced order and happiness did not last long. Very soon, Ven became a dictator and tormentor of one and all.

'"Ven has disappointed us. We were scared of anarchy and made him king, but now he himself has become a terrorist. We chose him to safeguard the interests of society, but now he is hell-bent on destroying society itself," the sages of the age discussed among themselves. They had been responsible for anointing Ven as king.

'"We should counsel him," the eldest among them proposed.

'So, they spoke to the king: "Respected king, people are dissatisfied and frustrated with your rule. We are here to request you to act with compassion, generosity and munificence. Follow the rule of ethics, so that the gods bless you and your populace. Pray to them to give you good sense, consciousness, ability and strength to rule wisely."

'Their words angered Ven. "You stupid, ignominious, wretched and profane old men! You are my subjects, yet you pray to another master and dare advise me to pray to him. Remember, you cannot live in peace, neither here nor in another world, if you disrespect and disobey your king. You behave as a woman of lose character, who does not love her husband and is enamoured of other males," Ven mocked them cruelly.

'"Fools, don't you know that all those gods, capable of giving boons and curses, live in the body of the king? Therefore, the king encompasses them all. Yet you clowns pray to those insignificant gods! Henceforth, everyone will worship only me and I will punish the unfaithful."

'He warned the sages, "Sinners, you consider yourselves the custodians of dharma. Now, hear me. I am dharma. Eulogize me and sing songs in my praise!"

'"Ven, you have become insane. You have lost your wisdom and power of reasoning!" a sage shouted.

'"Kill this worthless soul!" Ven commanded his soldiers.

'But before the soldiers could respond, the assembled sages cornered Ven and slit his throat.

'When she heard the commotion, Sunitha reached the spot. She mourned and sat beside her son's dead body. Ven was childless. Sunitha was worried about the imminent end of her son's lineage. She decided to protect his dead body, hoping for some miracle.

'Days and months passed. A kingless land again fell into anarchy. The land needed an authority to restore law and order. The sages discussed the matter first among themselves and later with Sunitha, and concluded that king Anga's lineage must be salvaged.

'Sunitha insisted that Ven's thigh should yield his progeny. The sages scraped out cells from Ven's thigh and churned them. These cells produced a man whose tendencies were cruel since inception. Sunitha took him away, and kept him in hiding. It is said that, since then, all humans involved in bad deeds tend to hide.

'The disappointed sages now scooped cells from Ven's arms. From these cells, they created a couple. The man was destined to expand his compassionate rule throughout the land and, hence, was called Prithu. Archi, the woman, became the wife of Prithu. The sages declared that Prithu would be the first master of Prithvi, the earth.

'When Prithu took the reigns of the land, it was barren, sterile and famine-stricken. Dying people cried before the king, "As a tree is consumed by a fire in its cavity, our bellies, burning with hunger, are destroying us. O king, please save us!" The cries of his people troubled Prithu. He contemplated and then arrived at a conclusion: "Prithvi has knowingly hidden cereals, medicines and metals inside her." Angrily, he shouted, "I will extract food and material from her!" Aiming at Prithvi, he mounted an all-annihilating arrow on his mighty bow.

'Trembling with fear, Prithvi ran away like a scared deer. She took the form of a helpless cow and ran for her life. Seeing her running away like this, enraged Prithu further and he followed her. Wherever she went, from heaven to hell, one universe to other, an angry Prithu chased the scared cow.

'Finally, an exhausted Prithvi stopped. There was nowhere to hide. She surrendered before Prithu and prayed for her life. "Prithu, what is my crime? What have I done? Why are you aiming to destroy me? If I die, how will you and your people survive?"

'"Prithvi, you are right: We will die anyway, either by starvation or by your destruction." Prithu wondered at the helpless logic that he had just uttered. He thought for a while and then threatened her, "In the beginning, all kinds of seeds and minerals were produced by Brahma. You have hidden them inside your belly. You don't care for us living beings. I am determined to penetrate your skin with my sharp arrows and release those seeds."

'For a few moments, both stood staring at each other, and then Prithu lowered his bow. Sensing that Prithu could now be engaged in conversation, Prithvi spoke with a little more courage.

'"Prithu, I have enough for everyone's need, but very little for anyone's greed. Except humans, none of my children exploit my resources or accumulate the produce. Humans have become like thieves. They amass everything in abundance, whether required or not. They spoil and waste, without realizing that even a mother needs nourishment and care. Therefore, I have hidden all resources inside me."

'Prithu understood what Prithvi was trying to say. "Your indiscreet burial of resources has put the lives of innocent creatures in jeopardy. What about them?" he politely asked.

'"Prithu, here comes your role: the role of a king." Prithvi hoped that the new king understood his responsibilities. "A king must prohibit destruction, pollution and over-exploitation of resources. He must try to sustain these for posterity. If a king fails in this duty, thieves roam freely and destroy the wealth of the earth."

'Prithu was beginning to understand, but he was not sure how to get the resources. Prithvi sensed it and offered him a way.

'"Prithu, have you seen a calf drinking milk from the udder? Humans should act like that calf."

'Prithu followed her directions and milked cereal seeds from Prithvi and held them in his hands. The learned sages milked the Vedas into their senses. The gods milked nectar, semen, grace and physical power into a golden bowl. The demons milked wine and other drinks and kept them in an iron vessel. The Gandharvas and damsels milked the sweetness of music and beauty and kept it in a lotus pot. Following them, all creatures milked the earth according to their need and obtained the essential products.

'Prithu became emotional, seeing a mother's capacity to give. He vowed to take care of mother Prithvi as his daughter. "The role of a king is akin to a father," he now realized that.'

~

'She is the greatest mother, our mother earth, Prithvi,' Krishna said. 'I wonder to think of her joy when she witnesses billions of her children playing and enjoying in her lap all the time!'

Kunti remembered nascent Karna's innocent face and the memory overwhelmed her. In her mind, she brought her face down to kiss her baby. But, before she could do so, a sweet fragrance filled her nostrils and refreshed her body, mind and soul. Every mother savours in her soul, the fragrance that emanates from her young and tender infant. Like a cautious mother, she wanted to have infinite amounts of that aroma. Suddenly, the memory of pushing the little basket into the river disrupted everything.

'What did I do? I abandoned him!' she almost cried out.

Krishna read the passing emotions on the face of Kunti.

'Aunt, only a mother can pass on that divine aroma to her child… Do you know what Brahma once said about Prithvi's fragrance?'

'"O Prithvi, in ancient times, your fragrance was implanted inside the lotus. That was then presented to Surya by the gods during his marriage."'*

'What does a child get from its father?' Kunti interrupted

---

*यस्तेगंधः पुष्करमाविवेश यंसंजभुज्ञः सूर्यायविवाहे। (अथर्ववेद12/1/24)

Krishna. She had four sons from four men, but their roles in her sons' lives had been limited to insemination only.

'Mother, you create life,' for the first time, Krishna addressed Kunti as mother. 'Like mother earth, whose revolution brings seasons and whose rotation turns a day into a night and a night into a day, a mother remains forever novel, forever unique, forever benign and forever dynamic. But mother, you alone cannot procreate. Your conductors are the sun and the space. Only when you join the sun and the space, you become *Dhyavaprithvi* and can procreate. Life always moves on two wheels, as Kashyapa had once said to his wives.'

'What did Kashyapa say to his wives?' Kunti asked.

'The mystery of the origin of the cosmos is the mystery of how one takes the form of many, and how many are merged into one,' Krishna began his tale.

'The Progenitor had made Brahma both the creator and the first creation of the cosmos. Brahma's consciousness created his nine *manasputra*s, or the mind-born sons. All nine sons were of twenty-five years of age at birth. They were: Atri, Mareechi, Bhrigu, Pulastya, Pulaha, Kratu, Kardama, Angiras and Vasishtha. Brahma, thus commencing the cycle of creation, wished that his *manasputra*s would produce various species. On his command, the *manasputra*s inhabited various parts of the cosmos. Thus, they were also called the *prajapati*s and were commanded to abound the cosmos with their progenies. Brahma also created a few women for them. Thus, Atri, Kardama, Bhrigu, Pulastya, Pulaha, Kratu, Angiras and Vasishtha married Anusuya, Devahuti, Khyati, Bhuti, Sambhuti, Kshama, Shraddha and Urja respectively. After some time, a daughter Kala was born to Kardama and Devahuti. She was married to Mareechi, a *manasputra* of Brahma.

'Later, when Brahma was in deep meditation, from his right thumb another *manasputra*, twenty-five-year-old Daksha was born. Daksha's wife was Prasuti, a daughter of another *manasputra* Manu. The young couple was ordained to fill the land, the sea and the sky with their progenies. Daksha was the chief among wagoners. Emulating his father and by exercising his will, Daksha fathered five thousand sons, called the *Haryaswaa*s.

'Procreation by will alone was a prerogative of the Supreme God and, by delegation, of his son Brahma's. Daksha's use of will to create sons was in violation of the cosmic law and thus was not liked by Brahma. He induced his other *manasputra* Narada to sort out this tricky affair. Thus, sage Narada went to meet the five thousand *Haryaswaa*s. He fired up the burning desire to become immortal in them, by knowledge and knowledge alone.

'"Sons, only by knowledge you can win over death," Narada convinced them. "Don't go back to your father, instead seek to decipher the secret of the cosmos and strive for the ultimate knowledge."

'Following the advice of Narada, the five thousands sons of Daksha set out in search of enlightenment and lost themselves in that eternal quest.

'A disappointed Daksha once again used his willpower and created one thousand more sons called the *Sabalaawaa*s. However, they too were persuaded by Narada to go on a quest to decode the mystery of the Universe. They too never returned.

When Daksha heard of this, he became mad with rage and cursed Narada, "Narada, you sinner, what have you achieved by fooling my sons and sending them on an eternal voyage?"

'Narada smiled, but kept mum. His smile fuelled Daksha's anger.

'"Narada, I curse you! You too will wander forever, like my sons who are wandering."

'However, cursing Narada could not dilute Daksha's anger. He met his father Brahma and registered his protest very strongly. Brahma listened to him patiently.

'"Son, procreation by will is not allowed to anyone except

the Supreme Lord and, by delegation, to me. If everyone uses this method of creation, it will create anarchy. You must not do it again. I can suggest you three other ways of procreation."

'His father's suggestion could not satisfy Daksha. He was a highly ambitious man. Creation by will, or *sankalpa srishti*, would have given him immense power. Any other method of procreation would take effort and consume a lot of time, he was sure.

'"Do you want to hear me out or not?" Brahma did not like his arrogant son's attitude. Daksha had no choice but to agree.

'"Son, you can procreate by three other methods. Through the mere look of an adept male, a female can conceive. This is called *sandarshana srishti*. In *sparsha srishti*, the touch of a capable male impregnates a female. Then, there is the most intimate method of creation, called *samparka srishti*. In this biological union of male and female, male semen fertilizes the egg present in a female's womb, then develops there and results in the birth of their progeny."

'"I want my progeny to bear my traits alone," Daksha demanded. "By these methods, will the progeny be entirely mine?"

'"Sorry son, I cannot allow that. If two living organisms are involved in procreation, then the progeny will bear the traits of both parents. In that way, evolution will be ensured. If I agree to your wish, it will interfere with the evolution of the species," Brahma replied. "Your child will carry physiognomies and properties of both of you."

'"I myself would like to give birth to my children. I should be both the mother and the father," Daksha protested.

'"I told you that is not possible," Brahma said irritatedly. "However, you may give the children your name and the lineage."

'A very unhappy Daksha returned to his abode.

'In time, Daksha and Prasuti procreated fourteen daughters. The eldest, Sati was married to Shiva. The individualist

Daksha neither liked his independent-minded daughter, nor his nonconformist son-in-law. After Sati, Prasuti gave birth to Aditi, Diti, Danu, Vinata, Kadru, Simhika, Krodha, Krura, Kapila, Muni, Anaayu, Kaala and Praadha.

'Slowly, Daksha came to terms with his other daughters, but he never made truce with Sati and Shiva.

'When Daksha's other daughters became of marriageable age, Daksha called them one by one and asked, "Daughters, it's time for you to join *grahastha* ashrama. Who would you like to marry? Do you have someone in mind?"

'Surprisingly, all of them chose Kashyapa, the son of sage Mareechi and his wife Kala, as their husband. Accepting their wish, Daksha married all of them to Kashyapa. Kashyapa and his thirteen wives were blessed with millions of children who inhabitated the land, the sea and the sky.

'Aditi gave birth to numerous Devas or the Adityas, including Indra and Varun. Diti gave birth to two sons, who were every inch the opposite of their stepbrothers, the Adityas. Diti's sons, Hiranyaksha and Hiranyakashipu, and their heirs, were called the Daityas. Danu bore the Daanavas, including Maya Daanava, Viprachiti, Sambara, Namuchi, Puloma, Asiloma, Virupaksha and others. Anaayu and Kashyapa's sons Vikshara, Bala, Veera and Vratasura and others were called the Rakshasas. Kaala gave birth to the Kalikeyas and Krodha bore the fierce Krodhavasas. Muni and Prada became the mothers of the Gandharvas and the remaining wives gave birth to various birds, animals and other creatures.'

⁓

'Once they attained adulthood, an intense fight began among Kashyapa's children, to capture the resources available in the universe,' Krishna continued. 'Based on their intrinsic characteristics and physical ability, the rivalry and the struggle among them became fierce and bloody.'

'Why did Kashyapa not stop his children?' Kunti asked.

'When a boy attains the age of fifteen and a girl the age of ten years, parents should treat them as their friends. It was not that Kashyapa did not try to unite his children: He educated them and taught them well. He counselled them to live harmoniously and stressed that nature provides enough for their needs and there was no need to shed each other's blood for their greed. But, his sons failed him.

'Soon, his children formed two prominent groups. Diti's sons were physically powerful and ready to put in hours of hard work, but they were *tamasik* in nature. These Daityas convinced the Daanavas, the Rakshasas, the Krodhavasas and the Kalikeyas to join their group. All of them shared a similar value system: They built grand civilisations based on majestic urban architecture, art and music.

'The Adityas were *rajasik* in nature. They were not as hard-working as the Daityas, but they were shrewder and a proud and arrogant lot. They created a civilisation based on the ethos of fine taste, opulence, grandeur and immortality. The Gandharvas, the Kinnaras and the Kimpurushas supported them.

'Another *manasputra,* Swayambhuva Manu and his wife Shatarupa began their connubial life to procreate human beings. Their children were supposed to be *satvik* by nature. Manu and Shatarupa had five children. Priyavrata and Uttanpaad were their sons and Aakuti, Devahuti and Prasuti were their daughters. As I mentioned earlier, Devahuti was married to Kardama and Brahma arranged the marriage of Prasuti with Daksha.'

'The children born to the same father can be so different,' Kunti commented, but felt embarrassed the moment the words left her mouth. There was hardly any similarity between Karna, Yudhishthira, Bhima and Arjuna.

Krishna smiled.

'Aunt, my guru once told me: The one who propitiates many gods, ancestors or humans, is in the dark. The one who takes pride in worshipping one omnipotent god has fallen into more darkness.'*

---

*अंधँतम: प्रविशंतियेअसम्भूतिंउपासते। ततोभूवइवतेतमोयउसम्भूत्यामरता: ॥

'Why so?' Kunti asked. 'Many monotheistic cults feel superior on this basis.'

'All organisms on this earth are made of the same elements. Compassion for all is the only path to enlightenment,' Krishna replied. 'This means that everyone is free to choose their own way of life. The more we know, the more humble we become.'

Kunti said nothing. 'Is there anyone whom I loved more than myself?' she wondered.

'Krishna, tell me about Aditi and Diti.'

～

'Despite the best efforts of their father Kashyapa, Indra, the leader of the Adityas and Hiranyaksha, the leader of the Daityas, became bloodthirsty sworn enemies of each other.

'"Why don't you tell your sons to behave nicely?" a frustrated Kashyapa asked Aditi and Diti.

'Aditi remained silent, but Diti gave her husband a hard look.

'"Ask Aditi. Her scheming sons always mock my sons. My sons respect you but you often ignore them and take the side of the Adityas. That's unfair."

'"Diti, I feel sad to see them fighting, but I don't lie. My sons are not scheming," Aditi snapped back.

'"Your sons always cry and shout for help, many times without reason. They fabricate stories and accuse my sons of tormenting them," Diti continued.

'"It is because your sons often beat my sons. My sons are few in number, but well-behaved; and yours are... " Aditi was not ready to back down.

'"The other day, Narada said that half of our literature will be filled with the cries of help from your sons, and the remaining half with someone's efforts to save them," Diti laughed aloud.

'Aditi did not like that. She shouted back, "Your sons are evil and work against dharma!"

'This was a huge allegation and Diti was not one to swallow it. "Kashyapa, Aditi's sons are so insecure that when my sons laugh among themselves, the Adityas take it for a battle cry. Let me tell you how mischievous Aditi's sons are. They are the progenitors of falsehood, an evil which has no precedent."

'Finally the sage found something to intervene on, "What? A lie?"

"'Kashyapa, you know that *vaani* or speech is for communicating the truth and the truth only. But Aditi's sons have set a precedent, using it to communicate falsehood, fabricated stories and to cheat others."

'Shocked, Kashyapa looked at Aditi for confirmation. The ability to speak was given to select species, only to communicate the truth. This was a violation of *rta*. But Aditi remained silent.

"'Now, she will not speak. Perhaps she may go on a hunger strike," Diti chided her sister.

"'Kashyapa, my children love music. They forget everything the moment they hear good music. The melody captivates them. When Indra and his brothers observed this, they conspired against my sons."

"'Tell me in detail," Kashyapa was curious.

"'Indra hatched a conspiracy in association with Agni and Varuna. They decided that they would request *Vaani* to sing, and when the Daityas become entranced, Indra would kill them. They all went to her and requested her to sing for them. She agreed. Why not? After all, she is also a daughter of Aditi," Diti mocked her sister and then addressed Kashyapa again.

"'But do you know what she did? She tricked Indra!" Diti laughed. "She sang the actionable part for the Adityas, but the benevolent part for herself. Thus, the Adityas' attempt nose-dived."

"'Then?"

"'Knowing this, my sons inundated *Vaani* with sin. Now, one can use *Vaani* to lie, but the user will become a sinner," Diti said proudly.

'Kashyapa shook his head in disgust and was about to leave the house, when Aditi retorted sharply.

'"Diti, your sons are mean. You and the sage know the reason very well. Children's behaviour is determined by their mother's deeds. We know how you conceived the Daityas: You forced Kashyapa to make love to you at an inauspicious and evil time, and your sins are manifested in your sons."

'"No time is ill-fated for making love with your husband. This is another lie to you are spreading," Diti could not bear more of this, and crying aloud, she ran to her hut. Aditi also felt embarrassed by her own speech, and wondered if she had gone too far. The ill-will between his wives also saddened Kashyapa.

'"The past comes back to haunt us. We are nothing but travellers in an unending cycle of death and birth. And what we earn, good or bad, we have to carry it forward," Kashyapa lamented. He could not meditate that evening.'

～

'What was Aditi saying? How were the Daityas conceived?' Kunti asked.

Krishna began his story.

'One day just before sunset, Kashyapa was meditating on the bank of a serene lake. Diti was sitting close by, silently watching her husband meditate.

'Kashyapa was a handsome man with a chiseled face, wide shoulders and broad chest. Around his waist, he wore a deerskin. The glow of the setting sun made him look like a golden *Kamadeva*. The romantic setting filled a voluptuous Diti with hitherto unknown lust. She tried to suppress her feelings, but the more she looked at Kashyapa, the more she longed for their physical union. When the urge became unbearable, she got up and silently stood behind the sage.

'Caressing his chest with her delicate hands, she huskily proposed, "Kashyapa, as an inebriated elephant trampling a banana tree, lust has overpowered my senses. Dear husband,

I am jealous of your other wives. You have gifted them many children. I too want my children. Fulfil my desire, please."

'Kashyapa looked at his desiring wife and slowly caressing her hand, he pulled her before him.

'"My love, I will fulfil your wish. One attains the fruits of dharma, artha and kama only because of his wife. My proud wife, I will do as you say and satisfy you. But…," Kashyapa paused for a moment and said, "just wait till the sun sets. This time is inauspicious. At this hour, your brother-in-law Shiva watches everyone with his three eyes, the sun, the moon and the fire. Though worldly senses do not touch him, yet he expects everyone to follow the law of *rta* or dharma. Wait till it becomes completely dark. Then, I will fulfil your desire."

'"My love, I cannot wait. I am burning with desire. I will die if you don't make love to me now." Diti embraced the sage, and slowly pulled down his deerskin. Looking at her yearning, Kashyapa propitiated the Lord and made love to Diti.

'Later, Kashyapa went for a bath and resumed his meditation. Diti too felt embarrassed, for forcing Kashyapa to act against his wishes.

'"Sage, have mercy on me. I know that I have wronged. I know that Shiva is benevolent and kind. Please appease him and request him to not kill my foetus. He is my sister Sati's husband and merciful. Assure me that he will not harm my children."

'"You chose an inauspicious time and did not heed my advice," Kashyapa said a little harshly. However, looking at his beautiful wife in tears, his heart melted. "Diti, let us forget the past. Don't worry. You will give birth to two powerful sons, but don't allow the reign of dharma to slip away from their hands."

'Diti eventually gave birth to twin sons who were physically very powerful and mentally resilient. Kashyapa named them Hiranyakashipu and Hiranyaksha.'

'For a few weeks after the showdown between Aditi and Diti, the atmosphere in the Kashyapa household remained very tense. Then, Aditi took the initiative and called Diti and Kashyapa to sort out the unpleasant issues.

"'Diti, let us find a way out and make our children live together in harmony. If Kashyapa approves, I have a proposal."

'At that moment Shatarupa, the mother of human beings, also arrived.

"'What do you propose?" an impatient Diti asked.

"'Let our children spend a few years with Brahma and receive education. I am sure that they will become more tolerant and accommodative. Brahma will surely help them."

"'Excellent idea. I will speak to Brahma," Kashyapa said approvingly. Diti also had no objection.

"'I would also like my children to join them," Shatarupa requested.

"'Why not? He will be happier," Kashyapa agreed.

'Thus, the Adityas, the Daityas and the Manavas stayed with Brahma for many years. When their education was over, Brahma called all of them to bid farewell.

'At that moment, the Adityas requested him, "Grandsire, give us a farewell sermon."

'Brahma looked at the Adityas, "You still want sermons? That's great. Now, listen carefully." Then, he uttered, "Da," and gesturing, asked, "Did you get it?"

'The supremely confident Adityas happily responded, "Grandsire, we got it. You said, *damanam*, to pacify." Brahma smiled. Did the Adityas get it right? Brahma left it to their wisdom.

"'Initiate us as well, Lord," Manu's sons then went forward.

'Brahma looked at them and uttered the same word, "Da," and gesturing, asked, "Did you get it?"

"'Understood, Lord. You said *danam*, to contribute." The Manavas were a little nervous, but they answered readily.

Brahma smiled. Did the humans get it right? Brahma left it to their wisdom.

'Finally, the Daityas' turn came. Politely, they requested Brahma to read them a sermon as well.

'Brahma looked at them and uttered the same word, "Da," and gesturing, asked, "Did you get it?"

'The Daityas did not take much time to decipher it. "Understood, grandsire. You said *daya*, to show compassion." Brahma smiled. Did the Daityas get it right? Brahma left it to their wisdom.'

As Krishna finished his tale, Kunti remembered her lonely days in Hastinapur. Sitting alone and looking up at the sky, she used to hear the thundering of the clouds. Did they not make the same sound?

'Madhav, when the clouds thunder, they continuously make the "Da" sound. I think that the Adityas indulge more in sensual pleasures, therefore Brahma asked them to suppress their desires and passion. The Daityas are physically powerful and perceived as cruel, so they were asked to show pity on others.' Kunti paused and then said with a smile, 'We humans are a hungry and greedy lot. We accumulate everything. Therefore, we were aptly told to donate. Am I correct?'

Krishna laughed, 'How can you be wrong, aunt?'

Then he became sombre. 'Aunt, I think Brahma should not have generalized. *Damanam*, *danam* and *daya* are essential for everyone. For a moment, imagine that Brahma is our mind, Diti is our intellect and Aditi is our conscience. The organic powers of humans are our demonic tendencies; they are therefore older and more powerful than the conscience and ethical inclinations. Thus, the perpetual war between demonic and godly tendencies.'

Kunti tried to decipher what Krishna was referring to.

'Every property has two extremes. The humans represent the middle, the neutral part, and it's beautiful to be a human being. Sometimes, the third aspect is better than the previous two. Like the absence of odour between the fragrance and the stench; like water between the acidic and the basic chemicals. The humans are beautifully placed between the gods and the demons.' He paused, 'But, it's difficult to tread the middle path.'

'What happened thereafter? Did they live peacefully together?' Kunti asked.

'Hiranyaksha and his elder brother Hiranyakashipu were very powerful, and soon they established their independent kingdoms. The Adityas, and Kashyapa's other sons also founded their own kingdoms or their areas of influence.

'However, in the race to occupy land, the humans were left behind. Swayambhuva Manu could not find any piece of land for his children. They were weaker than the Adityas and the Daityas, who had grabbed all the space.

'"Where should we live? There is no land!" Manu prayed to Brahma.

'"Scared of the evil deeds of Hiranyakashipu and Hiranyaksha, Prithvi has taken shelter in the deep galactic sea. Pray to the Almighty, only He can pull her back," Brahma advised.

'To get land for himself and his progenies, Manu began a difficult penance. Finally, a pleased Lord Vishnu agreed to help Manu.

'Lord Vishnu took the form of a cosmic boar as large as a galaxy. Its hair was longer than the biggest comet and its snout was bigger than the sun. The cosmic boar jumped into the galactic space and lifted up the earth. Holding it on the tip of its huge grinders, the cosmic boar had begun its upward journey when a shocked Hiranyaksha challenged it.

'"Is it for your amusement, boar?" he forced a laugh and hit the boar.

'The unperturbed boar continued its upwardly momentum.

'"Are you not ashamed of running away like a coward? If you are the Supreme Lord, then why are you running away like a thief?" the Daitya with yellow hair and long teeth shouted.

'The boar placed the earth in its orbit around the sun, and then emerged before Hiranyaksha.

'"Hiranyaksha, I grant you your wish. Come and fight me." Roaring and blazing like a hundred suns, the boar accepted Hiranyaksha's challenge.

'After a fierce duel, Lord Vishnu in the form of a great boar, killed the demon. Diti and Hiranyakashipu were devastated.

'"I swear that I will avenge my brother's death, mother. I will slay Vishnu."

'"Son, the shrewd Adityas have found their saviour in Vishnu. At this moment, they cannot be defeated. If you want to be the lord of the universe, you have to lie low for a while," Diti advised her son. By now, her hatred for Vishnu had reached manic levels.

'"Vishnu is the Supreme God. Nothing can move against his wish. He is the immutable law of the cosmos. I am sure that Hiranyaksha received redemption," Kashyapa consoled Diti and his son.

'"Kashyapa, what does that mean?" Diti did not like sage Kashyapa's sermon.

'"Diti, we are nothing but bundles of energy, separated from the supreme source of energy. Our assimilation back to that source, that is redemption. Till we integrate into Him again, we are ordained to move through the cycles of death and rebirth. Now, our son Hiranyaksha has been liberated from this unending cycle."

'Diti bowed her head and walked away. Kashyapa was not sure if she was walking away in agreement or in contempt. However, a bellicose Hiranyakashipu declared war on the Adityas and their associates. Leading an intimidating army, he went on a rampage and established his reign of terror over the three worlds.

'At that time, their children having left their parental house, Kashyapa lived alone with his wives. The fighting among their children caused a lot of pain, not only to the family, but also to the three worlds. Countless children lost their fathers, innumerable young women became widows and numerous parents lost their children. For years, the world heard of nothing but scheming, deceptions, wars and bloodbath. The Adityas (they had started calling themselves the Devas, the gods) and the Daityas were equally responsible for that. There appeared to be no end to this self-inflicting misery perpetuated by the children of Kashyapa.'

'"Do you know what a mother wants?" One evening, a pensive Aditi asked Kashyapa.

"Today I am saying this, but tomorrow when a sage repeats it, the whole world will listen to him," Kashyapa uttered an abstract reply, without looking at his wife.

'"Why can't you give a straightforward reply?" Aditi did not like the sage's abstract one-liners. "I don't get it."

'"I was contemplating my reply to your question," Kashyapa gently took Aditi's hand. "Aditi, the addition of each want makes things more complicated. Each want or desire brings sorrow with it."

'"You have got it wrong, old man. I am not asking for anything for myself. I am simply asking you a question. Do you know what a mother wants?"

'"I don't know who cursed her," Kashyapa chuckled, "but whenever *Vaani* is invoked, it's for a want."

'Aditi did not like this response and angrily went inside the hut. Kashyapa quickly followed to pacify her.

'"Darling," he said, cupping her face in his palms, "I am a father, I know what a father wants. You tell me what a mother wants."

'Aditi was not sure if she was happy with her children. They had gone berserk. "The achievements of my sons don't make me happy any more, because they are engulfed by greed, lust, envy and hatred. Kashyapa, a mother wants a child who is strong but compassionate. Like she holds at heart the welfare of her child, she wants her child to hold the welfare of the entire universe in his heart."

'Kashyapa smiled.

'"Kashyapa, is it possible to have a child who is devoid of greed, hatred, envy and lust? Someone who can enlighten the three worlds with his deeds, who can give life but never snatch it away?" Aditi asked.

'"Have you gone crazy, Aditi? Have not you seen my children? No one can guarantee how their children will behave," Kashyapa shut down the proposal without a thought.

'"Kashyapa, please. God cannot be so cruel, to not give us a benevolent son."

'Suddenly, Kashyapa realized what Aditi was asking for. He wished to help her. "What you seek, only Lord Vishnu can grant. Pray to him," Kashyapa advised his favourite wife.

'Aditi immediately immersed herself in rigorous penance to please Lord Vishnu. After many years of *tapa,* when she was nothing more than her "wish", the Lord appeared before her.

'"Aditi, I am pleased with your devotion. Tell me, what is your wish?"

'"Lord, I want a child who is unmatched in wisdom and power, yet whose heart cares even for a little sapling; One who is unsullied by partiality, greed, hatred, jealousy and lust; A benevolent being that lives for giving life to others and dedicates himself to the cause of others."

'"Aditi, only a self-burning source of light can nurture the world with its all-embracing benign magnanimity. So, I will create Surya for you. You will give birth to a son who will enlighten an entire solar system. He will be free from all the vices you mentioned. He will be the source of life. Without him, there will be no life." And thus, the Lord fulfilled Aditi's wish. Happy beyond belief, Aditi listened as the Lord listed the qualities of her future son.

'"He will rule the planets as he moves through the twelve

signs of the zodiac: *Mesha, Vrisha, Mithuna, Karkata, Simha, Kanya, Tula, Vrischika, Dhanu, Makara, Kumbha* and *Meena*, over a period of twelve months, and that will form a solar year," Vishnu explained.

'The news of this boon spread thick and fast. Everyone in the Universe waited for the birth of the star that would give and sustain life to an entire solar system. Soon, Aditi gave birth to a radiant baby. The entire galaxy of the *manasputra*s, their spouses and their progenies, and celestial deities blessed the newborn baby. The baby changed its glow and characteristics every month. Aditi felt as if she was the mother of twelve babies, who were merged in one body.

'Diti heard the news with some aversion. By now, the chasm between her and Aditi had become too wide and deep.

'"If Aditi has the 'source of light' as her son, Diti must embrace the darkness. Neither my sons nor I will seek a grand progeny from anyone. The Daityas are a proud race and will remain independent. We will survive by our own strength," she announced the Daitya philosophy to her sons.

'"We will be our own," everyone echoed.

'Diti advised Hiranyakashipu to go on penance and to ask for immortality from Brahma. Hiranyakashipu followed his mother's advice. A pleased Brahma asked the Daitya king to express his desire.

'"Grandsire, I want immortality."

'"Son, no one can be immortal in this body. Even I can't be immortal in this body," Brahma replied. Then, looking at a disappointed Hiranyakashipu, he explained: "Son, our body is a vessel and its decay is binding. Immortality can be achieved only through knowledge or sacred work. Diti knows this. Has she not told you?"

'Hiranyakashipu was very disappointed. Brahma saw his long and dull face and empathized with him.

'"Son, you may ask for anything, except physical immortality. If you wish, I can prolong your life."

'Hiranyakashipu thought for a while and then expressed his desire.

'"Lord, grant me this boon: That no one can kill me during the day or during the night; neither under a roof nor in the open; not by any weapon; I can't be burned by fire, not can I be drowned. Grant me that no god, demon, human or animal can kill me. I can't be killed on land, in the sky or in the water. I can't be killed by anyone produced by the three *srishties*: *sandarshana*, *sparsha* or *samparka*." He stopped when he thought that he had covered all his bases and outsmarted the creator.

'"Let it be so," Brahma granted him the boon.'

༄

'The Adityas soon discovered *soma*, a celestial drink that gave them strength and happiness. Diti countered this by encouraging her clan to have more and more children. Soon, the Daityas outnumbered the Adityas. They continued their fight for sustenance, honour and power, by all means. Hiranyakashipu promised that he would force everyone to forget the name of Vishnu. But, it was not destined to be so.

'Hiranyakashipu's wife was Kayadhu. She was the mother of Hiranyakashipu's four sons and one daughter. Their youngest son was Prahlad. Hiranyakashipu's daughter Simhika was married to Daitya Viprachitti. Their union produced a son called Ketu.

'Prahlad, the youngest son of Hiranyakashipu, was unlike the other Daityas. He was a sober boy and a thinker. From his childhood, he believed that Diti's philosophy was against the Divine.

'"Why does Vishnu favour the Adityas and not us?" This was a constant theme he used to ponder on, since his childhood.

'"Why can't we ask Vishnu to take our side?" Prahlad once asked his grandmother.

'"He will never do so. He likes sycophants," his grandmother replied.

"'I don't think so. He is the Supreme Being. Why would he need bootlickers?"

"'Where did you get this wisdom from?" Diti asked wryly. She sensed that the boy needed an immediate course correction.

"'This world does not run by Vishnu's writ. This world runs by the *rta*, the law of the cosmos," she said and paused, looking at the young boy. "Son, if you believe that He is the Supreme Being, then each and every manifestation, every phenomenon is His wish. Then, who are we? Are we not also his manifestation?" Diti challenged Prahlad. "Son, a person's basic nature decides their behaviour. We can't change our nature. With time, our nature becomes our dharma."

"'But there are things like good or bad nature. We can pray to Him to change our nature," said Prahlad.

"'Prahlad!" Diti was angry now, "Do you mean to say that we are people of a bad nature?"

'A scared Prahlad remained silent.

"'If you think we are bad people, I will give you an example," Diti almost shouted. "Have you seen a snake? Yes or no?"

"'Yes…" Prahlad could barely reply.

"'What is the dharma of a snake? Is it of a bad nature? Should it pray to Vishnu to change its character? Tell me!" Trembling with anger, Diti caught Prahlad by his shoulders. The boy was almost in tears. This softened Diti a little.

"'Son, can you ask a lion to live like a cow? If you start behaving like an Aditya, you no longer remain a Daitya. And remember, you are a Daitya and living like a Daitya is your dharma."

"We all belong to the same species: It's not a lion versus a cow," Prahlad said contemptuously.

"'Prahlad, you are now questioning our *maryada*. It is our declared policy not to appease anyone. We trust and believe that the Lord should treat everyone equally."

'Prahlad was not convinced. Diti alerted her son; Hiranyakashipu was worried. His intelligent and sensible son was going haywire. He decided to put Prahlad under some influential tutors, who would inculcate Daitya pride in the young boy. But, they also failed.

"'Son, it is all about identity. It was destined that we be born as Daityas. Then, it became our identity and dharma. If you ask Vishnu, he will advise you the same. It is far better to discharge one's prescribed duties, even though faultily, than to perform another's duty with perfection. Self sacrifice in following one's own dharma is better than engaging in another's dharma, for to follow another's path is dangerous,"* Hiranyakashipu tried to instil some reason in his son's head.

"'Father, I don't agree with your logic," young Prahlad remained unmoved. "I think what you said is about individual dharma, a person's quest for the ultimate knowledge. I wonder what you would say about the instance where individual dharma clashes with collective dharma. Then, what should one do? Are we not free born individuals first?"

"'You are wrong, my son. A family is superior to an individual, and the clan is superior to a family. I am shocked that you have got it all wrong," a frustrated Hiranyakashipu told his son.

Highly upset, Hiranyakashipu made it be known that whosoever praised Vishnu or sang his paeans would be punished with death. This deterred everyone, except Prahlad. An infuriated Hiranyakashipu finally decided to punish his son with the death penalty.

"'Take him to the highest mountain peak and throw him down. Let his death be as ordinary as his life has been," a disillusioned Hiranyakashipu ordered.

"'Prince, why don't you follow your father?" one daring executioner asked Prahlad.

"'You won't understand. This blind rivalry between the Adityas and the Daityas is snatching childhood away from children, youth from women and old age from mothers. We

---

*श्रेयान्स्वधर्मोविगुण: पर्धर्मात्सवनुष्ठितात्। स्वधर्मेनिधनंश्रेय:परधर्मोभयावह:।। (गीता 3.35)

must protest against this madness," Prahlad replied.

"'But what will happen to our identity?" the executioner demanded.

"'Is our identity so weak that it will melt away the moment we befriend the Adityas? What is the value of such a weak identity?"

'The soldiers did not reply. However, they followed the order of their king and threw Prahlad from a very high peak. To their surprise, when they went down to collect his remains, they found Prahlad alive, without a bruise.

'This event raised Prahlad's reputation everywhere. The miracle forced Hiranyakashipu to close the embarrassing episode quickly and conclusively. He called his daughter Simhika. In her childhood, Simhika had received a boon from a sage, that fire could not burn her. Hiranyakashipu asked her to hold Prahlad in her arms and walk into a fire. Everyone anticipated a cruel end to the poor boy and for Simhika to emerge laughing.

'What occurred was the contrary: Simhika's cries shattered the hearts of the bravest Daityas. Her father tried to save her from the flames but failed. Prahlad came out, shocked but without a single burn.

'This episode fanned the rumours that Vishnu was indeed saving the young prince. It initiated the division of opinion even among the Daitya royals. This enraged Hiranyakashipu no end. He decided to deal with Prahlad himself.

"'Tomorrow, before the entire court, I will kill the boy myself!" he thundered.

'The Daitya priest Virochana calculated an auspicious time for the boy's capital punishment. Everything was well-planned and the entire city assembled outside the court to see the slaughter of the prince.

'In the royal court, Prahlad was tied up against a tall stone column. To everyone's surprise, he appeared calm and cheerful: Faith had given him an insurmountable confidence. He was sure that nothing could happen to him.

"'Prahlad, you have been proved to be an incorrigible criminal and a traitor. Today, I will cut you into pieces," the king announced his judgement.

'Hiranyakashipu looked at the assembled crowd of stunned Daityas. He could sense the pulse of the people. He decided to ask Prahlad one last time.

"'Prahlad, you are my son and also a prince. In the presence of these thousands of proud Daityas, let me give you one last opportunity: Accept your sins and apologize for them. You can still save your life. Promise me that you won't utter the name of Vishnu again. If you obey my command, I will pardon you."

'The crowd applauded, to encourage the young prince to obey his father's command.

"'I stand for truth. Your threats are meaningless to me. Your sword cannot kill my ideals and my soul," Prahlad said, looking into his father's eyes.

'The crowd sighed aloud in disappointment. His son's humiliating reply infuriated Hiranyakashipu. Shouting in fury, he ran to kill his son with his naked sword.

"'Call your Vishnu! Call him! Let me see how he saves you!"

'Hiranyakashipu swiped his sword at the boy's neck. But before the sword could touch Prahlad's skin, a miracle happened.

'Tearing the stone column apart, a strange creature came out and bore the brunt of that powerful stroke. The strange beast was neither a man, nor a god, neither a demon nor an animal. The unbelievable spectacle stunned a bewildered Hiranyakashipu. The creature was a lion-man, with a lion's head and hands with huge claws. Its entire body was covered with lion hair, but its chest and legs were that of a man. It was neither a man nor an animal.

'Hiranyakashipu panicked: His strength melted like ice before that strange beast's power. The unique beast was none other than Lord Vishnu in his Nrusingha incarnation. He tossed the Daitya like a toy on the floor. Hiranyakashipu could not get up.

'The sun was setting. It was neither day nor night. The lion-man dragged the demon to the threshold of the court's main gate. There, Nrusingha placed the body of Hiranyakshipu on his thighs and tore open the chest of Hiranyakashipu with his claws and killed him.

'When Diti heard that her second son had been killed, she became mad with rage and left the palace. She took shelter in a dense forest and contemplated her next move. Vishnu had killed both her sons. Nothing can touch Vishnu, she knew very well. Her entire wrath became focused on Indra, her stepson.

'"Cruel, ruthless and immoral Indra planned and got my sons killed. Until I take my revenge, how can I be at peace?"

'Diti was too proud to worship Vishnu. That would have shattered the edifice of her Daitya philosophy. She had been devoted to only one man in her life, her husband Kashyapa. Determined to get a son who could slay Indra, Diti decided to take Kashyapa's help. She served Kashyapa with her exceptional love and devotion for many years. She knew how to please her husband.

'"My dear beautiful wife, I am pleased. You have served me with your soul and the senses. I will fulfil all your wishes: Tell me what you want," a delighted Kashyapa offered.

'"Lord, Indra got both my sons killed and has rendered me childless. If you want to grant me a boon, grant me a son who can slay Indra."

'The sage shuddered. However, he was obliged to honour his words. He decided to play it safe with Diti and put forward an impossible condition.

'"My beloved, for that, you must complete a penance to perfection, for a complete year. Only then will you have a son capable of killing Indra. However, even a small error in your penance will have an opposite effect. He will become Indra's friend forever."

'"Tell me the penance, and I will perform it," Diti did not have a choice.

'"Diti, for one year, you cannot think, speak or do any evil against anyone. Neither can you speak a lie, nor can you say a harsh word or curse anyone. You must not speak to evil people for a year. You will not touch any inauspicious object. During this year, you will bathe without entering into the water and you will not wear washed clothes. For one year, you should not eat or drink anything given by anybody. You will not sleep without washing your mouth, without bathing, without praying, without untying your hair. Once you receive my seed in your womb, you will neither indulge in sex nor think about its pleasure. You will perform penance with a daily prayer to get your desired son. This penance is called *punsavan*, and if you follow it for a year, you will give birth to the slayer of Indra."

'Diti was indomitable in spirit, and a resolute woman. She began following the difficult penance with utmost devotion. When Indra came to know about her penance, he was scared. Diti's penance had forced her to live in seclusion. It was severe hardship for a woman, living alone in a secluded forest. Indra decided to take benefit of her isolation. He arrived at Diti's hut in the disguise of a young ascetic. He started serving Diti by helping in her penance. His predatory eyes waited for a moment of slackness, but after eight months of spying, Indra did not have a single opportunity.

'Diti's pregnancy was now at an advanced stage. Indra had become frustrated and he even thought of killing Diti and waited for an opportune moment. As a result of the long penance, Diti had become physically very weak. It was the hottest month of the year, *Jyeshtha*. One evening, exhausted from a long day's work, Diti was very tired. Indra offered to fan her for a little relief. She hesitatingly accepted the offer. Soon, she fell asleep without bathing and washing her mouth. Indra got his opportunity and entered into her womb. With his golden knife, he cut Diti's foetus into seven parts. The foetus cried and begged Indra not to kill him.

'"Don't cry, don't cry," saying this to the foetus, a heartless

Indra further sliced the seven pieces seven more times. All the parts of the foetus prayed to Indra in unison, "Aditya, why are you killing us? We are your brothers."

'"Do you promise to be my friends forever, brothers?" the cruel Indra threatened them.

'Scared of an imminent death, all the pieces agreed.

'"Very well. Don't be afraid. I will not kill you. Now we are friends," Indra assured them.

'In the morning, when Diti woke up, she saw forty-nine radiant babies playing with Indra, who had abandoned his ascetic disguise.

'"Indra? What are you doing here? Who are these babies?" a surprised Diti asked.

'Indra fell down at the feet of his stepmother. He apologized and told her everything.

'"Mother, when I learnt about your penance, I came here in disguise with an ill intent. I was not following dharma and the moment you showed a little slackness, I sliced the foetus in your womb into forty-nine pieces. It's a miracle that they are still alive. It must be the grace of the Lord, extended to you after your tough penance. How could anyone kill a life blessed by Him?"

'Diti was very happy to see her babies and she forgot her revenge. Admiring her radiant babies, she even forgot the presence of the wicked Indra.

'"Mother, in ignorance, I committed this unpardonable sin. Please forgive me. I will always be a friend to these babies," Indra begged her forgiveness.

'This miracle and Indra's apology pacified a shocked Diti. She now had forty-nine sons. For a moment she looked at Indra, the sworn enemy of her clan, and then she forgave him,' Krishna thus ended his tale.

'How cruel! What happened to the Daityas after this incident?' Kunti asked.

'Aunt, young Prahlad understood the dilemma between practicing *sva-dharma* and following collective dharma. He understood and preferred his individual human relationship with the Supreme Being. Contrary to his father Hiranyakashipu's fear, that by following the Lord, the Daityas would lose their identity, Prahlad remained a Daitya forever, and an ideal and strong Daitya at that. During his time, Daitya culture flourished everywhere. There was prosperity in the three worlds and people lived in peace. He was considered more pious than the Adityas and than many of the great sages of his age,' Krishna explained.

∽

'What happened to Aditi?' Kunti asked.

'Aunt, do your remember Kashyapa's first thought when Aditi wanted to know what a woman wants?' Krishna asked Kunti.

'Yes: Desire makes things complicated and causes pain.'

'True. Unlike Diti, Aditi never experienced the death of her children. You won't find a more insatiable, scheming and cunning person than Indra in the whole of *Itihasa*. His lust for power was insatiable. Countless times, on a trivial pretext or at the slightest opportunity, he initiated wars against the Daityas, and conspired against the well-meaning sages and human beings.'

'Could he do so against Prahlad as well?' Kunti asked.

'No. You would be surprised to know that, later on, some of the virtuous Daityas became the lord of the three worlds. During these times, Aditi played her part to bring her progenies back to power.

After the demise of his father, Prahlad consolidated Daitya power. His successors expanded it and also concentrated on the development of their kingdom. Very soon, they left the Adityas far behind in their standard of social life, prosperity, art and culture. A jealous Indra once again waged a war against them. At that time, Prahlad's grandson Bali was the king of the Daityas. Bali was a brave and benevolent king, with a balanced head on his shoulders.

'Bali not only defeated the Adityas, but also diminished the glory associated with the coveted title of Indra. A worried Aditi advised the Adityas to rush to Brahma for their survival.

'Brahma meditated over the situation and advised them to lie low.

'"All are born out of Him, including me, Shiva, the Adityas and the Daityas. For Him, killing someone or saving someone, ignoring someone and admiring someone, all are meaningless. He is devoid of any attachment," Brahma paused for a moment.

'"Despite that, at the time of creation, annihilation and on certain circumstances, He bears one of the three *gunas*: *satva*, *rajas* and *tamas*. In my view, the present time is not apt to pray for his intervention."

'"What should we do?" Indra asked.

'"Right now, the Daitya influence is on the rise. Be wise, go and make peace with them. You will need their help for the task I have in mind. Once you have achieved your objective, you may vanquish them," Brahma guided them.

'This formed the basis of the great churning of the sea, from where many invaluable offerings were received and distributed among the Adityas, the Daityas and others. However, in the end, the Adityas seized the ultimate prize, the nectar of life, through much deceit and with the help of Lord Vishnu himself.

'This reduced the Daityas to a weaker and vulnerable position. Now they could be wiped out in a battle, while the Adityas became immortal.

'A bolstered Indra immediately declared a war on the Daityas. A ferocious Aditya-Daitya war commenced at the place of the sea-churning itself. Boosted by the power of the nectar, the emboldened Adityas attacked the Daityas, who fought ferociously, but the Adityas were far superior. In the end, the war became one-sided and the Daitya warriors began to fall like trees in a cyclone. This worried Brahma. His decision to help the Adityas was now making the Daityas extinct. He quickly dispatched Narada to ask Indra to stop the war.'

༄

'With power comes insecurity, and the same happened to Indra. Despite getting the nectar, he became increasingly more insecure. As a result, he looked at the whole world with suspicion. He tried to play tricks even on Lord Shiva.

'After Sati's self-immolation at Daksha's *yagna*, Shiva became aloof. Meanwhile a Daitya called Taraka tormented Indra no end. It was destined that Taraka could only be killed by Shiva's son. Therefore, at the behest of Indra, Brahma cajoled and persuaded Shiva to remarry. For the sake of the Adityas, Shiva agreed to marry Parvati, a daughter of Himachala, the king of the mountains. Parvati won Shiva's heart with her love and dedication.

'It is said that Shiva joyously made love to her night and day, but without ever shedding his semen. Indra became afraid. He foolishly thought that such a union would have produced a child of unbearable power. In haste, he collected his crony Adityas and interrupted Shiva's lovemaking. This interruption enraged Parvati and she cursed the wives of the Adityas to be barren forever, since she was thwarted while making love in the hope of bearing a son.

'Shiva tried to salvage his ejaculation: He placed his seed in Agni, the fire god. Since then, the ritual act of throwing an oblation into the consecrated fire during a *yagna* began. Agni took up Shiva's semen, from which the six-headed Skanda was born. Skanda finally killed Taraka.'

Krishna continued narrating the stories of the primordial mothers to Kunti.

'Is that why the children of the Adityas are born from male gods or sages, who create children unilaterally merely by the thought or sight of a woman, by ejaculating into a flower, a female animal or a river to produce a motherless child?' Kunti asked.

'Yes. That is why these children are called *ayonija*, born without a womb,' Krishna smiled

'Krishna, please continue Aditi's story,' Kunti reminded Krishna.

'These events took place between the birth of Diti's many sons and the final act of Aditi. After the debacle of the churning of the sea, for a long time, the scared Daityas remained in hiding, fearing for their lives. Later on, they began to try and find something to counter the nectar.

'Shiva had not liked the brazen cheating by the Adityas during the churning of the sea. Both the Daityas and the Adityas laboured equally in churning the sea, yet the Adityas got the finest yields, as well as the nectar. The poor Nagas, who were used as ropes around the mountain, got nothing. All the poison accumulated in the process was to be consumed by Shiva to save the world. This resulting imbalance of power, hugely in favour of the Adityas, greatly worried Shiva.

'Therefore, when the Daitya guru Shukracharya prayed to Shiva to impart to him the knowledge of making the dead come back to life again, Shiva agreed.

'"You can use it, but don't teach it to others," Shiva placed this condition before imparting the *mrit-sanjivani vidhya* to Shukracharya.

'With the help of this knowledge, Shukracharya could now revive the dead Daitya soldiers. This restored the power balance between the warring sons of Kashyapa, and the Daitya king Bali quickly regained his lost glory. After a lot of preparation, he attacked Indra to avenge his defeat. Indra and the Adityas could not withstand the onslaught of the rejuvenated Daityas.

'When Indra again ran to Brahma for help, Brahma refused to intervene, after learning from his past mistake. Brahaspati, the guru of the Adityas, advised them to hide in a secret and secure place until the Daityas did something silly and invited their own destruction.

'Daitya Bali was now the lord of the three worlds. The Brahmins declared him their new Indra. Bali did not disappoint anyone and proved true to all expectations. Across the ages, no one had seen a wiser, more benevolent and pious king than Bali.

'Bali ruled uninterruptedly for many years. Though he respected Aditi like his own grandmother and never gave her a reason to complain, she decided to leave Amaravati. The defeat of the Adityas had bruised Aditi's spirit.

'"So, at the end of many battles, Diti won the war," this thought agitated Aditi all the time. When it became unbearable for her to sit peacefully even for a moment, she decided to approach the Supreme Lord one more time. She started her penance in a secluded place.

'One day, sage Kashyapa returned to Amaravati after his long meditation. He saw Bali sitting on Indra's throne. Kashyapa's heart sank, seeing Bali in the place of his favourite Indra. He was devastated to see that not a single resident of Amaravati was unhappy with Bali. No one in Amaravati missed the Adityas. Everyone met Kashyapa with utmost veneration but did not express the least sympathy for Indra and his ilk. A crestfallen Kashyapa left Amaravati in search of his favourite wife Aditi.

'After exploring everywhere, he located Aditi in a secluded forest. He found her in absolute misery. Looking at her glum face, he tried to cheer her up.

'"Kashyapa, protect us!" she cried, holding the sage's feet.

'"Diti's sons have grabbed our wealth, prestige, splendour and power. My sons are hiding like criminals. Neck deep in this sea of sorrow, I don't have a reason to live. Please save us and help us regain our glory!"

'"Aditi, you are like the earth immersed in the deep sea. Only Vishnu can save you. I suggest you undergo a penance of twelve days, meditating on the *Varaha* incarnation of the Lord."

'With a lot of hope, Aditi dutifully followed her husband's advice. The Lord finally appeared before her.

'"Devi, I know what you wish for. I have sympathy for your sons, but I cannot go against a virtuous Bali. He deserves to enjoy his achievements. However, I will not disappoint a mother. Stay with your husband for a few years. I will be born as your son and bring glory back to you," the Lord blessed Aditi.

'After a few years, Aditi gave birth to a dwarf boy: the newborn was the Vamana incarnation of Lord Vishnu.

A couple of decades after Vamana's birth, on the advice of his guru Shukracharya, Bali planned a great *Ashwamedha yagna* at Bhrigukachchh, on the bank of River Narmada. When Vamana arrived there, thousands of people were participating in the *yagna*. Bali welcomed this dwarf Brahmin with utmost reverence.

'After the *yagna*, when Bali had donated to all the participating Brahmins, Vamana came forward. Bali humbly requested him to ask for anything in *danam*.

'"Great Bali, I know your illustrious lineage. Your father, king Virochana, and your grandfather Prahlad were great men. When his sworn enemies, the Adityas, came before your father disguised as Brahmins and asked his age in *danam*, despite being aware of that blatant cheating, great Virochana donated his age to them. You are his worthy son. I am sure you will not disappoint me," the dwarf Brahmin said.

'"Thank you for the praise, Brahmin. What can I do for you?" Bali asked.

'"Daitya king, I will be satisfied with only three steps of land. I don't need more than that. Grant me three steps of land."

'"Vamana, you are being foolish," Bali laughed. "You don't know when you will get another opportunity to ask for something from Bali. Ask for something more."

'"King, please don't underestimate the virtues of satisfaction. If one is not satisfied with his needs, he will not be satisfied with the entire wealth of the cosmos."

'Shukracharya was listening to their conversation. He realized that the dwarf was Vishnu in disguise. He shouted a warning: "Bali, you are being tricked like your father. He is Vishnu. Don't grant him anything."

'Bali heard his guru's warning, but ignored it.

'"Fool, don't agree to his demand. In two paces he will measure the entire cosmos. Then where would he place his third step? You will fail in this *danam* and land in hell for not fulfilling your promise," his guru was infuriated.

'Bali was made of a different metal. He raised his hand to lift a pot full of sacred water. The guru knew his pupil's weakness very well.

'"Bali, don't let your reputation destroy the Daitya clan. If you still fear for your reputation and are scared to break the promise, let me show you the reason. This body is a tree and truth and vow are its fruits and flowers. If there is no tree, how can there be a fruit or a flower? Saying no for survival, or not giving basic things necessary for self-existence is not a sin. To save one's life, one can withdraw from his commitment," Shukracharya counselled the Daitya king.

'"Forgive me, gurudeva," a firm Bali politely expressed his decision, "these excuses cannot deter me. There is no sin bigger than falsehood."

'This public defiance from his pupil incensed Shukracharya.

'"Bali, you are ignoring my advice. How dare you disobey me! I curse you: You will lose all your wealth, here and now!"

'Bali accepted the curse of his powerful guru with a smile. Taking the sacred water in his right palm, Bali promised to give the dwarf Brahmin three paces of land. Vamana measured the entire cosmos in two steps and then asked Bali, "Where should I place my third step? If you fail to give me the three paces you promised, you will fall into hell for not being true to your words."

'"Lord, I don't fear death or hell, I only fear ignomiry. Please place your third step on my head," great Bali humbly said, without a tinge of remorse.

'Bali's offer stunned the assembled people. The great Lord was pleased to see the supreme devotion of the Daitya king. A happy Vamana said, "Bali, I am happy that, despite knowing my reality, you did not deviate from the path of dharma. Whom I love, I take away their false pride, but you don't have any. You will be blessed forever."

'Vamana made Bali the lord of the netherland and blessed him, saying that he would regain the title of Indra in Savarni *manvantara*.

'Between Diti and Aditi, finally no one won or lost. In this infinite universe, does a win or loss on a little planet between tiny organisms really matter?' Krishna concluded with a big smile.

3

Independence

'Krishna, Diti and Aditi were primordial mothers. They were tasked with populating the earth. Their common husband was largely neutral to his children. Their progenies were struggling for survival and I can see that their existence was only for their children,' Kunti commented. 'Every act of Diti and Aditi's life was for their sons. For them, their husband was a sacred deity, to be invoked only for insemination. What about their individuality?'

'Aunt, how can there be a mother without a child? For a mother, her child is the most important. Motherhood is biologically the most important aspect of a woman,' Krishna replied.

After a brief silence, Krishna continued, 'I agree that their stories don't tell you the conflict that sometimes takes place between the myriad roles played by a woman. However, a woman's priorities depend on various factors. However, till her children become capable of looking after themselves, they remain the priority for the mother.'

Kunti nodded in agreement.

'Aunt, I will tell you Jabala's story,' Krishna said.

'Jabala was Brahmarishi Satyakam's mother. She was an attractive lady. Saintliness and clarity of heart, as well as the beauty of her nature, made her even more exquisite. She lost her parents at an early age and this led to a period of continuous suffering, because she was socially vulnerable.

She was exploited by men unknown to her, and became the mother of a son. Motherhood gave her life some purpose, but society considered her to be a virtueless woman. Unaffected by the way people treated her, she focused all her efforts on giving her son a stellar character. With a lot of hope, she named him Satyakam.

'When her son began playing with other children of his age, he started questioning her about his father and his *gotra*. He would return home crying and ask, "Mother, who is my father? What is my *gotra*?" She used to avoid answering him by diverting his attention to other topics.

'Slowly, such questions became a daily affair and one day when her son lost his patience, she started weeping. If there was one thing that could scare her son, it was her tears. He understood. "Perhaps my father is dead and his memory makes mother cry." He never repeated the question again.

'When Satyakam was old enough for formal education, he went to an Acharya for the brahmacharya sacrament. As was the custom in those days, the Acharya asked his father's name and *gotra* before accepting him for the initiation. When he could not answer, everybody including the Acharya ridiculed him.

'"Go back to your mother and ask," the Acharya advised.

'That day, Satyakam was unyielding. He was determined to know the name and *gotra* of his father.

'"I can't answer your question, my son. Don't ask me this," tears flowed from Jabala's eyes.

'"Mother, I just want to know his name and his *gotra*. I promise that I will not ask anything more. I will not ask what he does, if he is alive or not, or where he lives. I will not ask anything else; just tell me his name and the *gotra*. I need this minimum information to begin my education."

'A speechless Jabala looked at her son. She was helpless. For a mother, there was no misery bigger than that. Even the tears had dried up in that unfortunate mother's eyes. When Satyakam saw his mother trembling and about to fall, he rushed to help her. For many moments the two did not speak. Satyakam could not bear to look at her anymore and went motionless in his mother's arms. Something melted inside her and he could hear her heart pounding heavily. She squeezed him tightly.

'"Son, no one will teach you, no one," she said in a voice full of agony. A chill ran down the boy's spine.

'"No one will initiate you, son," Jabala's voice was now clear and firm, after arriving at a conclusion. She tried to smile. The sun was coming out from behind the clouds after years of gloom. The boy could see a sacred glow on his mother's face, as if she had been cured of a very old disease, as if somebody had lifted a heavy stone off her chest. An amazed Satyakam stood speechless. She stroked his hair.

'"Son, I have been effortlessly untruthful to people whenever they asked me about your father. I used to tell lies. I never felt that I was doing something wrong. But whenever you used to ask, I could not say anything. I never wanted to lie to you. Do you know, why I named you Satyakam?" I have always prayed to the Lord that you should never do something in your life for which you have to lie or be ashamed. This name, Satyakam, is the abstract of my motherhood, my lifelong humiliation, my biggest ambitions and the tallest dreams: the dreams that I have dreamt for you. Son, that's why I cannot lie to you."

'"Mother... ," Satyakam was speechless.

'"Son, today I will tell you the truth. The truth is that I don't know who fathered you. I lived a life that no one should. I slept with many men, willingly on a few occasions but mostly unwillingly. Neither do I know the names of all those men nor have I ever tried to know. Son, this is the truth, the complete truth. Now, know that you are your mother's son: Jabala's son."

'Satyakam's body shuddered for a while and he felt like he was witnessing the Supreme Lord himself. His eyes became moist with pride. Silently, he wept and embraced his mother tightly. Both mother and son remained like that for a long time. Then Jabala lifted her son's face and kissed his forehead.

'"Mother, now I don't need a guru. You just introduced me to the truth." Touching his mother's feet, he vowed, "Mother, I will never speak a false word and never commit a false act in my life."

'"But, you must go to a guru for your initiation," she insisted. Hesitatingly, he agreed.

'The next day, Satyakam went to the same Acharya again.

'"Acharya, I am Satyakam Jabali, Jabala's son. She is my mother and her name is my *gotra*."

'The Acharya hooted with laughter and asked him to get lost. Satyakam went from one Acharya to another. Everywhere, the same story was repeated. Nobody was ready to initiate him. But Satyakam had decided that he would not give a false introduction. The wisdom that he had received from his mother was invaluable.

'Finally, someone suggested that he should go to Haridrumata Gautama. Haridrumata Gautama was a renowned explorer of *Brahma vidya* and had a reputation of being a tough taskmaster. "What is your name?" he asked Satyakam.

'"Satyakam Jabali."

'"What is your father's name?"

'"I don't know. I asked my mother, even she does not know. Her name is Jabala, I am her son, Satyakam Jabali."

'The sage looked at him with his piercing eyes. Then, suddenly, he got up from his seat and hugged Satyakam. "Son, only a Brahmin can speak the truth so boldly and clearly. Bring the sacrificial firewood. I will give you the sacrificial thread right now."

'Gautama made Satyakam his pupil.'

~

'Krishna, when her children are young, a mother devotes most of her time to tending them. You may not realize it, but it affects her other roles,' Kunti said.

'Of course, aunt. It's easy to imagine that sometimes a craving for personal space overwhelms a woman, suffocated between her roles as a mother and a wife. Striking the right balance between her many roles becomes a challenge for a mother. Those who fail to do so, often want to run away like Sanjana.'

'Will you tell me about her?' Kunti asked. Krishna began his story.

'Sanjana was the eldest daughter of Vishwakarma and his wife Varastri. Vishwakarma, as you know, was the son of Prabhasvasu, the last of the eight *Vasu*s. Sanjana was extraordinarily beautiful, graceful in manners and wise beyond her age. Both her father and grandfather were the principal architects of the Adityas.

'Every morning, while taking a bath in a nearby pond, Sanjana used to watch the radiant rising sun, elegantly moving across the sky. Unknowingly, she fell into the habit of watching the sun, from the moment of its appearance on the eastern horizon until it became silvery white and unbearable to glance at. From a little bright crimson dot to glowing orange and then saffron and then red, she could tell the changing faces of the sun. Her close friends knew her secret.

'"Ask your father to help. We heard that he is building a palace for Surya," they used to tease her.

'Vishwakarma had gone to build a palace for Surya. Sanjana imagined posing many questions to her father. "What is he like? Does he look like us? Is he arrogant? What does he like and dislike?"

'When Vishwakarma returned home, he had many stories to tell about Surya. One early morning, when both Vishwakarma and Sanjana were walking near the pond, indicating the sun reflected in the water, Vishwakarma commented: "He looks so beautiful in the pristine water. Perhaps, even he likes the cool freshness of the clean water."

'"He looks beautiful even in the sky and his beauty grows by the day," Sanjana remarked and lowered her eyes.

'"He is the universal benefactor. Everyone likes him."

'"Is he married?"

'"Not yet. I heard that his parents are looking for a suitable match for him." Vishwakarma could see the glow on his beautiful daughter's cheeks. Sanjana did not hide her feelings.

"'How can a woman live with a ball of fire?" she wondered, laughing at her thought.

'Vishwakarma smiled and affectionately held her chin and shook it. "Should I talk to Kashyapa?"

'Sanjana did not reply but lowered her head.

'Vishwakarma was not joking. He sent Narada to find out the views of Aditi and Kashyapa.

"'Kashyapa, your son has excelled you in acquisition, containment and dissemination of wisdom. He gives nourishment to all," Narada praised Surya.

"'It's every father's wish, *Devarshi*. We are proud of our son," a visibly happy Kashyapa humbly acknowledged.

"'Will he remain a bachelor forever? Are not you thinking about his marriage?" Narada asked.

"'We are looking at some proposals. Finally, God's desire will prevail."

"'God willing, I have a beautiful girl in mind. She is suitable for Surya in every way."

"'Who is she?" Aditi was very curious.

"'Do you know Prabhasavasu?" Narada smiled.

"'Of course, Narada!" Aditi replied. "He is an old friend, and you know, his son Vishwakarma is building a new palace for Surya," Kashyapa gladly added.

"'Yes. I am talking about Prabhasavasu's granddaughter Sanjana. She is beautiful beyond description and has all the qualities you are looking for in Surya's bride."

"'Kashyapa, I am so happy to hear this. What do you say?" a delighted Aditi asked her husband.

"'Let's talk to Vishwakarma and Varastri," Kashyapa happily agreed.

"'I have already spoken to them," Narada winked. "In fact, I have also spoken to Sanjana. When I described Surya's exceptional character and beauty, her eyes glowed like the dew in the morning rays. In fact, she loves Surya very much and Vishwakarma also knows where her heart is."

'"Aha, then everything is settled. Let us ask Surya," Kashyapa concurred.

'When Aditi told Surya about Sanjana, Surya did not take long to give his consent. It was decided that the marriage would take place in the presence of all the Adityas, in the grand palace of the bride's father.

'As a gift to the newlyweds, Vishwakarma built another grand palace for them. Made of pure gold, the magnificently ornamented palace was a cosmic wonder in itself.

'The newly-married couple was madly in love. To Surya, Sanjana was the cosmic *Usha* with her fresh and youthful physical aura. She was the divine and soulful warmth for his heart and soul. She was the calming *Sandhya* who caresses lovers and makes them happy and satisfied. Surya could create hundreds of epics praising the beauty of his ladylove. From toenail to head, she was the epitome of an enchanting beauty. He used to call her *Varavarnini*, a beautiful woman who gives physical pleasure to her husband, with life-giving warmth in winter and comforting coolness in summer; and *Varaaroha*, a young woman whose contours, on a mere touch, give immense pleasure to her lover.

'As a couple they danced across all twelve *rashi*s, divinely gracing the universe and sending a message of eternal youth and timeless love to all. They made love in their seven-horse-drawn chariot in the day and in their palace at night. Together, they spent one month in each *rashi*, where the daytime was the celebration of lovemaking, and the night was spent under the stars, immersed in each other's soul and in the cosmic music.

'To Sanjana, Surya was the supreme Adonis. She could spend her life just watching his ever-changing glow from dawn to dusk. She adored the touch of his body and his intoxicating warmth sparked the fire of desire in her heart. For her, Surya the omnipresent was also *Savita* the creator of life, *Khaga* the wanderer of the sky, *Pusha* the nurturer, *Gabhastiman* the light source, *Suwarna* the golden, *Bhanu* the light bearer, *Hiranyareta* the cosmic seed, *Divakara* the light that wipes out darkness, *Haridashva* with seven coloured horses, *Sahastrarchi* with thousands of light rays, *Saptasapti* with seven horses, *Mareechiman* decorated with rays, *Tamobhedi* and *Timironmathan* the destroyer of darkness, *Shambhu* the source of blessings, *Tvashta* the destroyer of the world, *Martandaka* life-giver to the cosmos, *Anshuman* possessing rays, *Hiranyagarbha* Brahma the creator, *Shishir* naturally pleasing, *Tapan* the heat producer, *Ahaskara* creator of the day, *Ravi* prayed to by all, *Agnigarbha* the source of fire, *Shankha* the omnipresent and pleasing, *Shishirnashana* the destroyer of the cold, *Vyomanatha* the master of the sky, *Apa-mitram* the creator of water, *Vindhyaveethiplavangama* the high-speed mover in the sky, *Aatapi* the producer of heat, *Mandali* the possesor of rays, *Mrityu* the death, *Pigala* of brown colour, *Kavi* capable of watching three worlds, *Rakta* the red colour, *Sarvabhavodbhava* the reason behind every life, and *Vishvabhavana* dear to all.

'Their union blessed them with three children. The elder son was Vaivasvatha, the son of Vivaswaan or Surya. Later, he became Vaivasvatha Manu and established the Surya dynasty. The younger son was Yama, the god of death. The youngest among the children was Yami, who later took the form of the River Yamuna.

'The romance in the abode of love began to diminish slowly. Initially, the tidal energy of all-conquering youth allowed Sanjana to bear it all. But, with the responsibility of three children and Surya, Sanjana felt that her energy was quickly draining away. It was strange, with each day the *tapa* of Surya was increasing and Sanjana's ability to bear his resplendence was waning.

'It was not that her love towards Surya had diminished. "No, I still love him very much." Sanjana tried to figure out what was making her unhappy. "I adore my children, they are so precious and dear to my heart."

"'Then, what is the problem with you?" her alter ego probed.
"I feel that this is not the place for me. I am not happy here." She could express only this.

"'Surya is the benefactor of all. He hardly rests. Yet, he finds time for you and loves you. What are you complaining about?"

"'There is no problem with him. The problem is with me. I am not happy. Perhaps, I can bear his gleam no more."

"'His glow or his fame?" her alter ego laughed.

'She chose not to reply but thought, "Who am I? And what do I want to do?"

'Nothing remained hidden from Surya. He quickly found out that his wife was not at ease. One evening, he came back home early. Sanjana was standing on the balcony, leaning on a carved column. Quietly, Surya went behind her and clasped her waist with his hands. Kissing her on the neck, he asked merrily, "What are you dreaming about, darling?"

'Gently pushing him, Sanjana moved away. "What is troubling you, darling?" Surya tried to draw her closer.

"'Nothing," she replied and went to the opposite corner of the balcony. Surya followed her. "Sanjana, what has happened?" he was concerned.

"'Sanjana, to me nothing is dearer than you in this universe. Tell me why you are behaving like this," Surya waited for a while. When Sanjana did not reply, he said softly. "Tell me the reason for your gloom. I will fix it. If someone has offended you, I will burn him in an instant."

"'Surya, please don't get me wrong. I don't know what to tell you." Finally she broke her silence.

"'Don't you trust me? Whatever is worrying you, we may fix it together," Surya assured her.

"'How do I say that I feel suffocated in this house?" Sanjana thought. "But I have to say something."

"'It's your radiance that makes me uneasy," Sanjana said slowly, "I can no longer bear your radiance."

'A shocked Surya stood speechless. "Are you angry with me?

Tell me what I should do for you, suggest any penance," Surya begged.

"'No, it is not like that, Surya. I love you the most. You have committed no wrong." She paused and then said, "Please don't get me wrong. It's just that when you come closer, I feel like conflagrating."

"'I don't understand. Nothing has changed between the two of us, dear. What kind of trial is this?"

"'Surya, trust me. I cannot bear the heat you emit any more. It's only that."

'This made Surya angry. "We have been living together for so many years, and so happily. What has happened to you suddenly? How did you bear my gaze earlier?"

"'I don't know, Surya, but I am tired. Passing each day here is a big trial for me." She paused and then softly added, "We both love each other, but I don't know why my heart is not here."

'A gloomy Surya contemplated for a while and then said, "I don't understand, Sanjana. Let us talk together and solve this together."

"'Please forgive me, Surya. Can't you give me some more time and space?"

"'Sanjana, you knew me and my work before marrying me."

"'Can you not make this little sacrifice for me? A few moments ago, you said that I am everything to you."

"'Sanjana, you should be reasonable; I cannot change my nature." Surya paused and then said tersely, "Sanjana, you have enough space for yourself. I have never stopped you from doing anything. What else do you need? I see that you are talking irrationally."

"'Surya…," Sanjana tried to protest, but did not know what to say.

"'Sanjana, a family runs by the mutual commitment of both spouses. If what you have said is true, I will not come near you. I will wait for your call." Surya walked out without looking at his wife.

'A few days passed and Surya did not speak to Sanjana. Then, one evening, Sanjana went to Surya. Prudent and affectionate as he was, Surya welcomed her with open arms. She allowed herself to be immersed in his warmth. Surya kissed her gently, allowing her to speak her heart out.

'"Surya, I need some time to prepare myself for you. Let me go to my father's home for a few days. I need some time away from here to recharge my spirits and regain my resilience. I will come back soon."

'Surya happily agreed. "Take care of the children," Sanjana hugged him before departing.'

∽

'Sanjana went to an isolated dense forest. It was so dense that the sun's rays could not penetrate its green cover. It was a beautiful place: Lakes, ponds and waterfalls abounded. Tall and dense trees competed with the clouds in the sky. Sanjana had selected this place long before leaving Surya's abode. There was not even one animal in that amazing forest. The whole forest was covered with innumerable kinds of trees, plants, shrubs and flowers.

'Sanjana had never intended to go to her father's place. She knew that her parents would never understand her. "They will think that I have gone crazy. Leaving such a caring and loving husband and three lovely and young children behind! Are you mad?" She could hear her parents' voices in her head.

'"How selfish! You could not stay with such a doting husband and adorable children. If your love is true, why don't you change yourself instead of demanding that he change?" her alter ego challenged her.

'"I am Sanjana first, then anything else." She wanted to be firm about her priorities, but she remembered her young children, and her heart became heavy, imagining their sad faces. They were very young, and Surya was extraordinarily busy and had no time for them. "Who will take care of them?"

she wondered. Emotions dragged her almost to the point of repentance, but she was firm on her decision. "I cannot live there."

'"God, if only I had a sister who could take care of them in my absence. How will they live without me? I must do something for my children." This realisation changed her immediate priority. Something urgently needed to be done for the children. An independent life was possible only after finding an equally capable caretaker for them.

'"We cannot run away from the bonds of *karma*, but we can manage them," she thought. She sat there throughout the day, trying and failing to find a solution.

'Next morning, when she went to wash her face in the pristine and clear water of a lake, her image in the water looked at her. She tossed back her locks to wash her face again; her image copied her. She smiled at that. It was neither magic nor a new discovery; she had seen her image millions of times. But, that morning, she liked it. She began playing with her image. She giggled and so did her image; she smiled and her image copied her; she made faces and her image dutifully followed; she stuck her tongue out and the image copied her again. She made a cup with her palms and slowly called her name. The sound echoed and the image wavered in the cold water. Again, she called out, louder; the sound returned to her in equal measure.

'"If images could be real!" she wondered.

'She wished she could have forever remained a little girl, walking with her father and holding his finger. Vishwakarma's memory brought back his words as well.

'"All of us are the children of the Supreme Being and therefore have infinite creative capability. Everything is in abundance in this cosmos, Sanjana. We just need to tap that," the greatest architect had once told her. "Remember my child, there is nothing you cannot imagine and whatever you can imagine your can create."

That day she began to decipher the meaning of her father's words.

'"Sanjana, let me repeat my words. Like Him, our creative possibilities are also infinite. These abilities don't diminish because He is complete, and so are we, because we are His creation and thus an extension of Him. This cosmos is his creation and has come out of Him. He is not diminished because this grand cosmos has come out of Him, because this cosmos too exists within Him. Everything is in Him and He is in everything.* Just remember this *mantra*. One day, it will help you."

'The mantra was about to change Sanjana's life in that secluded forest. She now had the *sutra*. However, after a few moments in meditation, a negative thought disrupted her. She remembered what Brahma had once told Daksha.

'"Son, procreation by will, *sankalp srishti*, is prohibited. Only the Supreme Lord and, by delegation, I can do so."

'"If Daksha could not do so, how can I?"

'Then she saw an image of her father and his words echoed in her ears as if she was in front of him. "Everything is possible, Sanjana. Everything is possible. Just align yourself with that supreme source of abundance."

'She decided to begin afresh, first by unlearning everything and then focusing with a clear objective to create someone like herself. "Perhaps a clone, to take care of my children."

'Days passed and her meditation continued, until one day she felt her mind become as pristine as water. With a new vigour and energy, she meditated on her image in the lake. Gradually, her image began to take shape in her mind: Hazy at first and then slowly it became clearer and sharper. She did not rest until the image became so sharp and correct that she could see herself in totality.

'The next step was to give the image a physical body, mind,

---

*पूर्णमदः पूर्णमिदंपूर्णात्पूर्णमुदच्यते। पूर्णस्यपूर्णमादायपूर्णमेवावशिस्यते॥

mannerisms and thoughts. She started a conversation with her image. It was a painful and one-way communication, but she was determined: "One day, I will make it a reality."

'Finally one day, Sanjana transformed her imagination into a reality. On the bank of that divine lake, there stood Sanjana and, right opposite her, stood her clone.

'"What is your name?" Sanjana asked.

'"My name is Sanjana. I am Surya's wife and… ," the clone replied.

'"No." Sanjana did not like somebody taking her identity. She corrected her. "I am Sanjana. You are my image. I will call you Chhaya. Say, that your name is Chhaya."

'"My name is Chhaya," the clone replied.

'At this point, suddenly an unknown fear alarmed Sanjana. She wanted to achieve her objective. Though she had created her, watching an equally competent clone perturbed her.

'"What if she goes out of my hands?" she wondered.

'"You are my identical image. Do you know that I have created you to follow my commands?" She needed an assurance.

'"I know. I am grateful to my creator. I shall follow your commands." Chhaya's reply should have assured her, but some suspicion germinated in Sanjana's heart.

'"Chhaya, you have been created for a specific purpose," Sanjana wanted to be doubly sure. "I will live here in this forest. You have to play my role to perfection. Take care of my children, Yami, Yama and Vaivasvatha and also my husband Surya. Promise me."

'"I promise, I shall fulfil my responsibilities towards your children and husband as you would have done. They will never feel that I am not you."

'"Now, go to Surya and my children," Sanjana felt assured.

'"Leave everything to me. I will handle everything," Chhaya guaranteed Sanjana and left for Surya's abode.'

'Surya and his children were pleasantly surprised to find Sanjana back. The children clasped her legs with joy and Surya embraced and kissed her like a crazy lover.

"'Sanjana, my dear! I was about to go to Vishwakarma's place to bring you back. I am so relieved. Look at the children, they missed you so much. Yami and Yama hardly ate anything in your absence."

"'Mother, don't ever leave us again," the children begged her. "We will not annoy you again."

"'I am sorry, children. I will never leave you. I shall always be with you," she reassured them, planting kisses on their foreheads.

'Then, looking at Surya, she smiled enticingly, "Surya, forgive me. I shall not give you a reason to complain."

'Once again, the Surya household became a blossoming garden with the chirping of happy children and the laughter of a loving couple. A few years passed like this.

'One day, when Chhaya was sitting with the children, Yama started talking about his concept of dharma.

"'Yesterday, Acharya was saying that the *prana* is Brahma, the food is Brahma, the *vayu* is Brahma, the eyes are Brahma, and the vaak is Brahma. He explained everything so nicely. But he did not mention the truth. I think that truth alone is Brahma. What do you say mother?"

"'Oh, Yama. Enjoy your food. No studies at mealtime. Ask your doubts to your teacher tomorrow," Chhaya said.

"'Mother is right, Yama. Eat your food." Vaivasvatha supported their mother.

"'Yama talks about truth, dharma and law all the time," Yami complained.

"'So what is wrong in that?" Surya asked, entering the kitchen. "Truth is the axis of the cosmos. Truth is *rta*. The Supreme Being is devoid of emotions. He acts on the basis of truth alone, because the laws of creation can neither be arbitrary nor based on imagination, deceit and lies."

'He patted Yama's back and said, "I am happy son, make truth the core of your life."

'Surya's explanation scared Chhaya. So far, she had played Sanjana's role to perfection and was happy with the love and affection she had been receiving from everyone.

'"If Surya and Yama think that the gold standard to judge someone is truth and truth alone, then do emotions not matter to them? What if, tomorrow, Sanjana comes back? If she does not, what if one day they find out that I am an imposter? What will happen to me? Chhaya panicked. "What if Surya or Yama comes to know about me?" "Surya is a simple person, but he is an ardent follower of dharma. He is ever-sacrificing, consuming himself every moment to give hope and light to others. He demands nothing from anybody, he asks absolutely nothing in return. Dharma alone is his lifeline. Dharma gives him an innate strength that sustains him. Such a person, howsoever gentle he may be, will not tolerate a lie." Chhaya became very anxious.

'"Good. Then go and tell him that you are a clone. He will burn you instantly," her alter ego mocked Chhaya.

'"He will not burn me, he loves me," she sensed how weak her response was.

'"He loves Sanjana, not Chhaya. When he finds out that you are an imposter, he will throw you out of his house," her alter ego warned her.

'"My children will support me."

'"Why would they love you? You are not their mother, you are just a lookalike, a caretaker."

'Chhaya could not sleep that night: she wondered if it had been a mistake to take up Sanjana's role. "What is my identity? I don't have an independent identity. I am just a clone. There is only one difference between Sanjana and me: the children. These three children are not mine, they are Sanjana's children. I must have my own children to safeguard my interests. Then, if Surya knows my reality, he will never harm the mother of his children." So, Chhaya decided to have her own children.

'The next night, Chhaya prepared herself well to welcome Surya. A charmed Surya looked admiringly at his wife. In an instant, he pulled her towards him.

'"Your magic grows like the phases of a waxing moon."

'That night, they made love like young lovers. When a satisfied Surya was relaxing, resting his head on her bosom, he asked, "Sanjana, you have made my life beautiful. What can I do for you?"

'Gently stroking his chest with her soft fingers, she looked into his eyes and then lowered her head. "I need nothing but your love," she replied.

'"Tell me your wish, darling," raising her chin gently, Surya asked.

'With a little effort, she forced herself on top of Surya and caressing his broad chest, she said with an intoxicating smile, "If you are so pleased with me, grant me three children, two boys and a girl."

'"Sanjana, we already have three children, two boys and one girl! Why do you need more?"

'"Surya, you know I love children. My three children are now growing up. How much time does a boy need to become a man? I want my house to always have the joyous sounds and laughter of babies. Let's have more children, please."

'"I hope, after a few years, you will not ask for another set of children," Surya laughed and then obliged her.'

༄

'On the eighth night of the *Pushya* month in the year *Pramodoota*, when the *Asthami* moon was waning and the *Swati* star was in ascendancy in the sky, Chhaya gave birth to a baby boy.

'The whole Surya household was assembled there and, contrary to everyone's expectations, the newborn was a weak, mewling and thin boy, with a dark complexion and an ill-proportioned body. His eyes were yellowish-brown and he looked strange.

'Chhaya got the shock of her life. "Is he the reflection of my ill-will?" The thought almost killed her.

'When Surya saw the newborn, he too became worried. The infant did not bear any characteristics of his parents. In fact, he was diametrically opposite to the features of Surya or Sanjana.

'Chhaya noticed her husband's baffled face and said in a voice filled with guilt, "Surya, I expected him to be like you…"

'The ever-benevolent Surya affectionately lifted his son in his strong arms. "You are wrong, Sanjana. My son complements me perfectly: He is like my inseparable shadow, my *chhaya*."

'Kashyapa and Aditi came for the newborn's naming ceremony. Kashyapa drew the boy's horoscope. "He will scare his opponents. His enemies will never sleep in peace. He will be a strict disciplinarian, a tyrant. He will always move with a measured tread. He knows and values restraint. His name should reflect all his traits. I will call him Shanishchara," Kashyapa predicted.'

∽

'Time passed. Chhaya realized that she received a great sense of accomplishment in the company of Shanischara or Shani, as he was fondly called. The mother and son took special care of each other. Eventually, Chhaya gave birth to two more children. Her younger son Saavarni had a flaming complexion like his father's radiance. Tapti, the youngest among the three children, was a beautiful girl.

'Chhaya now had the responsibility of rearing six children. Quickly, her attention became divided between Sanjana's trio and her own. Her engagement with her own children became delightfully intense and fulfilling, whereas she started first ignoring and then disliking Sanjana's children, but the children were yet to feel it completely.

'"I am not wicked. My children need more time than

Sanjana's grown-up children," she told herself. But very soon, this thin curtain of dislike became a wall of hatred. Chhaya could no longer bear the sight of Sanjana's children. If she saw Vaivasvatha laughing, she did not like that; if some Acharya praised the academic acumen of Yama, she felt jealous; and if Surya dotingly cuddled his beautiful daughter Yami, Chhaya's skin burnt with irritation. This dislike slowly turned into an intolerable hatred.

'Chhaya now started discriminating heavily between the children: It began with unequal distribution of food, clothes, amenities and affection. She stopped taking Sanjana's children outside. Then, she began dealing with them in separate sets, her's and Sanjana's: She tried to isolate the two sets. But when the children did not follow her wish, one day she called her own troika.

'"Shani, both Saavarni and Tapti are too young to understand this, but you are a big boy now. At least you should not follow Vaivasvatha's commands. Instead making your siblings understand, you too follow Vaivasvatha, wagging your tail."

'"Mother, I like him. He takes care of us."

'"Shani, my son, you are so innocent. Vaivasvatha, Yama and Yami are different and older than you. They are cunning, evil and shrewd. You cannot recognize their true self. You, Saavarni and Tapti are too young and simple to understand this." She looked at the closed door. "They will harm you so subtly that you won't realize it."

'"But they are our brothers and sisters. Why would they harm us?" Saavarni was unable to understand why his own siblings would hurt them.

'"Saavarni, you are a foolish child. Use your brain. Before your birth, they had everything. Now they think that you are eating their share. Look at Shani, he is much younger than them, yet he is much smarter and stronger. He understands their cunning. Learn something from Shani."

'"Mother is right, Saavarni. Don't you feel that they hide

many things from us?" Bolstered by his mother's support, Shani happily took up the mantle of the leader of the pack.

'"In that case, should we not tell father how bad Yama and Yami are?" Tapti jumped with joy, imagining the plight of the two siblings, standing before a strict father.

'A confused Shani looked at his mother for guidance, but Chhaya tackled the tricky question herself.

'"Children, your father is a very busy man. He hardly has time for the family. How can he understand what's going on, specially when the three of them are so shrewd? He will not understand it the way I do, because I spend all my time with you."

'Chhaya looked at her children and then added in a hushed tone, "You should not share our secret talk with your father because he loves them more than he loves you. He will never trust you."

'"He loves them more than us! Why?" a heartbroken Saavarni almost cried.

'"Because they were the first babies," Shani showed his frustration to his naïve brother.

'In Shani, Chhaya had someone who would propagate her schemes. "One day, my 'dark and disproportionate' son will torment them," she thought confidently. "What had he said?" She bitterly remembered, "You are wrong, Sanjana. My son compliments me perfectly. He is like my inseparable shadow, my *chhaya*." Surya's words still offended her, though he had never meant any ill will with them.

'Shanischara was an imperious boy and he never liked the way Vaivasvatha used to broker peace among all the siblings. Vaivasvatha was a mild-mannered and mature boy. He disliked quarrels and tensions among siblings. As Surya was hardly available at home, unconsciously Vaivasvatha had taken up the responsibility of an elder in the house.

'Chhaya's insinuations encouraged Shani to dominate the siblings. Slowly, Vaivasvatha noticed that Shani was challenging him. Initially, there were heated conversations. Chhaya presided over the settlements and blatantly favoured Shani. An emboldened Shani began to ill-mouth Sanjana's children.

'One day, Yama and Yami were playing chess. Tapti was looking on from a distance. Slowly, the game became very exciting. Tapti came closer and advised Yama on his moves. Seeing this, an enraged Shani forcefully dragged Tapti back.

'"I have told you not to play with these wicked guys!" Shani shouted at little Tapti.

'"Why are you calling us wicked?" Yama got up and blocked Shani's path. Shani tried to push him, but Yama was stronger. When they were jostling with each other, Chhaya saw them.

'"Yami, Yama and Vaivasvatha, you are a bad influence on your younger siblings. As punishment, from now on, you will get food after everybody finishes theirs!" Chhaya screamed in anger.

'"This is injustice," Yami protested to her elder brother. "Why is our mother doing this to us? She always takes the youngsters' side."

'"Don't you think the youngsters should get the food first? Mother is right in doing so," Vaivasvatha presented his logic and consoled her.

'To the dismay of even a patient Vaivasvatha, delayed food slowly became leftover food and sometimes no food at all. The elder trio was puzzled. They were unable to understand why their mother was punishing them without reason. They could not understand why she did not admonish Shani and Tapti for their bad behaviour. When this stark discrimination became unbearable, one morning Yama raised the need to find out the reason.

'"Today, after lunch, I will ask her why she is doing this."

'"I am not sure. Maybe this is her way of educating us," Vaivasvatha tried to pacify him.

'"It can't be so. A mother should be like the stomach, which distributes nutrients equally among all the organs, without discriminating. But, our mother blatantly takes the side of

Shani, Saavarni and Tapti. This is bad for us, but not good for them either."

"'Why would any mother do that?" Vaivasvatha repeated the troubling quandary.

'The more they tried to be nicer to them, the worse their younger siblings' response became. Despite being generous and giving an extended benefit of doubt to his mother and Shani, now Vaivasvatha too felt like he was living in an alien home. Finally, Vaivasvatha agreed to discuss the matter with their mother.

'When Chhaya saw them coming silently to her room, she became alert, like a hungry leopard ready to pounce. "You should handle this calmly," she told herself.

"'Mother, we need to talk."

'She did not respond.

"'Mother, we don't know what our fault is. It has been months since you have spoken nicely to Yami, Yama and me. Please tell us our fault. We will follow all your advice. We apologize if unknowingly or knowingly we have done anything wrong. Do not be angry," an emotional Vaivasvatha prayed earnestly.

"'There is no question of being angry or pleased. You are hopeless. You have been incorrigible offenders. Like the sinners who perish in hell, you too will suffer."

"'But what have we done? Mother, before cursing us, you must tell us our crime," Yama said bitterly.

'Chhaya stared at Yama with fiery eyes. If Vaivasvatha was a docile boy adapted to silent sufferings, Yama was hard logic without emotion. She knew that if he continued speaking, she would be compelled to pour out all her hatred over him.

"'And that day you falsely accused me of stealing Tapti's food," Yami started crying.

"'Vaivasvatha, tell them to keep quiet when two elders are speaking…"

"'Mother, you have to listen to us," Yama said firmly. "You must tell us our crime. How can a mother discriminate among her own children in the way you do?"

"'Yama, please keep quiet," Vaivasvatha tried to stop Yama.

"'Let me say it, Vaivasvatha. She punishes us without fault and on the contrary, encourages the hostile mischiefs of Shani."

"'Yama, you don't know how to speak to your elders!" Chhaya shouted.

'An angry Yama came a few paces forward and stood before Chhaya, staring at her.

"'Mother, we are nothing but a small entity in this universe. We often are commanded by our senses. Our senses lead us to sin." He paused and then said like an old wise man, "There is a chain that connects weak things to the most powerful. For example, the senses are commanded by temptation, and temptation is commanded by the mind. The mind is commanded by wisdom. The soul is more powerful than wisdom. Cosmic illusion is more powerful than the soul. And the *parbrahma*, the Supreme Being, is the most powerful. That's absolute and that's the salvation…"*

"'Keep your philosophy to yourself. Parroting a few *shloka*s does not make you a Brahmarishi. I can't tolerate your nonsensical utterings!" an impatient Chhaya screamed at Yama.

"'Mother, following the path of our father, we are seeking wisdom to have a glimpse of that ultimate truth. We have never spoken a lie in our life. And you are accusing us of speaking lies, without showing us a single instance," a composed Yama said, looking at his mother's angry face.

"'Mother, those who nurture falsehood and those who promote falsehood, both destroy themselves. We know that we are following the path of truth, but we worry for you and our younger siblings."

"'How dare you call me a liar? Who are you to worry about my children and me?" Chhaya was quivering with anger.

"'Mother, do you know how the Daityas destroyed themselves? Their blind arrogance destroyed them. They used to believe

---

*पुरूषात् नपरकिंचितसाकाष्टासापरागतिः ।

that nothing is superior to them. They believed everything was for their consumption. They did not share, they did not preserve, they just blindly consumed for themselves. This conceit devastated them."*

'No one spoke for a while. Yama bowed down and rested his head on Chhaya's feet.

'"Mother, we love you and our younger siblings, but please don't do something that destroys all of us."

'Taken aback, Chhaya moved back a pace.

'"You vile Yama, you are cursing me and my children. I refuse to treat you at par with Shani, Saavarni and Tapti. What will you do? Now, get lost!" Chhaya kicked at Yama and he fell down.

'Vaivasvatha and Yami rushed to help Yama. But before they could reach him, Yama got up. Burning with pain, anger and sorrow, he raised his foot. Chhaya was shocked. Things had now moved out of control. In a fit of rage, she exploded: "Yama, you are a pampered and spoilt child. Your father's pampering has destroyed your conscience. You want to kick your mother? You will repent for this act, you insolent buffalo!" A catastrophic silence pervaded the room, and then Chhaya's shrill curse pierced the air. "Yama, may your foot fall from your body and provide fodder for the worms."

'In disbelief and utter fear, a shocked Yama put his hands on his ears, as if to block the curse. He looked at Chhaya and felt her frenzied hatred.

'"How could a mother…? How could you curse me, mother?"

'"I could have done worse, Yama," a remorseless Chhaya said.

'"I am your son…"

'"No. You are not my son. Are you listening? You are not my son. None of you are my children!"

'"Vaivasvatha, get him out of my sight, otherwise I will kill him!"'

---

*अतिमानेनतेवैअसुराकथंनुवयंजुहुयामइतिवदंतः पराबभूवुः ।

'A perplexed Surya heard what had happened to Yama. Vaivasvatha told him everything, right from the beginning. A sobbing Yama was difficult to console. The pain, humiliation and anger were etched across his face.

'"She always smiles when she sees Shani, Saavarni and Tapti. But the moment see looks at us, she scowls and scolds. Whenever I invite Tapti to play, she warns me not to play with Tapti," a crying Yami told her father.

'With every revelation, Surya became increasingly startled. He had no idea what was happening in his house.

'"What will happen to my foot?" a scared Yama asked. Surya closed his eyes for a moment and then set young Yama on his lap.

'"Yama, I cannot reverse her curse." Gently placing his hand on his son's head, Surya consoled his aggrieved son. "But I can modify it: Some flakes of flesh from your foot will fall painlessly on the ground. The worms will feed on them. You won't lose your foot and your mother's curse will also take effect."

'"She is not our mother," Yama firmly said, "she said it thrice."

'"Let me check that," Surya replied and kissing his son's forehead, he marched into Chhaya's chamber.

'Chhaya felt a scorching heatwave entering her chamber. Surya came in. His face was red hot and Chhaya could feel his intense energy parching her. He grabbed her arm and drilled into her with his laser-like gaze. Chhaya could see whirlpools of fire inside his eyes. Each cell of her body felt red hot like burning coal, and she trembled with fear. She realized that she could no longer keep her secret.

'In a thunderous voice Surya asked, "Sanjana, how could you curse your own son?"

'The searing heat had now become unbearable. She felt that if she did not reply quickly, his gaze would melt her soul.

'"He has been utterly abusive, arrogant and insubordinate," she tried to shift the blame one last time.

'In a sudden and uncharacteristic burning whisper Surya asked, "And did you say that they are not your children?"

'Chhaya was now gasping for breath. Despite her inherent coolness, she was now unable to bear Surya's radiance.

'"Will you please stay a little away? I will tell you everything." She could barely speak. This angered him further.

'"Tell me, who are you?" he hissed.

'"I am not Sanjana. I am Chhaya," she confessed. Surya got the shock of his life and his grip slackened on her arm.

'Chhaya ran away towards the door, but froze on seeing the children standing there, listening to her confession.

'"So, you are an imposter. Now, tell me, where is Sanjana?"

'Chhaya narrated the entire story with tears flowing down her cheeks. Surya and his six children listened to each and every word in incredulity.

'"Tell me the name of that forest," Surya asked amidst the worried cries of the children.

'"Vaivasvatha, take care of your brothers and sisters; I will bring your mother back." He hugged his children and rushed to find his wife.'

~

'When Surya reached that secluded and dense forest, it became illuminated. There was no sign of any airborne, aquatic or terrestrial animal there. For a long time, he wandered from one place to another, looking for some sign of Sanjana. Apprehensions about Sanjana's safety shrouded his heart. He looked at each and every shrub and bush and in every cave. He scanned every place where even a small animal could hide, but he could not get a glimpse of his beloved. Tired, he sat down on the bank of a large lake, whose clear water reflected the bright green and azure shades of a shining sky.

'"Sanjana… Where are you?" he cried aloud desperately, as if it was the last cry of a crestfallen lover.

'Once the echo subsided, an intense silence overpowered

everything. Surya felt as if time had stopped. Then, he heard the soft neighing of a horse. Surya got up and looked in the direction of the sound. A pristine white horse was looking at him from the far bank of the lake. Cautiously and with very slow strides, he walked towards the horse. The horse did not take its gaze off him for even a fraction of a moment. When Surya was closer, he found that it was a mare, unblinkingly gazing at him with her large, limpid eyes.

'Surya locked eyes with the mare, and then recognition hit his consciousness hard. How could he mistake those eyes? Those were Sanjana's eyes, inviting him to make love to her. In a flash, Surya transformed himself into a tall and regal stallion. He went closer to the mare and, with a soft neigh, rubbed his head against her exquisite neck. In turn, she brought her soft body against his and began rubbing it tenderly.

'The secluded forest became the playground of the mare and the stallion and their passionate mating was uninhibited and unrestrained. Long years of separation had fuelled their love and now they were not ready to disengage from each other. As a result of their impassioned copulation, the mare gave birth to a pair of twin sons, sporting equine faces on human torsos. Then, both Surya and Sanjana resumed their original form and again made passionate love. As a result, Sanjana gave birth to a son.

'The blessed couple was happy with their children and spent some time in the forest. Surya named the horse-faced twins, Naasatya and Dasra. They were not ordinary beings, but were destined to become divine physicians, the Ashvini Kumars. The youngest son was named Revanta. Later on, he achieved fame as a doyen of equestrian science.

'"Surya, I never recovered from the guilt of leaving my children. I am worried about them. Let us go back home."

'"Yes, Sanjana. Let us go," Surya agreed immediately.

'"Please pardon me, I should not have done what I did. My children paid a heavy price for my mistake."

"'No one can replace a mother, not even a clone,'" Surya smiled. "Sanjana, I too should have softened my unyielding attitude. Now, I recognize your needs and appreciate them better. Let us amend our past mistakes."

'With tears in her eyes, Sanjana wordlessly embraced her husband. They remained in their tight embrace for a while, and then Sanjana repeated, "Let us all go home."

"'Not all of us, Sanjana. Don't you think our sons should begin their education now?" Surya asked Sanjana. Her heart sank, but she understood.

"'Naasatya, Dasra and Revanta, it's time to be initiated into *brahmacharya*, to begin your studies. I have asked Narada to come here and take you to guru Brahaspati. Go and complete your education and make us proud."

'Sanjana blessed her sons, "Naasatya and Dasra, may you become the best physicians in the three worlds."

"'And Revanta, you will become the master of equestrian science," Surya added smilingly.

'Sanjana's heart broke when Narada came to take the three young lads to Brahaspati. "I wish we could have taken them home," She sighed.

"'Sanjana, everyone in this world is born with a specific purpose. Naasatya, Dasra and Revanta are no exceptions. Let them go to Brahaspati and learn. We don't know God's design: Living beings are nothing but cogs in His scheme. I am sure that all our nine children will serve some purpose assigned by Him."

'The three children bid adieu to their parents. Sanjana's tears continued to flow. "Nature demands all the difficult decisions from a mother, so why does it give a soft heart to her?"

'On their way back home, Sanjana asked Surya, "What kind of a schemer is God? Why does he put the head of a horse on a human torso?" Surya understood her pain and put his arm around her waist.

"'What else would the sons of a magical mare and an

enchanted stallion look like?" he replied, to make her laugh.

'She did not like his joke.

'"Our wants instigate us to take the form of an infinite number of animals. When I realized that an obsessive Surya was looking for me in that lonely forest, I could only think of becoming a mare to watch my lover silently. And, unable to bear the separation, and with a burning desire to copulate, he took the form of a stallion," she reflected quietly, and realized that those events were not dictated by God's wish, but were consequences of their wants.

'"Children bear the burden of their parents' actions, Sanjana," Surya kissed her forehead. Sanjana wiped her moist eyes. The new set of three babies was the fruit of their uninhibited and free love.

'"My sons are the creation of pure love, born of a moment when you were not Surya and I was not Sanjana. They are made of a love that is free from ego, ambition and all flaws. They will cure people of all blemish."

'When the couple returned to their palace, Vaivasvatha, Yama and Yami came running into her outstretched arms, but Chhaya's children remained hesitant. Sanjana understood their hesitation. "If I have to give equal care and love to all my nine children, the shadow has to go." She decided to end the individuality of her image.

'"Chhaya, your role ends here," Sanjana said in a clear and tranquil voice. "You don't have an existence without me. You have served your purpose and it's time you merge into me again."

'The moment Sanjana voiced her command, Chhaya lost her speech. For a brief moment, she looked at Sanjana with moist eyes, urging her to grant her freedom. She raised her hand to touch her children, when she heard Sanjana's call.

'"Come Chhaya, come."

'Shani tried to catch hold of his mother, but before he could reach her, Chhaya silently fused into Sanjana. In the light of

Surya, Sanjana's image wavered for a while and then it became still. Sanjana pulled Chhaya's three children into her arms.

"'Don't fear, my dear children. Your mother and I are one and the same. You are my children." With a little effort, Sanjana could wipe away the apprehensions of Chhaya's children, and very soon the Surya household became a happy and joy-filled home again.'

~

'Krishna, throughout my life, I struggled with the doctrine of Shwetaketu. Everyone accepts it for the sake of social order. Therefore, Karna was always ridiculed as *suta-putra*. The sons of Indra, Dharma, Vayu and Ashvini Kumars were called the Pandavas. Why does everyone discard a mother's right over her sons?' Kunti asked.

'Aunt, I agree with you. Tradition should facilitate human dignity and order, not the other way round. Traditions that lower the dignity of human beings must be discarded,' Krishna replied.

'Don't you think that my sons should just have been *Kunti-putra*s instead of Pandavas? After all, it's the mother who makes and shapes a child!'

'Aunt, there still exists a few societies who are matrilineal. However, most societies have now evolved along the patterns of patriarchy. These things evolve and decay, they are not permanent. Maybe, in the future, people will accept matriarchy as a norm. Who knows?' Krishna smiled.

'Krishna, I never fought against any wrongdoing, be it from Pandu, the Kauravas or my sons. I am a weak woman. But tell me, was there ever a woman who questioned the right of the father over the child? A woman who had rejected the Shwetaketu doctrine and given her child her name?'

'Aunt, you know about Jabala, but her case was extraordinary, as the identity of the father was unknown. I will tell you an ancient story that explains who should be the real guardian of a child,' Krishna said.

'Sage Angiras was one of the mind-born sons of Brahma. His wife's name was Vasudha. She was a large-hearted lady who took care of her husband's students like a mother. True to her name Vasudha, she provided shelter, warmth, food and water to the residents of the ashram. From a new *brahmachari* to an old *adhvaryu*, anyone could come to her and resolve his issues. Their faith in her earned her the nickname Shraddha, the faith.

'It is said that once, in a fit of rage, Agni the fire god renounced the world and left for an unknown place to do penance. Without fire, all creatures suffered a lot. During that time, Angiras volunteered to perform Agni's duties till his return. This saved Agni from a big sin. When he returned and found Angiras performing his duties diligently and efficiently, a happy Agni offered the status of fire god to Angiras.

'"Angiras, I am pleased with your services. You deserve my place among the pantheon of gods."

'"Agnideva, academics give me immense joy. I don't know anything except learning and teaching. If you are pleased with me, then accept me as your pupil and give me sacred knowledge."

'"A pupil like you is always welcome, son," a pleased Agni said. "But I would like to gift you something. Please ask me for anything. If you so wish, you may consult Vasudha."

'Angiras looked at his lovely wife. Standing under a cherry blossom tree and holding its tiny branch, Shraddha was looking at him. Their eyes met and they spoke wordlessly.

'"Father, let your kindness bless us with a son of extraordinary wisdom and brilliance," they prayed to the radiant Agni, who was standing against the background of a glorious red sun in the sky.

'"Your wish will come true," Agni blessed them. A delightful radiance spread in the sky from east to west.'

∽

'In time, Shraddha gave birth to a boy, and they named him

Brahaspati. From early childhood, the boy exhibited virtues of patience, calmness and wisdom. In a few years, he grew up to be a tall and well-built young man. His broad shoulders and strong bones, his radiant big eyes and his broad forehead delighted his parents. Despite his sturdy physical appearance, the boy's face was delightfully innocent. He was also a gifted orator: His voice was sweet and ever pleasing.

'"He will become a great scholar," Angiras proudly predicted to everyone.

'Shraddha and Angiras provided the best education to him. Very soon, Brahaspati surpassed his illustrious father in knowledge. Philosophy and its various branches, polity, science, fine arts, logic, medicine, yoga, mathematics, astrology, politics, aerodynamics, theology and others, there was no subject that Brahaspati had not internalized. He was the best pupil any guru could ever have. Very soon, Brahaspati took charge of his father's ashram. His fame soon reached everywhere. Hundreds of *brahmachari*, from all the three worlds, made a beeline for his school.

'Angiras relished the boundless joy and pride that emanated from the deeds of his young son. One day, when the proud father was sitting under a *peepal* tree, teaching a batch of young students, a golden chariot stopped nearby. Seven white horses were attached to it and its golden flag had an elephant and a thunderbolt, indicating that the chariot belonged to Indra, the king of the Adityas.

'Indra greeted Angiras with utmost respect and sat near him. Angiras apologized to his students and asked them to reassemble some time later. Indra was known for his haughtiness, swagger and arrogance. His exaggerated show of humbleness alerted the sage.

'"Great sage, you are a *manasputra* of Brahma and nothing is hidden from you," Indra bowed in respect. "Daitya Vrashparva has cunningly approached Usana to be his priest and the guru Usana has accepted his offer. This has increased Daitya power immensely, and we are worried and feeling insecure," Indra informed the old sage.

'Angiras was not sure what Indra was up to.

'"Great sage, I have thought a lot about our position and discussed it with Brahma as well. We both feel that we must have your son Brahaspati as our guru and preceptor to counter Usana," Indra proposed.

'Proud Angiras' eyes became moist with emotion: Being the preceptor of the Adityas was a big honour. He realized what Nataraja must have felt during his cosmic dance. To Angiras, it felt like the universe was nothing but a tiny ball, which could fit in his hand. With an immense sense of gratification, he indicated his son.

'"Indra, why don't you ask Brahaspati?" Indra thanked him and walked towards Brahaspati. The procedure did not take long and Brahaspati was anointed the priest and guru of the Adityas.

'Indra's choice was perfect. Soon, Brahaspati restored the balance of power between the warring stepbrothers. He was a match for Usana, who later became famous as guru Shukracharya. Battles turned into wars, and the Adityas and the Daityas remained engaged in fierce conflict for many years.'

∽

'"Angiras, Brahaspati's friends have become parents and a few are now grandparents," Shraddha reminded Angiras one day.

'The old sage nodded in response but did not reply.

'"Why would you worry? You and your son are married to these scriptures," Shraddha expressed her annoyance. "Don't you see that he is aging? We must find a suitable match for him."

'This time, Angiras took Shraddha's worries seriously. "I completely agree, dear, but our son is mature enough and he should appreciate this, after all, he is the guru of the Adityas. Let's urge him to settle with a girl of his choice."

'Brahaspati listened to his parents patiently. Buried under the stress and expectations of the divine responsibility bestowed upon him, he had completely forgotten about this aspect of life.

'"Whom should I marry?" he asked.

'"We don't know a girl befitting your stature and virtues, my son," Shraddha earnestly said.

'"Your mother is right, son," Angiras seconded his wife. "Go and find a girl of your liking."

'Brahaspati also consulted Brahma.

'"Son, make a tour of the globe. One day, you will find a girl of your choice, and you will recognize her when you see her." Smiling at the guru of the gods, the creator then added, "This journey will make you wiser."

'A happy Brahaspati cheerfully began exploring the globe, to find the most suitable match for himself.

'At about the same time, a vivacious maiden was bathing in the sea around an isolated island. She was enjoying the refreshing coolness of the water and the warmth of a caressing sun. Her sun-tanned frame was blessed with divine curves. Her gorgeousness could ignite passion even in ascetics. Alas, on that island, there was none to admire that ravishing beauty, except the creator.

'This woman longed for a male companion. Under the shining blue sky, as she enjoyed the caressing tides of the sea, she appeared to be an integral part of that strikingly beautiful panorama. Immersed in the bliss of nature, she closed her eyes and prayed for a man. When she opened her eyes, she found Brahma standing before her.

'"Taara," he called her with utmost affection. "My dear child, your wish will be fulfilled. Brahaspati will be your husband. Go and explore the globe, and you will receive twofold happiness and joy in this marriage."

'Without deliberating much on Brahma's cryptic words, Taara accepted the wish of the Lord and started her voyage in search of an unknown Brahaspati.

'Destined to meet, the two lovers thus began their journey in opposite directions. On their way, they met many prospective persons. They interacted with all kinds of creatures, but did not find the destined and designated match. With every interaction, their expectations soared. "Not this. Not this," the mantra kept them moving, on a search, till it ended on a coral beach in a far corner of the world.

'Standing on that coral beach, Taara suddenly heard a voice calling, "Gurudev Brahaspati!" She turned towards the sound and saw one sage running after another, who was walking with fast strides. The moment she turned, Brahaspati turned to respond to the call and their eyes met. For an eternity, they forgot the caller and what he was saying. Unaware of their surroundings, their eyes spoke.

'Tall, masculine and broad-shouldered Brahaspati and stunningly beautiful Taara came together with an intense desire. An arduous search had ended and the dams of their desire were breached. The couple spent many days in physical intimacy and then got married. Angiras, Shraddha and Indra were overjoyed. The newlyweds commenced their married life in Brahaspati's ashram.

'However, their honeyed nights did not last long. Very soon, Brahaspati became involved in the time-consuming and energy-sapping political conspiracies between the Adityas and the Daityas. Indra was a busy schemer and fond of his brainstorming sessions. He was a self-indulgent and greedy king who never cared that his companions had other responsibilities as well. When an idea enticed him, whether day or night, Indra would summon his entire team, to scheme against someone or the other. These sessions were never for the welfare of the people, but only to propagate his selfish agenda and continue his dominance as the lord of the universe for eternity.

'Brahaspati, being the guru, chief counsellor and the priest, was sucked into these meetings full-time. The constant stress and pressure, to meet the ever-growing expectations of his king, had made a simple, hardworking and truthful Brahaspati old before his age. Brahaspati's hair turned grey and he looked older. This perfectly suited the agenda of Indra, who secretly envied the cerebral brilliance of a much younger Brahaspati.

'Brahaspati's involvement in politics and academics meant that he hardly had any time for his young, voluptuous and yearning wife. His intellectual wit and wisdom, that had once charmed Taara, quickly evaporated into thin air, and his masculine touch, that had enlivened Taara's nights, also waned.'

~

"Aunt, before I take this fascinating story of Brahaspati and his beautiful wife Taara forward, I have to tell you the story of Chandra's birth." Krishna paused.

"Chandra?"

"Yes. Chandra played a major role in the married life of Taara and Brahasapati. Like it generates the powerful waves by attracting the ocean water, Chandra's attraction brought turmoil in Taara's married life.

'Once upon a time, there was a young and exceptionally beautiful woman called Sheelvati. Her husband Ugrashrava was a wicked man, afflicted by leprosy. Despite that, Sheelvati served him with complete devotion. Her husband's jealousy and insecurity made him think that, one day Sheelvati would leave him for a healthy young man. Therefore, he always insisted on accompanying his wife whenever she went begging.

'Dutifully, Sheelvati used to carry her foul-smelling husband in a basket on her head, whenever she went out. Yet Ugrashrava always abused her and cursed her. With the passage of time, Ugrashrava's physical condition deteriorated, but Sheelvati's love and compassion for him never diminished. The more Sheelvati took care of him, the worse his abuses became. He began torturing her by falsely accusing her of infidelity and hatching conspiracies to kill him.

'One evening, Sheelvati was returning home after begging,

carrying her husband on her head. In front of the last house in the lane, an attractive woman opened a window and offered her alms. Sheelvati refused to take the offering and walked past hurriedly. However, a glimpse of the beautiful donor agitated Ugrashrava's heart.

'"Why did you refuse to take alms from her?" he asked his wife.

'"She is a prostitute. How can I receive alms from her? It's not clean money."

'"You fool! She was giving you so much money!" he cursed his wife. "She is so beautiful, isn't she?" shamelessly he asked Sheelvati. "After many years, today I felt an urge for a woman. Take me to her."

'"My lord, what are you saying? It would be a sin!"

'"Don't you understand? I want to spend a night with that beautiful lady. Take me to her!" Ugrashrava shouted.

'"Lord, how can I?" a horrified Sheelvati cried out and entered their home. Placing her husband carefully on his bed, she stood there shuddering with apprehension.

'"You miserable woman! How dare you disobey me?" he shouted and fell off the bed in his agitation.

'Carefully, Sheelvati tried to gather him up, but Ugrashrava kicked her.

'"Lord, I don't have money to give to that prostitute," with tears in her eyes, she succumbed to his pressure.

'"You liar!" Ugrashrava looked at her with burning eyes. The room was dark, yet she could see his red eyes. "You are a beggar. Go and beg her for my pleasure. She will oblige. Take me to her and beg," trembling with anger, Ugrashrava commanded.

'A shocked Sheelvati remained silent for few moments. Ugrashrava had become relentless. When Sheelvati did not respond soon enough, like a maniac, Ugrashrava moved down on to the floor and struggled to come to his feet.

'Forced by her husband, a perplexed Sheelvati quickly placed him in the basket and left. It was pitch dark and the prostitute's house was a few hundred yards away. Ugrashrava was still restless and was kicking his limbs out of the basket, cursing and abusing his wife to make her walk faster.

'When they reached the prostitute's house and Sheelvati was about to place him on the ground, he tried to kick her hard one last time. However, he missed his target and banged his foot on something else. A coarse male voice cursed him like thunder.

'"Listen, you despicable fool, whosoever you are! You have given me excruciating pain. I curse you: You will die when the sun rises tomorrow morning!"

'The curse stunned the couple. Hearing the noise, the prostitute came out with a lamp in her hand and saw an old and weak sage, Mandavya, trying to stand up on his feet.

'The dark curse echoed in the minds of Ugrashrava and Sheelvati. She became speechless with fear and Ugrashrava caught hold of her legs. "He has cursed me to die. I will die when the sun rises tomorrow morning," he started crying. "Sheelvati, save me. I beg you, Sheelvati. Save me," trembling in panic and crying like a frightened boy, he prayed. "Sheelvati, I don't want to die. Save me!" He continued repeating his words till he fell unconscious.

'Silently, Sheelvati lifted her husband's body and returned. "When the sun rises tomorrow morning, he will die." The curse of Mandavya was irreversible. Sheelvati looked at the lines on her palm and decided that she would not let that happen.

'Holding a pot of water in her right hand, and pouring water into her left palm, she spoke: "If I have worshipped my husband as my only god and loved him more than anything else, then may the sun never rise again!"

'Her words reverberated all over the cosmos and instantly halted the movement of the sun and all other celestial bodies, plunging the universe into an absolute stillness. Time came to a standstill; The movement of every celestial body ceased. The celestial wanderer Narada told Indra the reason for this catastrophe. An enraged Indra raised his thunderbolt to kill Sheelvati.

"'Don't try that," Narada warned him. "Killing a chaste Sheelvati would not end her curse. On the contrary, it would complicate the problem."

"'Should I go and request her?"

"'That won't help either. She will never let her husband die. Here, we are in a quandary. We can neither overturn Mandavya's curse, nor can we reverse a chaste woman's curse. Only Brahma, Vishnu and Mahesh jointly can resolve this predicament."

'A worried Indra and his companions went to the trinity.

"'There is no way out unless Sheelvati revokes her curse," Mahesh said.

"'Why would she revoke her curse?" Brahma argued.

"'Sheelvati's philosophy and conduct is embedded in *rta*. Only an equally chaste woman can convince her to revoke the curse. I suggest that you request virtuous Anusuya to help. She may be able to convince Sheelvati to revoke her curse. Indra, you don't have much time. Go to Anusuya at once, and ensure that the sun becomes mobile for the well-being of all," Vishnu advised Indra.

'Indra and the other gods rushed to the ashram of Atri and Anusuya. Sage Atri was one of the *manasputra*s of Brahma. His wife Anusuya was a revered scholar. She was a peerless, chaste and virtuous wife. Her father was Kardama, another of Brahma's *manasputra*s, and her mother was Devahuti. At the time of this incident, despite many years of marriage, the couple was childless.

"'Mother, you alone can save the universe. Please help us!" they pleaded.

'Anusuya meditated for some time, weighing her options and contemplating the consequences.

"'I will convince Sheelvati but..."

"'But?"

"'...I have one condition: Let the trinity in person request me to intervene in this matter."

'Indra had no option but to agree to her demand. He invoked the trinity to appear in person.

"'Anusuya, speak your wish," Vishnu said.

'Anusuya bowed before them and said with utmost reverence: "It is my duty to follow your command. In return, I beg you to grant me three boons."

"'Anusuya, what kind of bargain is this?" Indra became agitated.

"'Indra, this is a woman's prayer. Please let me ask," Anusuya politely told Indra. "Please grant me three boons," she prayed to the trinity.

"'Anusuya, we will bestow you the three boons you have in mind, but first go to Sheelvati. This chaos must not be prolonged. We will wait here for you," Vishnu advised Anusuya.

'Anusuya swiftly went to Sheelvati's hut, where she found her sitting near her husband's body. "Daughter, take heart. Nothing will happen to your husband. I understand your sorrow and feel your pain," Anusuya took a shattered Sheelvati into her arms.

"'Mother!" Sheelvati cried. Someone had finally come to share her grief. She cried for a long time while Anusuya consoled her.

"'My child, your curse has put the world in danger. Please understand its consequences and withdraw it," Anusuya persuaded Sheelvati. "Please allow the sun to rise."

"'Mother, my husband will die. How can I allow that to happen?"

"'Child, trust me like your mother. Have faith. Give me the threads of your life: I would never let any harm befall my daughter," Anusuya tried to assure her. "Faith is stronger than everything else. Believe me. Nothing will happen to your husband. Now, allow the sun to rise."

'Sheelvati looked at Anusuya. The turmoil inside her heart

was unbearable. Shaking with apprehension, she got up, eyes still focused on Anusuya.

'"Trust me. Nothing adverse will happen to your husband," Anusuya reassured her.

'Sheelvati took some water from a pot. She cupped her palm and poured some water into it. She looked at her dying husband. Imprinting his image on her heart, she closed her eyes and said: "If I am a chaste and virtuous wife, let the sun rise now."

'In an instant, the eastern sky came alight in a flare of orange and red. The celestial bodies resumed their movements and dawn descended slowly, revitalizing the universe. Tumultuous cheers from outside shook Sheelvati's home. She looked at her husband in horror: He had died. Her mourning cries pierced the heart of the sky, but Anusuya did not stay there. She rushed to the place where the trinity was waiting for her.

'The happy and joyous Adityas greeted her. The trinity looked at her affectionately and blessed her, "Ask your three boons, Anususya."

'"Nothing is impossible for you, yet you gave me this honour. You always magnify the small virtues of your devotees: You are the cause and source of everything in this cosmos."

'Looking at the lotus feet of the Lord, Anusuya asked, "My first wish is to have Ugrashrava come back to life again. My second wish is to make him healthy, young and devoted to his wife."

'"So be it," said the trinity in unison.

'"And the third boon, my child?" Mahesh asked.

'Anusuya smiled and looked at Atri. He was looking at her with pride. She knew her wish had his assent. She went closer to the trinity. Her heart's desire made her emotional and choked her voice. Her heart seemed to grow with boundless maternal love and her breasts seemed to fill with milk, ready to feed the world. The universe appeared so tiny before her. The trinity appeared like infants.

"'I wish to have the three of you take birth as my sons,'" she fell at the feet of the trinity.

'No one except a mother could dare to ask for this. No poet with the greatest of imagination could ever muster the courage to make the creator sit on a mother's lap. Feeding the Progenitor as her child, playing with him in her courtyard, having him come back to her, crying and complaining about little things: That is bliss,' Krishna became emotional. 'What a joy that emotionless God must have felt while playing like a child on a mother's lap!'

'Granting her the three boons, Vishnu said, "So be it, mother. In some time, Brahma will be born in your womb as Chandra, the moon. I will be born as Dattatreya, your second son, the son of Atri. Shiva will be born as your third son and the world will know him as Durvasa."'

∽

'Atri and Anusuya were overjoyed. Chandra grew up as an extraordinarily handsome man. He was so good looking and well-mannered that Anusuya often worried for him. An ever curious, intelligent and disciplined Chandra was a much-sought-after pupil among the learned sages of the age. Parents of marriageable girls had started making a beeline for the doorsteps of Anusuya.

'Chandra's parents were renowned sages, and they provided him with the best education. He was a brilliant student, and very soon Atri and Anusuya realized that they had taught Chandra everything they knew.

'"Chandra, we have taught you everything we know. Now, I want you to study under other gurus. Spend the remaining four years of your brahmacharya ashrama in learning and teaching," Atri advised.

'"I was also thinking along the same lines. Should I join Agastya or Vashishtha?" Chandra had some gurus in mind.

'"They are two of the best gurus on earth, but I would

recommend you to learn from Brahaspati, the preceptor of the gods," Anusuya suggested.

"'She is right,' a delighted Atri seconded his wife's recommendation. "Chandra, you may find Agastya and Vashishtha more or less like us. But Brahaspati may teach you an entirely new perspective of life."

"'It will be an exciting learning experience indeed," Chandra happily consented and, turning to Anusuya, he smiled, "Mother is always right."

"'Leave your habit of buttressing the ladies behind," his mother admonished him affectionately.'

༄

'Brahaspati welcomed Chandra like his younger brother. Chandra was much senior to his other pupils and after a brief discussion, Brahaspati was convinced that Chandra would prove to be a great asset to his school.

"'Chandra, I accept you as my student, but on one condition."

"'Anything for learning, gurudeva! If it's not against the *rta*, I give my word."

'Chandra's reply pleased Brahaspati. "I would like you to teach a few classes as well. You know, I am pulled every which way between my duties as preceptor and the head of this school. If you can share some of my responsibilities here, it would be very good for the pupils and also for the school."

'Chandra bowed his head in acceptance. That evening, during the communal feast, Brahaspati introduced Chandra to his beautiful wife Taara. She could not take her eyes off the handsome Chandra. The attraction was instant and strong, like high tide on a full moon night.

"'His moon-like face pulls me like the sea waves. His masculinity, his broad chest, chiseled figure... indeed he is an incarnation of Madana," Chandra had already made a place for himself in Taara's thoughts. Wave after wave of erotic fantasy washed across Taara's mind. Unmindful of and oblivious to her thoughts, Chandra continued savouring the food.

'"Why are you not eating anything?" Brahaspati touched Taara's shoulder lightly.

'Chandra looked at Taara, who hurriedly picked up a morsel. In the process, the drape on her shoulder slipped down, exposing the milky valley between her full and firm breasts. Chandra's gaze rested there for a while and then he swiftly looked away. Taara was observing him. There was something in those eyes that made Chandra's heart pound faster and harder. He lowered his gaze but it did not help. The milky valley lay exposed before him. He looked up again and found those searching eyes tugging at his heart.

'Unaware of these nascent tides of attraction, Brahaspati was engaged in talking to other teachers and pupils. After some time, he stood up to make a statement. "My dear fellow residents, we have decided that Chandra, our new colleague, will be in charge of the ashram during my absence, and he will also take a few of my classes." Everybody applauded this announcement: Brahaspati could not register that the most enthusiastic appreciation came from neither a student nor a teacher, but from his own wife. But Chandra noticed that: There was no end to his perplexity.

'"She is an extraordinarily beautiful lady," he thought, lying in bed that night, as sleep stayed far away from his eyes. "Those eyes, my God! What was not there? A search, a call, an enticement, an admiration, a thirst, a curiosity, an invitation and a familiarity: What was not there in those beautiful eyes? Those were like a whirlpool, pulling me down."

'He felt ashamed of his own thoughts. Anusuya's face replaced Taara's. "It is just natural affection from the guru's wife. She was courteous and took some extra care of me. Isn't it normal for the first lady to give more attention to a newcomer?" Reluctantly, his heart agreed to this argument. When sleep finally overpowered him, by then a tiny part of his heart had been smitten by the love bug.

'A good night's sleep served Chandra well and he almost forgot Taara's provocations. But when everyone sat down for lunch, Chandra's eyes looked for Taara. She was not around: Her absence perturbed him. Brahaspati, as usual, was talking about his leader's generosity and describing how busy he was. Chandra found that boring. When they were about to finish the meal, Brahaspati announced that for the next few days, he would remain in Amaravati to discharge his priestly duties.

'"Chandra will look after the ashram. Since he is new, Acharya Vararuchi will guide him in administrative and disciplinary matters. I will ask Taara to brief him on matters of housekeeping."

'That evening, Taara called Chandra to the hermitage. He felt a hitherto unknown nervousness. His heart was already bouncing and his excited mind was unsure of these new expectations. "Why am I not behaving normally?" he wondered. She was his guru's wife, but his heart was not ready to address her as *guru-mata*, like everyone else in the ashram so intuitively did.

'From a distance, he saw Taara was waiting for him near the main gate. He could see the contours of her finely-shaped body. Her *uttariya* was bright yellow in colour, and she had knotted it tightly around her breasts. A beautiful corsage was pinned to her blouse. She was a *Rati* incarnate, in the orange-saffron rays of the setting sun. She had adorned her hair with flowers, and this enhanced the magnetism of her chiseled and glowing face. Her shapely legs were covered in a tight *sari*. When he reached closer, he could spot a tiny band around her narrow waist.

'Taara's gaze made him uneasy and he lowered his eyes. He greeted her and stood at a respectable distance. Taara smiled and her big eyes scanned him thoroughly. "Come, Chandra. Come inside: I will show you the granary."

'She led him into the hut and stopped at the granary door, almost blocking Chandra's way. Smiling at him, she signaled him to move in. Chandra hesitated and then gestured at her to give way. She grinned and moved slightly away. Chandra could feel her perfume and warmth: The heady mix was intoxicating.

'The granary was huge and divided up to store different kinds of grains. While explaining the varieties, quantum, menu and issue and audit procedures to him, she stood very close, almost forcing him to breathe her exhale. And he realized that he liked it.

'When he was about to leave, she passed him Brahaspati's baton. While giving it to him, she carelessly touched his hands and giggled. Her touch was electrifying and shook Chandra. "From tomorrow, you are taking his place," she whispered, and her eyes expressed much more than her words. An enchanted Chandra returned to his hut.

'The night was warm and humid. Chandra was unable to sleep. The touch of her fingers, her provocative smile and dancing eyes had stirred each and every cell of his body. He almost gasped for breath, remembering her aroma. He opened all the windows and doors but her intoxicating scent did not go away. The air inside the hut felt unbearably warm. He came out on the porch to cool down. Far from his hut, slightly towards the north, the big door of Brahaspati's house was open, and someone was standing by the window. He kept gazing at her. The silhouette by the window remained unmoved. Then, suddenly the wind blew and the clouds dispersed: The silvery rays of the moon brightened the night, and Chandra recognized Taara.

'That night, they stayed awake, witnessing the hide-and-seek of the clouds and the moon. The night changed its hue constantly: from dark to silver and then gray again. Both Taara and Chandra pretended to be laborious skygazers and spent a night that left their hearts longing for more.

'The next day at lunch, Taara told Vararuchi: "Acharya, Malavika is not well today. I will take Chandra to the riverbank and show him how we fetch water for the ashram."

'Vararuchi agreed. He too liked the young son of Atri. He was so courteous, handsome, intelligent and humble. He found Chandra's keen interest in ashram management laudable.

'Chandra happily accompanied Taara to the river. "Dry days in the *chaturmas* are so prickly," Taara looked Chandra in eyes. "Let's go for a swim," she suggested.

'Without waiting for his reply, she jumped into the river by the deserted bank. A mesmerized Chandra looked at her gracious frame, appearing and disappearing in the water like a mermaid. His throat became dry and his breath became heavy. Taara called him again to join her. His ethics made his legs heavy, but an uncontrollable urge to go closer made his heart fly.

'"Come, Chandra, come. It is so cool here," she called. He smiled at her, but did not move. She waited for a while and then called him again, but he hesitated. She swam back to the bank and stepped out of the water.

'"God! She looks breathtaking!" Her wet clothes exposed her delicate curves. She did not try to cover herself, instead she came closer to him.

'"Water or me, what scares you?" she teased him and ran away to the river again. To her utter disappointment, a shy Chandra remained unmoved. On their way back, Taara walked slightly behind Chandra. He walked with a faster pace, nervous and anxious.

'Later, the evening became unbearable for Chandra: Time seemed to stand still. He prayed for an early night, to avoid the gaze of his guru's wife. Taara went past him many times, but did not bother to look at him. During dinner, she behaved like Chandra did not exist and talked to Vararuchi. Her behaviour confused Chandra. "Am I getting it wrong?"

'The night was once again warm and humid. Chandra gazed at Brahaspati's house: There was no movement. He went inside his hut and tried to sleep but failed to do so.

'"I will check once, only once," he told himself and went out.

'The air was still and the night was passing quietly. The doors and windows of Brahaspti's house were shut. "I was wrong. She never meant that. I was mistaken." Cursing himself for his stupidity, he returned to his hut, leaving the door wide open. He tried to sleep again, but her image, on the riverfront, her wet curvy body, her smile, her eyes kept playing in the dark. There was no respite for Chandra.

'"Just one more time, I will go and check," he promised to himself. "I will stay outside only for a moment. Then I will sleep."

'He stepped out again. The whole of creation was sleeping in the silent darkness. He walked a few paces towards Brahaspati's house. He wanted to convince himself that, like him, she too was awake and restless. But there was absolutely no movement. After an hour or so, he returned to his hut, looking back many times, slowing his pace. At the door, he stood still, trying to feel the weight of her gaze on his bare back. The moon had come out and the courtyard was bathed in silver moonlight. There was no sign of Taara.

'"Why am I mad about her? Who is she? If someone sees me doing this, what would they think? If she does not care for me, why should I?" He decided to abandon his tender search. Lying down on a coarse mattress, he cussed her for enticing him. For long, he tried to rationalize her perceived advances. He was sure that she desired him: he could not detach himself from her magic. Like a bird trapped in a net, the more he struggled to free himself, the more he became entangled.

'Well past midnight, when his attempts to sleep failed, he decided to check one last time. "It will confirm that she is not interested."

'The moment he stepped outside his hut, someone moved behind the nearby bushes. An alert Chandra quickly slipped into the bushes, but there was no one. The moon was struggling against the clouds and Chandra against his desires. Carefully, he moved towards the entrance of the preceptor's hermitage. When he raised his head to look at the main door, his heart leapt into his mouth.

'Taara was standing there, her right hand tenderly resting on her slender waist, looking at him. For a few moments no one moved. Then, Taara walked slowly towards her naïve lover. She slowly touched his fingers and then holding them in her right hand she drew Chandra after her. There was a big orchard behind the hut. They entered the orchard and silently stood near a thick mango tree.

'"What were you doing at my gate?" she whispered in his ear. Chandra felt the warmth of her breath on his neck. She was so close to him that he could not reply. Her warmth and fragrance stirred him. Taara leisurely pushed him towards the thick trunk and placed her soft palms on the tree trunk, encircling Chandra.

'"Now, you are my captive, Chandra." Chandra could feel her heaving breasts touching his bare chest. She asked again, "What were you looking for, Chandra?"

'Chandra could no longer remain a pretender: Holding her lean waist in his arms, he rubbed his rough cheeks against her soft ones. Grabbing her forcefully, he planted his lips on hers and began kissing her like a passionate, thirsty and frantic lover. Taara reciprocated even more fervently and the two bodies melted into each other.

'Chandra had never known such pleasure, such happiness and such ever-mounting desire. The more he loved her, the more he longed for her. For Taara, Chandra was the man of her dreams: A harried preceptor was nowhere close to a vigorous, witty, charming and sturdy Chandra.

'In Brahaspati's absence, the two lovers merged their souls during the lonely nights. Taara and Chandra took extra care to keep their romance secret. They performed their ashram duties diligently and to the satisfaction of all. There was no reason for any doubt.

'When Brahasapti returned to the ashram, the two lovers felt irritated. However, they knew that their reunion was only a few weeks away. When the meetings dried up, the two lovers became desparate to unite. Despite their frequent disorientation from their assigned duties, an unsuspecting Brahaspati and others in the ashram remained clueless about the intense chemistry between them.

'A few weeks later, Brahaspati again went to Amaravati. Like the previous times, he again briefed Chandra to take care of the ashram and kissed Taara goodbye.

'That night, the two lovers met passionately and vowed never to be separated again. Once the highly impassioned tide of lovemaking subsided, resting in the arms of Chandra, Taara asked: "How long will we meet like this? I don't fear if someone knows about our love, Chandra, but what is the future of our relationship?"

'Chandra wrapped her in his arms and kissed her. Frankly, this question had never occurred to him.

'"Chandra, I want to live with you; Not for a week or two, but forever. There is nothing I love more than you. Look into my eyes, caress my soul, you will find nothing there except my love for you." Passionately, she kissed Chandra on his temple, nose, cheeks and lips, and all over his face.

'Chandra, in turn, gently placed her on the mattress. Kissing her wet eyes, he tried to convince her. "Taara, trust me, my dearest. I will find a solution."

'"Chandra, how long can we hide this? The moment Brahaspati knows about it, all hell will break loose." She scrutinized his face and then said, "There is only one way out. Brahaspati is not around for a week. Let's elope and begin our new life together,"

'Chandra hugged her tightly and agreed. "We will be together, forever." He kissed her and said, "Taara, Vishvakarma has built a palace for me. We will start our new life there." Taara liked the idea.

'The next day, they prepared to escape. Taara told Vararuchi that he might go to Amaravati to be with Brahaspati. The elopement remained a well-kept secret for a week, till Brahaspati returned from Indra's palace.

'His wife's infidelity stunned the preceptor of the gods. For a day, he closed himself in a dark room, deliberating over the incident that had snatched away his peace, prestige and faith. He decided to launch a search discreetly. He was determined not to publicize it. Therefore, Indra and the others were not informed. Somewhere in his heart, Brahaspati was still hopeful that Taara would realize her mistake and decide to return. After a few weeks, the search party informed a distraught Brahaspati that Taara was happily living with Chandra in her paramour's abode.

'Brahaspati decided to talk to Taara. He reached Chandra's palace and requested her to return. Taara remained silent but a cold Chandra responded: "Brahaspati, Taara and I love each other. She wishes to stay with me. We are happy together. Kindly return to your place."

'"Swine! How dare you talk to me like this? You are a sinner. She is my wife, your guru's wife. She is like your mother,' an angry Brahaspati retorted.

'Chandra chose not to reply. His silence emboldened Brahaspati. "A vile creature, you are a shame in the name of Atri and Anusuya!" a furious Brahspati shouted.

'He then looked at his wife. "Taara, you are my wife. I love you so much." He counselled her, "It is a sin to live with any other man than your husband. This is against dharma. Come back, please." Chandra and Taara did not utter a word, instead Taara walked away and disappeared inside the palace.

'Chandra looked mockingly at Brahaspati. Brahaspati's face had darkened with humiliation. For a moment, the disgrace stunned him, then he decided what was good for all of them.

'"Chandra, call her. I want to speak to her."

'"I respect you Brahaspati, heed my advice. Don't call her, it will cause you further embarrassment."

'"You thief! You will teach me what is good and what is bad? Call her!" Brahaspati shouted.

'Before Chandra could react, Taara came out and stood

between the two men. Holding her head high, she brazenly looked at Brahaspati.

'"Taara, let us go home," Brahaspati pleaded.

'She did not reply, but firmly held Chandra's hand. The guru of the gods went numb. Clearly, his pleas had no impact on Taara. He gently held Taara's hand. "Taara, let us go home," with tears in his eyes, Brahaspati requested her again.

'Taara did not move and Chandra became infuriated. He pulled Taara towards him. Taara left a disgraced Brahaspati's hand and stood behind Chandra. No one said anything for a while, then Brahaspati left, holding his head in shame.

'This humiliation broke Brahaspati. He stopped meeting people and confined himself to his hermitage. A worried Vararuchi went to Indra and told him everything. Indra came to console and help Brahaspati.

'"Gurudev, an unchaste woman like Taara must be deserted. Shun her and forget her. You deserve a better partner. If you agree, I will find a better match for you," Indra, the king of gods assured his preceptor.

'"Indra, Taara is my wife," patience was Brahaspati's virtue. "I married her with the promise to never abandon her. That wretched Chandra has misguided her. It's a matter of time. Eventually she will return to me."

'"For how long will you wait, gurudeva?" an impatient Indra asked.

'"I don't know, but I will wait."

'"Gurudeva, we can't allow you to live in disgrace and in depression. Apart from a husband, you are also the preceptor of the gods. I will free Taara from the clutches of that offender. I will deal with that despicable creature myself."

'Indra quickly assembled his army. He was determined to punish Chandra for this grave sin. However, the tumultuous march of the Adityas' army alerted the Daityas. The preceptor of the Daityas, Shukracharya approached his king Vrashparva.

'"Vrashparva, Brahaspati's wife Taara has eloped with his

student Chandra. Brahaspati is devastated and secluded. The Adityas are ashamed and low on self-esteem. We must take advantage of this situation. Such an opportunity does not come often. This is a perfect time to defeat the Adityas."

'Vrashparva immediately agreed. Taara eloping with Chandra was a great humiliation for the Adityas. A cunning Vrashparva decided to embarrass the Adityas more by offering his support to Chandra and Taara.

'"Acharya, you go to Chandra and offer our active support to him. This will be a double blow to the Adityas," Vrashparva requested his guru.

'Endorsing the decision of his king, Shukracharya went to Chandra and offered their assistance. It comforted a worried Chandra. Lonely and helpless, Chandra immediately accepted the Daitya's help. In no time, a Daitya battalion took charge of Chandra's security and Vrashparva assembled his ferocious army to counter Indra.

'This imminent war between the two superpowers alerted Brahma. In an instant, the creator appeared before Chandra, who paid his respect by placing his head on Brahma's feet. Taara also rushed to pay her respect. "Taara, tell me if it is right for a married woman to live with someone else?" Brahma asked without wasting a minute.

'Taara remained silent.

'"Atri's son, tell me if it is right?" Brahma asked Chandra.

'Chandra also remained silent.

'"Is it acceptable, what both of you have done?" Brahma asked again.

'Taara remained silent.

'"We love each other, grandfather. We are very happy together. Taara was not happy with Brahaspati. So, is it wrong if we decided to live together?" Chandra pleaded.

'"Chandra, Taara and Brahaspati married after knowing each other well. That marriage was destined to give happiness to everyone. They married without any pressure from anyone. A marriage is based on mutual faith, trust and cooperation, and patience makes it stable. A lot of effort is required to run an institution. If people keep deserting married life at the tiniest of excuses, it will bring down our entire social structure."

'"Taara and Chandra, you have abandoned the path of dharma and succumbed to bodily lust. Your stupidity has almost started a war between the Adityas and the Daityas. Think about it," Brahma cautioned Taara and Chandra.

'The couple remained silent.

'"I command Taara to go back to her husband and take care of his house." Then Brahma looked at Chandra and said, "You will not be without a companion. In time, you will also find a suitable spouse."

'"Grandfather, Taara was not happy with Brahaspati. She is happy with me. We love each other. Why must she go back to an unhappy place? I will not leave her," Chandra was unhappy with Brahma's command.

'"Chandra, you can't put the world in danger for your lust."

'"Grandfather, I refuse to obey your command," Chandra was not ready to budge.

'"Chandra!" an irritated Brahma shouted. "You disobeyed my command." Brahma raised his hand and Chandra's handsome face became blemished. "Chandra, this dark spot will remain with you forever, reminding you and the world that immoral acts always end in bad consequences." A horrified Taara cried out. Chandra's face had been sullied permanently.

'"Children, love should not be a burden on anybody's soul. And, more importantly, it must not bring calamity on others." Brahma then brought Taara to Brahaspati's ashram.

'"Son, do you remember that I had told you that this match would make you mature? Our greatness lies in forgiving. You have shown that throughout this trial. I bless you, that you will always be remembered as the wisest among all." Putting Taara's hand in his, the creator blessed Brahaspati.

'He then turned to Taara. "Taara, I had also blessed you with two-fold happiness from this marriage. You got that. Now, it's time to seek forgiveness from Brahaspati. Be faithful to him."

'Brahaspati and Taara bowed before the Creator.

'When everyone left, Taara touched Brahaspati's feet cautiously. She was carrying the weight of her pregnancy. "Forgive me, Brahaspati," she said with eyes full of tears.

'"Think of it as a bad dream and forget it," Brahaspati hugged her.

'"I am a polluted woman: An unchaste woman, not worthy of your love," Taara said.

'"No," Brahaspati held Taara affectionately. "Taara, a woman is never polluted. Dharma says that a woman is cleansed of the sin of adultery by her monthly curse. Her menstruation flushes out impurities from her body and makes her pure again. If you love me, that is enough for me."

'Taara could sense the feelings of her big-hearted and virtuous husband. Now, he looked so adorable to her. She embraced him tightly, never to leave him again.

'"Life should never be a prisoner of the past. It moves on," Brahaspati promised, holding Taara's hand.'

∽

'Taara gave birth to a baby boy. Brahaspati's ashram resonated with joy. Brahaspati was very happy and quickly invited his parents to bless the newborn. Indra and his fellow Adityas also came with divine gifts for their preceptor's newborn son.

'A huge gathering was to witness the naming ceremony of the infant. Angiras and Shraddha had invited a galaxy of sages, including all the *manasputra*s of the Creator.

'"We have assembled here for the naming ceremony of this blessed child. It is his fifth *samskara*. These are the necessary sacraments of life. Now, call the proud mother," Angiras began the ceremony.

'Holding the infant, wrapped in a golden cloth in her arms, Taara arrived. Wearing a golden sari, she looked extremely graceful, glowing with the aura of motherhood. Behind her came a delighted Brahaspati.

'"Let both the parents sit before the sacred fire. We will now begin the naming ceremony," Angiras invited the couple to sit near the *yagna*.

'Seven great sages began the *yagna*. The Creator and Angiras made the horoscope of the infant. "Brahaspati, *Ba* is the initial syllable for the infant's name. Now, you can give him a name beginning with the letter *Ba*," the Creator pronounced. Brahaspati closed his eyes to think of a good name for the infant. But before he could pronounce anything, a sharp voice protested.

'"Brahaspati has no right to name my child. I am the father of this boy. I will name him," an angry Chandra appeared near the altar. The seven great sages paused the *yagna*.

'Taara looked at Chandra and then at the infant who was joyfully enjoying the warmth of her lap. The newborn was destiny's child, beautiful beyond description and the bliss of his mother's heart. He was smiling at her with glowing eyes and happy lips.

'"Scoundrel! How dare you step into this sacred place? You thief! I forgave you once; If you fear for your life, turn around and run away." Trembling with anger, Brahaspati looked for his water-pot. He held it in his right hand and was about to curse him, when Chandra replied.

'"Brahaspati, your threats cannot scare me. Accept the truth. How can you assert my lineage as yours?" Chandra was not ready to leave his claim.

'Chandra's firmness had shaken Brahaspati, but he did not show it. Indra came forward to help his preceptor.

'"Traitor, stand here and face my mace. You have sullied the sacred *guru-shishya* relationship. You cheated your own guru and stole his wife. Now you want to claim his son as well!" Indra thundered.

'"When truth is at stake, I fear none. Indra, the *rta* controls everyone, including the Creator. And the truth is that this is my baby," Chandra stared at Indra.

"'Are you listening? He is my son. Give him to me. Don't refuse me my right!" Chandra demanded.

"'A cheat and a turncoat calling himself a guardian of dharma!" Indra laughed aloud. "Come on friends, let's throw this criminal out of this sacred venue," he commanded his comrades. The moment Indra jumped at Chandra, Durvasa, a firebrand sage and Chandra's brother, came in between the two.

"'Indra, you fool! Without examining the truth, how dare you punish Chandra?" Indra stopped. He was well aware of the sage's powers. Angiras and Atri came forward.

"'Both Brahaspati and Chandra claim the newborn as their biological son. Without examining the truth, we cannot decide who is the real father of the child. So far the child has passed four *samskaras* of life: His *jatakarma*, the birth rituals, his *seemantonnayana*, satisfying the cravings of the pregnant mother, and his *punsavana*, the fetus protection, these three *samskaras* have been performed by Brahaspati. But no one knows who did the *garbhadhana,* the conception of the fetus,"Angiras said.

"'Only the creator and the mother know who the biological father of a child is. I believe that the question of parenthood should best be decided by the mother," Atri said.

'Angiras nodded in agreement.

"'I will go a step further, sage," Angiras continued. "Only the mother should have the right to name her child."

"'Well said," Atri seconded. The entire assembly was listening to the learned duo. Atri and Angiras, father of Chandra and Brahaspati, were trying to resolve the dispute between their sons.

"'Only Taara knows who fathered her child," Angiras looked at Taara and requested her, "Daughter, would you like to come with us?"

'Taara got up with the infant in her arms. She walked slowly towards the two sages and took her place near the two.

"'Revered guests, this is my child's naming ceremony." She looked calm and composed. "My guardians have asked me to come to a secluded corner to reveal the name of my son's father. I refuse to obey them. Motherhood is unknown to males and they can neither experience nor understand this. Unfortunately, the decision-makers here are all male. Therefore, as a proud mother, I refuse to go to a private place to disclose the name of my son's father. I will announce his name right here, in this crowded assembly. I have not committed any sin. Brahaspati ignored me and Chandra supported me when I needed support. I don't bear any ill will against either of them. I respect both of them. I respect Chandra for being my companion when I needed him. I respect him for showing the courage to fight against the world for me. I respect my husband, for showering his unconditional love, for accepting me despite knowing my wrongs. Yet, I feel ashamed standing here as a person under trial. "Why should a father alone have all the rights over a child? Why should these rights not belong equally to the mother?"

'She looked at the presiding sages and said, "People like Angiras and Atri are rare. They are wise. Therefore, they are ready to give a mother her due. Their presence gives me courage to stand before you. First, I will do what a father traditionally does. I will name my child. I name him Budha, the wise. Please accept Budha as one among you and bless him."

'The galaxy of the *manasputra*s, the Adityas and the sages applauded Budha's naming.

"'I will also call him Saumya, the son of Soma or Chandra," briefly she looked at Chandra, thanking him for this wonderful gift.

'Angiras blessed Taara and Budha.

"'Let us all pray for the boy. I bless him with intelligence. He will possess the wisdom of Brahaspati, the courage of Taara and the beauty of Chandra. I bless him; he will never be a cause of an inauspicious event. He is blessed to generate prosperity for all. I bless this baby that it will provide all living beings with the ability to choose the right way in life, and illuminate their path in all situations through life."

'Everyone present blessed the child.'

4

Love and Retaliation

'Krishna, perhaps that was a different age. Taara appears so strong and sure about herself,' Kunti commented.

'Why do you say so?'

'Those were great men and women. These great stories of legendary women happened because exceptional men supported them. Alas, my generation does not have many,' Kunti's voice was full of dejection.

'Aunt, you are so naïve,' Krishna laughed. 'We are the prisoners of our time. Time decides the prism through which we see the present and the past. The present always looks for its heroes in the past. Tomorrow people will praise the great persons of our age,' Krishna smiled. 'Don't we praise the people of Treta?'

'Were they not great people? They were blessed, those who lived when Lord Ram was the king!' Kunti said.

'Aunt, why do you think everything was great then? Was there not a Soorpanakha for a Sita, a Kaikeyee for a Kaushalya? If Kaikeyee went overboard to protect the interests of her son, Sumitra sent her son on exile to support Ram; if Meghanad's wife chose to die after her husband's death, Mandodari and Tara preferred to remarry. How can life be monochromatic, aunt?' Krishna laughed.

'Tell me more about the mothers in Treta,' Kunti said.

'Let us begin with Kaikeyee,' Krishna began the story of the mothers of the Ramayana.

'King Dasaratha of Ayodhya had three wives, Kaushalya, Sumitra and Kaikeyee. Kaushalya was the chief queen, but Dasaratha hardly frequented her palace. The king was no ascetic, as he patronized hundreds of concubines; and at a ripe age, he married the much younger princess of Kaikeya.

'Occasionally, the queens met one another and exchanged courtesies, but most people in the palace knew that it was a façade. Kaikeyee was extremely proud and arrogant, and the old king adored her the most. Her arrogance was reflected in every step of her walk, in each and every word she spoke, and in every twitch of her eyebrows.

'The second queen Sumitra was a princess of Kashi. She had never been a favourite of Dasaratha. After his marriage to Kaikeyee, the king ignored her completely. Despite his neglect, Sumitra had not lost her vivacious, radiant and enthusiastic character.

'Kaushalya's son was Ram and Kaikeyee's son was Bharat. Sumitra had two sons, Laxman and Shatrughna. Laxman was like his mother, a straightforward, tough and effervescent person. Since childhood, he had an intense affinity for Ram. His twin brother Shatrughna was charming, quiet and obedient, but he was lazy as well. He was very close to Bharat.

'How come an old Dasaratha married a much younger Kaikeyee?' Kunti asked.

'Kaikeyee's father Ashwapati was the king of Kaikeya. Dasaratha defeated him in a battle and married his beautiful daughter. After their marriage, Dasaratha returned the kingdom of Kaikeya to Ashwapati with full honour.

'The stunning beauty of Kaikeyee had enamoured Dasaratha. She was the crown princess of Kaikeya, well trained in civil and military administration. Charming, witty and high-spirited, Kaikeyee had floored an aging Dasaratha, who was desperate to cling to his fast-fading youth. After his marriage, Dasaratha stayed for one more month in Kaikeya and Kaikeyee's charisma engulfed his senses and coloured his vision and wisdom.

'After a month-long fiesta, Dasaratha left for Ayodhya with his new bride. Chests full of gems and jewels, livestock including cows and bulls, and maidens were part of his convoy. On the way, when the caravan was crossing the Hindu Kush, a fierce tribe living in the neighbouring hills ambushed the convoy. It happened despite Dasaratha having sent an advance party to clear the way. This sudden attack dispersed the royal guards.

'Dasaratha knew that the ambush was aimed at plundering the royal wealth. He decided to give the treasure to the invaders, but Kaikeyee opposed this surrender. She immediately sent a few speedy riders to call back the advance party. She reasoned that they could hold the tribesmen till their cavalry arrived. The skirmish became fierce and many of Ayodhya's men perished. The invaders were closing in. Dasaratha's charioteer was swiftly driving the chariot away from the battle, when suddenly, a javelin pierced his back and killed him. This terrified Dasaratha. Kaikeyee took the reins of the chariot and manoeuvred it out of the skirmish.

'This incident made Dasaratha forever indebted to his new bride. At night, resting in his royal tent and holding Kaikeyee in his arms, Dasaratha whispered, "Kaikeyee, Ayodhya is indebted to you forever. Tell me what you desire, I shall grant that."

'Kaikeyee's mesmerizing eyes smiled at the king but she said nothing.

'"Please tell me what I should do for you Kaikeyee. Ask for two wishes, not one," the king was desperate to repay his debt.

'"I shall ask you, when the time comes." Despite his flattering insistence, Kaikeyee kept mum.

'Once Kaikeyee arrived in Ayodhya, the environment changed quickly inside the palace. An enchanted king's inclination towards his new queen alienated his elder queens. Even in household matters, Kaikeyee's words and authority became paramount. The palace servants sniffed it out quickly and joined her camp. Dasaratha not only preferred Kaikeyee's suggestions in household matters, but in administration as well. Very soon, the two elder queens became marginalized.

'Within a few months of her arrival in Ayodhya, Kaikeyee successfully persuaded Dasaratha to invite her younger brother

Yudhajit to join the royal court of Ayodhya. The influence of the Kaikeya commanders in Ayodhya grew rapidly. Dasaratha also appointed many of them in powerful positions in his army. This culminated in the appointment of Yudhajit as the chief of the army.

'These interventions gradually reduced the power of the old king, while enhancing Kaikeyee's dominance in administration and defence. It also increased indiscipline in the army, as factionalism grew between the native and foreign commanders. Yudhajit could not control the rising corruption in the army and in the civil machinery. It caused a sharp fall in the state revenue. Soon, the payment of salaries to a swelling army from the state exchequer became difficult.

'For a long time, Yudhajit successfully kept the king aloof from the affairs of the state. But an alert Ram began to question the growing corruption in the army, their atrocities on peasants and their inability to counter the Rakshasas. Kaikeyee and Yudhajit did not like this. When anarchy became intolerable, sage Vishwamitra approached the king to control the unrest.

'"King, I am sure that you are aware of the brutal murders, loot, kidnapping, and other terrorist activities being carried out by your soldiers and the Rakshasas in many parts of your kingdom. Their acts are so ghastly and cruel that the villagers have deserted their ancestral lands. The Rakshasas have disrupted people's lives and have made it impossible for the villagers to live in peace. The Rakshasas are small in number, but your army's inaction has made them invincible. Those who could not run away from their ancestral land have started adopting the Rakshasa way of life and have become one of them."

'Dasaratha had very little idea about all of this. He appeared clueless.

'"King, send prince Ram with me to punish these criminals and restore peace. Ram's victory will reinstate people's faith in your rule."

'"Sage, I am aware of the situation. You should avoid poetic exaggerations to make the situation look worse. Our army has control over our land," Yudhajit intervened. "We have taken the atrocities committed by the foreign terrorists very seriously. We are sending our forces there. At the same time, we don't want to appear panicked by a handful of Rakshasas. The migration of the masses, that you spoke so gravely about, is mainly because of better work opportunities in Ayodhya."

'"Stop talking nonsense, Yudhajit!" Vishwamitra shouted. "Have you ever visited these areas? Do you know how many people have already been killed? If your counter measures are so effective, then why are those bloodthirsty Rakshasas becoming stronger day by day? Why is your army afraid of a handful of Rakshasas?"

'"Brahmarishi, please forgive me," Dasaratha intervened to pacify the angry Vishwamitra. "If what you say is true, I order Yudhajit to march immediately to punish the evil Rakshasas."

'"No, I don't need him. I only want prince Ram to come along," Vishwamitra refused the king's offer.

'Dasaratha then offered himself to lead the army, but Vishwamitra refused the proposal.

'"King, either Ram accompanies me or no one else does."

'The politician in Dasaratha raised its head. A victorious Ram would silence an arrogant Yudhajit and if he failed, Kaikeyee's demand to elevate Bharat could be met.

'The head priest Vashishtha finally interrupted to remove the logjam. "King, the sage himself is capable of dealing with the Rakshasas. Ram will learn a lot from him. Don't hesitate. Allow Ram to go with him."

'Yudhajit became upset and angry about this open humiliation. He was aware of the delicate situation in the border areas, but he could not understand why Vishwamitra was asking for Ram. Kaikeyee too wondered why the sage demanded for Ram so forcefully.

'"He is certainly trying to develop a new power centre in

Ayodhya. Why? Perhaps to challenge us," she discussed with her brother and son.

'"Perhaps he knows that Ram is not happy with our army. Maybe he wants to show Ram what's happening in the border areas. His school was in that area. Through Ram, he can impress upon the king for some financial help. Maybe he wants to re-establish his school," Yudhajit offered his opinion.

'"Should I go along with Ram?" Bharat asked.

'"There is no need for that. If the purpose is to show Ram what's going on in the fringe areas, your going won't serve any purpose. Secondly, the sage will not take you along," Kaikeyee refused Bharat's suggestion.

'But what followed was beyond the wildest imagination of Kaikeyee and her brother. Ram not only killed the ferocious Rakshasas led by a fierce Tadaka, but also established himself as the messiah of the downtrodden. The liberation of Ahilya gave Ram the status of a living god overnight. All of that happened in the rural areas, away from the glare of the royal courts. But, Ram's next miracle happened right there, in the court of Janaka, the king of Mithila.

'There, he broke the prestigious bow of Lord Shiva and humbled the rebel sage Parashurama in a crowded royal assembly. Ram won Sita's hand in the *swayamvara* organized by her father, Janaka. Sage Parashurama bowed before Ram and prayed to him as an incarnation of Lord Vishnu. Ably guided by astute Vishwamitra, these events elevated Ram's stature to mythical proportions.

'His marital relationship with a strong and influential kingdom like Mithila gave Ram immense political clout. To counter it, a worried Kaikeyee quickly planned her son Bharat's marriage to Sita's sister. However, Janaka had already decided to marry his younger daughter Urmila to Laxman. Therefore, Bharat got married to a niece of Janaka, Mandavi. The youngest prince Shatrughna married Shrutakirti, a sister of Mandavi.

'Ram had always been a darling of the people of Ayodhya.

After his return from Mithila, the demand to make him the crown prince grew exponentially.

'This presented a complex situation before Dasaratha. The people were with Ram, the army was under Yudhajit and Kaikeyee wanted Bharat to be the next king. Dasaratha decided to go with the people's choice. But, it was not easy. With the army strongly backing Yudhajit and Kaikeyee, Dasaratha found himself helpless. Whatever little control he had over Ayodhya was because of people's faith in the Ikshwaku dynasty.

'By a stroke of luck, at about the same time, Ashwapati fell ill and Yudhajit decided to return to Kaikeya. Bharat and Shatrughna accompanied him. Dasaratha decided to take advantage of their absence, which gave him the courage to act swiftly.

'"I can not betray my ancestors," he decided. "I have to be free of this Yudhajit-Kaikeyee nexus."'

∽

'Dasaratha's misery had started when Ram went to Siddhashrama with Vishwamitra. That day, after Vishwamitra had left with Ram and Laxman, Dasaratha had gone to Kaikeyee's palace for a night's stay. There, she had asked him the most obvious question that had baffled him as well.

'"King, why had Vishwamitra wanted Ram alone? Why did he refuse to take the army?"

Listening intently to the stories of Treta mothers, Kunti realized that informed people make correct choices. Arjuna had also chosen the unarmed Krishna over his huge army of eighteen million soldiers! She looked at Krishna. 'Who is he?' she had always wondered. 'Is there a connection between him and Ram?'

She listened in rapt attention as Krishna continued his story, going back to the events after Ram's departure for Siddhashrama.

'"I am not sure," Dasaratha replied honestly. "Maybe Vishwamitra thinks that Ram is enough for a tiny Rakshasa band."

'"Is it so simple?" Kaikeyee paused, looking sternly at the old king. "No. It's not that simple. If your love for Ram has suddenly blossomed… " she tried to make her voice less vicious. "If you are trying to hatch some wicked plan with Vishwamitra against my son, then my dear king, you should be very, very careful." Kaikeyee's voice was cold and the king shivered.

'"Are you joking, Kaikeyee? Do you see any chance of him winning against those dreadful Rakshasas?" He smiled unassumingly. "Is not it good? If he fails, even the puritans will not question Bharat's ascension to the throne."

'"What if Ram returns victorious and Vishwamitra fights for his claim?" Kaikeyee looked very apprehensive.

'Dasaratha did not reply.

'"Dasaratha, if you are involved in this, then start counting your days," she snarled. "Declare Bharat your crown prince tomorrow. This will save you from all future hassles," she commanded the old king.

'Dasaratha remained silent. He was not sure if Ram would be able to defeat those Rakshasas alone. "Vishwamitra would not pick Ram without reason. What is the game plan of that wily king-turned-saint? Does Vishwamitra know something about Ram that we don't?" Dasaratha was not sure.

'He decided not to plant any suspicion in the mind of his highly ambitious and powerful queen.

'"Kaikeyee, my spies tell me that Vishwamitra does not have an army. I repeat: I don't see Ram decimating or even containing Tadaka and her men. I don't see any reason for you to worry. I am equally eager to announce Bharat as my successor, but think, after sending Ram to the battlefield, would such an announcement go down well with the people? Have patience dear, we may have good news soon."

'After that night, life had become increasingly difficult for old Dasaratha. Yudhajit and Kaikeyee had mounted pressure on him and no news had been available from Siddhashrama.

'The next morning, he woke up with fatigue, back pain and a throbbing headache. He picked up a mirror from the side table and looked at himself. His own image terrified him. Overnight, he had become old: A lifeless wrinkled face with white hair and white beard stared back at him! In disbelief, he closed his eyes and then slowly opened them again. His dull and gloomy eyes looked ghostly.

'"Ah! The last chapter of my life has started. A useless, passionless and helpless chapter! Cruel time is snatching away everything that gives pleasure to me!" His attention went to what Kaikeyee had said last night. "Without power, in this old age, who will care for me?"

'The king was not sure when power had slipped away from his hands. "My army does not listen to me; the priests and Brahmins listen only to Vashishtha. Trade is completely controlled by the Kaikeya traders loyal to Kaikeyee. I am left with nothing." These thoughts troubled the old king. Then he realized why Vishwamitra had only wanted Ram. "Only Ram can help me." For the first time, the king realized that if someone could support him in Ayodhya, it was Ram.

'He tried to imagine how Ram and Laxman were faring in those dreaded jungles against the horrendous Rakshasas. He could only say a little prayer, "Let him be safe. Let him come back victorious."

'"Once he comes back, he will help me. I will regain control over the palace and the kingdom," Dasaratha reassured himself.

'Despite his careful moves, Kaikeyee and Yudhajit were quick to anticipate and neutralize the few minor administrative and military tweaks designed by Dasaratha. Very soon, Dasaratha realized that his efforts were proving futile. Frustration, anger and helplessness pushed him to take shelter in the pleasure of women and wine. Despite endless desires, his body was now succumbing to age faster than he liked. The body's sluggish response to the mind's cravings made him yearn more and more for his lost youth.

'Then came the news that changed things from bad to worse. After slaying the Rakshasas and redeeming Ahilya, Ram had become a legend. His deeds became the subjects of folklore. For the first time in his reign, Dasaratha saw the common people of Ayodhya rejoicing over Ram's extraordinary achievements.

'One afternoon, when Dasaratha was contemplating his future moves, a maid came in. "Lord, commander Yudhajit and the queen are waiting at the door."

'"Send them in," Dasaratha dispatched the maid.

'Without much ado, Kaikeyee raised her concern, "King, I am sure that Vishwamitra is conspiring against my son. He is busy making Ram a hero, and here you are delaying the announcement to make Bharat the crown prince, on one pretext or another."

'An angry Yudhajit immediately snapped at his sister, "Kaikeyee, I cannot suffer a fool. This is the time to act. Ram is away and the king is incapacitated. Call Vashishtha and declare Bharat the king of Ayodhya."

'Dasaratha looked at the scheming pair. This wicked conversation fuelled his anger. For the first time since he had married Kaikeyee, he shouted at them. "Don't forget that I am the king. How can you talk like this?"

'Fortunately for Dasaratha, before anyone could react, head priest Vashishtha entered.

'"Congratulations, king! Janaka, the king of Mithila has sent his messengers. Ram has won the hand of princess Sita in a *swayamvara* after humbling hundreds of kings and the mighty Parashurama. King Janaka has invited you all to the wedding ceremony at Mithila."

'Dasaratha heaved a sigh of relief. Ram had saved him.

'Later, Dasaratha and the marriage party from Ayodhya joined Ram and Laxman in Mithila. They returned with four brides, one each for Ram, Bharat, Laxman and Shatrughna.'

'Since that time, Dasaratha had played his cards well and held them very close to his chest.

'"Now that Bharat and Yudhajit have left for Kaikeya, it is time to implement the plan," Dasaratha decided.

'Ayodhya saw a lot of hectic activity and reshuffling of officers in the administration, the day after Bharat's departure for Kaikeya. With exceptional haste, invitations were sent to important people in the kingdom, friendly neighbours, sages and tributary kings, requesting them to attend an emergency meeting. A few important names missing from the invitee list were Sita's father and uncle, and Kaikeyee's father and brother.

'The grand assembly was organized in a large hall. All tributary kings, sages, ministers, village headmen, important officers, prominent citizens, merchants and people of Ayodhya attended the assembly. In a regal voice and a tone befitting the grandeur of the occasion, the king addressed the assembly.

'"Revered sages, kings, chiefs and fellow people of Ayodhya, consciously following the path shown by my ancestors, I have always placed the interests of the people of Ayodhya above all. The provident care of wards is possible only through the valour, vision, will, wisdom and action of a king. I have served you all for long and now, with your permission, I wish to rest my tiring body.

'"I firmly believe that the best man should lead the state. Otherwise, it shall be injustice to the people and the land. A decision that affects millions of people cannot be left in the hands of any rigid arrangement or a commitment made in the past. The past must not dictate future decisions. Therefore, in the presence of all of you, I wish to propose the name of my elder son Ram to look after my people after my retirement. As you know, Ram's attributes and his valour supersede even those of Indra. He will prove to be a worthy king and to have a king like him will be an honour for all of us.

'"This is my proposal and I request all of you to think over it and give me your considered opinion."

'Unexpected as it might be, the proposal was acceptable to everyone present. Everyone was aware of Ram's deeds. There was not a single dissenting voice. A visibly happy Dasaratha accepted the unanimous decision of the assembly with folded hands and spoke in a humble and gracious voice.

'"I am grateful to you for supporting my proposal. With age catching up with me, I want to leave early. This pleasant and pious month of *Chaitra* is also called the *Madhumasa,* the sweetest month. Look around you, nature has blossomed in all possible hues and colours. Therefore, I wish to crown Ram tomorrow." He paused. "It also coincides with his birthday."

'In the evening, Dasaratha called prince Ram to his private chamber.

'After an affectionate hug, he advised his son: "Ram, I know virtues come naturally to you, yet being a loving father, let me say a few things. Son, always be humble and stay in command of all your senses; always judge matters only after getting all the details from indirect and direct sources. Always keep your ministers and commanders happy. A king who gathers a huge treasure and armoury, and considers his subjects, his ministers and his army to be his friends, is never defeated. Therefore, my son, always follow good conduct and constructive policies."

'Ram nodded in agreement.

'"Ram, everyone in Ayodhya wants you to be the crown prince. Tomorrow morning, the anointment ceremony will be completed." Dasaratha looked concerned and then cautioned Ram.

'"Ram, I am scared. Nowadays, I see terrible dreams and bad omens. I witness comets and lightning even during daytime. Astrologers say that I will be the victim of Sun, Mars and Rahu. You know that when these three planets turn against us, a king falls into the worst of times and may even die."

'Ram became concerned and looked at his father inquiringly.

'"Son, I will not find peace until you take charge. Circumstances, a man's luck and the human mind, all these can change at any time. My mind says that your coronation must be completed immediately. Tomorrow morning is the most auspicious time for your coronation, therefore, my son, be prepared. You are required to be vigilant. Ask your faithful bodyguards to protect you tonight, as often auspicious moments are marred by terrible interruptions."

'Ram was surprised to hear these words, but Dasaratha persisted.

'"Ram, before Bharat returns from Kaikeya, you should firmly establish yourself as the king. Son, I have no doubt that Bharat is virtuous, pious and respectful to elders. However, as I said, the human mind is very unstable. And many a time, the best of men fall prey to jealousy and competition."'

༅

However, Kaikeyee had other ideas. She made that night the longest and the most painful one in the history of the Ikshwakus.

'The king's announcement, making Ram the future regent, had enraged Kaikeyee. She immediately sent her trusted messenger to call Dasaratha at once to her chamber. The king's response was quick.

'"My beloved queen!" King Dasaratha tried to soothe his loveliest and most powerful wife. "What have you done to yourself? Please don't make yourself distraught and don't distrust me. I say it under oath, my dearest, whatever makes you happy, I shall do that."

'Surrendering before Kaikeyee, an infirm king sat on the ground close to her. Looking into the bleary eyes of the king, Kaikeyee firmly reminded him of his promise.

'"Lord, no one has done me any wrong. If you remember, long ago, you had promised to give me two boons. If you are a truthful king, then grant me my wishes."

'The old king guessed it wrong: He deduced that the queen wanted some compensation. Feeling a little more courageous and relaxed, he smiled and then moved closer to her. Raising her head from the ground, he placed it on his lap and began caressing her hair.

'"My dearest, I remember very well. Ask what is dear to you," playing with her fingers gently, Dasaratha assured his incensed wife.

'"Lord, your assurance gives me hope. Please oblige me. My first request is to announce Bharat as your successor and the second is to banish Ram from the kingdom for fourteen years, during which time he should live in the forests far away from Ayodhya."

'The king could not believe his ears! "Is this a dream, some black magic or is Kaikeyee under some ghostly influence?"

'But Kaikeyee was not done yet.

'"Lord, if you honour your words and the great tradition of your ancestors, then fulfil my two wishes immediately. If you don't, then there is no reason for me to live," Kaikeyee tried to stand up.

'Dasaratha tried to make her sit down near him, but quickly realized that she was burning like a log. His wily mind cautioned him to stay calm and bargain hard with an adamant Kaikeyee.

'"Kaikeyee, my dearest! Ram is virtuous, kind-hearted and brave. Be magnanimous, please be kind and bless him."

'His words made Kaikeyee furious. Like an injured snake, she looked into the king's tired eyes and hissed. "What is wrong with my son?"

'Dasaratha was terrified to see the warped expressions of his beautiful wife. His mind tried to find ways to deal with her subtly, but failed. That open contempt of his command was unimaginable. Dasaratha suddenly realized that the woman had robbed him of his prestige, authority and persona.

'The moment lingered and then the king's stored complexes and frustrations erupted. In a voice trembling with unmanageable anger, he shouted", '"O merciless hellcat Kaikeyee! You vamp!

Always planning to destroy my house! O sinful and wicked spirit! Tell me, what wrong have I caused you? What wrong has Ram done to you? Now, I realize, I brought you here only to ruin my home. I never knew, in the guise of a queen you're actually a fanged cobra!" The king got up, shaking with anger, but stumbled. With a lot of difficulty, he supported himself against a nearby wall.

'"Now, listen to me." His tone was harsh. "Ram is my eldest son and is revered by one and all. I can leave Kaushalya, Sumitra or this crown but I cannot leave Ram. Shun this sinful wish."

'Seeing no change in her expression, the king clenched his fists and his face became contorted. "You sorceress! Tell me how I can make you happy! Tell me how I can please you!"

'Realizing that he was losing, the king made one last attempt. "Kaikeyee! How could you even think of banishing him?"

'Kaikeyee's fiery gaze unsettled the king. Dasaratha felt dizzy and grabbed a chair to steady himself. Taking a deep breath, he tried to clear his head and attempted sanity. He touched her hand as a gesture of peace, but it was colder than ice. The king was looking for some warmth desperately, one ray of hope, a few kind words from Kaikeyee, but he got nothing. He felt a storm building inside him. Controlling himself, he again tried to convince her.

'"Dear Kaikeyee! I am old and almost on my deathbed. Be kind to me. I will give you everything you wish for, but don't demand the impossible. It will cause me instant death. Darling, have mercy on Ram. He loves you more than Bharat. Don't destroy him."

'She inspected the defeated man sitting before him.

'"King, if you deny me what you had promised, then you are a shame. Your deviation from your words will ruin the prestige of your grand clan forever," Kaikeyee pronounced in a stern and clear voice.

'The king avoided her stare and responded in a pacifying tone, "Kaikeyee, I love Bharat as much as you do. I will announce

Bharat as my heir tomorrow. But, my beloved queen, please take back your demand to banish Ram for fourteen long years. This is a sin. People will also condemn it."

'Kaikeyee looked at him without lowering her gaze.

"'Good or bad, dharma or sin, I don't care. Ram's exile is non-negotiable. I am firm that it is better to die than to beg before a haughty Kaushalya."

"'My beloved queen, don't ruin my prestige. Try to understand. I made the announcement in a crowded assembly, not in a deserted place. How can I disown it?"

'Kaikeyee did not like this and, like an injured lioness, she attacked. "King, what about the promises you made to me? You must know the consequences of your deeds. I will repeat my two wishes three times and then, if you deny them, I will consider myself an abandoned wife and shall give up my life here and now."

'The king could not counter her threat. With unfocused eyes and an unsettled mind, he could utter only curses.

"'If you wish so, I abandon you. I repent taking you as my wife. I also abandon the son borne by you."

'The king's threats had no effect on Kaikeyee.

"'King, there is no use saying all this. Even abandoning us won't free you from your given word," Kaikeyee said very calmly. "Call your beloved Ram immediately and begin preparations for his exile. Send him away for fourteen years and make me free of fear, and only then, I will allow you peace."

'At dawn, a pale Sumantra entered Ram's palace. The hardworking and cheerful minister looked unusually worried and ashen-faced. He ushered Ram to the chariot and drove him to Kaikeyee's palace.

'Royal officials and workers had started gathering on the streets. Overnight, the whole town had been painted afresh. Colourful flags and banners covered the streets. The air was scented and smoke from *yagna* altars wafted like low-lying clouds. When people saw Ram's chariot, they greeted him enthusiastically. There were workers everywhere, on highways, lanes and squares. Temple bells were ringing. Near the gate of the palace, Brahmins, priests, ministers, army officers and merchants had begun to assemble.

'When Ram reached Kaikeyee's palace, he sensed a discomforting quiet. The palace looked like a ghostly place. Inside, in Kaikeyee's private chamber, Dasaratha sat on a chair with a pale face and dry lips. When Ram prostrated himself before them, Kaikeyee did not respond and Dasaratha could only utter, "Ram!"

'"Mother, what is the matter? Why do both of you look so upset? How may I help?"

'Kaikeyee stared at Ram and said in a sweet voice. "Ram, there is something troubling your father's heart. He loves you the most and therefore he hesitates to pronounce an unpleasant truth."

'"Mother, your wish is my command."

'"Ram, you know that truth is the pivot of dharma. It is the key. Therefore, pleasant or unpleasant, one must follow the truth under all circumstances. Son, your father had granted me two boons. Favourable or otherwise, it is your dharma to follow them. And if you promise to do so, only then will I tell you these boons. They will release your father from this unbearable pain."

'Kaikeyee's words were unusual and incoherent, but a steadfast Ram could sense that something terrible was about to happen.

'"Mother, whatever he desires, I will obey. Tell me without hesitation."

'Kaikeyee quickly told Ram about the two boons she had asked for.

'"Ram, your father loves you a lot. For him, your separation is unbearable. At the same time, he also wants to honour his promise. This dilemma has made him pathetic. Only you can release him from this despicable situation."

'An informed Ram was relieved. In a flash, he decided his duties.

"'I shall follow your desires very happily," Ram paused, "and leave Ayodhya immediately.'"

'Aunt, an audience with truth is amazing,' Krishna told Kunti. 'It liberates you. Kaikeyee was correct when she said that truth is the pivot of dharma. She was revealing the truth. Nobody knows what will happen tomorrow, but many a times, hard paths lead to the discovery of the purpose of life.'

'Exile is not unknown to us,' Kunti thought. Her sons were sent on exile for twelve long years, followed by a year in complete hiding. She knew how horrible those thirteen years had been for her, living in Hastinapur under Dhritarashtra and his scheming son Duryodhana.

'What was the reaction of Kaushalya?' Kunti asked.

Krishna smiled. He knew why Kunti was asking that question.

'Royal decorum allows only a defined conduct within the *maryada* of one's position. It forbids royals from expressing their private feelings in public. Ram's mother Kaushalya had always been very dignified, but the sudden reversal of fate and this highly undeserved and harsh punishment tore the veil of her gallantry.

"'Ram, perhaps I would have been happier being childless. I suffered my persecution with a faint hope, of seeing you as king one day. But Kaikeyee has strangulated even that faint hope. Now, I have to hear the taunts of the younger ladies and keeps forever, and have to live at the mercy of a scheming Kaikeyee."

'Ram hugged his dejected mother but before he could say a word of comfort, she complained further.

"'Ram, many a times, I have been treated worse than Kaikeyee's maids. Even my own servants or maids are scared in the presence of Yudhajit or Kaikeyee. In such an environment, how shall I live without you? Once you go away, these vultures will eat me alive. In the Ikshwaku dynasty, only the eldest son succeeds his father to the throne. Ram, if you know the essence of dharma, you must stay back, claim your right, and serve your people."

'Ram tried to pacify his mother.

'"Mother, without the king's wish, how can I stay in his kingdom? Even if you consider the opinion of the elders in the assembly, the final decision to anoint me rested with the king. Now, if he does not wish so, I don't have a claim. My stay will cause a vacillating king more pain and that will not augur well for Ayodhya's future."

'Kaushalya was not convinced.

'"Mother, father needs you more than anybody else, in these circumstances. If you abandon the king, who will support him?"

'"Ram, wait," Kaushalya demanded. "If your father's command is so sacrosanct to you, what about your mother's? He has asked you to go on exile, I am commanding you to stay in Ayodhya and fight for your rights." Kaushalya paused and then added, "If you decide to relinquish us, I will fast unto death and cause you the most painful infamy."

'Ram understood the pain of his mother. Gently putting his point forward, he consoled her.

'"Mother, the role you envisage for me is not the complete truth. When we see beyond our selfish drives, only then can we understand that these two vehicles, the throne and the body, are only for the service of the people. The exploitation of a certain authority, and the pleasure derived from it, are momentary and not worthy of my time. Here, drowning deeper in palace politics, I will not be able to do justice to the role I see for myself. Let me go." Ram hugged his mother and said, "Fourteen years will fly very fast, mother. Then, we will be together again. And you will not regret this, I promise."

'"Ram, I will follow you to the jungle like a cow follows her calf." Kaushalya wiped away her tears and said, "If you have pledged to live in the forest to follow your dharma, how can I distract you from your true path? And why should I?"

"'Mother, I am young and capable. I can take care of myself. But look at the king: He will not survive without you. Take care of him, mother. He needs you more than I do."

"'Ram, if you will not listen to me, then please leave and come back safely after fourteen years. I will pray to the Lord for your safety and well-being. Let me say a few auspicious words to you." Kaushalya continued, "Ram, nobody can stop you: Remember this forever. My son, remember to follow the truth, so that you walk on the path of great souls. My son, you are a lion among men. Let the dharma, the right action that you so attentively obeyed, protect you." The old mother's eyes were full of tears, but she blessed her brave son.

"'Ram, let the wisdom and the deeds, that you are so faithful to, protect you. The weapons that you have obtained from your gurus, let those weapons protect you. Ram, my son, I bless you. Let all the wisdom you have imbibed, do good to you, let your valour be proved, may you get immeasurable illustriousness in the forest, may your path be everyone's path."'

࿂

'In the afternoon, Ram, Sita and Laxman went to meet the king before their departure.

'Kaikeyee's chamber was crowded with people. Many ministers, including Sumantra and Siddhartha, were there. Vashishtha was sitting near the king, who was crumpled on the bed. Kaikeyee was sitting opposite Vashishtha. Many palace women were standing a little farther away. Ram held the hands of his father and then, in a soft voice, sought his permission to leave Ayodhya. Dasaratha had to make an effort to open his eyes.

'The blurred vision of the king settled on his elder son's face. Dasaratha tried to clear his throat and then, in a wavering tone, he spoke: "Ram, I have committed a sin. I have become a prisoner of my own words. I faltered in my dealings with a virtuous man like you. Please forgive me." He gazed at Ram and then said in a low voice, "It is better if you imprison me and take over the throne."

'Holding his father's hand little tightly, Ram replied with an affectionate smile.

'"Father, I pray to God for your long, happy and healthy life. I have decided to fulfil your command. It is unfortunate for a young son to leave his father when he needs his care. But, my dharma is to leave Ayodhya." He paused and then added, "Sita and Laxman are also going with me. I assure you, after fourteen years, we will come back to serve you."

'A deep pain moved the old wrinkles on the king's face. Suddenly, his voice rose and, looking at Kaikeyee with frantic eyes, he pronounced: "No! They will not go anywhere. If you have decided to go, then you go alone. Sita and Laxman will stay here. This evil Kaikeyee has demanded your exile, not my daughter-in-law's."

'Dasaratha closed his eyes. A few drops fell from the corner of his closed eyes. The king murmured to everyone present: "Tell Sumantra to go with Ram. Ask him to take the best horses and men. My entire army shall follow Ram. Let the most beautiful maidens, efficient and sweet-talking maids and guildsmen follow Ram. My armoury, spies, artisans and entertainers should also go with Ram…"

'Everyone turned their surprised gaze on the king. Dasaratha's voice grew louder, as if his authority had finally found voice.

'"Ram is going to live in solitude in those dreaded forests. So, send my treasury and the granary with him. He will perform *yagna*s with the sages in the wild and make the forests habitable. Provide him everything he desires. Then, let my dear son Bharat rule Ayodhya and make its citizens happy."

'Ram held his father's hand. "Father, I do not need… " Before Ram could complete his sentence, a visibly angry and distraught Kaikeyee stood up and shouted aloud.

'"King, nobody drinks wine devoid of its taste; Then why

should Bharat accept a kingdom without the treasury and the men?"

'For the first time, a smile appeared on Dasaratha's face.

"'Kaikeyee! My dear, don't torture me with your ever-growing demands. You never placed this condition while demanding Ram's exile. How can I accept your unjust calls?"

'The king's reply made Kaikeyee hysterical. She began hurling abuses at the king.

"'King, let me not venture out to explain what kind of worthy princes your clan has had. Had not Sagar banished his fool of a son? Ram should also be banished like him, with the clothes on his back."

"'Shame on you, queen!" a usually taciturn Siddhartha shouted at Kaikeyee.

'Siddhartha was the oldest minister in the royal council. He was considered a yogi among the ministers. The king had always held him in very high esteem.

"'Queen…," the old minister regained his calm. "Please don't compare prince Ram with prince Asmanjas. This comparison is unwarranted and completely wrong. Asmanjas was evil personified. He used to throw children playing on the road into River Sarayu for his sick entertainment. One day, a rebellion broke out and people forced the king to choose between the prince and the people; they threatened to desert Ayodhya in case the king chose the prince. Then, Sagar, after verifying the facts publicly, denounced his son and banished him from his kingdom. Queen, you are trying to compare light with darkness. This is unacceptable."

'The highly charged atmosphere affected an otherwise calm, mature and wise Sumantra. He was the king's confidant and also an advisor. But, at that moment, the natural calmness of his face had disappeared; indignation was written all over his voice.

"'King, even if you water a *neem* tree with milk, it will not give you sweet fruit. You have always preferred sensual indulgence to the interests of the state. Ethical, social and state codes should control everyone's behaviour, including that of a king. But ever since you married queen Kaikeyee, you have always preferred her interests, whether just or unjust, over the state's."

"'How dare you say this?" Kaikeyee was furious. "You, a lowly servant, dare to speak about me ..."

'Sumantra ignored Kaikeyee and addressed the king.

"'King, every culture has its decorum and dignity. Children learn from their parent's conduct. Unfortunately, the queen has got her idiosyncrasy from her mother."

'The allegation stunned everybody, but Sumantra did not stop.

"'Once upon a time, happy with the services of Kaikeyee's father, one sage gave him a boon. Because of this boon, the king could understand the chatter of birds. The sage, while blessing him, also warned him of immediate death, in case the king revealed to anyone what the birds spoke. One morning, when Kaikeyee's parents were sitting in the garden, a bird chirped. Hearing her chirp, the king laughed aloud. The queen suspected that the king was laughing at her and asked him to explain. The king tried to assure her that she was not the cause of the laughter and that it was the bird that made him laugh, but the queen did not believe him. Despite the king's many efforts, she could not be pacified. She insisted and when the king did not budge, she sat on a hunger strike. The king did his best to pacify her but she was adamant to know why he had laughed."

'Then, the king told her that if he revealed what the bird had said, then he would die instantly. Even after knowing this, the queen was adamant to know what the bird had chattered. The king was very disturbed and sought advice from the same sage."

"'"King, if your partner does not believe you, and instead behaves recalcitrantly, defying all decorum, then you should drive her out of your palace,' the sage advised."

"'Following the sage's advice, Kaikeyee's father exiled his wife, far away from his palace and his life."

"'So, I speak to you, wise king! You too, should act in a tough manner. Otherwise, you will skittle away not only your dearest sons and daughter-in-law, but also the sympathy and respect of your people. My Lord, if you do not act now, I see a catastrophe befalling Ayodhya."

'Deep silence followed the harsh words of Sumantra. Ashen-faced royals looked at the old minister with bewildered eyes. For few seconds, silence prevailed, as if a big dark storm was brewing before a disaster. Then, Kaikeyee screamed.

"'Throw out this lowly man! Imprison him!" she shouted at the guards. In a moment, many guards appeared at the door of her chamber.

'Laxman quickly took out his bow. Sensing an impending showdown with the fiercest prince, the guards hesitated. The king remained speechless. Ram tried to calm the atmosphere.

"'Amatya," he addressed Sumantra, "I have always respected you as a sage among the ministers. But what you just said makes me sad. Your words pile more agony on my parents, who are already suffering so much. To obey their command is my duty, and I am doing this happily. If my mother wants Bharat to be the king and me to live in the forests, then it should be like that."

'Sumantra did not reply and stood before the king with folded hands. Kaikeyee's wrath had accumulated in her red eyes. Ram turned to Sita and Laxman and said, "Let us go."

'Once they left Ayodhya, the king's health deteriorated faster. When Sumantra informed Dasaratha that Ram had crossed River Ganga and there was no hope of his return, Dasaratha's faint hope for survival extinguished. On the fifteenth day of Ram's exile, Dasaratha left this world.

'Dasaratha's demise created panic and uncertainty in the palace. Kaikeyee came to see the dead king and remained there for some time. Kaushalya became silent and Sumitra was busy consulting the sages and Vashishtha about the king's last rites.

'Bharat and Shatrughna returned from Kaikeya. When Kaikeyee told Bharat what had happened, he became agitated. Fuming with anger, he charged his mother for orchestrating a catastrophe. Then, he went to Kaushalya and convinced her of his innocence. Initially, both Sumitra and Kaushalya suspected him, but the way Bharat mourned Ram's exile and cursed his mother for everything that had happened, made them amend their opinions. After that realization, Kaushalya and Sumitra went to Bharat and requested him to occupy the vacant throne.

'Within three days of his return, Bharat had transformed everyone's opinion about him. His firm and clear stand in rejecting Kaikeyee's demands, his resolve and explicit commitment to bring back Ram, his ethical and just ways, won over everyone. Bharat became dearer to all.

'What Kaikeyee's malevolence had failed to do, Bharat's righteousness achieved in a short time. People began to say openly that Bharat would surely make a worthy king until Ram returns from exile. Siddhartha and Sumantra went to Bharat and requested him to honour the late king's commands and accept the crown, but Bharat firmly rejected their request.

"'I can't follow your advice as it does not calm my heart. My conscience and belief say that I must go to Ram and request him to come back and be our king. We will all go to him, apologize and bring him back to rule Ayodhya." 'Bharat tasked himself with reuniting the family. The chariots of Bharat and Shatrughna, followed by the ministers and the priests, led the convoy. The queens had their separate chariots, so had the princesses. Noisy, happy and elated with optimism, the convoy of Ayodhya went to bring back the exiled Ram.

'For more than a month, Bharat and the others tried their best to persuade Ram to return to Ayodhya, but he did not agree. He advised Bharat to take care of the kingdom, according to the wish of their parents. But, Bharat steadfastly refused to sit on the throne and instead offered to live in exile in place of Ram. Finally, Ram agreed that he would take the reins of the kingdom, but not before serving the full fourteen years of exile.

'"Bharat, abandon your hesitation. Go to Ayodhya with a free mind and serve the people. When I return, I will do the same."

'"If that is the order of my king, I shall abide by it. But I must have your support," Bharat requested.

'"Bharat, take the guidance of guru Vashishtha and king Janaka. Shun all worries and serve Ayodhya sincerely," Ram said, placing his hand on Bharat's shoulder.

'"Ram, I will serve the people as your humble servant. Give me a symbol of yours to support and guide me," Bharat prayed with folded hands.

'Overwhelmed by the love of his younger brother, Ram got up from his seat and hugged Bharat. Bharat requested Ram to hand over his sandals.

'"Lord, placing your sandals on the throne, I will serve as a caretaker of your kingdom for fourteen years. But, if you do not return at the end of the fourteenth year, I shall immolate myself. This is my vow."

'Ram promised to return after fourteen years.'

~

'Aunt, in all our stories, we show the victory of good over evil. But we never announce complete annihilation of evil. This is because both the *satva* and the *tamasa* are equal and permanent *guna*s of God. The victory of the good only indicates that the balance between the *satva* and the *tamasa* has been re-established correctly. In the flow of the time, this balance is disturbed time and again, and when that happens, the struggle between the 'good' and the 'bad' resumes, and to set the balance right, time and again Vishnu reincarnates himself. All our endeavours are aimed towards establishing this creative balance.'

'Krishna, you mean to say that Soorpanakha was also a victim of circumstances? Does this absolve her of her bad deeds?'

'No, aunt. To decide what is right and what is wrong, *prakriti* has gifted us with a conscience, the consciousness and cognition.

Don't we humans instinctively know what is good or bad? Many a times, we knowingly embrace the "bad". How can we absolve ourselves from our 'bad' deeds?' Krishna responded.

'Tell me more about Soorpanakha. We only know what she did at Panchavati when she met Ram and Laxman. She is often portrayed as a woman who, for her lust, had destroyed her entire clan. If she was of such a lowly character, why did Ravana care so much for her?' Kunti wondered.

'I will tell you the story from the beginning, aunt,' Krishna smiled.

> 'It begins with a sage called Pulastya. He was also a *manasputra* of Brahma. Young Pulastya was an embodiment of all good virtues, and his eminence was recognized all over the land. Pulastya built his ashram near a delightful lake, under the shelter of mount Meru. The ashram and its surroundings were full of natural beauty.
>
> 'The beauty of the place and the lake attracted many youths from nearby areas. They used to flock to the place and engaged in their amusements. They would play music, sing and dance and make a lot of noise, which caused a lot of annoyance to the sage. Initially, he tried to cope with the situation, but later it became too much to handle. Irritated, first he tried to chase away the youths. Soon, he realized that they were not very obedient and hardly cared for him. Furious, Pulastya finally cursed the polluters: "After tomorrow, if I see any girl in this area, she will become pregnant."
>
> 'The announcement had its desired effect. Hearing Pulastya's curse, young maidens got scared and people began avoiding the place.
>
> 'In those days, a righteous king called Trinbindu ruled the mountains. His young daughter was a beautiful and daring girl. Her name was Ilvila. She did not pay heed to the sage's warning. One afternoon, under a clear sky, when she was swimming in the lake near the sage's ashram, Pulastya saw

her. His curse materialized and she became pregnant.

'A worried Trinbindu and his wife arrived at the sage's door to apologize and request him to revoke the curse. But, that was not possible. The troubled king then requested Pulastya to marry his young daughter. The sage obliged the king and thus, Pulastya and the princess got married.'

At this juncture of the story, Krishna smiled again and asked, 'Do you know aunt, Trinbindu was an Ikshwaku king?'

'Ram's clan?' Kunti was astonished.

Krishna smiled and continued the story of Soorpanakha.

'Sage Pulastya liked to chant Vedic hymns in a melodic voice. He had this belief of clairaudience of his child growing in his wife's womb. Thus, when a son was born to the princess, the sage named him Vishrava. Because of his mother Ilvila, Vishrava was also called Vishravas Ailvil.

'When Vishrava grew up, Pulastya sent him to the best teachers. Soon, a young Vishrava became as renowned as his illustrious father. Sage Bhardwaja got his daughter Devavarnini married to the young and virtuous Vishrava.

'Soon, Vishrava and his wife were blessed with a son. This son was named Vaishravan. Unlike his father and grandfather, Vaishravan was not interested in academics. At an early age, he established a huge business empire around the world and became the richest person on earth. The Yakshas accepted him as their leader and gave him the title of Kuber. He also became a close friend of Indra.

'During that time, Daitya Sukeshi's three sons, Malyavan, Mali and Sumali were building their empire in and around Lanka. Their growing influence and power made Indra envious. To check their authority and growth, he went to Shiva for help, but Shiva refused to help him against the sons of his friend Sukeshi.

'After Shiva's refusal, Indra went to Vishnu for help. As a result, a series of vicious wars began. In a fierce battle, Vishnu killed Mali and forced Malyavan and Sumali to go into hiding. This war reduced the power of these Daityas to naught. Indra gifted the fort of Lanka to his friend Kuber, who in no time made it the most opulent place in the world.

'Malyavan and Sumali were desperate to get their lost prestige and the fort of Lanka back. After seeing the opulence of Vishrava's son Kuber in Lanka, and gauging Vishrava's influence and power, Sumali decided to use his daughter Kaikasi to win back the lost influence and power of the Daityas.

'"Kaikasi, my daughter!" Sumali counselled his daughter, "You are young and beautiful. It is the right time for you to get married. We all desire that you marry the most worthy man."

'A pink glow of happiness appeared on Kaikasi's face.

'"I have found a suitable match for you. Pulastya's son Vishrava is a young man." Sumali added, "I wish my grandchildren to be as intelligent as Vishrava and as radiant as you. Go and propose to Vishrava, I am sure this relationship will be most gratifying for you."

'Kaikasi was a proud girl. She was well-educated and very beautiful. She had grown up listening to the stories of the great opulence and grandeur of her paternal and maternal clans. Vishrava was well-known in both the worlds and was still young. She decided to follow her father's advice.

'She met Vishrava on a splendid beach on the western coast, when the sun was setting and the weather was cool. After a short acquaintance, Vishrava found her charm irresistible. She was like the waves of the sea where he always wished to surf. She inspired him to do all the wild things a man could desire, unlike his predictable and disciplined wife Devavarnini.

'Vishrava found a match in Kaikasi. She was well-travelled. She knew many languages and was familiar with various cultures. Her uninhibited conduct and passionate attitude towards life enticed the sage. Vishrava found it hard to ignore this beauty with a face like the full moon, a narrow waist and elegant limbs. They married immediately.

'In a few years, Kaikasi gave birth to four children. The eldest among them was a boy. He was so attractive and graceful that just one look at him told the world that he was born to rule.

'"What should we call him?" Kaikasi asked her husband.

'"Rayivaan," Vishrava replied. "He will be the best amalgamation of *Rayi*, material opulence and *Prana*, spiritual magnificence."

'"So beautiful!" Kaikasi exclaimed. "In our language, we will call him Raivana." She looked at her husband and asked, "Is it okay?"

'"If you want to call him Raivana, I suggest you say Iraivana."

'"Iraivana? You mean the god or the king?"

'"Of course Iraivana the king."

'The boy was so intelligent and strong that they also named him Dashgreeva. He inherited intelligence from his father and valour from his maternal grandfather. Unlike Kuber, he was strongly built, handsome and had a strong interest in martial arts, literature, philosophy and music. He was indeed a source of joy for both sides of the lineage. Vishrava hoped that one day Dashgreeva would carry forward the legacy of his father and grandfather. Kuber was a great son and the wealthiest man in the world, but Vishrava had always longed for a scholarly son.

'Dashgreeva surpassed everyone's expectations. At a very young age, Malyavan and Sumali took him under their wings. Ambitious Kaikasi filled him with the desire to be more opulent than Kuber, more knowledgeable than Vishrava and mightier than Indra. Malyavan and Sumali inspired him to bring back the lost pride and glory of the Daityas. Malyavan was a great warrior himself. Under his tutelage, a young Dashgreeva became an unconquerable swordsman. Pleased with his brilliance, Shiva started calling Iraivana, the Ravana.

'Vishrava and Kaikasi's second son was named Kumbhkarana. Pulastya gave this name to him affectionately, after noticing his huge ears. The big boy was passionate about military technology and used to spend long hours in Malyavan's laboratory.

'Kaikasi's third child was an attractive girl. They named her Suparna. Kaikasi fondly called her Chandranakha because of her beautiful and round nails, but her brothers used to tease her by calling her Soorpanakha, a girl with nails as big as a shovel. She was not beautiful in the classical sense, but her long ebony hair, bright black eyes and strong, tall and lean physique made her very attractive. The uninhibited and free environment of Sumali's home made her a free spirit.

'The real apple of Vishrava's eye was his youngest son, Vibhishana. He was very shy and inclined towards academics. Vishrava encouraged his scholarly attributes. His siblings ridiculed him for this, but he was a determined boy and pursued his studies very seriously.

'All the children grew up quickly. Ravana became the master of ten arts, thus, justifying his name Dashgreeva. He could sit for hours in discourse with his father during the day, in the evening he would sail towards the small eastern islands, winning them with the might of his sword; and before dawn they had to drag him from the dens of professional damsels, where he was found lying drunk.

'Kumbhkarana and Soorpanakha never liked Vishrava's preaching. They obediently followed Ravana, who had, by now, snatched Lanka from Kuber. Ravana started calling himself a Rakshasa. Very soon, a frustrated Vishrava stopped following their progress. Stories of their misconduct and criminal behaviour reached Vishrava's ears, but he left it either to destiny or advised aggrieved people to approach Sumali for the redressal of their complaints.'

∽

'A powerful tribe of the Kalikeyas lived in the eastern islands, not far from Lanka. They were fierce warriors and mercenaries, with a strong sense of independence. The Rakshasas considered their islands to be useless. Therefore, Ravana never attempted to bring them under his direct control. Instead, he was happy to get them as paid soldiers at minimum wage. He also encouraged many children of the Kalikeya nobles to stay in Lanka for their education and granted them generous scholarships.

'Vidyutjinnha was one such Kalikeya youth. He was tall, dark and very handsome. He was studying in Lanka's royal school and everybody was impressed by his eloquence, charming manners and athletic achievements. A highly ambitious young man, Vidyutjinnha was a master swordsman. Soorpanakha met him during an annual school competition and the moment their eyes met, she fell in love with the charming Kalikeya youth.

'It was a new experience for a young and naïve Soorpanakha. She was tired of living under the grand patronage of her mighty brothers. Her every wish was fulfilled by them, but it had increasingly made her pensive. Despite attaining youth, she was still treated like a doll, or at best as a young sweet girl. Her brother Ravana could move the world upside down to fulfil her wishes, but failed to treat her as a grown up woman with an independent mind.

'It was very different with Vidyutjinnha. With him, everything was so informal and equal. To her, he was suitably powerful, talented and intelligent. At her tender age, his being a penniless Kalikeya youth was immaterial. He had an animal magnetism that pulled Soorpanakha with great force and ease. His body like molten copper, chiseled to perfection, made her heart weak. For Soorpanakha, he was the best creation of nature.

'A glimpse of him, a thought of him and the desire to be with him, could make her heart pound heavily. Walking past the manicured lawns and gardens of the school with him, were her most pleasant moments. They had blissful moments, lying together on cool nights on a sea beach. Even more exciting for her was running away from the palace, waiting for him anxiously at isolated places on the beach or in some dreadful cave.

'Those moments of innocent adventure and fun gave her soul the freedom that it longed for. Those moments of togetherness, away from worldly chaos, were her own. In those moments of bliss, sometimes time moved too quickly, and sometimes it seemed to conspire against her. Her favourite pastime was to compare the fragrance of Vidyutjinnha's body with the bouquets of wines so fondly brought by his connoisseur brother from around the world.

'"Let us elope," she proposed to Vidyutjinnha after an intimate hour on a dark beach, where only silvery waves moved. The sky was silent and the sea was calm. The moon was lovingly caressing them with a shy smile.

'"Why don't you speak to your brother?" Vidyutjinnha held her closer.

'She looked at him with her big eyes, "Let's run away to your island. We will have our own small place where we will live like this forever."

'"Suparna, that will be like invoking death for the Kalikeyas. I don't want that. Your brother is a wise and brave fellow. He loves you. If you tell him about our love, he may sanctify it," he insisted.

'Soorpanakha was not so sure about that, but Vidyutjinnha forced her to discuss it with her brother. Soorpanakha hesitated to speak to Ravana. Instead, she reluctantly broached the subject to his wife, Mandodari, who did not like the idea of a princess marrying a pauper. She cautioned Ravana to restrain Soorpanakha. Mandodari warned her husband that the episode might bring embarrassment upon him. When Ravana tried to take the side of his sister, Mandodari dismissed Soorpanakha's love as a stupid adolescent adventure. She also ridiculed Ravana's proposal to allow Soorpanakha to stay for some time with the Kalikeya boy, in order to understand him better.

'"She is an impulsive girl. Encouraging this affair would be detrimental to an innocent Suparna."

'Ravana decided to speak to his sister to put an end to her

affair. Narrating the stories of the prestige and power associated with his clan, Ravana tried to counsel his sister, but she refused to listen to his arguments.

'"Dashgreeva, you are our guardian. Do you wish to control my life? Do you want to take away my right to choose my husband? Is this not against Rakshasa tradition?" she argued.

'Ravana reasoned to make her understand.

'"Suparna, the Kalikeyas are primitive, uncultured, poor and resourceless. You will not be happy there. I am not opposing your love, but how can I approve of my sister settling down with a poor orphan? Let this phase of infatuation fade away. Tomorrow, you may get a better man than Vidyutjinnha. I am not in favour of you taking such big decision under emotional impetuousness, in your innocent adolescence."

'"Brother, do you see any fault in Vidyutjinnha? Don't you find him capable?"

'"No. To me, he looks like a youth lost in this majestic Lanka. He is ignorant of the ways of the world and is very emotional."

'"What is wrong with that?"

'"These attributes, added to his poverty and his lack of lineage, become burdens. He is not a man who can ensure my sister's luxurious way of life in this arduous world."

'"Is this a condition?" Soorpanakha said sarcastically.

'"Chandranakha, there are a few more issues. Do you know that he killed his own mother on his father's instigation? His mother was a Rakshasa and a Lankan. What he has done was against the ethos of Rakshasa culture. I cannot imagine him as my brother-in-law."

'An angry and fuming Soorpanakha left the room.

'That night, she eloped with Vidyutjinnha. The night sea was calm and the moonlight was sufficient to navigate. Vidyutjinnha coxed the dinghy. Soorpanakha was surprised to see around them a large number of small dinghies appearing out of nowhere. The sailors were obviously his Kalikeya fellows.

'"How did he arrange hundreds of men to help?" she thought

and looked at him. He winked mischievously and grinned.

'After arriving in Ashma, the Kalikeya capital, Soorpanakha found out that Vidyutjinnha was the crown prince of Ashma. He had kept his identity a secret in Lanka. Now, she knew that the man she and many Lankans thought was an orphan, was in fact a king in waiting. His father was on his deathbed and the Kalikeyas were waiting for his return to crown him their next king.

'The next three days went by like a dream. Soon, she became the queen of Ashma. The celebrations were not spectacular, but here she was the queen and her beloved was with her.

'The dream did not last long. On her fourth night with Vidyutjinnha, sixteen hundred Lankan warships besieged Ashma. Boats of different shapes and sizes harboured in the shallow water and thousands of Rakshasa warriors, armed with axes, javelins, maces, bows and arrows attacked Ashma. Ravana himself, with Kumbhkarana, was leading the Lankan naval force.

'A ferocious battle took place and within a few hours, many thousands of Kalikeyas and a few hundred Rakshasa warriors laid down their lives. Then, Vidyutjinnha came forward and proposed a duel with Ravana to save innocent lives. Ravana quickly agreed. For an hour, both the warriors faced each other with extraordinary gallantry, dexterous riposte and remise, and lightening movements. Ravana was injured, but finally managed to cut off Vidyutjinnha's neck with a swift stroke of his sword.

'The battle ended. Soorpanakha decided to immolate herself with her husband's dead body, following the Kalikeya custom. She climbed up on the wooden pile prepared for Vidyutjinnha's cremation. Holding her beloved's head on her lap, she waited for the pyre to consume her. A tearful Ravana requested her not to do so.

'"Suparna, everyone has to follow the clan dharma, otherwise the clan dies. You did not follow that. Therefore, this tragedy happened. Let bygones be bygones. Give up this dreadful and impetuous decision of self-immolation."

'"No, Ravana! Now the Kalikeya is my clan and this is my clan dharma."

'"Don't abuse your precious life, Suparna!" shouted Ravana, and holding his sister in his mighty arms, he swiftly removed her from the pyre.

'Soorpanakha protested but then she slowly calmed down. Ravana embraced her and said many soothing words. He requested her to come back to Lanka.

'Soorpanakha refused, "Dashgreeva, I cannot leave the Kalikeyas now."

'Ravana thought for a while before speaking.

'"Very well. I give you the entire main land south of the River Godavari. Go to Janasthan with all your people. That place is fertile, beautiful and full of minerals. I will instruct Khara to assist you in every way. Take all your people there and be their goddess."

'Soorpanakha agreed.'

~

'When she reached Janasthan and made it her permanent residence, Soorpanakha was pregnant with Vidyutjinnha's seed. Soon, she gave birth to a boy. Very affectionately, she named him Jambumali.

'Soorpanakha never forgave Ravana and the Rakshasas for Vidyutjinnha's murder. She wanted the annihilation of the entire Rakshasa clan, but she was helpless. Time was not on her side. Ravana had put his trusted trio of Khara, Dushana and Trishira in her service, thus effectively ending any possibility of a rebellion. However, Soorpanakha took great care in nurturing her son. When he was young, Soorpanakha told him how Ravana had killed his father. Soorpanakha encouraged him to avenge his father's death. An angry Jambumali vowed to retaliate and went to please the sun god.

'Providence plays bizarre games with creatures. The death of Vidyutjinnha had changed Soorpanakha. The young and emotional princess died that day in Ashma, and what came out of that tragedy was a different woman. After her arrival in Janasthan, she used to stay alone. Not many had seen her in public. But, slowly, everything changed. The shy widow slowly transformed into an aggressive and cruel lady.

'Perhaps, a lack of control and excessive power at her disposal made Soorpanakha into what she became infamous for. She never took an interest in any other Kalikeya man after the death of her husband, but she had short affairs with many local tribal youths. Later, stories of these tribal youths disappearing mysteriously began to circulate in Janasthan. Stories about Soorpanakha inviting young boys to her palace and later murdering them became common. When locals began avoiding her palace in Janasthan, she started roaming around the place in search of young boys. Her servants forcibly abducted anyone who resisted her advances.

'With advancing age, she tried to look younger and adopted insane ways to remain young. She was fond of using various types of ointments and medicines made by chemists from plants, animals or human organs.'

∽

'When Jambumali left to pray to the sun god, he chose Panchavati, a beautiful forest garden, as his place of penance. He began his penance in a bamboo grove, in a secluded corner of the forest. He prayed to Surya to give him a weapon that could destroy the Rakshasa race. After many years of penance, a pleased Surya offered him an unconquerable scimitar. That scimitar descended directly from the sky and began revolving around the grove inside which Jambumali was meditating. However, this success made Jambumali arrogant and he vowed that he would accept the weapon only if Surya presented him the weapon in person. So, he sat inside the bamboo grove, waiting for Surya to appear.

'At around the same time, following the suggestion of the sage Agastya, Laxman, Ram and Sita came to Panchavati to spend their final year of exile. By that time, Janasthan was a two-decade-old well-settled Kalikeya garrison.

'In Panchavati, Laxman had chosen a place with five huge dense trees for the huts of Ram, Sita and himself. There was a pond nearby, full of lotus flowers, swans, cranes and other birds. Herds of deer and flocks of peacocks made the place majestic. The hill nearby was blossoming with trees, climbers and creepers.

'The huts were to be located near the hill, encircled by the woods, close to a big cave. From this place, the surrounding area could be watched, but it was extremely difficult from the outside to get a hint of the inner cordon. The armoury was close to Ram's hut and Laxman built his hut a little away in the southern corner. Laxman built this extensive hermitage as a huge leaf-house. Strong walls of stone and mud, and pillars of strong wood supported the roof, which was made of long bamboo sticks and boughs of the Sami tree, and fastened with strong cords. The roof was well covered with reeds, blades of *kusha* grass and *kasa* flowers. The ground was levelled and coated. The walls were painted and decorated aesthetically.

'River Godavari was very close. *Sharad* was about to end and *Hemant* about to begin. The nights were becoming colder, but the days were pleasant and the sun was very enjoyable! Hidden in the haze after sunrise, the fields looked mysterious and the grass remained wet most of the time. Later in the day, the plains looked so bright, noisy with crying cranes.

'In the evenings, when the sky was clear blue and noisy with chirping birds loudly announcing their homecoming, Laxman used to sit under one of those five big banyan trees that had given the place its name, Panchavati. It was his routine in the evening. From the top of these five trees he could keep an eye on the surroundings of their camouflaged hermitage. So far, they had not encountered any Kalikeyas. Laxman often wondered how far away their battalion was.

'One evening, Laxman went to collect fruits from the jungle. While returning, darkness had almost descended over the plains. Carefully holding his basket of fruits, Laxman was treading the difficult path when he saw a strange scene. A radiant and big scimitar was encircling a bamboo grove at great speed. Without giving it any thought, Laxman reached out and grabbed the handle of the scimitar. The shining scimitar was made of a metal unknown to him. Its shine was peculiar. An excited Laxman wanted to examine its sharpness and swiped it at the same bamboo grove it had been circling.

'The scimitar moved with extraordinary speed and, in a fraction of a second, it cut the bamboo grove and the person sitting inside it into two. The poor fellow did not even get the chance to scream. A horrified Laxman inspected the dead body. Covered in blood, it was the body of a young Kalikeya man. He was wearing expensive clothes and gold ornaments. Laxman looked around and searched the body for any identification marks. The youth was wearing a pendant around his neck and a strange symbol was inscribed on it. Laxman kept the scimitar with him and returned to the hermitage.

'Back in the hut, he told Ram and Sita about the incident.

'"My God!" Sita screamed. "This is an inauspicious omen. Let us leave this place as soon as possible."

'"What happened was unfortunate, Sita," Ram said calmly. "Don't panic. We shall be more vigilant." Then he turned to Laxman, "You did not kill him knowingly, so don't feel miserable. Now, we should be more careful."

'Ram discussed the incident with Jatayu, his father's friend and the leader of the local tribe, the Geedhas. Both of them went along with Laxman to see the dead body. Jatayu recognized the body of Jambumali.

'"Oh God! This is not good. She will take revenge," he whispered.

'Ram and Laxman looked at him questioningly.

'"It's Jambumali, the son of Soorpanakha," a horrified Jatayu revealed the identity of the dead man. "The weapon Laxman used is unknown. Don't tell anyone what happened here. No one should know who killed Jambumali," Jatayu advised.'

༄

'A few days passed in apprehension. They were more vigilant and asked Jatayu to alert his men. They received news that Soorpanakha had hurriedly returned from Lanka after hearing about her son's death.

'One night, Laxman was on patrol duty. Staying awake for the whole night was not new to him. He had passed most of his nights in exile like that. Threat was a constant companion in the jungle.

'Past midnight, Laxman took out his sword and inspected the whole compound again. There was nothing. But, the moment he turned towards his hut in the far corner, he sensed a pair of eyes on his bare back. An extensive experience of martial art years of living through silent nights had made him over-sensitive to the slightest disturbance; Instantly, he moved a pace to the right and then turned around. His eyes searched near and far but could spot no one. Perplexed, he remained still for a couple of minutes, his eyes trying to pierce the darkness, his ears attentive to the faintest sound, but they could sense nothing.

'For the first time in the jungle, Laxman felt that his limbs were fatigued. He began inspecting each and every stationary object with an unwavering focus, but he could not find anything unusual. "We need to be more careful," he reminded himself.

'A couple of days passed and nothing happened, but Laxman was in no mood to lower the guard.

'"The Rakshasas are better trained for night movement. You have practiced the same for the past fourteen years, so let me assume that you can sense them better!" Ram laughed.

'But before a nocturnally active Laxman could meet any Rakshasa, Ram met Soorpanakha on a sunny morning by the bank of River Godavari.

'That morning, Ram went for his bath a little late. He swam in the river longer than usual. When he stepped out, he sat for a while on a big stone, basking in the sun. Then, he noticed her. She was staring at his wet and bare body. Their eyes met. Ram had never experienced such shamelessly inviting eyes.

'She audaciously inspected him from head to toe, admiring his chiseled body and long limbs. A visibly embarrassed Ram looked for his clothes. She laughed at his coyness. Ram felt a strange and strong revulsion for her. Her body flaunted signs of a long and luxurious life. Her skin was fair but her limbs were too fleshy. She was wearing a lot of ornaments with sparkling jewels, and a robe made of rare deerskin, with an intoxicating fragrance. Her flesh was oozing out of her tight clothes. She was also wearing a tiara made of gold. Heavy layers of ointments on her face made her look strange. Since leaving Ayodhya, Ram had not seen a lady wearing such heavy make-up.

'She came closer. She did not have the mature and assured walk of a middle-aged woman, but the artificial gait of a woman trying to walk like an adolescent. Ram felt awkward, but he greeted her with folded hands. She flashed a broad smile and stood closer, making him feel uncomfortable. Ram took a couple of steps back. She introduced herself and he reciprocated.

'"What is an exiled prince doing in our forest with a big armoury? Ascetics don't carry such huge piles of weapons," she observed.

'"Princess, we are new to these forests. We are no ascetics, but Kshatriyas. These weapons are for self defence."

'She did not waste any time and proposed to him. "Ram, you are in my area and therefore my guest. Since many days,

I have been watching you. The moment I saw you, I fell in love with you. We Rakshasas believe that a girl has the right to choose her partner. I am of marriageable age and unmarried. Ram, make love to me and be my lover!"

'Ram did not hesitate in his reply. "Princess, I have taken a vow to have only one wife. I cannot betray my wife's faith. Kindly excuse me."

'He tried to walk past her, but she obstructed his path.

'"Ram, I am the ruler of this land. Refusing a willing girl's request is considered a sin here. You are living in my area and thus you are my subject. You don't have the right to refuse."

'"Princess, I have a very high regard for you and your culture. I have already told you the reason why I can not consider your request." He paused and then added, "I believe that these forests belong to everyone."

'His steadfast refusal annoyed Soorpanakha.

'"Ram, you are a prime suspect in my son's murder," she said in a harsher tone. "Ravana has also ordered me to kill you by any means. Contrary to my duty, I have been kind to you. If not for me, Khara and Dushana would have killed you and your wife long ago."

'Ram remained silent. Soorpanakha then softly prayed, "Prince, follow me. I will make you the king of Janasthan. You will be treated with utmost respect in Ravana's court." She tried to grab Ram's right hand.

'"Ram, it is a sin to refuse a woman." She moved closer to him. "Think of what you will get after receiving my favour. Mighty Khara and Dushana will be your assistants. The world's best warrior Meghanad will call you *matula*; ferocious Kumbhkarana and wise Vibhishana will honour you as their brother-in-law. Ram, I will always be faithful to you. You will get everything you wish."

'"Princess, I am sad to hear about your son." He looked at her and said, "It is also not wise to force your desires on an unwilling person. What kind of joy will you get from that? I have absolutely no desire to be intimate with you. Please find someone who can reciprocate in equal terms."

'She stared at him, as if trying to reach some conclusion.

'"What about your brother?"

'"You may ask him. He is not with his wife," Ram replied instantly.

'"Very well. I will see him," she said and left immediately.

'Ram remained standing there. The past few moments had been absurd. No woman had ever treated him like that. He was just a piece of meat for her, someone who could satiate her hunger in the best possible way. He felt sorry for her. Then, he realized what he had done: He had involved Laxman in it.

'Soorpanakha had been watching them since a few days. When Khara's spies told her about them, she could not resist taking a look at both of them. No one was sure who had killed Jambumali, but his place of meditation was not very far from Laxman's hut. Soorpanakha, in a fit of rage, had gone to kill the princes. But the moment she had seen them, she had forgotten about her son's murderers.

'That night, she saw a male with a fair complexion, wearing nothing but a cloth covering his legs! His strong body, broad shoulders, long arms and narrow waist mesmerized her. But more than these, she liked his big eyes.

'She turned down Khara's proposal to attack the hermits. "It will be shameful to attack two lonely princes. Let me deal with them," she told Khara. However, Soorpanakha could not muster the courage to go to their hermitage and meet them together. Instead a voyeuristic urge forced her to follow their movements outside their hermitage. She waited all day, just to have a glimpse of them. Her desire was like an uncontrollable river, urging her to break all barriers. A mere look at those handsome princes fired a tornado of desire in her.

'Soorpanakha now knew that the male she had seen that night was the younger prince, Laxman. The elder one was Ram, who was with his wife Sita. She had not seen her yet. The big question was, getting to one or both of them. Soorpanakha's imagination ran wild and deep. Many a times, she looked at herself in the mirror and, each time she found herself lacking something. They were young and she was getting older. Soorpanakha summoned the best of her designers, dressers and make-up girls. But even their best efforts could not make her confident enough to face the young princes.

'Soorpanakha had followed Ram from his hut to the riverbank. She watched his bulging arms, his broad and shining chest, narrow waist and his sturdy long legs. It was a body moulded in the best fashion and was well-honed with years of hard work in the forest. What she liked most was the scant hair on his bare body. She watched him swimming in the river: He was very agile and fast. Soorpanakha could not take her eyes off, until she found him out of the water.

'But her worst fear came true and the elder prince refused her. "How dare he do that?" Her anger and irritation subsided a little when Ram indicated that Laxman was available. "Perhaps willing too," she optimistically thought.

'She was now waiting for the younger prince. Soorpanakha weighed her options. She would have approached the younger prince wherever he was, but she wanted to meet him in private. She had heard many stories about young Aryan men being shy in front of their elders. She decided to wait near those five banyan trees where Laxman used to sit every evening.

'After his encounter with Soorpanakha, Ram rushed to their hermitage. He told Sita and Laxman everything, and apologized for involving Laxman in it. Sita was scared. For the first time, someone had so nakedly desired her husband, and she sensed it as a bad omen for the coming days.

'"This is not a laughing matter, Ram. She is Ravana's sister. The slain Jambumali was her son. They have a huge garrison here and we don't have any soldiers with us. We should not forget that."

'Ram knew what she meant.

"'Ram, appeasement can never win evil. How long can we make a fool of her? Let us be ready to fight the Kalikeya army and deal sternly with this mad princess," Sita argued.

"'Ram, I cannot forget that I accidentally killed her son," Laxman added. "I have been unable to understand her. But, I am sure that she would not mind sacrificing her entire army to get you. The battle with the Rakshasas is now inevitable. There is no need to string her along any longer. It will vitiate the environment."

'Ram did not agree. "Laxman, the Rakshasas and the Daityas do not mind free copulation, but they don't force you to indulge and they respect your decision. When I refused, she just nodded and turned away."

"'No! It was not an explicit no. You left a window open. She has some hope of getting you through Laxman," Sita was very worried.

'Soorpanakha followed Laxman like an animal follows another in oestrus. She could feel his broad shoulders, mesomorphic back and legs, the swing of his hard, toned and muscular buttocks. She felt hot blood gushing through her body. When Laxman sat down to meditate at his chosen place, she approached him.

'Sitting in lotus position, Laxman looked like *Kamdeva* incarnate. His eyes were closed and his spine was erect. His big eyes, long and thin nose, proportionate features, broad forehead and matted long black hair gave him a puerile aura. He had coiled his matted locks on his head. Looking at his tranquil face for a few seconds, Soorpanakha lost her breath. Suddenly, she thought that he was even more attractive and handsome than Ram. She licked her lips and went closer.

'Laxman sensed movement very close to him and opened his eyes. He was not surprised to see her. He cautioned himself, "I should not get angry."

"'Charming prince!" her smile broadened and she quickly sat in front of him and introduced herself.

'Laxman asked a few questions about her clan and herself. Quickly, he realized that she was not interested in his questions. Her eyes were roving all over his body. He was filled with repugnance at the thought that a woman was trying to entice him for purely physical pleasure.

'"Laxman, I am a perfect match for your masculinity and handsomeness. You will not find a girl like me. You will be dearer to Ravana and my powerful relatives. Accept me and rule these forests."

'Laxman tried to simultaneously engage her while avoiding her physical advances, but nothing came to his mind. Soorpanakha observed his puzzled expression and mistook it for the natural inhibition of a young man.

'"My charming prince, lady luck is smiling on you. Come with me!" She moved forward and held his hands.

'Laxman gently removed his hands from her grip and, to the best of his diplomatic ability, tried to pacify her.

'"Princess, you deserve a better mate. A king can keep you happy, not a servant like me. I am just a servant to my master. I don't have the means and ability to keep you happy. You should speak to Ram and propose to him. He is wise enough to know your worth and may consider your request."

'"Ram says that he will not take a second wife," Soorpanakha was irritated.

'"A beautiful maiden like you can make him do anything."

'A puzzled Soorpanakha went back to Ram. Now she was fearless and decided to face Ram in his hut. As she walked, rage began to fill her head. Laxman discreetly followed her.

'Soorpanakha entered the hermitage. Laxman shadowed her, realizing that the farce had gone too far and was now threatening to become an ugly tragedy.

'Soorpanakha passed by the rooms and looked in the courtyard. On the left side of the courtyard, Ram and his wife were sitting on a bench and were laughing together. The moment she saw them laughing together, she lost her mind.

In a fit of rage, she shouted in anger and pain.

'"Ram, you ignored me for this ugly, thin and old woman! You dishonoured me. You did that because you prefer her to me. I will put an end to it. I will kill her!"

'Before they could understand what was happening, Soorpanakha took out a sharp dagger hidden beneath her clothes and rushed at Sita. A horrified Sita cried out. Laxman jumped between them, and before Soorpanakha could do any damage, he took out Jambumali's scimitar.

'The moment Soorpanakha took another step towards Sita, her son's scimitar defaced her. Her long nose was cut off and blood came gushing out. Sita was scared and ran into the inner rooms. Soorpanakha, with all her might, chased her. Laxman tried to pull her away. From the courtyard, Ram shouted, "Laxman, help Sita!"

'Laxman cut off Soorpanakha's ears with two sharp hacks of her son's scimitar. A scared and injured Soorpanakha ran outside. Laxman chased her with the bloody scimitar in his hand. She turned back and looked at him in horror and screamed. Soorpanakha, blood flowing from her nose and ears, ran away into the darkness and disappeared.'

'Aunt, everyone knows what happened after that,' Krishna said. 'Ravana did not like what happened to his sister and he decided to retaliate by abducting Sita.'

'And it all led to the annihilation of the Rakshasas. Soorpanakha's curse destroyed Ravana and his clan,' Kunti sighed.

~

'Krishna, in the Ramayana, we come across three different races, the Manavas, the Rakshasas and the Vanaras. You have told me about one Manava mother and one Rakshasa mother. Tell me about one Vanara mother.'

'Aunt, the most prominent among the Vanara women is Tara. She was a great woman and mother. She is considered one of the five greatest women of all time. Unlike Kaikeyee and Soorpanakha, she succeeded in protecting her son's interest.'

'Tell me about her, Krishna,' Kunti insisted.

'When Ram and Laxman were wandering from one forest to another in search of Sita, they met an old tribal woman called Shabari on the bank of Lake Pampa. She advised them to meet Sugreeva.

'"Who is he?" Ram asked.

'"Ram, he and Bali are the sons of the famous Vanara king Rikshyaraja," Shabari told Ram. "His kingdom was called Keesh-Kondha. Keesh is the aboriginal tribe living in that area. Kondha or Konda is the word for a hill in their language. The river flowing nearby is Keesh-Na, the river of the Keesh. The Vanaras are a powerful race. They are fiercely loyal to their leader."

'Shabari saw Laxman's expression and quickly explained, "Laxman, don't mistake this with slavery. This loyalty is related to a deeper sentiment, towards a pious duty and sacredness. The Vanaras respect bravery."

'Shabari told them the story of two feuding Vanara brothers.

'Once, king Rikshyaraja went out hunting. On that hot summer afternoon, he felt thirsty after walking for miles in a dense forest. After a fatiguing search, he found a pond. In the clear water of the pond, the Vanara saw his own image and mistook it for an equally powerful enemy. He jumped into the pond to fight with him, but there was none. A disappointed Rikshyaraja came out of the pond and quenched his thirst.

'When he was drinking water from the pond, he again looked at his image. To his utter surprise, he found that he had transformed into a beautiful maiden. The moment he realized this, he also lost all his past memories! When this beautiful maiden Rikshyaraja was walking through the woods, Indra saw her. Her beauty charmed Indra so much that he descended on earth and became her lover. Once, the semen of

Indra fell on her hair. The boy born out of that relationship became famous as Bali.

'After a couple of years, when the young lady Rikshyaraja came out of the woods, Surya saw her. Captivated by her charm, Surya also fell in love with her. His semen fell on her beautiful neck, and thus was born the younger brother Sugreeva.

'From his early childhood, Bali was an aggressive, confident and powerful youth. He enjoyed royal games like hunting and duels. A meek and sagacious Sugreeva was his ardent follower. He was more interested in philosophy and academics. For Bali, the end always justified the means. Sugreeva was not so sure about that. In fact, he was always intimidated by the powerful personality of his elder brother.

'Bali loved his meek and obedient brother Sugreeva. After the death of their father, when Bali became king, he appointed Sugreeva as his heir apparent. Sugreeva had the rights and authority of a crown prince, but, in important matters, Bali always ensured his supremacy. Sugreeva never complained. He was not very ambitious. If Bali enjoyed the luxuries of the kingdom, Sugreeva was the hard-working royal.

'When the Daitya noble Maya got her daughter Mandodari married to Ravana, Maya's two sons also joined Ravana's court. Their names were Dundubhi and Mayavi. However, Ravana quickly found out that both the brothers were difficult to handle. Both were conspirators of the first order and were very mischievous. A number of complaints piled up against them and Ravana decided to throw both the brothers out of Lanka.

'Ravana very wisely convinced Mandodari of the need for a separate Daitya kingdom for Dundubhi and Mayavi. For a long time, he had cherished the dream of controlling the western coast. It was very important for marine trade, but the dominant and notorious Vanara tribe was the biggest hindrance there. Ravana had earlier tried to make peace with them, but soon learnt that he could not make them docile.'

'Impossible! Ravana could not defeat the Vanaras!' Kunti was surprised.

'Yes. In fact, in a duel between the two hulks, Bali defeated Ravana. That caused a lot of embarrassment to the Rakshasas. Ravana did not try a prolonged military campaign against the Vanaras because he knew that wiping them out was no solution, as no Rakshasa was ready to work in the harsh living conditions of the Rishyamuka mountain range.

'Therefore, a shrewd Ravana convinced his wife Mandodari to make Dundubhi the provincial head of the entire west coast. Dundubhi was like a raging bull, always ready to fight. He also had a strong sense of pride in his physical power and used to boast a lot about it. He immediately liked the rugged terrain of the Rishyamuka and settled there with a few hundred Rakshasas.

'He was wise enough not to get into a direct fight with Bali early on. An arrogant Bali was also not bothered about the presence of a handful of Rakshasas in the neighbourhood. In the beginning, Dundubhi focused on getting his men settled near the coast and on developing a working port. But, very soon, he became frustrated with the attitude of the local tribes. For the Shabaras and the Vanaras, sea business was a stupid idea. Thus, a failed Dundubhi was compelled to poach Bali's kingdom.

'The most influential sage of the area, Matanga, was aware of this danger brewing in his neighbourhood. Initially, he tried to remain aloof from it and advised the local Shabara tribes accordingly. But when the Rakshasas adopted criminal ways and attacked the Shabara homes and abducted their women and children, a pained Matanga approached Bali for help. But, Bali had always been suspicious of the sage's preaching and his influence on the local tribes, including the Vanaras. Bali not only rejected Matanga's request, but also rebuked him. The angry sage returned to his ashram. Realizing that a corrupt and powerful king would never protect them, he began imparting lessons in archery and taught the art of poison-making to the native Shabaras.

'The tribal Shabaras were very fit and agile folk. Living on trees, climbing mountains and running on difficult terrain were natural to them. They quickly adapted to the bow and arrow and were ready to revolt against Bali.

'Very soon, tribal poisonous arrows killed many intruding criminals. Sage Matanga built sentry posts at strategic locations in the Rishyamuka range and deployed the Shabara sentries. The Rakshasa spirits were made morbid by the Shabara guerrilla tactics, when Matanga's formidable archers forced Dundubhi's Rakshasas to flinch away. Then they had no option left but to plunder Vanara territory.

'Initially, Bali avoided the advances of Dundubhi, partly because he knew that Dundubhi was a close relative of Ravana and also because Dundubhi's earlier victims had been poor Vanaras. These underprivileged people belonged to a different tribe of the Vanaras, who assume a totem of the lion-tailed macaque and called themselves the Rikshas.

'These poor tribes, terrorized by Dundubhi, soon began flocking the streets of Bali's capital Kishkindha. Bali was already unpopular among the poor. But no one dared to raise a voice against Bali and his cruel army.

'When Kishkindha's streets were flooded with refugees, criminal activities in the capital became rampant. Bali's royal court became a place of complaints and intense debate. Instead of punishing Dundubhi, who was the root cause of the problem, Bali started imprisoning and killing the refugees. When it did not reduce the refugee inflow and he failed to reduce the anarchy and chaos on the streets of his capital, an incensed Bali sent his henchmen to torment the villages of the refugees. Bali's henchmen killed many village leaders. Somehow, their leader Jambavanta could save his life. In frustration, Bali's henchmen torched village after village. This made sage Matanga furious.

'The anarchy in the kingdom fuelled criminality and it made Dundubhi stronger, as all sorts of criminals joined him. He had started abducting rich Vanara traders. He used to extract huge ransoms in lieu of their release. Devastated rural folks refused to help the royal forces in capturing Dundubhi or his men. Very soon, the traders began avoiding Kishkindha.

'Bali woke up only when Dundubhi abducted Samudra, a powerful chief of Kishkindha's guild of traders. This forced Bali to go himself to punish Dundubhi. Bali attacked Dundubhi's citadel with all his might. A huge army of Vanaras attacked the villages surrounding Dundubhi's fort. That fort was in Rishyamuka and very close to Matanga forest. Hearing the attack of Bali, Dundubhi ran away in trepidation and hid himself in the forest. When Bali could not find Dundubhi, he went on a rampage. He ordered his forces to kill all the villagers sympathetic to Dundubhi, and his forces torched as many villages as they could and slaughtered men, women and children mercilessly.

'This barbarism enraged the sage. He ordered his guerrilla force to launch an attack on Bali's forces. Meanwhile, Bali had found Dundubhi hiding on a peak of the Rishyamuka range. Sensing no escape, Dundubhi challenged Bali to a duel, which an arrogant Bali could not refuse. A rough duel started between the two heavyweights, matched in power, skill and cunning. In the end, Bali broke Dundubhi's head with his powerful hands and killed him.

'While Bali was searching for Dundubhi, the Shabara guerillas with their sharp and poisonous arrows were killing Bali's soldiers. Under Matanga's leadership, they pushed out Bali's army from Rishyamuka. When the guerrillas reached Bali, he had just killed Dundubhi in that fierce duel. Hundreds of Bali's men also witnessed their king fighting with the Daitya. They were rejoicing in the victory of their mighty lord when invisible Shabara archers attacked viciously.

'An injured and frightened Bali got the shock of his life. He was standing on the peak of the mountain and there were deep gorges all around. He could not see the enemy, but felt the showers of their lethal arrows. He had not seen such a torrential rain of poisonous arrows before. His soldiers were dropping like flies. There was no place to run. Standing on the hilltop and looking down at the deep chasms, death appeared imminent to Bali. Fear struck him hard and his head started reeling. Before falling down unconscious, he saw the dark lord of death about to stab him. After that, Bali developed hypsophobia and never went to Rishyamuka again.

'When Mayavi learnt about his brother Dundubhi's death, he vowed to avenge it.

'In disguise, he arrived at Bali's court and introduced himself as a Lankan trader. Bali welcomed him as a respected guest. Tall, dark and handsome Mayavi was the connoisseur of royal etiquette. He was charming enough to woo the rustic Bali. Mayavi's introductory gifts were intoxicating enough to impress the king. Young, supple and lithe dancers and musicians from different parts of the world charmed Bali like never before. An infinite number of intoxicating drinks, stimulating herbs and hallucinogenic drugs pleased and relaxed Bali.

'Bali never was an enthusiastic visitor to the royal court. He never liked long debates between the aldermen and the counsellors. These were the topics permanently delegated to Sugreeva. With the arrival of Mayavi, Bali's once in a blue moon sojourn in royal court also ended. The king was now keener to try out new drugs and new women, and Mayavi never disappointed him.

'Sugreeva was too meek to question his brother's conduct. But, when a major chunk of revenue went into the black hole of wine, women and drugs, Sugreeva was alarmed. Many public works programs were postponed and new plans were withdrawn. Payments to the army became irregular. Four senior ministers, Kesari, Tar, Mayand and Dwividha discussed the matter with

Sugreeva in private. Sugreeva did not know how to put it to Bali.

'When the situation was about to get out of hand, he decided to take the help of Tara, an intelligent and smart wife of Bali and the mother of a young boy, Angad. Quick-witted and virtuous, Tara had a sweet tongue. Tall and elegant, she had big mesmerizing eyes. Sugreeva often wondered about those eyes. They were sparklingly charming and so expressive that Sugreeva always thought that she hardly needed a voice. Her enigmatic smile would play a thousand games with Sugreeva's emotions. In response, he always found himself faltering in his expressions near her. On his part, Sugreeva never dared to step out of his *maryada*. Sugreeva always thought that his wife Ruma was inferior to Tara. Though Ruma was much younger and her slender features perhaps more lithe than Tara's, he never found that sparkling wit and the flash of a thousand stars in Ruma's eyes.

'Tara's father Sushena was a senior minister in Bali's court and she persuaded Bali to appoint her brother Tar as a senior commander in Bali's army. Tara's enthusiasm for life was a combination of her sharp brain and suave upbringing. Early in her adolescence, Tara fell for the manliness of a young Bali. When Sushena learnt about the romance between the two, he consented happily. The marriage had a positive impact on Bali temporarily.

'Tara's dominance in the royal palace was a sum of her grace, beauty and conduct. Despite that, Bali frequently indulged in sensual pleasures. Initially, Tara protested, but Bali was incorrigible. Tara compromised with her situation and utilised her time in rearing her son Angad and to look after the affairs of the state. But now, under Mayavi's spell, seeing Bali sinking into drugs, wine and women, Tara had become apprehensive of his health and well-being. Her son's future was at stake, as Sugreeva was the crown prince, not her son Angad.'

'That day, Sugreeva was nervous while meeting Tara. He looked again at the folder he was carrying. He hoped that he remembered all the facts explained by the ministers. He knew her, but his statements and apprehensions were very vulnerable to her sharp queries.

'Tara welcomed him as usual and sat very close to him. Sugreeva found himself unsettled. With trembling hands, he opened his folder and then looked at Tara. She was looking at him. Her glowing skin and sparkling eyes rattled the prince and sweat beaded on his nose. He dragged himself back to the present and pushed forward a paper.

"I know you are worried about the balance sheet," she said. "Sugreeva, sometimes I wonder what would have happened to this kingdom without you. You are the most faithful brother this world has ever seen."

'Sugreeva nodded and tried to focus on his job.

"Bali does not listen to me these days," Tara desired Sugreeva's support and Sugreeva nodded in sympathy. He knew why it was so: Mayavi's magic was ensnaring Bali. The latest reports about his conduct were very alarming. Many young Vanara girls were being abducted for the pleasure of the king and his friend, and now the intemperance of the king was knocking on the doors of the aristocratic Vanara families.

'The sadness in Tara's eyes troubled Sugreeva. For the first time, he felt as if he had something to offer her.

"I know about the evil influence of Mayavi on him. Let us both go to Bali and try to make him understand," he suggested.

"It's useless to advise him. I have tried a lot. Even Angad has begged him to change his way of life, but he never listens." She looked at Sugreeva in desperation. "Sugreeva, you have to do something to break Mayavi's spell over your brother."

"How can we do that?" Sugreeva felt weak. The mere thought of standing up to his brother made him feel frail. Since childhood, he remembered that Bali had always boasted,

"Sugreeva, I have a boon. Whosoever fights me in a duel, half of his power is transferred to me."

'Tara was extremely sharp and knew her ways. Bali's indulgence was demeaning her status as well. Angad was mature enough to understand his father's sins. She always feared that such indulgences would certainly be fatal for Bali and were detrimental to a young Angad's prospects. Tara wanted Bali to live longer and Angad to succeed to the throne in his father's lifetime. She feared that in case of Bali's premature demise, a consensus of the Vanara chiefs would favour Sugreeva over a young Angad. That was the reason why she got her father and brother promoted in the royal court. Sushena and Tar combined to make a formidable team with Tara, to take care of the interests of young Angad. Tara never hesitated to undermine whatsoever little authority Sugreeva had. But to tame Bali, she knew Sugreeva's help was required. Tara told him her idea. If Bali could be separated from Mayavi, it was in the best interest of Kishkindha. Sugreeva was also convinced. So, without wasting any time, he agreed to help Tara.

'The chief of the Kishkindha trader's guild, Samudra, was the wealthiest man in the kingdom. His harem was said to have the best collection of beautiful women from all over the world. He also had four wives and the youngest among them was considered to be the most beautiful woman in Kishkindha. Samudra had purchased her from Mayavi, who had brought her from a town in the Mediterranean. Her fair skin, ravishing looks and suave mannerisms made her the most desirable woman among the youths of Kishkindha.

'This woman was called Thalia. When she walked on the streets of Kishkindha, the Vanaras jostled each other to have a glimpse of her and to reach her. Stunningly exquisite, Thalia was the dream of every youth in Kishkindha. For Samudra, she was a prized possession. Despite being worldly-wise and a renowned miser, he never hesitated to spend his fortune to keep Thalia in a good humour.

'After that meeting between Sugreeva and Tara, things moved quickly. Tara began to take an interest in Samudra's ladies, especially Thalia. In the beginning, Samudra saw a proud queen's friendship with his wife apprehensively. Samudra was well aware of the age gap between them, as well as his wife's permissive attitude. But the queen's warmth and Thalia's enthusiastic response put him quickly at ease.

'Later, in a royal ceremony, Tara introduced Thalia to Bali. Bali could not take his eyes off her curves. Her tantalizing beauty and Mayavi's stimulating drugs made Bali restless. Mayavi also noticed Bali's condition.

'That night, Bali returned very late to his room. Tara knew that Thalia's magic had worked. Bali spent the night with Tara, as if she was Thalia. A heavily drugged and drunk Bali kept on uttering Thalia's name in his disturbed sleep.

'Next morning, Bali woke up with a heavy head. His choicest maids took him to the pool, but Bali's mind was stuck on Thalia. All the beauties walking nearby reminded him of Thalia. That day, he could not think of anything except Thalia.

'Later at night, he could not resist the temptation to ask Tara about Thalia. Tara then described what a scintillating beauty Thalia was. Bali requested Tara to invite Thalia to his palace, revealing his desire for her. Tara first showed her anger and annoyance, but later agreed to fulfil her husband's wishes.

'Thalia had heard a lot about Bali. He was the king and a friend of her mentor. Learning that the king likes her made her shiver with excitement. Bali was the ultimate prize in Kishkindha. She had often compared him to many of her past lovers including Mayavi, and secretly longed for the sovereign.

'Years ago, when she was captured by Mayavi's men and was forced to become a slave, she had thought about ending her life. But that thought changed the moment her eyes met Mayavi's. He was a magician and a short conversation with him floored Thalia. She decided to become a tool in the hands of the master craftsman.

'Mayavi was an accomplished artiste, well-travelled and experienced. His knowledge about different cultures was bewildering. Mayavi trained her in the various arts and etiquettes of the aristocrats. Mayavi sold her when they were passing Soorparak port. Then, she came to know why Mayavi had been training her so hard. A trained and beautiful slave fetched many gold coins in the market. Mayavi was indeed a shrewd investor.

'Samudra, a pot-bellied Vanara trader, purchased her. He was filthy rich, but old. Despite Samudra's blind spending on Thalia's comforts, she was not happy with him. Her youth was an ever-rising flood and Samudra's age was a weak embankment. Unlike the places she had lived in before, Kishkindha was very primitive.

'Her life changed again when one afternoon she saw Mayavi at Kishkindha. Samudra had invited Mayavi to a celebration at his house, and seeing him again triggered a volcano of emotions in her. She began looking for ways to meet her past lover and mentor. Mayavi too had sensed her state of mind and reciprocated enthusiastically. Soon, the two old lovers had their own secret rendezvous. Slowly, an emboldened Mayavi began visiting her residence at night. So far, they had hidden their meetings from the world.

'With a trembling heart, Thalia waited for Bali in his palace. Tara had arranged the meeting. Bali entered the room with his heavy footsteps and his companion stood outside the gate. She knew that it was Tara. Bali stopped near her. His torso was bare, barring a few gold chains studded with the costliest gems. He was a tall, sturdy and masculine man. She liked his body: His arms were long and she could feel those bulging muscles.

'After that day, Bali and Thalia met frequently. But, unknown to the design of the queen and Sugreeva, Thalia began to court both her lovers. One was an accomplished artiste and the other was a brute operator, and she liked both.

'During that period, Samudra had to leave on business.

This gave the lovers prolonged opportunities to spend time unabashedly. Bali and Mayavi both were oblivious to the secret of the other. One night, Bali could not sleep. He was restless. When huge gulps of wine and doses of drugs did not soothe his nerves, he rode to Thalia's house. There, to his utter dismay and shock, he saw Thalia and Mayavi together.

'Like a volcano, a furious Bali attacked Mayavi, but he somehow saved himself and ran away. In a fit of rage, Bali killed Thalia, but his wrath did not subside. Mayavi had disappeared like camphor. Bali launched an intense combing operation to find him. Then, one day, one of Bali's spies spotted Mayavi near Mount Durdura. Bali was a proud warrior. He vowed to punish Mayavi with death.

'Tara encouraged Bali to chase and kill Mayavi, "Bali, that son of Maya has brought infamy to you. As a devaputra and true warrior, you must slay him."

'"Tara, my love! Even if he hides behind God, I will kill him," Bali promised.

'With a mace in his hand, Bali marched towards Mount Durdura. Sugreeva accompanied him till they arrived near the escarpment, signalling the end of Kishkindha's limits.

'"Sugreeva, let me complete my task. You return to Kishkindha. Go and take care of our land and the family. If I don't return by the end of the year, then presume I am no more."

'Sugreeva offered to accompany him, but Bali steadfastly refused. A disoriented Sugreeva returned to Kishkindha. He deployed a platoon of soldiers at that escarpment with strict instructions to stay alert.

'Contrary to everyone's expectations, Bali did not return even after one year. This period was turbulent for Kishkindha. Influential ministers, led by Tar and Sushena, troubled Sugreeva. Both of them were very dominant and consistently conspired against him. Fortunately, some of the executives were well-meaning and wise. Therefore, routine administration did not suffer, but the palace politics became worse. Sugreeva became trapped between his intentions and the manoeuvres of his adversaries. The caucus of powerful counsellors was difficult to break. Most of them liked Bali, as he never delved into the affairs of the state. This had provided the counsellors enough freedom to pursue their selfish agenda. Now, they were reacting with variance to Sugreeva's scrutiny.

'Opposition from the counsellors and the ministers made Sugreeva's life miserable. His opponents often threatened his confidants of dire consequences after Bali's return. Tara continued to be an enigma to Sugreeva. She had always been warm to him personally, but on matters of state, she always behaved like an opposition and never offered an inch of space. In all royal functions, she was still the supreme authority. Tara used to mark this distinction in public only. Inside the palace, she was warm and affectionate to Sugreeva. Deciphering Tara's behaviour had become Sugreeva's biggest pursuit and the more he tried, the more it confounded him.

'Sugreeva was still hopeful of his brother's return, but he had started searching for comrades loyal to him. Both Bali and Dundubhi had earlier harassed the Riksha tribe. Sugreeva invited their leader Jambavanta to his court and honoured him. Jambavanta was an experienced campaigner and a wise old man. Soon, Sugreeva placed him in charge of various welfare schemes. This further alienated Tar and Sushena.

'Under such stressful conditions, Sugreeva passed the prescribed year. With each passing day, hope of Bali's return diminished. Yet Bali's terror was so overpowering that, often in his dreams, Sugreeva saw a bloodthirsty Bali drinking his blood. Sugreeva often used to walk alone on the path that went to Mount Durdura. Sitting near the escarpment, he imagined different scenarios in the rare event of Bali's return. The Durdura caves were full of beasts. No Vanara had ever gone there. It was a prohibited place, fit only for beasts and canines.

'"How can Bali, despite his unparalleled physical strength, endure Durdura?"

"'Bali is a slave to drugs and wine, how can he survive in these ravines, caves and chasms where no human lives?"

'Sugreeva's heart was finding solace in his conclusions. Finally, he decided: "I cannot surrender to this anarchy. I have to be bold and win over this phobia."

'After a long logical debate with himself, he became certain that Bali was no more. Very soon, Kishkindha's meeting points, streets, courts and the palace became centres of gossip, debating the need for a permanent king. There were different opinions about Bali's possible return and a powerful faction led by Sushena was optimistic about it, but Jambavanta and others believed that Bali was no more.

"'How long can we wait for Bali?" worried counsellors met to discuss the matter.

'Tara was worried. She could not decide what to do. Angad was young and Sugreeva was the crown prince. Bali had left the responsibility of the state with Sugreeva. Tara finally decided not to oppose Sugreeva in public, provided he declared Angad his crown prince. Sugreeva had no problem in doing so.

'Then, the unexpected happened. One day at dawn, Bali returned to Kishkindha. He kicked open Sugreeva's door. Before Sugreeva could see him, Bali hit him hard with his mace.

"'Scoundrel, get up you wily rogue!"

'A trembling and stumbling Sugreeva could not understand what had happened. Bali was not ready to listen to anything. A crowd was gathering outside Sugreeva's palace.

"'Treacherous villain, you are not fit to live. I left this kingdom, believing you to be my trouper. But you captured my kingdom and told everyone that I am dead! Lowly animal! And you thought, I would not come back!"

"'Bali, my brother! I am still a caretaker. You don't know how happy I am to see you back!' Sugreeva prayed with folded hands.

'Hearing that, Bali forcibly dragged Sugreeva out of his palace.

"'Cunning swine, yes, you are happy to see me back!" Bali laughed aloud and twirled his mace in the air.

"'Bali! My brother! It was you who had asked me to take care of the state. Now you are back, it is all yours."

"'You beggar! What do you think? Bali is naïve and a fool. Look around. Show me a single person among your loyalists who can stand here in your support!"

'Bali looked around with his merciless eyes. Not even one head was raised. Even Sugreeva found it hard to look at Bali. Seeing his enemy down and out, Bali thundered. "Sugreeva, punishment for treason and betrayal is death. I would have torn open your chest with my claws. But we were born to the same father, so I will give you a chance! Run Sugreeva, run for your life and save yourself, if you can."

'Sugreeva again tried to pacify him by attempting to hold his feet, but Bali thrashed him with a powerful stroke of the mace. Blood began to flow from Sugreeva's mouth.

"'Arrest this traitor!" Bali yelled.

'Sugreeva then realized that he was in grave danger. The royal bodyguards and the assembled crowd stood like statues. Sensing that, Bali took out his sword and leaped on Sugreeva, and he fled to save his life and took shelter in the Rishyamuka mountains.

'What followed was more tragic. Burning with rage and the desire for retaliation, Bali forced Sugreeva's wife Ruma to live in his harem and kept her there along with his other women. It was the gravest punishment he could have given to Sugreeva. That humiliation broke Sugreeva's honour and pride. Bali did not stop there. He sent his mercenaries to kill Sugreeva, but Hanuman and Jambavanta's intelligence and timely help saved him.

'Bali continued sending his band of killers to murder Sugreeva, but he was not successful. Slowly, Sugreeva developed a good network of informers to stay alive.'

'Shabari completed the story of the two feuding Vanara brothers and advised Ram, "Ram, make Sugreeva your friend. He will help you in Sita's search."

'Following Shabari's advice, Ram and Laxman proceeded to the Rishyamuka mountain where Sugreeva was hiding. When his spies saw Ram and Laxman wandering near the Rishyamuka, they were not sure if the two men were mercenaries sent by Bali. So, they sent Hanuman to verify the real identity of the two warriors.

'Hanuman quickly found out that the two armed men were the exiled princes of Ayodhya. Ram also liked the quick-witted and smart Hanuman and immediately offered his friendship.

'"Ram, Sugreeva will be very helpful to you. Make him your friend and help him."

'"I will do that gladly,' Ram smiled.

'At Rishyamuka, Sugreeva welcomed Ram. Hanuman formally introduced them. Sugreeva appeared to be a gentle and cultured man. Ram was calm and he assured Sugreeva of all help. Despite that, Sugreeva was not ready to believe in Ram's capabilities.

'After a long discussion with Jambavanta and Hanuman, Sugreeva came back to Ram and proposed, "Ram, I have not an iota of doubt in your abilities. In fact, I am honoured to have your support." Then he became quiet, not sure whether to speak or not.

'Ram comforted him, "Sugreeva, what is bothering you?"

'Sugreeva hesitated a bit and then said in a low voice, "Ram, Bali is a monster with unmatched physical power. You look ordinary in appearance. I am not convinced that you will be able to defeat him."

'"Friend, how can we dispel your apprehensions?"

'"Ram, I know that no one can defeat Bali in a duel. You are an archer par excellence. I wish to test the power of your shot." Sugreeva indicated some nearby trees. "Look at these seven huge *Tamala* trees standing in a line. They have been here since time immemorial. Their trunks are very thick. I request you to shoot at the trunk of one of the trees. If your shaft pierces the trunk of a tree, it will give me confidence that you can send an arrow through Bali's heart."

"'I will do so, if it helps you," Ram said with a smile. 'He positioned himself opposite the first tree. Then, he pulled his bowstring and its sound echoed across the mountains and valleys. Like lightening, that arrow not only pierced the trunk of the first tree, but it also pierced the remaining six trees and then returned to Ram's quiver.

'A stunned Sugreeva had never witnessed such an artistic and powerful display of archery. Amazed by Ram's skill, he felt scared and relieved simultaneously.

"'Ram, no one can match you in archery, but brute Bali is so powerful that he can move a mountain. I have a buffalo named after Dundubhi. Bali can lift it like a lamb. If you can do so, I will be assured that you can defeat him in a duel."

'Laxman was furious to hear this and demanded to see the buffalo at once. He looked at Ram and then said angrily, "What kind of a man is he? Does he not know your one arrow can kill him?"

"'Laxman, it's not him but Bali's terror speaking. We have to free Sugreeva from that trepidation."

'A giant black buffalo was brought before them. Before Sugreeva could even utter his request, Ram went and lifted the animal high over his shoulders. Then, in front of the bewildered eyes of the Vanaras, he propelled that huge buffalo many metres away into a gorge.

'Sugreeva and the others stood speechless for a while. Then, Ram put his hand on Sugreeva's shoulder and gently assured him, "Sugreeva, if you are convinced, we may consecrate our alliance and let the fire be our witness."

'Hanuman quickly arranged the holy fire. Both men took an oath of friendship and promised to help each other. Sugreeva promised to help Ram search for Sita and Ram vowed to make Sugreeva the king of Kishkindha.

'"King Sugreeva, believe that your bad days are over. Soon, you will be reunited with your wife and have your kingdom back. Have faith in yourself."

'The mere thought of confronting Bali unnerved Sugreeva. "Ram, I cannot stand before him. He will kill me. I urge you to challenge him in a duel and kill him."

'"Sugreeva, my friend! For your honour and pride, you must challenge Bali and defeat him. Only then will you win the admiration, confidence and loyalty of your people."

'Sugreeva said nothing but remained unmoved.

'"Sugreeva, trust me. My bow, *Kodanda* is invincible. It will protect you. Follow your dharma, go and fight."

'Sugreeva went to challenge Bali.

'"I don't like this man. He is timid and unsure of himself. How will he be helpful to us? Bali seems like a better choice between the two," Laxman was not impressed by Sugreeva.

'"Laxman, means are very important to me. I cannot take assistance from a wrongdoer," Ram explained.

'As things turned out, Sugreeva was no match for Bali. In no time, a bruised and injured Sugreeva returned to Ram. He was limping and blood was visible on his thighs and back.

'"Ram, what kind of a friend are you? Did I not tell you, he is not my brother but my death? He hurt, ridiculed and humiliated me. I request you again to go and kill Bali and prove your friendship."

'"Sugreeva, my friend! A will to fight and win is the most potent weapon of a warrior: You need to acquire it," Ram advised and then added, "I shall assist you in that pursuit."

'Ram spent many sessions with Sugreeva, coaching him about the nuances of a duel. This exercise was more mental than physical: Stories, history and philosophy, Ram left no stone unturned to motivate a beleaguered Sugreeva.

'"Sugreeva, believe in your strength and skill. Both Bali and you are equally strong. Nothing separates you two, except your self-created mental block. Bali dominates your consciousness so much that you cannot dare to stand before him. Once you realize that Bali is not invincible, you will win the combat. You ought to be always alert and conscious in a battle. A warrior must remain cognizant and vigilant in a fight."

'Ram encouraged Sugreeva, "Friend, reorganize yourself. Look at Bali's weaknesses. Observe him and look for chances to hit back. He is an overconfident warrior. If you fight consciously and remain focused, you will win."

'Sugreeva nodded. Ram wrapped his arm around his shoulder and assured Sugreeva, "Trust me, I will not allow Bali to kill you."

'After a couple of days, everyone observed a sea change in Sugreeva. A timid and clumsy Sugreeva transformed into a roaring hurricane. A distinguished gait, agility and grace became apparent in his demeanour. The ripples of this transformation began to reach Kishkindha.

'When, in a few days, Sugreeva challenged Bali again, Tara tried to counsel her husband. Bali's overconfidence worried her.

"Bali, think again. You defeated Sugreeva so effortlessly, yet he is banging at our door again and challenging you. Why? How does a timid rabbit, who never had the courage to come out of Rishyamuka, dare to challenge you not once but twice?"

'Bali smiled, but said nothing.

'"Bali, our spies say that Ram is invincible in battle. He killed fourteen thousand Kalikeya warriors alone in Janasthan. Pay heed to my advice and make truce with your brother. If you love me and have Angad's welfare in your mind, don't invite Ram's wrath."

'Bali smiled and reassured her, "Tara, why will Ram fight against me? There is no issue between us."

'"Bali, why don't you understand? Sugreeva has promised to help search for Sita. They have suffered the pain of having their wives abducted, and they understand and share each other's pain. What I heard about the princes makes me worried. Ram helping Sugreeva is bad news for us."

"'Tara, you have a chicken's heart. Let me defeat Sugreeva in a duel. Then Ram will understand who is worthy of friendship."

"'Bali, I am scared. Listen to my heart's voice. Please make peace with Sugreeva. Forgive him. He is your younger brother."

"'Peace with Sugreeva? Are you mad? Tara, how can I ignore a challenge from that faint-hearted Sugreeva? I have to punish my challenger. Ram may be brave, but how could he pass on his virtues to that coward?" Bali hugged his wife and assured her.

"'Bali, have you ever thought why Ram needs Sugreeva? He needs the Vanaras to help him win back his wife. In lieu of that, he is helping Sugreeva get his wife and throne back. Bali, please understand this. Make peace with Ram. Offer your help in finding Sita. It will augur well for all of us."

"'Tara, I am not against Ram or his friendship. But, let me first deal with Sugreeva. If I let go of his challenge and approach Ram for friendship, generations will taunt me as a coward. Tara, like a good wife, you have advised me. You have done your duty, now let me go and do mine."

'Realizing that Bali was not listening to her, Tara finally said, "Bali, have you ever thought what will happen to Angad and me, if something happens to you?"

'Bali smiled, but said nothing and left to face Sugreeva.

'Ram, Laxman and Hanuman were standing behind a dense row of trees when a roaring Bali arrived for his duel with Sugreeva. A fierce fight began. Each wanted to kill the other, and tried to find the other's weakness. For a brief period, Sugreeva defended himself well, but then he began feeling breathless. Bali had begun to hit him more frequently.

'However, the direction of the fight reversed soon. A noisy Sugreeva pulled down his heavier brother on the ground and sat on his chest. Bearing down on Bali with all his might, Sugreeva got a chance to lay his hands on his opponent's neck. He began strangling his elder brother. Bali was losing his grip and was about to faint when, in a desperate attempt, he threw Sugreeva off and freed himself. This chance was enough for an enraged Bali. Within seconds, Sugreeva was lying under him, struggling for life.

'Ram waited for a while. "Can Sugreeva show strength and courage again?"

'Sugreeva was still fighting bravely, but Bali was on top of him. Then suddenly, Ram saw that Bali was sitting on Sugreeva's chest and throttling him. There was hardly any time left to save Sugreeva. "He is about to die," Ram realized. "His life is in danger. I will take the entire blame on myself but never let my friend die."

'With an unbelievable swiftness, Ram took out a sharp arrow and shot it from his *Kodanda* bow. Like lightning, the arrow pierced Bali's broad back. In disbelief, Bali looked back and saw Ram coming out from behind the bushes.

'"This is not fair, Ram. Why did you snipe me?"

'"Bali, a person under the influence of lust loses all piety and fails to realize the exigencies of time and place, and also loses any sense of *artha*, *dharma* and *kama*. A younger brother's wife, the wife of the son, and sister, all these three are like your daughters. Therefore, killing a lecherous person who forcibly keeps his younger brother's wife is not a sin. Sugreeva was ready to return your kingdom to you, yet you made every effort to kill him. Bali, you were on adharma's side and about to kill my friend…"

'A dying Bali accepted the situation quickly. He nodded in agreement and prayed, "Ram, promise me that no harm will be caused to my son and my wife."

'Indicating Tara, Bali urged Sugreeva, "Sugreeva, this daughter of Sushena is proficient in politics and capable of solving any tricky and complex matter. Take her advice in important matters, you will never repent. Ram, my son should not pay for my sins. I am putting him under your tutelage. Please protect his interests."

'As Bali lay dead, a grief-stricken Tara requested Ram: "You are an ardent follower of dharma. I am an orphan and I don't have a future, except to join my slain husband in heaven. So, have pity on me and allow me to join my beloved Bali. This won't make you a sinner."

'"Queen Tara, shun such pessimism. This world is a creation of God and no one should violate His law. You will enjoy the fruits of life as you have been doing. Your son, Angad will be the crown prince. So leave this gloom and arrange for a befitting send off for brave Bali."

'Led by Laxman, the Vanaras kept Bali's body in a royal palanquin. Every clan and every family of the Vanaras was present on the last journey of the departed king. At a lonely place on the bank of a river, funeral logs were arranged. With the help of Sugreeva, Angad placed his father's dead body on the logs and, following their tradition, cremated his father.

'Tara thought hard about her future. Under Bali, she had all the rights and the authority of a queen, but now she was at the mercy of Sugreeva. During the mourning period, she became restless.

'"Ruma's return to Sugreeva as his wife is sure, but what about me?" Tara began to see herself more and more as a persona non grata in Sugreeva's palace. "Who am I, the mother of Sugreeva's enemy's son?"

'The mere thought of losing power made her shudder. Angad was still young and under the influence of Sugreeva.

'"Sugreeva can convince him to do anything, can even make him relinquish his right to the throne." The more she thought, the more nervous she became. She realized that, in fact, it was she who was about to lose everything.

'"What will happen to me if Sugreeva does not honour his commitment to make Angad the crown prince?" She tried to control her nerves. She was not one to go down without a fight. But, as long as those two princes were there, Sugreeva was unconquerable. Then, it dawned on her; she had been disregarding her charm and magic over Sugreeva in this battle. It gave her a possible way out.

"'If Bali can keep both Ruma and Tara, why cannot Sugreeva? Unlike Ruma, Tara herself will surrender before the new king. This will make it easier for a righteous Sugreeva." With that thought, her plan got wings and her dreams appeared possible. What she needed was resolute support from her father and brother. About Sugreeva, she was confident of her magic.

"'But Ram?" She remembered what Ram had promised to a dying Bali. "He is dharma incarnate and he has promised Bali to protect our interests." Tara tried to decipher Ram's assurance and gave a serious thought to marriage with Sugreeva.

"'It will protect my son's interests, and also mine. It has the sanction of our tradition as well." But the question remained: "Will Sugreeva honour our custom of marrying the widow of his elder brother? Following tradition is not lust. More so, I am ready to be his wife."

'She decided to consult her brother Tar and father Sushena.

"'Tara, Ram has promised to make Angad our crown prince. He will do everything to keep his word. I don't see any reason for you to worry. Let me talk to Sugreeva about your marriage," Sushena was convinced and Tar was also in agreement.

'Without wasting any time, Sushena approached Sugreeva. As expected, Sugreeva expressed no objection to Tara's proposal, but was apprehensive about what Ram would think. Sushena approached Ram to clear Sugreeva's doubts.

"'Ram, do you think society's age-long traditions should be followed and protected by the king?"

"'Yes, of course," Ram was forthright as usual. "If traditions don't harm people's right to life and don't restrict their spiritual growth and preserve social cohesion, why not?"

"'I am sorry to report this, Ram, but, queen Tara is worried. King Sugreeva is scared of your rebuke. He thinks that you won't approve of his marriage with his brother's widow. He is hesitating to marry Tara. She feels that he is doing this merely to appease you. Perhaps in your culture it is not legitimate. His predicament defies our age-old tradition."

'"Sushena, King Sugreeva is not here. Therefore, I would not like to express any opinion in favour or against him. If a widow agrees to remarry, I welcome that. It will make the widow's life better, provided both of them agree. If both Tara and Sugreeva want to marry each other, why should I have any objection?"

'Tara was absolutely right about Sugreeva. After receiving Ram's consent, he immediately agreed to marry Tara. Once the prescribed mourning period was over, Sushena quickly arranged for their marriage. Ram politely declined the invitation to attend their marriage and also Sugreeva's request to live in a lavish palace at Kishkindha.

'"I cannot disobey my father's command. Friend, enjoy your good times but don't forget your duties."

'Sugreeva's ascension coincided with the first shower of monsoon. Ram gave Sugreeva four months to prepare for the expedition.

'Sugreeva indulged in sensual pleasures. His time was mostly spent with the choicest of wines and women. Ram's protection and friendship had made him free from enemies, both internal and external. His long ordeal in the forests had fired his lust. Tara's attraction triggered his passion for uninhibited and lustful sports. She was a connoisseur in all womanly arts. Supremely confident, she knew no one who could resist her attraction. After finding Sugreeva at her feet, she felt triumphant. Bali or Sugreeva, it was immaterial, the true authority of Kishkindha remained queen Tara.

'When monsoon arrived in Kishkindha, Ram shifted his base to Pravarshan hill. Pravarshan was one of the greenest hills in the western range. Ram spent four months like forty years, immersed in Sita's thoughts.

'Finally, the four painful months of monsoon got over. On the western hill, the huge fort of Kishkindha could be seen shining brightly. Some activities were visible near the checkposts and

Ram could spot a figure or two patrolling, but the big northern gate of the fort was still closed. Ram wondered when the gate would open and Sugreeva would come out.

'Neither Sugreeva nor any of his messengers came out. The northern gate remained closed. No caravan left the fort. The southern pathway was still deserted. The sentries at the checkposts and the guards on the fort beats remained busy doing their chores.

'Laxman had never been impressed by Sugreeva. With each passing day, Ram also started wondering about Sugreeva's commitment.

'"Laxman, threat to life is the surest tool to wake up the spirits of the meek. Sugreeva's memory loss demands a harsh reminder. Take your bow and arrow and remind him of his vow. Convey my message to him that the path on which Bali was sent is still open."

'The sentries at the northern gate opened the doors for Laxman. Looking at an angry Laxman, no one dared to ask him anything. A couple of sentries walked ahead to guide him to the royal palace. News spread like wildfire. A curious crowd of Vanaras gathered on both sides of the street. Hearing this, Angad ran to his uncle's chamber.

'The wine and women from the previous night still had some effect on Sugreeva the next morning. When Angad informed him about a furious Laxman, it took him a while to decipher his meaning. The moment he realized it, all his energy left him. With trembling hands, he held Tara's arm. Tara looked questioningly at her son and husband. With fearful eyes, a terrified Sugreeva requested Tara to manage the crisis.

'The huge gates of the palace were flung open for Laxman. Once inside, two maidens led him to the inner court. On the way, Tara obstructed his path. Laxman stopped and looked at her sternly.

'"Where is Sugreeva?" he demanded.

'She remained unmoved. Laxman did not know how to deal with a queen like her.

'He became angrier, "Please give way."

'She smiled, as if testing his patience. Laxman was puzzled. Tara teased Laxman in a seductive tone. "Young prince, why did you not inform us about your arrival? We would have at least arranged a proper welcome for our liberator."

'"I need to meet the king, urgently," Laxman did not like the way she addressed him.

'"The king has just woken up and is taking a bath. I will give you company till he gets ready.'

'Laxman refused, "I will wait here."

'Immediately, the servants arranged chairs and a table. A variety of drinks and food were served in no time and Tara almost forcefully made Laxman sit on a chair.

'"I apologize, if knowingly or unknowingly we have committed a mistake."

'"Call that selfish and insensible king. He has dishonoured his commitment."

'"I apologize on his behalf. Trust me, he has not forgotten his duties…"

'"Please ask him to see me at once," Laxman was not satisfied.

'Tara sensed his mood well and requested, "Laxman, you are young and single. You are unaccustomed to the pleasure of marital life and the company of beautiful women. You are accustomed to hardship. Therefore, it is difficult for you to understand all this. Accustomed to the luxuries of the palace, king Sugreeva was forced to live in the forests under constant threat to his life. Can you imagine his plight? Now he has got the palace back. Is it not normal for him to satiate his tired limbs and thirsty soul?"

'Laxman was still agitated. Tara tried to pacify him. "Laxman, trust me. The king has not forgotten his promise. It is just a lapse on his part that he woke up a little late…"

'"A little late?" Laxman was angry. "What has he been doing

after getting back the throne, except indulging in wine and women? What kind of conduct is this? Ram has been very patient and Sugreeva is taking undue benefit of that."

"'Prince, believe us. The king's devotion to Ram is absolute. Our entire army is at your disposal. We are just waiting for your command."

'That softened Laxman slightly. Tara's argument assuaged him though he was not sure that whatever she had said was completely true.

"'Queen, he has not tried to approach us even after the rains!"

"'Laxman, this is not entirely Sugreeva's fault. We, the ladies of the palace, wanted him to be with us as much as possible, before he goes to war. Now he has had his fair share of well-deserved rest; I am sure he will march off with an unwavering focus."

'At that moment, Sugreeva appeared along with Hanuman. The moment their eyes met, Sugreeva fell at Laxman's feet.

"'Forgive me, Laxman! I had become a slave to my senses. Whatever punishment Ram decides, I will accept that."

'Sugreeva's apology pacified Laxman. "Sugreeva, know this, that Ram can decimate your empire in a moment. If you think he is dependent on you and begging for your help, you are wrong. You are lucky that despite your laxity, he still has not shown you his anger. If you have any sense and shame left, then go to Ram and seek pardon."

'Sugreeva quickly summoned all his chiefs and asked them to summon the Vanaras. He addressed them with a lot of passion and a focused purpose. He motivated them by invoking valour, courage and the rich tradition of loyalty; he threatened them with severe punishment on failure. Later, Hanuman and Laxman, along with Sugreeva and Jambavanta, chose members for the search teams.

'Each team was given twenty-five members. Once the announcement was made, Tara along with Angad, went to see Ram.

"'Ram, you are the guardian of my son. I put him under your guardianship, like Sumitra did for Laxman. Trust me, Ram. My son is worth his salt and he will serve you like Hanuman."

'Ram smiled and blessed Angad and he also volunteered to join the search and requested Ram to give him an opportunity.

"'Lord, everyone thinks that I am good for nothing. Be kind and give me an opportunity to prove myself. I am ready to serve in any team, under any leader."

"'Dear Angad, you are as dear to me as Laxman. Don't ever think that we do not hold you in high esteem. You are a worthy son of a brave father. But, you are the crown prince of Kishkindha, how can I risk your safety?"

"'Lord, if it is so, I am ready to relinquish my title. Please give me a chance," Angad pleaded.

'Ram looked at Tara, who quickly nodded in agreement.

"'Ram, be his guru. From this moment, you are his mother, his father and his guru as well."

'Ram affectionately patted Angad on his back. "Brave prince, you should join Jambavanta's team, that will go to the south in search of Sita. He has the best team. Your participation will make the team even better.'

5

Sacrifice

'Krishna, motherhood is divine. People say that a son may be a bad son but no mother can be a bad mother. However, none of these stories could comfort my burning heart. Are there women whose ideals one can follow and find peace?' Kunti asked.

'Aunt, no story, no emulation can provide you solace: It comes from within. If you are at peace with the outside world, as well as the world inside you, you are living in bliss. This means that we should neither have unrealistic expectations from others nor from ourselves. Who are we in this big scheme of the universe, aunt? Nothing and no one. If we know this and act accordingly, offering the fruits of our karma to Him, welcoming whatever comes from Him, then we would be the happiest. There is only one act that gives permanent peace: The act of "giving", or "sacrifice".'

Krishna smiled and then continued, 'All these stories took place in different eras, when people lived under different conditions. Therefore, their acts, their ideals and their beliefs should not be weighed according to the standards of today. But the three stories that I am about to tell you are the stories of sacrifice. These mothers earned reverence through sacrifice.'

'Aunt, tomorrow sceptics may ask why a soldier goes to the battlefield. Why should we glorify the martyrdom of a soldier? Today, we see it as an act of selfless valour, showing loyalty to the motherland or your king. Therefore, I urge you to listen to these stories with compassion. Please also consider that the highest human virtue is to sacrifice self-interest for the welfare of others. This "giving with love" gives permanent peace. Actually, motherhood is all about giving and that is why it is so special.'

'Krishna, sages say that to be free from the clutches of sorrow, men should abandon bonds. I understand what they are saying, but it's so difficult to follow. But, perhaps in the role of a mother, a woman attains that state,' Kunti said.

'So, which are the three stories you will be telling me now?' Kunti asked.

'First, the story of Sita; then the story of my mother Devaki, and then again the story of my mother Yashoda.'

'Your own mothers?' Kunti laughed.

'Aunt, for every child, their mother is the greatest. I am no exception.' Krishna smiled.

'Let us begin with Sita.'

~

'Taking a dip in the sacred River Sarayu was the first thing in king Ram's daily routine. This dawn was no different. After the bath, Ram offered prayers to his ancestors. Then he asked the charioteer to take him to the palace. When his chariot was about to reach the palace garden, he heard a recital of his own paean in sweet melodious voices. The singing was masterly, and metered to perfection, as prescribed in the *Sama Veda*. Ram could not remain seated in the chariot. Slowly, he walked closer to the two singers.

'Two adolescent boys, with a *veena* on their lap, were sitting under a *peepal* tree, unaware of the world and lost in their music. Their rhythm, voice and modulation were extraordinarily pleasing. Quick, medium and delayed, all three frequencies were used, and their rhythmic voices, perfectly nuanced in seven tones, merged soulfully with the tune of their *veena*. Spellbound, Ram lost sense of time.

For a long time, he stood there floating on the magical musical waves woven by the two boys. He regained his composure when the boys stopped singing.

'"I would like to enjoy their music in the royal court. Call all the sages, learned men, musicians, singers, teachers, poets, writers, astrologers, mathematicians, masters of grammar and words, painters, dancers, gurus of science and philosophy. Call all those men and women who are interested in music and words. Let the world know about this great poem and this masterly music," Ram summoned his minister and instructed him.

'The next day, in a huge public hall inside the royal palace, when everyone assembled, Ram called the two boys. With great affection, he made them sit close to him. The boys looked pleasantly innocent. With smartly-tied hair, saffron robes and floral wristbands, their faces radiated confidence. There was something soothing about those lovely faces: A look at them had a calming and relaxing impact on the mind and the soul.

'The moment the boys started the *aalaap* together, sweet melody filled the air. Their voices were delightfully pleasant. The enchanted listeners merged their souls into the music. Despite hearing them for hours, no one was satiated. The entire assembly and the king himself could not take their eyes and ears off the boys. Their fixed gazes were drinking in the nectar of the innocent yet celestial exquisiteness of the boys' art.

'A few in the assembly murmured, "Look, how they resemble our king."

'"Except the tuft on their head and their saffron attire, there is hardly any difference," someone else agreed.

'Like everyone else privy to that musical fiesta, Laxman was also mesmerized by their talent. Their uncanny resemblance to Ram also puzzled him. He had lived all his life with Ram as his shadow. Their mannerisms reminded him of a young Ram in Vishwamitra's Siddhashrama. They appeared so similar to a teenaged Ram: Intense positivity, graceful movement of limbs, confidence in appearance and action, face glowing with the strength of purity, and focused commitment to mission, they indeed were the king's youthful incarnation.

'Lost in his thoughts, perhaps for the first time in his life, Laxman failed to hear Ram's call. By the time he turned his head to respond to his elder brother's call, Ram was already addressing Bharat.

'"Kaakustha, award these two young talents with eighteen thousand gold coins each. If they desire anything else, that should also be provided to them." When Bharat went forward to award them, the pair humbly refused to accept the gold.

'"Prince Bharat, we don't need gold. We are forest dwellers and get enough for our sustenance there. What will we do with your gold?"

'"Then accept it for your parents," Bharat insisted.

'The boys politely refused, "Prince, our mother never accepts gifts."

'"Then take it for your guru," Bharat offered.

'"He will not take it either," they replied.

'Who were these two young ascetics? The assembly became curious.

'"Who is your guru?" Vashishtha asked in a sweet tone.

'"Brahmarishi, we are sage Valmiki's pupils."

'"I see," Vashishtha said. He closed his eyes for a few moments, as if trying to join a few dots. "Is he accompanying you?" he asked.

'"No. He lives on the bank of River Tamasa. Nowadays he is creating the sixth and the concluding part of a poem."

'"How long is the entire poem?"

'"Its five parts contain 24,000 verses in 500 chapters."

'Ram's youngest brother Shatrughna looked at the boys and then at Ram. "They are his son," he thought, remembering a night when he was in Valmiki's school, but kept mum.

'Ram was about to say something, when the younger boy requested, "If you liked the initial part, we can sing the complete poem for you."

'"Wonderful. I would love to," Ram immediately agreed. "Let's arrange for that."

'That night, Ram could not sleep. His heart knew who the two boys were, but he did not dare to ask. Those two dreadful days kept coming back to haunt him.

'"Creation has strange ways of bringing back past karmas to us. We may forget our past deeds, but she brings the consequences back to complete the karmic cycle," Ram kept tossing and turning in his bed.

'Fourteen years ago, Laxman had accompanied a pregnant Sita in a royal chariot to the faraway dense woods on a second exile—she had been completely ignorant about her banishment—and now these two young boys appeared in his court, resembling him so much. Ram's body was wet with sweat.

'"I am certain these are Sita's boys." The thought thrilled Ram but the very next moment it scared him. "Where is Sita? Is she alive?"'

~

'After Ram's coronation, he and Sita had spent many months of marital bliss in Ayodhya. As a result, Sita became pregnant.

'One afternoon, Sita broke the good news to her husband. In those intimate moments, Ram lovingly looked at her slightly swollen face and limbs, radiating with a motherly glow. Watching her pink face closely, he cupped her cheeks in his palms, and gladly said, "Wonderful, beautiful...." For a long time, his big adoring eyes lovingly admired his wife's beauty.

'"Sita, you have given me the greatest joy of my life." He kissed her forehead and said in the most affectionate voice, "Only a mother can salvage the souls of her husband's forefathers. Sita, you have released me from my *pitra rina*."

'He paused for a while, "Sita, tell me what you desire. Tell me, what is in your heart? I will fulfil whatever you ask for."

'Back in the present, after fourteen years, this memory hurt him like hellfire. His own boast resonated in his ears. History was repeating itself in the cursed Raghuvamsa.

'Many decades ago, in his moment of weakness, his old

father had asked his young bride Kaikeyee the same question. Kaikeyee's wish not only caused Dasaratha's death, but also exiled Ram, Sita and Laxman for fourteen years. The curse had separated Kaikeyee from Bharat, her only son.

'Unknowingly and unintentionally, asking Sita to desire something had led to similar consequences. If a chaste Ram did not have any degree of Dasaratha's lecherousness, Sita did not have any degree of Kaikeyee's guile and wickedness. Kaikeyee was ready to wreak havoc in her home for the sake of her ambitions, but Sita was so different.

'Ram's soul revolted. The facade of the ideal king suddenly melted in the angst of his heart.

'"All your life, you have released your frustration and stress on an innocent Sita and a loyal Laxman. And in less than a year, merely on some hearsay, you threw Sita out of Ayodhya again."

'That evening, fourteen years ago, when Ram had asked Sita to wish for anything, a pleased Vaidehi replied, "Ram, I wish to spend a few days on the bank of River Ganga where pious, learned and pure-hearted wise sages live. Old people say that a calm ambience, wise and soothing words, and being close to the nature are good for a baby in the womb."

'Ram was listening gladly and nodding in agreement.

'"Ram, I would like to give birth to the baby here, with you around me. But before that I wish to spend some time on the bank of River Ganga. So, arrange for my travel as early as possible; maybe tomorrow."

'Ram vowed to fulfil his beloved wife's desire, "So be it. Sita, I would have loved to accompany you. But as you know, we are preparing for a war against Lavanasura. Laxman will take you there tomorrow morning."

'Later in the evening, Ram met his group of ten spies to learn about the affairs of the state. Vijay, Madhumatta, Kashyapa, Mangal, Kul, Suraji, Kaliya, Bhadra, Dantvakra and Sumagadh were his trusted spies. Even Laxman was not included in these closed-door meetings.

'It was a business-like meeting. Ram's favourite spy Bhadra began the reporting.

'"Ram, people are happy. They praise you. They say you built the bridge over the vast sea, a feat unimaginable even for the gods and the demons. In public, they praise you for killing Ravana, the tormentor of the three worlds. But in private, they grudge that after killing Ravana, you accepted Sita back without question. Rudely they wonder how you could be at ease while making love to Sita. Ravana squeezed Sita in his arms when he abducted her; he took her to Lanka and kept her there for a year. Devoid of sexual morals, those immoral Rakshasas always surrounded her. Why, after knowing so much, does Ram love Sita?"

'"Ram," Bhadra continued, "they say: now we have to suffer likewise from our ladies, because people always follow the king."

'Bhadra's report agitated Ram deeply. He could not speak for many moments. Then he asked his other spies, "Please tell me, if you also have heard similar talk?"

'The majority of them supported what Bhadra had just said.

'That night, Ram did not go to Sita's palace. He called his brothers for a talk. The three brothers Laxman, Bharat and Shatrughna entered Ram's meeting chamber on receiving the command. For the first time in his life, Ram's face was devoid of glory. He was immersed in his thoughts. In a heavy voice, he told them what had happened.

'"Brothers, you three are my lifelines. I rule this land because of your support. You know the art of administration, you respect the morals and you also know your dharma. We are mature and trust each other. Therefore, I have shared this bad news with you." With firmness in his voice he continued, "Now, what I am proposing is to be accomplished together by all of us."

'The three younger brothers looked anxious and uneasy. For Bharat and Shatrughna, that was an unknown Ram. A worried, graceless and unsure Ram was unnerving them.

"'I know it is false," Ram said, "but there is a lot of evil and debauched propaganda going on, blemishing Sita's character and casting aspersions on my conduct."

"'Ram…" Laxman tried to intervene.

"'Laxman, first listen to me. You know everything about our exile and fight with Ravana. You also witnessed how Sita proved her innocence in that trial by fire. She came out unscathed from the burning logs. In front of all the assembled Rakshasas, Vanaras, and sages, Agni, Vayu, the moon and the sun declared her unblemished. Even the core of my heart knows she is chaste. My faith in her never diminished, never. Now, similar gossip about her stay in Lanka has resurfaced. I see a political design behind this propaganda. People are condemning my conduct and making Sita a scapegoat. I am distraught and want a solution."

'He paused and then looked at Bharat, "Bharat, you know this more than us. If denouncement and smear become public, the person falls into the worst hell; and he remains there till such stain is removed forever."

'Looking at Laxman, Ram said, "Laxman, try to understand. Why do we do so hard work throughout our life? Just to establish our reputation and illustriousness, why else?"

"'Ram, giving importance to the hearsay of some unknown, irresponsible and perhaps frustrated men is foolishness. And, as you said, if the motive is political, let us deal with it politically. Casting aspersions and devising a quantum of punishment for an innocent queen is an unpardonable sin."

'Ram thought hard. He knew that Sita was innocent. But the *maryada* of the crown was non-negotiable.

"'And if Sita stays and political power goes into unworthy hands ready to torment the people, then that would be the worst injustice to the people of Ayodhya."

'Finally, Ram decided.

"'Laxman," Ram said calmly. "To avoid public sacrilege, I can put an end to my life and even leave you. Discarding Sita is an option I am open to."

'For a few moments, no one spoke. Bharat and Shatrughna were looking at Ram and Laxman.

'"Laxman, tomorrow morning, you escort Sita out of the palace. A few miles after crossing River Ganga, on the bank of River Tamasa, you will find sage Valmiki's ashram. Take Sita to the dense forest near his ashram and leave her there. Tell her my command and return swiftly without wasting a moment."

'"Ram, this is injustice. How can you…?" Laxman got up from his seat.

'"Laxman, obey my orders. I don't want any further discussion about my decision." He paused, "You know it very well, Laxman. Any hesitation in compliance hurts me."

'"Ram, you are not being rational here. You cannot please everyone in your kingdom. Ram, you are a king. Suppose, if tomorrow, someone criticizes you, would you renounce your throne?"

'"Laxman! My brother, I bind you with the pledge of my honour and my life. Please don't oppose what I have decided."

'"Ram, I request you to reconsider your decision," Laxman pleaded with folded hands.

'"Don't utter a word now," Ram was upset. "Laxman, if you say so again, I will treat you as my enemy forever."

'A crushed Laxman sat down on the floor with his head in his hands. Ram went to him. Softly caressing Laxman's hair, he said, "If you love me, take Sita to the forest tomorrow at dawn."

'Ram paused for a while and moved to the window. Looking outside into the dark, he said, "Sita wants to see the ashram of the sages on the bank of River Ganga. Laxman, her wish must be fulfilled before the banishment."'

※

'That was fourteen years ago. Now, in Ayodhya for a few days, Ram and the residents enjoyed the music and singing of the two boys. Their Ramayana recital made people revisit the past and present of their king's life. Then it revealed to them that

Kusha, the elder and Luv, the younger one, were Sita's sons.

'Ram called his trusted minister Sumantra.

'"Go to sage Valmiki and give him my message. If Sita is of pure character and pious, if she is void of any sin, then after the sage's permission, she should come here and prove her innocence before the people of Ayodhya. You rush to his ashram and let me know her intentions. Let Janaki come to the royal court and uphold her virtue, remove my blemish and become the queen of Ayodhya again."

'When the minister conveyed Ram's message to Valmiki, the poet replied, "She will come to the court. Obeying her husband's call is the dharma of a married woman."

'Everyone in Ayodhya said that Sita would soon return to Ayodhya and undergo the virtue test. Ram invited all well-known sages in and around Ayodhya to witness Sita's ordeal.

'The invited sages came, praising the king. Following Valmiki, many worthy poets created new songs in the praise of their king's illustrious life. Sages, known or unknown, were present in Ram's court, eager to witness Sita's trial. Vasishtha, Vamdev, Jabali, Kashyapa, Deerghatama, Durvasa, Pulastya, Shakti, Bhargav, Vaman, Markandeya, Maudgalya, Garg, Chyavan, Shatananda, Bharadwaj, Suprabha, Narada, Parvat, Gautam, Katyayan, Suyagya and Agastya, all were present in Ram's court.

'Thousands of people, including the Vanaras, the Rakshasas, learned Brahmins, lionhearted Kshatriyas, rich Vaishyas, devoted Shudras, flocked to Ram's court. To witness Sita's tribulation, all kinds of seekers and experts in knowledge, action and yoga, the three branches of dharma, also arrived.

'A worried and apprehensive Laxman was in charge of the arrangements. His heart stopped beating when he saw Valmiki arriving in the court. A few paces behind him was Sita. Laxman looked at Sita's face. She was not the same beautiful girl, full of vitality, who he had first seen in king Janaka's garden and during her *swayamvara*. Standing here was a stone-faced Ahilya, beaten throughout her life by the brutal hands of man-made traditions, bigotry, ego, ethics and morals.

'Without his knowledge, his tears wetted Laxman's cheeks. He had been her best friend and companion for many years. Both had sacrificed their lives in service of a man and his ideals. "What have we done to her?" he cursed himself.

'Laxman tried to stop his tears. Sita, with folded hands and her head bowed, was entering the hall now. Her weathered face was devoid of any expression.

'"Look," said Bharat. "Behind Valmiki, she looks like Shruti following Brahma."

'Bharat's comment stunned Laxman. "Call her a goddess and torture her to death. Shame!" he was about to shout, when he saw everyone in the court stand up. The king was entering the court.'

~

'In the last few days, Laxman had established a good acquaintance with Luv and Kusha. Sita had nurtured them very well. They were music maestros at such a young age, but they were great warriors as well. Laxman was not very fond of music, but by a mere look he could differentiate a warrior from a trooper.

'He came to know about the hardships that Sita had gone through in raising them. He never got a hint from the boys of any ill will towards the people of Ayodhya and the royal household, for their inhuman treatment of Sita. She had not nurtured them that way. However, the boys were well aware of their father's iconic deeds.

'He remembered how Ram had addressed them: "The sons of Sita." They were indeed the sons of that lioness.

'Once he asked Kusha and Luv, "What if the king asks you to stay with him in Ayodhya?"

'Baffled, the boys looked at him. There was no readymade answer.

"'If mother also agrees to live here..." Luv said.

'But Kusha's answer surprised him. "Father is the guru and the guardian of his sons. We should follow his command."

"'Luv, do you agree with what Kusha says?" Laxman asked.

'For few moments, Luv remained silent. Nodding slowly, he confessed, "Kusha is right. But I wish mother also joins us."

"'You don't know your mother, sons," a sad Laxman thought. "She is different. She will suffer everything but not compromise with her self-respect. She had the courage to jump into the fire, because she had loved only Ram. She was ready to give her life because her commitment and her character were questioned. She did not think for a fraction of a second before leaping into the soaring flames because that crowd of the Vanaras was mocking her. You don't know your mother, sons."

"'But why is she here again after so much humiliation?" Laxman was puzzled, "Why should she be here to bow before this crowd of male chauvinists?

'He remembered their last conversation near Valmiki's ashram. Fourteen years ago, when he conveyed Ram's command to her, she fell down and lost consciousness. But once she regained her wits, on the contrary she consoled a crying Laxman.

"'Laxman, I suffer because I love Ram. I cannot see him sad, or under duress. You know all this. If he feels this separation will cause him good and it will restore the prestige of Ayodhya's crown, let it be so." Laxman's helplessness had made him numb.

"'Laxman!" Sita said suddenly, "Tell me, if someone asks me why Ram has abandoned me, what should I reply? If the women in these ashrams ask me what my crime was, what should I reply?"

'Her inevitable query stunned Laxman. The world was spinning around him. He caught hold of the chariot for support.

"'Laxman, suicide is one option to avoid this humiliation," Sita said calmly. "I would have jumped into River Ganga, but that's not possible for me. Laxman, perhaps you don't know,

I am pregnant. If I kill myself, the bloodline of my husband ends."

'This revelation unnerved Laxman. He looked at Sita. There was not a hint of anger on her face.

'"Laxman, I am determined to give birth to my child. You go back to Ram and give him my message. Tell him to try to stay clear of defamation, as he always has done. Tell him to treat his people well. I shall always pray for his good."'

~

'The noise in the royal court brought Laxman back to the present. In the attire of a forest dweller, her calm and composed figure was looking so pure and distinct from the Treta's polluted minds. Silently, Sita stopped opposite the king's chair with hands folded together and head held high. The entire assembly was silent now, waiting for the next scene to unfold.

'Valmiki walked closer to the king's throne and stood beside her.

'"Kaakustha, Sita is virtuous and the embodiment of dharma," he addressed Ram in a clear voice. "Look at her. She is the pious wife whom you deserted for fear of being disparaged."

'Valmiki's words warmed the hearts of many like Laxman.

'"Perhaps for the first time in her life, somebody may bring justice to her," Laxman prayed.

'A great galaxy of seers was present in the court. These were the learned men who determined the codes of social and political life that would remain for centuries to come. Many among them were associated with celebrated women. Sage Jabali was the son of Jabala. She was honest and fearless enough to admit before the world that she was not sure who had fathered her child. In an increasingly paternal Vedic society, sage Jabali got his name from his mother. Then there was Shatananda, whose mother Ahilya had suffered a stony curse from her husband Gautama. It was Ram who liberated her. Old sage Pulastya was also present there, whose son Vishrava married Kaikasi, the mother of Ravana.

"'Righteous king, the twins of Sita are your sons. I have never uttered a single false sentence ever in my life. Trust my words."

'Like a burning lance of red-hot iron ready to pierce the sky, Valmiki raised his right hand and swore, "King Ram, I have performed penance for innumerable years. If Sita has the slightest of vice, let my penance go waste. My mind, voice and action have not committed any wrong ever, knowing this and also knowing that Janaki is unblemished, I seek justice for her."

'The sage's thunder stunned the assembly. Only Ram remained emotionless.

'Coming closer to the throne, Valmiki then spoke in an affectionate tone, "Ram, I took her under my guardianship because I was convinced of her piousness. Ram, her conduct is pristine and no vice has ever touched her. Her husband is her god. Ram, I also know you love her and believe her chasteness is beyond doubt. You left her because a politically motivated scandal forced you to do so."

'Ram looked at the sage but said nothing. A little annoyed, Valmiki offered a truce.

"'Ram, no blot has ever touched Sita, she is the epitome of pure conduct. If you are still scared of a scandal then let her help you. She will prove her purity here in this open court."

'Valmiki paused for a while and then announced, "O professed and virtuous Ram, Sita is here to prove her purity, to release you from the bondage of public humiliation. Command her to do so."

'Laxman could not believe his ears. "What has happened to the sage? How many times will she go through this?" His soul craved to cry aloud against this injustice.

'Finally, the king stirred on his chair. He spoke after a brief glance at Sita.

"'Sage, you know the essence of dharma. I don't have any reason to disbelieve you. I trust your words. Sita had proved her purity once before. I also know these twins are my sons." The king continued, "But I will accept her only when she proves her virtue before this assembly."

'Sita heard the words. She knew Ram very well. Ram had always believed her. The king's words were harsh but not unexpected. She smiled on a strange thought: "The king has accepted Luv and Kusha without a test but for me he wants another ordeal." She looked at her sons. Quietly sitting between Ram and Bharat, they were witnessing the drama.

'"They will get their due. They look happy." Her existence suddenly became calmer.'

~

'It was a bizarre coincidence that the night when Sita gave birth to the twins, Ram's youngest brother Shatrughna was also present in Valmiki's ashram. He was on his way to Mathura to fight the Rakshasa king Lavanasur.

'It was a rainy night in the month of *Shravana*. Hearing the news of the twin births, Valmiki arrived immediately and admired the newborns. Beautiful and radiant, the twins looked like the young moon. Valmiki took a handful of reeds and whits and sanctified them with *mantra*s. He passed the sacrificial grass and reeds to one of the old matrons.

'"Scrub the elder baby with the grass and chant the *mantra*s. The baby will be known as Kusha." Then he gave the grass whits to another elderly nurse and instructed, "Scrub the younger one with whits and chant the *mantra*s. We will call him Luv."

'The elderly women in the ashram scrubbed the newborn babies while chanting the sacred hymns. Sita was happy. Though she did not have the opportunity to name her sons, the scholarly sage was a worthy name-giver. Considering her condition, and her own origin, the names Luv and Kusha were so apt. "What else would you call Sita's sons?" After many months, she had a hearty laugh.

'At midnight, Shatrughna was woken up by a gentle knock

at his door. When he opened the door, he heard the sounds of Vedic hymns and the names of Ram and Sita. Before he could ask, the messenger told him about the birth of Sita's twins.

'Without waiting for a minute, Shatrughna went to Sita's hut and congratulated her.

'"Congratulations, Sita. Kosala's future king is happy and healthy at birth."

'The whole night, he stayed in Sita's hut admiring the beauty of the infants.'

~

'"Shatrughna must have told Ram about their birth, but he never bothered to see us." A thorn deep in her heart pained Sita again. "He never bothered for them for fourteen long years and today he is happily sitting with them on the throne. And their mother stands before them all as an accused!"

'Valmiki had offered her for the ordeal asked for by her husband, and her sons were two among many mute spectators of this tragedy. Between Ram, Valmiki and her sons, she searched for her place, but could not find it.

'"Who am I? A daughter, a wife or a mother? Perhaps none."

'Though her parents never hinted at that, she used to hear the gossip even in Mithila. She was Sita, the furrow, born of ploughing the land. It was said that when Janaka was tilling his fields, and the metal bottom of his plough dug the land, she had appeared miraculously as a newborn baby.

'The whole of Mithila city was there in the gayest dresses and filled with boundless joy. Then the royal herdsman brought a thousand and one ploughs and the bullocks. Among those ploughs, one hundred and eight ploughs were for senior nobles and were made of silver. The horns of the bullocks pulling them were tipped with silver and adorned with white flowers. The plough held by the king was made of gold and the horns of the bullocks attached were also tipped with gold.

'When the ritual began, the king took the handle of the

plough in his left hand and a golden goad in his right. He made one furrow, passing from east to west. At the same time, the nobles made three furrows and the rest of the ploughmen followed. Then, suddenly when people looked west to see whether the king had completed his furrow, they saw him holding an infant in his arms. Everyone was surprised when the priest told the crowd that a girl child had sprung miraculously from the furrow made by the king.

'However, Janaka and his beautiful wife Sunayana never mentioned this story to Sita. She was the joy of their life. But once she attained puberty, all her liberties were taken away from her.

'The bow ceremony to select a husband for her was her father's idea. Since she first met Ram in her father's garden, the mere thought of anyone other than Ram breaking the bow sent a chill down down her spine. But as it was destined, after everyone else failed, Ram broke the powerful Shiva's bow.

'Her marital palace in Ayodhya was full of intrigue. They were soon exiled from the palace. They tried to settle in different forests but most of the forest-dwelling sages were misogynistic and chauvinistic. She remembered how Anusuya, the wife of sage Atri, indoctrinated her in the ideal dharma of a married woman. Paternalistic traditions never allowed Sita to be Sita, the woman. First, she was a daughter, then a wife, then an abducted woman, then an estranged wife, then a mother and single parent, and now again left at the mercy of her grown-up sons, a guardian and a long-separated husband.

'With a last look at her sons, she said, "Children, I have done my due. Only the greedy ones keep their children chained to them forever." She knew that she was faking it. Her heart wept, "They are merely fourteen and have forgotten me! Till last week, I was the whole world for them and today I am nobody."

'The moment of truth was close. True, all of them loved her. But, their love was often a convenient companion of their individual, political and social ambitions. And on her part, her love was absolute. Only love, nothing else ever mattered to her. If Ram was happy in shunning her, she was happy to be banished. She took the pain and the agony, believing that it would make him happy. She was ever ready to sacrifice herself for his repuatation, for his social causes and for his political wins.

"'I am the daughter of the earth. Where else can a person find warmth and protection like in a mother's womb? There is no place other than a mother's lap when one longs for peace and comfort. None," she firmly decided and looked at him.

'Ram's charm was still intact. Not even an iota of it had diminished in the last fourteen years. "I love this man." The feeling of seeing him, of seeing him well, filled her heart with joy. "They will live happily together," she thought.

'Trials and ordeals never worried her. She had faced them all through her life. Her life had been a big ordeal since birth. Before Ram, before the gods, she had proved her piousness once. There was no need to do so again. The assembled cast of sages and people of Ayodhya did not deserve that.

"'I cannot live with Ram," she decided. "Without faith, no relationship can exist. Why is a *maryadapurushottama* not strong enough to face his citizens and protect his wife? If he is a righteous king, then why does he insult a woman? Why is he setting a precedent for countless false trials and tribulations for women in future? Why should I be setting such a prejudiced and biased precedent? No, I shall not."

"'But a refusal before the people will lower the prestige of Ram," someone inside her persisted. "I will do it and do it in my own way. Not the way they want."

'She walked past Valmiki and reached just under Ram's elevated throne. Looking directly into his eyes, Sita announced: "Ram, I don't owe anyone any trial. However, if it puts you at ease, I will do my bit. If it is true that except you I have never thought about anyone as my male companion, then let mother earth open up and give me space inside her."

'The moment Sita pledged this, thunderstorms and tremors shook Ayodhya. The earth opened up right under where Sita was standing; and before anyone could react, she was gone.'

～

'Sita's story is very tragic,' Kunti wiped her tears. 'I wonder how many people could follow the highest standards of public probity set by Sita and Ram.'

'Aunt, whenever I recall the story of Sita and Ram, I remember two cardinal aspects of their relationship. The first and the strongest was their mutual love. Only a man like Ram can accomplish what he did by getting his love back from Ravana. Second, they knew that, for a larger social good, they had to sacrifice their mutual comfort. Sita did that many times. Many people criticize Ram for her second banishment. But, in many places in her story, we get the hint that for her safety and for the continuance of Ram's ideal rule, it was necessary to send her to Valmiki's ashram. Aunt, big ashrams have always been very powerful: politically, financially, academically and for the security of people.'

'Then why did Ram insist on another public trial for Sita?'

'Aunt, when Valmiki's epic was sung in public and Luv-Kusha had grown up, Ram took another chance to bring Sita back. However, he misjudged the power of his political enemies. They were still very strong. The only weapon in their hands was the period an abducted Sita had spent in Lanka. They played that card again. Therefore, Ram assembled everyone. He had more belief in Sita than in himself.'

'We too are the victims of this politics, Krishna. I can understand,' Kunti said with a lot of pain in her voice. 'Now, tell me about Yashoda and Devaki.'

'Aunt, you know both of them. What is there to tell?' Krishna smiled.

'No, I want to hear from you,' Kunti insisted.

'Aunt, I think when the competition for resources becomes intense and human greed turns violent, the suffering of a mother becomes more tragic,' Krishna said. 'I will begin with the story of Devaki.'

'Ahuka was a great man of the famous Vrishni dynasty. He had two sons, Devaka and Ugrasena. Devaka had four sons and seven daughters. My mother Devaki was his youngest daughter. Devaka's brother Ugrasena also had a big family, including nine sons and five daughters. Kansa was Ugrasena's eldest son.

'Aunt, your father, the Yadu prince Shoorsena was Devaka's contemporary. He married your mother Marisha. You know this. You are ten brothers and five sisters. My father Vasudeva is the eldest among the siblings and you are the eldest among the sisters.'

'Shoorsena had a dear friend called Kuntibhoja. Kuntibhoja was childless and had expressed many times his wish to have a daughter. Understanding his emotions, Shoorsena happily gave you away in Kuntibhoja's lap. Kuntibhoja raised you with the compassion of Marisha and the protection of Shoorsena. His care and affection transformed you from Prutha to Kunti.

'Shoorsena integrated two big kingdoms, Mathurmandala and Shoorsenmandala, and developed Mathura as his capital. He also invited all Vrishni and Yadu princes to settle in Mathura and appointed them in suitable royal posts. He set up a system of collaborative governance and appointed Ugrasena as his successor.

'Your elder brother and my father, Vasudeva was also known as Aanakadundubhi. It is known that at his birth, a rejoicing nature created a musical symphony and the sky resounded as if the gods were playing the divine drums. Vasudeva had many queens. Prominent among them were Pauravi, Rohini, Bhadra, Madira, Lochana and Ila. Now, he was about to marry Devaki, the youngest cousin of Kansa.

'Kansa enthusiastically participated in the marriage. Vasudeva was his friend and Devaki was his beloved sister. Devaka adored his daughter and gave her four hundred elephants decorated with gold ornaments, fifteen thousand decorated horses, eighteen thousand chariots and two hundred maidens as wedding gifts. After the auspicious wedding ceremony, when

Devaka's family put the bride and the groom in a chariot driven by seven white horses, a visibly elated Kansa requested his friend Vasudeva to allow him to drive the bride's chariot.

'"Vasudeva, my friend, this relationship has further reinforced our friendship. Both of you are dearer to me than my life. As tradition says, the bride's brother should take her and her husband to their new home. Let me have this opportunity to drive the bridal chariot to your palace."

'Everyone happily approved of the affectionate gesture from Kansa. Mighty Kansa took the reins of the horses in his hands and began driving the bridal chariot that was covered with millions of flowers. The groom's party thus started their return journey with the bride. The procession was passing very pleasingly, with a symphony of conchshells, bugles, drums and kettledrums.

'Halfway to Vasudeva's palace, when the chariot of the newlyweds was moving at a leisurely pace, amidst the happy chattering and laughing of the relatives, a deep voice came from the sky and resonated everywhere, stunning the marriage party.

'"Stupid Kansa, beware!" it said. "The eighth son of your sister Devaki whom you are carrying to her new home with such love and affection, will be your slayer."

'For the next few moments, stupefied, all three looked at one another, unable to fathom what they had just heard. Everyone in Mathura was terrorized by the demonic ways of Kansa and perhaps secretly wished his death. But it is also true that personally he loved Devaki the most.

'"Why me?" A baffled Devaki suddenly shuddered with fear. The prophecy from the sky struck all of them like a thunderbolt. But before she could react further, excruciating pain forced her to scream aloud. Kansa had caught hold of her hair and dragged her towards the driver's seat and was about to kill her with his sword.

'Frightened, she closed her eyes. She heard her husband begging for her life, "Kansa, my friend, the world knows you as the greatest warrior and a valiant prince. Such calls must not perturb you. That may be a farce. Have patience; don't get infuriated into killing your own sister. It's a sin."

'Devaki opened her eyes. Kansa looked a little confused, unable to decide what to do.

'Vasudeva further stressed upon him, "Kansa, think of your reputation. Killing your newlywed and helpless sister will mar your reputation forever. The Vrishni dynasty will not be known for your greatness but for this act of momentary and sinful wrath."

"'Vasudeva, how do you expect me to leave her after hearing that prophecy? Tell me, is my life more precious or my committing a sin? Why should I wait for her eighth son? I will annihilate the root itself," Kansa moved forward with his sword.

"'Kansa, my friend, listen to me. The nature of the mind is frivolous. On hearsay we accept something in one moment and the next moment we reject that," Vasudeva pleaded. He was trying to buy time. "The five things that influence our decision are form, taste, smell, sound and touch. Then the mind processes these senses and decides as it suits it. Why should a wise person like you be affected by a sound from the sky? Humans are superior to animals because they can wisely analyse and process the information received by the senses. Please don't act in haste. Think over it," Vasudeva tried to calm Kansa's wrath.

'When, despite his best efforts, Kansa could not be pacified, Vasudeva decided to commit something to the future, to avoid Devaki's murder, that appeared imminent.

"'Kansa, you don't have any danger from Devaki. If the voice from the sky is true, the danger is not from her but from her eighth son. The child is not here yet. Who knows Kansa, if Devaki will bear children or not? Or what if the eighth child is a girl? It's all futuristic and uncertain. For an uncertain thing, don't blemish all the ages to come."

'Vasudeva then firmly vowed, "Kansa, do you believe me?

Today, before you, I promise that I shall present all of her children to you to decide their fate."

'Vasudeva's promise worked. Kansa left Devaki's hair and grabbed Vasudeva's collar.

'"I know you don't lie, Vasudeva. I trust your words and trust you will honour your promise. But if you ever falter or try to cheat me, I will extinguish the entire Yadu clan." Satisfied with Vasudeva's promise, Kansa allowed them to go to their palace.

'Vasudeva and Devaki had three blissful months of matrimony and then Devaki became pregnant.

'"Men don't realize what they are promising," an apprehensive Devaki complained.

'"What do you mean?" Vasudeva was a little irritated.

'"Vasudeva, with your wise words that day you saved my life. How could you promise giving newborn babies to that demon for slaughter?" She caressed her stomach with affection, "A new life is living in my womb and I know its fate is Kansa's sword. Can you realize the sufferings of such an unfortunate and terrified mother?"

'"Devaki, I love you. That day, the most important thing was to save your life." He looked at her belly and said with conviction, "I still feel Kansa will not kill a newborn. How can anyone be so hardhearted? Do you think if I place our newborn in your brother's hands, he will kill it?"

'"You are too naïve, Vasudeva. Kansa is not human. He is a demon. If you think he will show any mercy to our child, you are ignorant."

'Hanging between despair and the hope, the couple passed the next six months in anxiety. Whenever Devaki forgot Vasudeva's promise, she used to weave a million dreams about her first baby. She decided that she would name it Kirtimaan.

'"You said Kansa is a demon," Vasudeva was puzzled, "yet you have named the child before birth."

'"Vasudeva, mother means hope. A mother is an eternal optimist. You will not understand it."

'"So you too are hopeful that Kansa would let this child live," Vasudeva quizzed his wife.

'"I don't trust Kansa. Demons like Kansa, who are addicted to unrestricted sensual gratification, are never truthful, so they can never be trusted. I don't trust him at all." She paused for a while and then said with hope, "But I trust God."

'When their first son was born, honouring his words, Vasudeva immediately presented the child before Kansa.

'"I know how painful it is, but this is the only way," he consoled Devaki before leaving for Kansa's palace.

'Many things had changed in Mathura during that year. When king Ugrasena opposed his son's demonic acts and refused to anoint him as the crown prince, Kansa imprisoned his father and became the king of Mathura. For a remorseless Kansa, imprisoning Ugrasena was an easy task, as he believed that Ugrasena was not his biological father. It was rumoured that Kansa was a child of rape. A Gandharva had raped his mother in a garden, and as a result, Kansa was considered illegitimate and ostracized by the people of Mathura. For this reason, Kansa hated the Yadavas. When he became powerful and got the opportunity, he captured the throne. Setting aside the Yadu tradition of not wearing a crown, Kansa declared himself a sovereign king and wore the crown. To consolidate his political power, he married the two daughters of Jarasandha, who was the most powerful king in Aryavarta during that time and was also famous for his tyrannical rule.

'Kansa gladly received the firstborn of Devaki and Vasudeva. The radiant face of the newborn reminded him of infant Devaki. For a moment, he became a little compassionate and looked at his brother-in-law. Truthful to the core, Vasudeva was standing before him with his head down.

'Kansa felt elated with pride. "I am the supreme," the thought passed his mind. "Shoorsena's son is standing helpless before me like a mouse cornered by a clever cat."

Boons & Curses

'"Dear Vasudeva, you need not present this child to me. The prophecy says Devaki's eighth son will kill me. This little one is harmless. Why should I kill this infant unnecessarily? You can take him back."

'Taken aback by the demon's generosity, a relieved Vasudeva returned home.

'"Look, this is what I had said. Kansa did not kill the baby," brimming with joy, he told Devaki.

'Devaki also became very happy and cuddled the infant. Feeding the child, she looked at her husband. Both were thinking the same thing, "How long?" Her own words echoed in her mind, "One who cannot control the senses, cannot be steady in his determination."

'At that time, sage Narada visited Kansa's court.

'"Kansa, I thought you are a wise man and an alert monarch. Are you sleeping?" Narada asked with a lot of sarcasm. "There is a great conspiracy going on against you. You are being projected as a demon. The Yadus, the Vrishnis and the Yadavas of Mathuramandala are conspiring against you. Your friend Vasudeva knows it all and is an active member of it. They call themselves demi-gods and have branded you a demon. They are projecting it as a war between good and evil. They say that you are the devil incarnate and thus need to be removed. Beware of their conspiracy."

'Narada continued, "Kansa, in your previous birth, you were Kalnemi, son of the greatest demon Hiranyaksha. In a battle, Lord Vishnu killed you. Your brother Andhaka was slayed by Indra. They are spreading the word all around that Vishnu is about to take birth to kill you."

'Narada's information infuriated Kansa. Earlier, Kansa was afraid of the eighth child but after Narada's information, he decided not to take any chances.

'"God cannot be trusted. Why the eighth? Any child may slay me," Kansa concluded. He went to Vasudeva and Devaki at once and arrested and put them in one of his worst prisons.

Snatching the infant from Devaki's hands, Kansa banged his head against the prison wall and killed him.

'Narada did not keep his conversation with Kansa a secret. Very soon, the whole of Mathura knew that the eighth son of Devaki would be the Lord incarnate and he would slay the demon Kansa.

"'What does this mean?" In their dark and secluded prison cell, Devaki too heard the rumour.

"'We have to be patient. Our eighth son is our only hope," Vasudeva consoled her.

"'How is it possible?" she cried. "Shackled in these iron chains, how can you think of procreation? I am against it. Let us not have any children. Why should we produce children? To be killed by Kansa? It's a sin, Vasudeva. I am against it."

"'Devaki, do you want to stay forever in this prison? Do you want people to suffer forever in the hands of that demon? If there is an iota of truth in that prophecy and my heart says it's true, then our eighth son will be the liberator of the world. We have to suffer for the sake of that prophecy; we have to suffer for the hope of millions of people. Devaki, we have to suffer for that."

"'Bearing eight or more lives in my womb, and then giving all of them to Kansa to slay, how can I do it?" she cried. "Vasudeva, how can you propose this? You don't know what it takes to give birth to a child."

'For a long time, Vasudeva did not utter a word. Sitting silently, he contemplated his karma.

"'Devaki, if everything depends on our eighth son, then we have to give birth to him," Vasudeva said in a firm voice. "Devaki, I know your trauma, going through this unbearable pain year after year. Perhaps no one else could have suffered such an ordeal. You have to bear all that pain to discharge your duty. It's your and my karma to bring our eighth son into this world. A son who will liberate us, a son who will free this world from Kansa's brutalities."

'Inside the prison, shackled in iron chains, Devaki gave birth to one male child every year, and Kansa killed them one after another. The brutal killing of the newborn babies inside the cell slowly cemented Devaki's determination to give birth to her eighth son. Day by day, her faith became firmer that her eighth son would annihilate the devil.

'In seven years, Kansa killed six children of Devaki. Meanwhile, through brutal power and sometimes through diplomacy, he broke the solidarity of the Yadu, Bhoja and Andhaka clans. Very few sympathisers of Vasudeva now remained in Mathura. Many of them migrated across River Yamuna and settled there.

'"Do you believe a newborn can kill that demon?" Vasudeva's long-suppressed doubt finally came out.

'"We need to plan how we can save our eighth child," Devaki had an idea, provided the other queens of Vasudeva also agreed to share the burden of sacrifice.

'When she became pregnant for the seventh time, Devaki experienced a joy hitherto unknown. This life in her womb was the precursor of the ultimate child, for whom they were suffering so much.

'Meanwhile Vishnu summoned Yogamaya, his internal potency.

'"Yogamaya, at the present moment my plenary expansion Sesha is in the womb of an imprisoned Devaki. Vasudeva's other wife Rohini is living in Gokula. Arrange the transfer of Sesha from the womb of Devaki to the womb of Rohini. After this arrangement, I will personally appear in the womb of Devaki as her eighth conception. I will be called Krishna."

'"And what will Sesha be called?" Yogamaya asked.

'"On account of him being forcibly attracted into the womb of Rohini, he will be known as Sankarshana. He will be the source of all the spiritual power or the *bala*, therefore he will also be called Balarama."

'Yogamaya nodded and was about to leave when Vishnu added, "And you shall appear as the daughter of Nanda and Yashoda in Gokula."

'Following his command, Yogamaya put both Rohini and Devaki under her spell called *yoganidra* and transferred the foetus. When this was done, everyone in Mathura thought that Devaki's seventh pregnancy had been a miscarriage.

'Kansa visited the prison and laughed aloud in Devaki's face, "Kansa's terror causes miscarriage. New life is now scared to take birth. Let us see if your eighth survives to be killed by my hands."

'Even Devaki was not aware of Yogamaya's act. She wept inconsolably.

'"This is not a good omen, Vasudeva. I don't know what happened. I took all care…" She kept on crying for many days.

'When Devaki conceived for the eighth time, she was very nervous for the safety of her foetus.

'"I will find a way to transport the eighth child out of this prison. We have made so many sacrifices. If we die and he survives to kill Kansa, even that will be a huge miracle," she told Vasudeva.

'Vasudeva encouraged her. "You need not worry, Devaki." He reassured her, "I don't have an iota of doubt that the child in your womb will slay Kansa and diminish the burden of the world." Devaki hoped and listened. The moment of truth was not very far.

Kunti smiled, 'Krishna, after that point I know the story. I have heard it more than a thousand times and the more I hear, the more I like to hear it again and again. Let me, for the sake of my own pleasure, reiterate this divine story of your birth.'

Krishna smiled but said nothing.

'Then, on a pitch dark and rainy night, you took birth. The parents saw the wonderful newborn with four hands, holding the conchshell, the club, the disc and the lotus, decorated with the mark of *shrivatsa*, wearing the jewelled necklace of *kaustubha* stone, dressed in yellow silk, wearing a crown bedecked with the *vaidurya* stone. Glancing at an abundantly decorated child, both the parents were overpowered by multiple emotions.

'"Lord, your form existed before this cosmic manifestation," Devaki prayed to the newborn. "Your forms are eternal and all-pervading. Kansa has already killed your six elder siblings, I am praying to you to rescue us from his cruel hands."

'The newborn smiled, "I know you are concerned about me and afraid of Kansa. Take me to Gokula and exchange me for the daughter of Yashoda, who is about to take birth."

'At Krishna's birth, by the influence of Yogamaya, all the residents of Kansa's palace, all guards and the doorkeepers were overwhelmed with a deep sleep. Iron shackles opened, as well as the gates of the prison. Vasudeva wrapped the little child in a cloth, kissed the forehead of Devaki and came out of the prison.

'The night was dark and the sky was thundering. It had been raining incessantly since many days. Vasudeva knew the way from where he could cross the river. He walked out of the prison compound. Suddenly, a big serpent spread its hood over Vasudeva to protect the father and the son from the pouring rain. Vasudeva kept walking and reached the bank of River Yamuna. It was not the Yamuna he had imagined. The water of the Yamuna was roaring with soaring waves and the whole span was full of foam. Guided by some divine instruction, Vasudeva, without hesitation, walked into the river. The big serpent, Sesha followed him. The river gave passage to him and he reached the other side safely with his newborn son.

'That dark night the rain was relentless. Like Mathura, everybody was under deep slumber at Gokula. Silently, Vasudeva entered the house of Nanda and then the inner chamber of his wife Yashoda. She had just given birth to a baby girl. Without hesitation, Vasudeva exchanged his son for the baby girl and returned to Mathura. The serpent was still shielding them from the rain and once again the Yamuna gave way to him and he reached his cell without any difficulty.

'He then gave the little girl to Devaki and clamped the shackles on himself. The moment she took the newborn girl in her arms, Devaki wept.

'"What happened?" an exhausted Vasudeva asked.

'"I can never forget Yashoda's sacrifice. I feel ashamed. To save our son, this little beautiful baby will soon be killed by that demon."

'"We don't understand the ways of God," Vasudeva tried to console Devaki. "The kind of things that happened on my way to Gokula, I know there is nothing human about it."

'"What had happened?" Devaki was about to ask, when the baby girl began crying and the guards entered the cell.

'Kansa came running with a naked sword in his hand. Nervous and agitated, he pushed open the prison gate and entered the cell.

'"Here it is! The cruel end of my life, that has tormented me for the last eight years." He tried to snatch the child from Devaki.

'"No. Please don't kill her. You have killed so many of my children, all as bright as the shining star. I never begged. Please leave her," Devaki cried, "Kansa, I beg you. You are not destined to be killed by a girl child. Excuse this little one and let her live."

'A little perplexed, Kansa snatched the child from his sister's arms. It was a baby girl.

'"I know what kind of tricks Vishnu plays," he shouted. In utter cruelty, he then mercilessly dashed the little girl against the prison wall.

'To everyone's surprise, the little child did not hit the wall. Instead she rose up into the sky and appeared with eight arms, holding a bow, lance, arrows, conchshell, disc, club, lotus flower and the shield in her hands.

'"So you are Vishnu. Come on and kill me," Kansa drew his sword and shouted like a madman. The goddess laughed and that laughter stopped the heartbeat of Kansa.

'"Fool, can you kill me? You?" The goddess laughed again. "The child who will kill you has taken birth." She laughed again and rose higher. A livid Kansa swung his sword in the air in an attempt to catch the deity. She kept on laughing and then disappeared. A scared Kansa shuddered with fear. He was perplexed.

'"So the prophecy was wrong," he thought. "Do the celestials also run false propaganda like humans?" He was confused. "It appears that God too speaks lies."

'Feeling terrible for his sister, Kansa politely offered an apology.

'"Devaki, my sister! Please forgive me for killing your children. You know I never intended to harm them. It was the false prophecy that caused me to do these ghastly acts."

'He looked at Vasudeva, "I am releasing you and Devaki immediately. But, you cannot leave Mathura."

'With tears flowing, Kansa fell at Devaki's feet. Soft-hearted Devaki and Vasudeva did not curse cruel Kansa.

'Vasudeva said, "Kansa, you believed that this materialistic body and the world is everything. This wrong conception was because of your ignorance. If the killing of our children has enlightened you, I am happy for you."

'Vasudeva's words relieved Kansa of his guilt and he returned to his palace.

'The next day, when Kansa narrated this entire incident to his counsellors in the royal court, they advised him otherwise.

'"King, don't forget what the magical girl said before disappearing. We must make arrangements to kill each and every child born in the last ten days. We should execute this plan indiscriminately and everywhere. King, if you neglect a disease in the body, it worsens and finally eats away the body. We have to be careful and kill all the infants."

'The counsellors scared Kansa with all the possibilities linked to his slayer. An alarmed Kansa immediately agreed. Thus began a huge operation, intended to kill all the children born within the last ten days. Kansa sent his mercenaries everywhere.

"'Let an active search be made for young children anywhere on earth and let every boy be slain without remorse."

'Nanda's wife Yashoda had given birth to a baby. She was very tired from the labour of childbirth; therefore she fell fast asleep immediately and could not see the newborn. Later, when she awoke, she found a male child happily looking at her. Thus, she would never know that she had given birth to a girl child.

'When the cowherd men (the gopas) and their women heard about the birth of a boy at Nanda's place, they were overwhelmed with joy. Dressed in their best clothes, they reached to congratulate the couple. Sprinkling a mixture of turmeric powder, oil, yogurt, milk and water on the boy and everyone present, the gopis blessed the newborn, "Dear child, you will live long to protect us."

'Rohini, one of the wives of Vasudeva and the mother of Balarama, also blessed the infant. The birth ceremony of the newborn was celebrated with opulence and there you were named Krishna.

'After your birth ceremony, Rohini returned to Mathura, entrusting Balarama to the care of Yashoda. Nanda also decided to go to Mathura to pay the annual tax to Kansa. When Vasudeva and Devaki got this news, Vasudeva immediately went to meet his old friend. He took an assurance from Nanda that he would not reveal this secret to Balarama, that Yashoda was not his mother. Indirectly he also enquired about Krishna and his well-being and hinted to Nanda that he should move farther away from Gokula for the safety of his clan. Nanda also expressed his sympathy towards Vasudeva.

"'Friend, I know you are aggrieved because cruel Kansa has killed all your sons. Although he could not kill your daughter, nobody knows where she is. We all are bound by our past karmas," Nanda said in ignorance, unaware that Vasudeva was your biological father.

'When Vasudeva returned to his palace, he was mentally

drained. He and Devaki wept for hours, not knowing what their son's fate would be.'

~

'Krishna, Devaki, Yashoda and I were so deeply associated with each other's life, yet we never met even once. Is that not a strange coincidence?' Kunti asked.

'This is the game that fate plays with all of us. Sometimes you suffer for your whole life, expecting that great moment of salvation, and sometimes you treat every moment of your life like salvation. Therefore, the wise say that we should live fully in the present.'

'But is it entirely in our hands? Who does not want to enjoy each moment of life? People around you won't allow you to do so!' Kunti said with some harshness.

'Aunt, you still have some bitterness left,' Krishna said. 'What perturbed you yesterday during dinner was the bitterness that Bhima showed towards Dhritarashtra and Gandhari. Aunt, forgive everyone. Forgive your relatives, friends and foes. Forgive everyone that ever had any karmic bond with you. Only then will you attain permanent peace.'

'I don't have a large heart like Yashoda, Krishna. She sacrificed her daughter to save your life and yet she loved you, nurtured you like no mother ever had,' Kunti sobbed.

'Begin with this moment, aunt,' Krishna suggested. 'Leave the fascination of Hastinapura, leave the attachment of your sons. Advise Dhritarashtra and Gandhari to follow *Vanaprastha* ashram. Ask your heart if you are willing to leave this palace and join them in the forest. I can see that your work here is over.'

Kunti lowered her head and remained silent for a long time. Lifting her head with a smile, she then requested: 'Tell me about Yashoda, Krishna. Maybe that will give me courage to sacrifice and to not to be greedy any more.'

'Aunt, mother Yashoda transformed me, a cowherd, into Krishna. Those sixteen years, when she was my mother, mentor, friend, guide and guru, were my formative years.

'Happiness is a state of mind, aunt. It is about understanding what brings everlasting happiness. A person chasing his dreams blindly cannot be happy. Happiness may come from a clear and unbiased understanding and affirmative action. But, the greatest joy is the joy of giving. When you provide love, compassion and goodwill, without expecting in return, you experience permanent happiness and open the floddgates of abundant cosmic love. A mother like Yashoda understands it the best.

'A mother gives her sweat, blood, flesh and everything to procreate. Does she desire anything from her progeny while conceiving? No. A mother never desires anything from her baby. It's a relationship of pure bliss, pure happiness. Only when we superimpose our unfulfilled desires, our ambitions and our business interests on our child, and use him as a tool to accomplish these, do sorrows arrive. Then, no happiness remains permanent, it always comes with a huge cost.

'Aunt, a mother soaks herself in the little moments of her child's small glories. Listening to his tales, enjoying his mischiefs and allowing him to roam free with his friends, while supervising his every moment, she does this with her complete love and devotion.

'Kansa was hellbent on killing me. Therefore, Yashoda could not afford to be careless, even for a moment. When I was barely a month old, Kansa sent Putana to kill me. After Putana's failed attempt on my life, mother Yashoda spent each day of her life taking care of only my safety and my well-being. The anxiety associated with this responsibility became a constant companion for her. But this anxiety could never diminish her pure affection for Dau or me. All the residents of Gokula were considered sympathisers of Vasudeva and therefore always were under constant pressure and threat. In such an environment, making my childhood as happy as possible was Yashoda's only pursuit. And today, I wonder how she did it so easily.

'I was so restless that Yashoda would try to protect me from the cows, bulls, monkeys, water, fire, birds and snakes while she was executing household duties. She enjoyed the complaints she received from her gopi friends for my naughty childish activities.'

'Yes. And I have heard that she was not unaware of your true identity. There is a story, I once heard from Balarama,' Kunti said

> 'Once your friend told her that you had eaten some clay. A worried Yashoda caught hold of you and asked if you had eaten the clay. You simply refused, but she insisted, "Just open your mouth. I will check."
>
> 'You immediately opened your mouth, just like an ordinary child. Yashoda looked inside your mouth and witnessed the opulence of creation. She saw the entire universe, including the solar system, the earth, its rivers and mountains, inside her son's mouth. This cosmic manifestation struck her with awe and she wondered who Krishna actually was.
>
> 'But the next moment she thought, "It may be the cosmic mystic power attained by my child or maybe he is Vishnu! How does it matter? For me, he is my baby." She immediately took you in her arms and breastfed you.'

Krishna's eyes became moist. He said nothing, but continued looking at Kunti's face, that looked so serene and peaceful now.

An emotional Kunti continued, 'Kanha, Satyaki once told me another story.

> 'Once, Yashoda was busy churning butter and singing songs, thinking of her son's beauty. It was a hot summer day and she was drenched in perspiration. Suddenly, Krishna appeared there and asked his mother to stop churning and let him suckle her breast. Yashoda took him on her lap and started feeding him. While Krishna was suckling, Yashoda was smiling, enjoying the beauty of her child's face. That little labour brought perspiration on little Krishna's forehead. Yashoda kissed his forehead affectionately. Suddenly, the milk kept on the stove began to boil. In a hurry, Yashoda quickly put Krishna aside and ran to the kitchen. Her leaving him unattended made

Krishna very angry. He picked up a stone lying nearby and broke the butter pots and went outside.

'When Yashoda returned and saw his mischief, she smiled.

'"Oh my boy! Where are you hiding? Your mother can find you very easily."

'She saw him hidden in a corner behind a box. He was eating butter from a broken pot. Silently, Yashoda went behind him. But Krishna somehow sensed her and ran outside. She chased him. It took her an entire hour to catch hold of the child. Exhausted, she thought of strapping the child's hands with some rope. She collected ropes from the house and began tying Krishna. The more she tried, the more rope she used; finally, she could not tie the child. Exausted, drenched in sweat and breathing heavily, she sat close to him. Krishna looked at his mother and smiled. Then, he fastened himself with the ropes. A mighty pleased mother had tears of joy in her eyes. She freed the child and took him in her arms.

'Kanha, they talk about many other manifestations of your childhood that are extraordinary. In the end, for Yashoda you always were her little Kanha, isn't it?'

'It is like that, aunt. Irrespective of his age, the child always remains a little baby for his mother.'

Kunti was so immersed in Krishna's childhood memories that she didn't hear Krishna's comment. She continued in her rhythm.

'Kanha, incidences like pulling down a pair of huge *arjuna* tress when you were bound to a wooden mortar by Yashoda, killing demons like Vatsasura, Bakasura and others, or subduing the Kaliya Naga in the waters of River Kalindi: People started talking about you as a child prodigy with divine virtues. But despite your heroics, Yashoda always remained worried for your safety and happiness.'

'Krishna, you began a social revolution in conservative Vrinadavan. You empowered cowherds by inspiring them, by encouraging and organizing them against Indra, and refused to give him a part in the annual puja. You started Govardhan puja in Vrindavan, thus rightfully highlighting the importance of the cow in a predominantly cowherd's society. You took a stand against orthodoxy, and then Kansa came to know about your true identity.'

'Yes, aunt. Slowly, the social change transforming Vrindavan was noticed by the outsiders and these events convinced Kansa that I was Devaki's eighth son,' Krishna said with a smile. 'He sent a senior Yadava noble, Akrura to get me and Balaram to Mathura. Mother Yashoda opposed it tooth and nail. But, everyone thought it was good for the security of the gopas. Mother Yashoda became overwhelmed with anxiety.

'Condemning Akrura, she said, "Akrura, you are behaving contrary to your name. My child is so young and innocent, how can we allow you to take him to Mathura? Why is cruel Kansa calling him? It cannot be for a good reason."

'But Akrura did not listen and Nanda baba could not protest. Yashoda followed Akrura's chariot as far as she could. I too wanted to face Kansa. Looking back at mother would have made me emotionally weak, so I did not look back. Her son had grown up now. I knew my behaviour must have hurt her.

'Later, when she heard that I had slayed Kansa, she hoped that one day I would return, but it could not happen.'

Kunti saw a tiny little teardrop at the corner of Krishna's eye. This was perhaps the only time that someone saw Krishna crying.

It took Krishna a few seconds to compose himself. He turned his face to Kunti and said, 'Aunt, when she learnt that I was Devaki's son, she told Nanda baba:

> "Nanda, I will not cry. Devaki has sacrificed a lot. She has suffered more than anybody on this earth. She deserves her son's company. I am content; Krishna gave me ultimate bliss: Perhaps I am the most fortunate woman on earth. Till I live, I will cherish and savour this joy of motherhood that Krishna gave me. He gave me the joy of rearing a child. He filled my

life with abundant joy. That is enough for me.'

'Yashoda smiled, "Krishna has truly grown up, Nanda. Till yesterday, a mother's lap was his biggest protection, today he has become the protector of all."

"Are you angry with him?" Nanda baba asked.

"Why should I be? I enjoyed my motherhood. I am blessed." With moist eyes, Yashoda continued, "I raised him in complete bliss, he was such a joy. What more do I need? Nanda, do you know what life's biggest delight is? It is to see your baby to grow, to see him take those first tiny steps, to relish his pure giggle, to see him trying to talk, to gradually feel that he is getting stronger, smarter and skilled. Oh Nanda, Krishna has given me the kingdom of this universe. Why should I complain?"

"He did not come to see you once. Are not you sad?"

"No, Nanda. Not at all. It is a huge joy and satisfaction to witness your child growing strong wings and flying. His happiness is mine. Tomorrow, when he will do good things for the people, they will say, look, here is Yashoda's son. This is the biggest reward for a mother."'

Krishna suddenly became quiet. Kunti had never seen Krishna so silent and lost in his thoughts.

She embraced Krishna, 'Don't worry for her, Krishna. A mother's reward is not what her son does for her or what great deeds he accomplishes in his life. Her reward lies in those years of innocent childhood, when the child and the mother compliment each other.'

Krishna looked up with moist eyes. Kunti placed her hand on Krishna's head and said with a lot of affection, 'I understood, Kanha. Now I understand your advice. When the child becomes capable, a mother's biggest elation is to let her child fly and admire his flight.'

Krishna smiled.

Let the son follow the mother's command and his father's pledge

Let the spouses communicate in sweet words
Let the brothers live together in harmony
Let their honeyed tongues take a common benevolent oath
And let them be committed to it.*

---

*अनुव्रत: पितु: पुत्रो माता भक्तु समना:, जाया पत्ये मधुमतीं वाचं वदतु शांतिवाम । मा भ्राता भातरं द्विक्शनमा स्वसारमुत स्वसा , सम्यनच सव्रता भुत्वा वाचं वदत भद्रया ॥ (अथर्व वेद)

Bibliography

Singh, Bhagwan. (2002) *Upnishadon kee Kahaniyan*, National Book Trusts, India, New Delhi.

Wilkins, W.J. (2012) *Hindu Mythology*, Rupa Publications India Pvt. Ltd., New Delhi.

Rao, V.S. (2016) *Navagraha Purana*, Jaico Publishing House, New Delhi.

Prabhupada, A.C. Bhaktivedanta Swami. (2011) *Krsna*, The Bhaktivedanta Book Trust, Mumbai.

Zimmer, H. (2011) *Philosophies of India*, Joseph Campbell (ed), Motilal Banarasidass Publishers Pvt. Ltd., New Delhi.

Doniger, Wendy. (2015) *The Hindus: An Alternative History*, Speaking Tiger Publishing Pvt. Ltd., New Delhi.

Megh, R.K. (2015) *Vishwa Mithak Saritsagar*, Vaani Prakashan, New Delhi.

Calasso, R. (2013) *Ardor*, Allen Lane, Penguin Books, London.

Valmiki, Maharshi. (2009) *Shrimadvalmikiya Ramayana* (Part I & II), Gita Press, Gorakhpur.

Shrimadbhagwat Mahapurana (2014), Volume I & II, Gita Press, Gorakhpur.

Rai, Kubernath. (2011) *Ramayana Mahatirtham*, Bharatiya Jnanpith, New Delhi.

Pattanaik, D. (2010) *Jaya*, Penguin Books, Gurgaon, India.

Glossary

1. *Aalaap* Cadence, high pitched beginning of a song
2. *Adharma* Opposite of dharma
3. *Adhvaryu* Head priest in Vedic rituals
4. *Ashram* A school run by sages/priests
5. *Ashwamedha* Horse sacrifice
6. *Bala (balaa)* Force
7. *Brahacharya Ashrama* The phase of life for attaining knowledge, up to 25 years of age
8. *Brahmacharya* Celibacy
9. *Brahmarishi* A sage who knows the Brahma
10. *Brahmchari* A celibate
11. *Bua* Father's sister
12. *Chaturmas* Four months of rain
13. *Chhaya* Image
14. *Daanam* Donation/charity
15. *Devaputra* Son of god
16. *Devarshi* Sage Narada's other name
17. *Dharmaraja* Another name for Yudhishthira; also Yamaraja
18. *Geedha* A species of vultures
19. *Gotra* Clan name/lineage from one of the manasputras of Brahma
20. *Guna* Characteristics
21. *Guru-shisya* Teacher-pupil
22. *Ikshwaku* Name of Ram's clan
23. *Ishwara* God
24. *Jambu-dwipa* Asia
25. *Jyeshtha* Summer month in Indian Lunar calendar *(May-June)*
26. *Kaakustha* Prince of Ikshwaku clan
27. *Kamadeva* Cupid (Indian god of romance)
28. *Madana* Another name of Cupid
29. *Manasputra* Mind-born son of Brahma
30. *Mantra* Sacred hymns

31 *Maryadapurushottama* The best among the dharma-following souls
32 *Maryada* The ethical sphere
33 *Matula* Mother's brother or father's sister's husband
34 *Moha* Attachment
35 *Mrit-sanjivani vidhya* The science of making the dead live again
36 *Nataraja* Another name of Lord Shiva
37 *Neem* A tree
38 *Neeti-shastra* Science of Policy
39 *Niyoga* Sex with an other man with the approval of the husband, for getting a son
40 *Peepal* A tree
41 *Pitra rina* Father/ancestors' debt
42 *Prakriti* Nature/Attitude
43 *Putra* Son
44 *Raghuvamsa* Raghu's descendants, Raghu's clan
45 *Rahu* One of the nine planets in Indian Cosmology; originally the head of a Daitya
46 *Rajasik* Related to the royals
47 *Rashi* Constellations
48 *Rati* Wife of Kamadeva/Madana
49 *Rta* The cosmic law
50 *Rudra*s Deities (eleven in number)
51 *Sal, sami, ashoka, chandana, kutaja, champaka* and *naga* Trees
52 *Samparka Srishti* Creation by copulation
53 *Samskara* Sixteen essential rituals of the Vedic people
54 *Sandarshana Srishti* Creation by a mere glance
55 *Sandhya* Evening
56 *Sankalpa Srishti* Creation by will
57 *Saptarshies* Seven sages (manasputras of Brahma)
58 *Satva* Truth/Light/The best of the characteristics of a yogi
59 *Satvik* Related to the ascetics
60 *Saavarni manvantara* An epoch named Saavarni
61 *Sharad* and *Hemant* Two seasons after four months of rain
62 *Shravana* A month in the Lunar calendar
63 *Shrivatsa* Vishnu's symbol
64 *Shruti* Four Vedas

65 *Sparsha Srishti* Creation by touch
66 *Suta-putra* Son of a charioteer
67 *Swayamvara* A ceremony where a girl chooses her groom
68 *Tamala* Tree
69 *Tamasa* Darkness, also a river
70 *Tamasik* Characteristics associated with darkness/evil
71 *Treta* The third epoch in Indian Mythology
72 *Triloka* Three worlds
73 *Usha* Dawn
74 *Uttariya* Cloth to cover upper body
75 *Vaani / Vach* Speech
76 *Vanaprastha* The phase of life between 50 to 75 years of age, when a person is expected to detach from, but guide, society
77 *Varaha* The boar
78 *Vasus* Deities (eight in number)
79 *Veena* A musical instrument
80 *Yagna* A sacred ritual usually associated with offerings in fire
81 *Yoganidra* Deep slumber often equated with complete relaxation, associated with Lord Vishnu